Jo

Winter's Night

"All right, let's get started," Barnes told the group after Vazques sat at the table with Trembulak and his other men. "We're going to review every detail of the plan so you'll all know what you're supposed to be doing during the operation. During the past four months we've met with each of you several times and discussed the parts of the plan that directly affect you. Now its time to tie all the pieces together."

"I have a copy of the complete plan for each of you. You can follow through them as we discuss the different elements," explained Leland as he handed each man a thick computer printout.

"Are you going to tell us which government we will be attacking, or don't you trust us with that information yet Barnes?" asked Trembulak sarcastically. "You told me this was an ambitious plan to overthrow a government, but I was never privileged to know which government I will be destroying!"

"If you shut your fucking mouth for two minutes, I'll tell you, Trembulak. The objective of this operation is the simultaneous military overthrow of the governments of the United States and Russia."

Journey Through A Long Winter's Night

by

Richard D'Onofrio

Commonwealth
Publications

> If you purchased this book without a cover, you should be aware that this book is stolen property. It was reported as "unsold and destroyed" to the publisher, and neither the author nor the publisher has received any payment for this "stripped book."

A Commonwealth Publications Paperback
JOURNEY THROUGH A LONG WINTER'S NIGHT

This edition published 1996
by Commonwealth Publications
9764 - 45th Avenue,
Edmonton, AB, CANADA T6E 5C5
All rights reserved
Copyright © 1995 by Richard D'Onofrio

ISBN: 1-896329-19-5

No part of this book may be reproduced or utilized in any form or by any means, electronic or mechanical, including photocopying, recording, or by any information storage and retrieval system, without permission in writing from the publisher.

This work is a novel and any similarity to actual persons or events is purely coincidental.

If you purchased this book without a cover, you should be aware that this book is stolen property. It was reported as "unsold and destroyed" to the publisher, and neither the author nor the publisher has received any payment for this "stripped book."

Designed by: Jennifer Brolsma

Printed in Canada

*To my Mom and Dad,
they always knew I could do it and spent their
time and patience convincing me,*

*And for Nancy
who had the patience and encouragement that
helped me complete this,*

*And for all of my friends
who helped me with this work,
especially Kathy K.*

*This is for all of you,
Thank you*

'As a child I walked with my mother
in the deep snow,
On a journey through a long winter's
night,
And at the end we found our home,
Where I felt the warmth of the fire,
And the tranquility of sleep'

Anonymous

Chapter One

The bright morning sunlight streamed through the windows of the large White House conference room located beside the President's Oval Office. A tired and troubled President Joseph Rockwell sat back in a burgundy leather chair after he wrote notes on his pad. He listened carefully to the opening remarks of a few of the thirty experienced advisors seated at the long wooden table with him. After the President's National Security Advisor informed him Russian military units were suddenly being massed in that nation's northern and southern regions, Rockwell decided to fly back to Washington from Oregon late the previous night.

While he was in Portland, Rockwell and his economic advisors met with the governors and mayors of the western states. The governors pleaded with the President to provide more financial assistance to their states. They cited rising unemployment and welfare costs as drains on their budgets. Both the governors and mayors expressed their displeasure after Rockwell announced the declining economy was the primary reason his advisors were proposing a substantial reduction in the financial assistance previously provided to the states. Rockwell also warned he might reduce the government's financial support of programs such as Medicare and Medicaid. Then he advised the governors to consider establishing health care programs for the elderly and disabled in their states.

"These blue areas are where Barakov is currently staging his military forces, Mister President," explained General Roberts of the Defense Intelligence Agency. He stood beside a metal easel that supported a large diagram of Russia and the nations around it. "We refer to the northern area as the Leningrad Military District. The southern area is the North Caucasus Military District. Barakov has assembled a variety of military units at those locations. They consist of two thousand armored personnel carriers, five hundred tanks, six hundred pieces of artillery, two hundred rocket launchers, and six divi-

8   D'ONOFRIO

sions of attack helicopters. We have confirmation that he's already placed those units on an alert status."

"How close are those forces to their respective borders?" asked Rockwell as he studied the map, and the position of red flags depicting various Russian military forces.

"Most of them are within ten kilometers of their borders, Mister President," replied Colonel Buynicki of the National Reconnaissance Office.

"So, why are they staging those forces so close to the border, Colonel?"

"They could use their missiles to destroy high valued targets in Bosnia like factories, until that government ends the fighting in Herzegovina."

"That assessment would make sense," agreed Roberts. "If they use the missile launchers, the other military forces could be there only to protect those launchers from attack."

"I don't understand what's going through Barakov's mind," sighed the President as he carefully studied the map and the position of the Russian forces.

"He could be worried the escalation of fighting in Bosnia and Crotia may spill over into his nation," speculated Edward Jamison, the Director of the Central Intelligence Agency. "With NATO threatening to use air strikes to stop the Bosnia Serbs, Barakov may be sending a message to the Serbs. He might be telling them to stop the fighting while warning them he doesn't want any problems in his own nation."

"But why mass such a large force at the border? What's Barakov planning to do with them? Move into Bosnia if he feels threatened?"

"But they would have to fly over the Ukraine, Belarus, Latvia, and Lithuania to get to Bosnia or Croatia, and that might cause diplomatic problems for Borakov."

The Deputy Director of the Central Intelligence Agency slid a green folder across the table toward the President. "That's a summary of Russian military radio communications we intercepted Mister President. They indicate the Russians may be preparing for some

JOURNEY THROUGH A LONG WINTER'S NIGHT 9

type of military action. We just don't know what they have in mind."

"We may be reading the situation incorrectly," commented Todd Solomson, a State Department foreign affairs advisor who was an expert about Russian matters. "The Russians may be justified by the military build up we're seeing in those areas. We've had several intelligence reports that described ethnic fighting in the region south of the North Caucasus Military District. Barakov must be concerned about the civil wars in Georgia, and the five year old conflict between Armenia and Azerbaijan. He may be positioning his troops to prevent any new fighting in those areas."

"What do you think, Curtis?" Rockwell asked his Secretary of State, Curtis Wilcox. "Is Barakov preparing for an offensive strike, or is he just being cautious?"

"I don't believe Barakov is going to do anything to jeopardize his position or cause any political turmoil in Russia. The economic and social reforms he's proposing for his nation are already making him unpopular. He knows a military strike on a nation that was once part of the Soviet Union might get him impeached, or might start another revolution."

"I need your recommendation, Curtis. I've got to do, or say something in a situation like this."

"I think we should put together a statement that can be read at the State Department press conference this morning, Mister President. I suggest we word it to say you're extremely concerned about the situation and you're carefully monitoring it."

"I agree, but I should be the one to read it to the press. Get something put together for me, Andy, and call a news conference in the Rose Garden at noon," the President told Andrew Raymond, the White House Director of Communications.

"I think you should call President Barakov and tell him you're concerned by what's happening, Mister President," suggested foreign affairs advisor Dona Riddell as she read her notes. "We're guessing at what's going on over there. It could be the Russian military forces are engaging in training maneuvers."

10 D'ONOFRIO

"What do you think, Curtis? I don't have a problem calling Barakov if you think it will help."

"I tried to contact him while you were on the way back from Oregon, Mister President. His advisors said he wasn't in Moscow and they didn't know where to reach him."

"That's bull shit! He doesn't want us using NATO air strikes to protect the United Nations troops and civilians in Bosnia, but now he's preparing his military forces to defend his own nation!"

"We may still need a policy to deal with the situation, Mister President," warned Rockwell's National Security Advisor, Peter Komoroski. "We better have something ready if the Russians do move into Bosnia to stop the fighting."

"He's right, Mister President," agreed Wilcox. "But, we've got to consider what position we want to take. Do we condemn the Russians or sanction their activity at that point?"

"I think we may be over reacting to this situation, Mister President," commented Kennith Dunnells, Vice-President Bradford Benson's personal advisor.

Komoroski appeared angered by Dunnells' statement as he slammed his pen down onto the top of the wide mahogany table. "I don't know how you can sit there and make a statement like that after everything that's already been said here. What do you think is going to happen if Barakov's military forces, or the Serbs in Bosnia, suddenly move against the Ukraine, Belarus, and Kazakhstan? The governments of those new republics retained control of their nuclear weapons after the breakup of the Soviet Union."

"You're concerned one of those governments is going to fire a nuclear tipped missile at their attackers?" asked Vice-President Benson with disbelief in his voice. "No one is that insane."

"I'm sorry, Mister Vice-President, I don't have such an optimistic view of this situation. Who's going to stop those new governments from using their SS-25 nuclear tipped missiles to defend themselves?"

Rockwell knew his inexperienced vice-president still

JOURNEY THROUGH A LONG WINTER'S NIGHT   11

did not have a full understanding of the events that occurred during the breakup of the Soviet Union. He was even more concerned Benson was not trying to learn more about the situation, although Rockwell repeatedly warned him to do so. The President realized he himself could not be an expert in every area of the government and foreign affairs. When making decisions and deciding policy he relied on his experienced advisors to provide information and guidance. Rockwell, unlike his vice-president, did attempt to have more than a cursory knowledge of all domestic and foreign issues that affected the nation.

Rockwell won the primary elections in every state, easily defeating his closest rival to become his political party's candidate for President. After the elections, Rockwell began a search for a vice-presidential running mate. His party's political strategists ignored Rockwell's concerns Benson was an inexperienced legislator. Instead, they applied pressure and forced Rockwell to offer the forty-four-year-old representative from Nebraska the vice-presidency. They choose Benson over several more experienced candidates, hoping his blonde hair and boyish face would attract the younger voters during the election.

After Rockwell defeated the incumbent President, Benson found himself in a job without goals or objectives. His schedule consisted of speaking at college functions, giving lectures to various civic organizations about his party's accomplishments,and attending fund-raising events for his political organization. Although they were menial tasks, several of Rockwell's advisors believed they were well beyond Benson's capabilities.

"The cold war is over, Pete, and Barakov is getting rid of the old Russian leaders who swore they'd bury this nation," said Benson triumphantly with a smile. "Barakov is even replacing the hard line military commanders while he's establishing his new democratic government."

"The Russian military leaders may see their prestigious careers coming to an end, but I don't think they're too willing to accept it," added Rockwell uneasily as he

12 D'ONOFRIO

pictured Moscow's gold domed buildings with heavy snow swirling around them in his mind. "When we were in Moscow last February, I got the impression they didn't agree with the democratic changes Barakov proposed."

"Maybe we should consider putting the Strategic Air Command bombers back into the air as a precaution, Mister President," suggested Frank Palmer apprehensively. He was the President's Personal Advisor who served with four of the previous administrations.

Katherine Bardeck, the Assistant Secretary of State, stared solemnly at the President as she warned, "No, that won't help the situation, Mister President. The United States is definitely not their target, and that action may send the wrong kind of message. If nothing else it'll raise the level of tension when we're perceived as going on the defensive because of the Russian's actions."

"I agree with Kathy, keep the bombers on the ground," said Rockwell after he thought about his advisor's suggestion. "It took months to get the flights suspended and I don't want to have to resell that plan after we resolve this situation."

Sharon Lingard leaned toward the President from the chair beside him and said, "Ten minutes until your meeting with the Federal Communications Committee, Mister President." Lingard was the President's Event Secretary, and the person he relied on to get him to his various meetings.

Rockwell momentarily looked to his right when eight news camera men entered the conference room with a White House public affairs officer. Everyone in the room attempted to ignore the camera men as they set up their equipment. When the President's advisors saw the bright lights of the video cameras they suddenly appeared more attentive as Rockwell asked for more information and each person's final thoughts about the situation.

After everyone expressed their opinion the conference room was quiet as the advisors waited for Rockwell's decision. "Based on your evaluations and opinions, I don't think we should do anything else than issue the press release. Keep me abreast of the situation and find me if anything else develops. Thank you all for your

JOURNEY THROUGH A LONG WINTER'S NIGHT 13

help." The President stood and watched as Wilcox placed his folders into his briefcase. "If this blows up in our face I don't know how we'll be able to present our budget modification proposal, Curtis."

Rockwell stood and adjusted his tie in a gold framed mirror Thomas Jefferson had used, as he waited for Wilcox's reply. Rockwell's critics and supporters agreed he was the strongest and most dynamic president of the past sixty years. Now into the third year of his first term, the forty-seven-year-old Rockwell had lost twenty pounds from his six foot frame during the past three months. Every morning he noticed more gray hairs intermixed with the black ones on his head, which he attributed to stress. Rockwell was a devoted family man and it was his wife and twenty-eight-year-old daughter who supported and encouraged him through the difficult decisions he had to make. Even with their support he was beginning to feel the stress and pressures of the Presidency.

"What budget modification proposal are you referring to, Mister President?" asked Dunnells as he and the vice-president prepared to leave the conference room.

Rockwell stepped aside when several members of the White House staff frantically cleaned the conference room for the next meeting. Then members of the kitchen staff began moving fresh coffee and pasty into the room. "Why don't we step into my office to discuss this," replied Rockwell, then he motioned to Curtis Wilcox and the group walked into the Oval Office.

Sharon Lingard followed the men and arranged several piles of papers on the President's desk as other secretaries walked into the office and handed her official communications.

"I don't want anyone else knowing about this yet," the President warned Dunnells and Benson. "I'm seriously considering a plan to divert some money from select areas of this year's budget. I may need some funding for an economic stimulus package I'm considering proposing to Congress."

"We cut back spending and eliminated everything nonessential before Congress approved the budget, Joe,"

14 D'ONOFRIO

said Benson who looked confused by Rockwell's statements. "Where can you find anything to cut?"

Rockwell lifted a thick report off a long wooden table covered with summarized briefings prepared by his staff and various government agencies. "This is a plan my personal advisors have been putting together during the past three months. It provides the details for an immediate reduction in the number of men and women in all of our armed services."

"I don't think we can justify laying off military personnel so you can use their salaries to help the economy, Joe," said the Vice-President, who seemed angered by Rockwell's startling revelation. "Why didn't you tell us you were considering this plan before now?"

Rockwell could see the shock on Dunnells' and Benson's faces, so he chose his next words carefully. "Because I really don't know how to proceed with this plan now that I have it. We both know there's no other area of the budget we can cut without pushing the nation deeper into the recession."

"I am your Vice-President Joe. You should have asked my opinion about this idea before your advisors started working on that proposal," whined an angry Benson as he stared at the President.

"You're right, I should have told you about it. At first I didn't think the amount of money we could save would be appreciable. I never imagined how much we can save by cutting our military forces by a half, or even by a quarter."

"That's a large number of people to put in the unemployment lines Mister President, and that's exactly what you'll be doing," commented Dunnells as he squinted while analyzing the idea. "There's no jobs in the private sector for them, and many of those people may end up on welfare."

"Our military leaders aren't going to like this plan, Joe, and they're going to oppose it, and us," warned Benson nervously.

"I've already considered that, Brad. If we go with this plan we'll see savings in the amount of food, ammunition, gasoline, aircraft fuel, spare parts, and cloth

JOURNEY THROUGH A LONG WINTER'S NIGHT 15

ing all the services purchase," explained the President. "If the services work more efficiently with their enlisted personnel we can save millions of dollars if we reduce the number of civilians they employ."

"I don't like this plan, the more I hear about it, Mister President," confessed Dunnells apprehensively. "You're talking about putting career military people out of work. You may even force the private sector suppliers that depend on military sales and contracts to lay off their employees because they won't have the orders to maintain their payrolls."

"You're right, that may happen in the short term."

"The number of people you directly or indirectly put in the unemployment lines may be greater than any financial benefits you derive from this cutback," said Benson. He knew the unemployed workers would never re-elect Rockwell when they remembered it was his administration that reduced funding to the military. If Rockwell could not win the next election Benson knew he would never have a chance to become the next President.

"No, I don't see that happening. In the long term, after we use the money we save to revitalize the economy, those people will have jobs when businesses begin expanding."

"This plan isn't going to make us popular with anyone," Benson disgustedly told the President.

"Popular or not, Brad, if I decide to approve this plan, it's going in whether you like it or not," commented Rockwell as he threw the report back onto the table.

Dunnells appeared concerned by Rockwell's warning and he walked to a window and watched the people lined up in the hot sun waiting to tour the White House. "I know how the people are going to react when you start closing the military bases in their home towns, Mister President. They're going to reject you, Brad, and this administration."

"The people out there aren't as stupid as you make them out to be," countered Wilcox who was angered by Dunnells' criticism. "We've burdened those people with increased taxes, and now we're cutting back services they all took for granted only a few years ago. Now they're

16   D'ONOFRIO

asking why billions of dollars are still being spent to fund our military when a coalition force like Desert Storm can handle the same problems."

"I just don't think Congress will go along with this cutback, Curtis," interrupted Benson as he nervously rubbed his hands together. "This directly affects the people they represent."

"I won't let Congress block this plan because of fears they won't get re-elected if they support it. With or without their support, I'd like to use half the defense budget to cut the personal income tax rates. Then I want to improve the welfare and job training systems, and overhaul the unemployment and public service job programs."

"That's too drastic an approach, Joe. If you want to make such radical changes we should do it in stages, spread over years."

"We can't spread out a military cutback like that, we need funding to help the economy today. What would you do if you were in my position?" Rockwell asked Benson after he walked to an office window and stared at the red and yellow roses planted outside. "Even if we attempt something like a troop reduction now, there's no guarantee it's going to help. Two years from now we may be forced to reduce our military forces by three quarters and raise taxes again."

A Presidential aide rushed into the office with several other people trailing behind her carrying various briefing and intelligence reports. The aide handed the President a folder and as she turned to leave Rockwell asked her, "What's this Rachel?"

"That's a summarization of the Democratic response to your health care proposal, Mister President. You asked for it to be delivered as soon as we completed it."

"That's right, thank you," said the President as he quickly flipped through the six page report. "We can't even agree on a plan to help the sick and dying in our own nation."

"The benefits of putting thousands of military people into the unemployment lines may not be politically justified, Mister President," Dunnells cautioned Rockwell with an uplifted eyebrow. "The members of our own party

JOURNEY THROUGH A LONG WINTER'S NIGHT 17

may not get re-elected when the unemployment rate rises after your cutbacks."

"I've considered that, but my main concern has to be for the people. Not all my decisions can be based solely on the political ramifications." The President paused, and looked at Wilcox after he saw the concern and disappointment in Benson's face. "Curtis and I will review the plan again, then I'll give it to you so you can read it. We'll all discuss it before I present anything to Congress."

"Well, I guess that just about does it," Benson sarcastically told the President as he attempted to express his anger and frustration over the situation. "I've got to get out of here. I'm leaving for San Francisco this afternoon. I'm giving a speech at Berkeley tomorrow night and attending a fund raising dinner Saturday night."

"Where am I this week?" the President asked Lingard as he watched a large group of men and women walking into the adjacent conference room for the next meeting.

"You're in Rhode Island for the Naval War College graduation this weekend."

"That's right. We're flying up Thursday morning, doing some quick sightseeing, and flying back here Sunday night after the ceremony."

"I still don't know how you convinced the Secret Service to let you stay in that hotel on an island, Mister President," said Wilcox with a laugh.

"I don't see why they made such a big deal of it. We've vacationed on Nantucket, and Catalina for that matter. Our friends own the hotel in Newport and we want to stay with them."

"Reynolds told me you're letting him park your helicopter on the island in case there's a problem. I think that relieved some of his concerns. "

"I've got to get moving," Benson interrupted disgustedly as he intentionally looked at his watch. "I've got a meeting with my staff in five minutes. I'll see you both next Monday morning."

"Have a good trip," replied the President as he shook Benson's hand, trying to coax an emotion other than anger from him. Benson and Dunnells then walked out

18   D'ONOFRIO

of the office and into the wide White House hallway without speaking.

"I'm not sure he could take your place if anything happened to you, Joe," confided Wilcox in a low voice, then he signed heavily. "I'm sorry to say, I don't see him maturing like we thought he would in his position as Vice President."

"I've seated the FCC committee, Mister President, and they're waiting to meet with you," Lingard reminded Rockwell as she handed him the agenda for the meeting. "This is going to be a long one."

"I'll be back later this afternoon with an updated report on the Russian military. I'm headed to the Capital and then over to my office," Wilcox told the President, then he walked out of the office.

As they angrily discussed the President's ideas, Benson appeared surprised when he and Dunnells rounded a corner and he walked into Marine General Burlson and Army General Murtagh.

"How are you, gentlemen?" he asked mechanically as he briskly walked between the two men he despised without any further comments.

"Now there goes a god damn ignorant and uninformed man," remarked Murtagh several seconds later as he turned and watched Benson standing in the hallway talking to Dunnells. "Can you see him as Commander and Chief, trying to tell us how we should be using our men and equipment?"

General William Murtagh was a five star general appointed by President Rockwell to command the United States Army as a member of the Joint Chiefs of Staff. The fifty-nine-year-old general had an impressive military career that began at West Point and included combat experience in all the American conflicts during the past forty years. He was shot several times in Korea and served four years as a field commander in Vietnam. He commanded a brigade during the invasions of Grenada and Panama, and helped plan the invasion of Iraq.

"Take it easy, Bill," warned Burlson as he looked around guiltily when several large groups of White House staff personnel walked past them.

JOURNEY THROUGH A LONG WINTER'S NIGHT   19

"I get upset when I think he can't handle a job like emptying the trash cans in the Pentagon, yet he's the damn vice-president."

"Don't push him or he may run to the President and complain about you again." Burlson was sixty-two years old and was planning his retirement for the end of the year. He was afraid his association with the outspoken Murtagh might endanger his chances for a promotion, and a larger pension, before he retired.

"I really don't care what that piss ant says about me anymore," Murtagh confessed with a laugh. "I'd like to send him and all the other politicians running our government straight to hell together."

Burlson seemed shocked and troubled by his companion's unexpected statements, and he quickly looked around again to see if any of the military officers walking past them heard the comments. "I would've thought that after all your years in the military you would have become accustomed to the politics in this city by now."

"Who, me? I can't stomach the people running our government."

"Why do you dislike the elected officials so much?"

Murtagh suddenly guided Burlson to an antique wooden desk in the hallway, and stepped closer to him as groups of reporters and cameramen rushed past them. "I even hate being in this damn building, Jeff. The White House is the epitome of the politics I believe are slowly destroying our nation."

"You never told me you felt this way before, Bill. The military has been struggling to work with the politicians since before they signed the Declaration of Independence. As far as the politicians go, you and I both know it's the ones with the most prominent connections and money that get themselves elected every year."

"That's my point. Every four or eight years a different scheming politician moves into this building with some grand idea of how we should run the government and the military. We should have a constitutional amendment that requires politicians to be former military men, corporate officers, or successful business men. They should be experienced men who have made tough deci-

20 D'ONOFRIO

sions before they can become the elected officials that run this country. Anyone with the right connections can become the President of this nation, and that's what infuriates me. Look at Rockwell, he wasn't even in the military. He was a governor for twelve lousy years and now he's the damn President. He doesn't have any business or military background, yet he's trying to tell us how to make the United States more competitive."

"But you've got to remember the people did elect him President. When I compared him to all the other candidates, I voted for him, too."

"If Rockwell wasn't the President, it would be someone else just as unqualified. We always leave the presidency and the tremendous responsibilities that go along with it to the person who was the least distasteful to us during the last election."

"I'll have to agree with you on that," sighed Burlson as he thought about the pre-election television debates, "it's unfortunate but true."

"Think about it. What real requirements are there before someone can become a senator or representative?"

"None, and you're right, most of the people we elect don't have any idea how to help this nation. Many of them are in it only for themselves."

"Exactly, look at how many get arrested for taking kick backs and for tax evasion every year. Things like the House banking scandal and the sexual antics of those officials upset me the most."

"But those things have been going on forever. It's just the press makes the public more aware of them today."

Murtagh shook his head and clenched his fist as he became angrier, attracting the attention of several of the catering staff walking past him. "Just because that kind of thing has been going on forever doesn't make it right. The elected officials don't care about the people, and they don't come in here with any new ideas or wisdom."

Burlson realized Murtagh's angry comments were brief, a departure from his usual oratorical reply to questions asked of him. "I believe some politicians have good ideas. Some present new programs for helping the people."

JOURNEY THROUGH A LONG WINTER'S NIGHT 21

"No, none of them have any idea how to help this nation. If they did, they'd be considering ways to use the military to help strengthen this nation. They're overlooking vast amounts of knowledge and skills that can help the people and industries of this country. They're either too ignorant, or they just can't see the potential in the branches of the military. But that's all going to change."

"Change how?"

"The incumbents and all the other politicians of this nation are going to be out! I can see a tremendous and surging wave of fresh clean water washing away the politicians of our nation."

"You mean the voters will be electing new officials?"

"Something like that."

"I don't think I understand what you're saying, Bill," said a now confused Burlson. "How can the military help the country?"

Murtagh smiled and calmed himself as he began walking in the corridor decorated with antiques of prior Presidents. "I'm sorry. I think I'm just upset that we're here to discuss using combat troops who fought remarkably well in both Iraq and Panama as flag bearers during the fourth of July parade."

Burlson agreed with Murtagh's comments as he shrugged his shoulders, hoping to express his own feelings of hopelessness. "Come on, Bill, we don't have a choice," he sighed as he led Murtagh into a conference room. Inside the President's public relations staff was waiting to discuss the upcoming holiday events with them.

Chapter Two

That same afternoon, a car slowly pulled into a trash filled alley between two long, run down brick apartment buildings in a ghetto of Havana, Cuba. After the driver parked the car he pulled a small machine gun from under the seat and placed it under his belt. Then he buttoned his green jacket as he spoke to his passenger who nervously looked around at the groups of people sitting in the building's shade in the oppressive heat.

Casimir Trembulak had never been to Havana. He did not expect to see the massive crowds of unemployed people attempting to stay cool outside the building. The drunken derelicts sitting against the building in the alley made him uncomfortable as they stared at him when he stepped from the car. Although Trembulak had the distinguished look of a corporate executive, he was responsible for organizing many of the terrorist attacks that occurred around the world during the past ten years. The forty-six-year-old Trembulak was already a major leader of the Palestine Liberation Organization. His desire to crush the nation of Israel and reclaim the land for his Palestinian people led him to join the organization as a hired gunmen. After participating in several assassinations on busy city streets in Europe, Trembulak quickly realized the work was much too dangerous for him. He plotted to quickly attain a much safer position of power in the terrorist organization. To do so Trembulak ambushed and murdered a long time and very close friend, the man's pregnant wife, and their three children. Then he blamed the Israeli government for the killings. Trembulak quickly assumed his dead friend's high ranking leadership position in the organization. Now he planned and directed his organization's terrorist activities from the safety of a fraudulent business office in Paris.

Trembulak often diverted portions of his organization's funds specifically allocated for training his men and purchasing weapons. He then used the money to purchase tailored suits, fine silk shirts, expensive shoes,

JOURNEY THROUGH A LONG WINTER'S NIGHT   23

but he especially enjoyed the look of gold on his body. Although Trembulak thought of himself as a brilliant tactician, many of his men died senselessly during terrorist attacks because he lacked a thorough knowledge of military strategy. Trembulak considered the men expendable and their deaths did not disturb him. He knew other willing men could be recruited to do their job. The killing of innocent people in Israel and the occupied territories would continue as long as he could find men willing to die for their cause.

Trembulak and the man with him walked past the large groups of Cubans pointing and talking about them. When they reached the end of a stench filled alley littered with garbage, they cautiously walked into an apartment building. Trembulak stepped over a drunk passed out on the floor, and another vomiting on the gray cement floor in a long unpainted hallway lit by a single light bulb. The smell of dried vomit, and urine on the walls and floor in the oppressively hot hallway forced both men to cover their mouth and nose with their hands. Many apartment doors were open, and radios and televisions were blaring in some, while people screamed at one another in others. After the two men found the apartment they were searching for, Trembulak's companion pulled the machine gun from his jacket and knocked on a rotted wooden door frame.

An armed guard opened the door an inch, then opened it wider after he recognized the two men. They walked into the apartment after checking the hallway to ensure they were not being followed. Trembulak saw five of his men seated around a brown Formica topped metal table in the apartment's sweltering kitchen. He did not know the four men standing together in the living room commenting about the yellow and red flowered wallpaper peeling off the walls.

"This is the man I told you about, Colonel Andres Vazques of the Cuban Army," Trembulak told his men as he placed his hand on his companions' shoulder. "Castro agreed to lend him to us for this operation. Besides being proficient with many types of weapons, he has worked extensively with all kinds of explosives. I

24   D'ONOFRIO

know this man's reputation, and I'm confident he'll lead his men to victory."

"You're late, Trembulak, and I don't fucking like that!" commented one of three men dressed in brightly colored shirts and shorts who walked into the kitchen and startled both Trembulak and Vazques.

"Tell this asshole not to point that weapon at me, or I might just stuff it up his fucking ass!" added the tactless man as he stared into Vazques' eyes coldly.

"It's all right, Vazques, I know these men," said Trembulak as he placed his hand on the machine gun and forced him to lower it. "This insolent one is Major Barnes of the United States' Army. The other is Major Vechesloff of the Russian Army. I don't know the man with them."

Barnes took Trembulak's derogatory comment as a compliment and laughed as he placed a folder on the kitchen table. Although he had no finesse when dealing with people, Barnes built his reputation in the United States Army by completing even the most difficult missions assigned to him. He spent two years in Vietnam with an American intelligence unit. His sadistic methods of obtaining large amounts of valuable information from captured enemy soldiers disturbed his commanders, but they always overlooked his brutal tactics. After Vietnam, Barnes traveled around the world to various military installations where he gathered intelligence information about the Russians and North Koreans. During the attack of Grenada and Panama, Barnes commanded a unit of paratroopers. When Operation Desert Storm concluded, Barnes and his unit received several commendations after destroying thirty Republican Guard tanks with shoulder launched missiles.

Barnes was an excellent military tactician, and one of the most trusted men in the Pentagon, where he was now stationed. Many of his critics said the muscular, handsome man's only flaw was that he had no compassion. Others warned the forty-three-year-old man was ruthless and would stop at nothing to get the power and prestige he craved. Those people never imagined what Barnes would really do for power.

JOURNEY THROUGH A LONG WINTER'S NIGHT   25

"That's Colonel Leland. We'll be working together until the end of this operation," Barnes told the men as he tried to intimidate them with his brusque attitude. "You don't want to fuck with him either."

Power and control were the two stimulants that Barnes needed and craved as though they were addictive drugs. In Vietnam he always volunteered for the more dangerous missions, living for days on the pure adrenaline high and fear that accompanies combat assignments. The justification behind the combat missions never concerned him, and the reason was irrelevant and inconsequential to Barnes. Although he came from a poor family of six children, Barnes has little use for money. He would do anything that would give him power and control, and the chance to dominate other people's lives. The tattoo of a naked woman's body hanging from a noose on one arm, and the bloody severed woman's head on his other arm should have provided people with some insight into the man's mind.

Leland frowned when Barnes pushed his way between Vazques and Trembulak, striking the Cuban soldier's body roughly with his shoulder as he walked passed him. "I'll be your liaison," Leland told the two men as he raised his hand to them, but it was a gesture they both ignored.

Barnes and Leland first met when they were assigned to the same commanding officer in the Pentagon. Although he was not as muscular, or as tall as Barnes, the red haired Leland still prided himself on his well exercised and developed body. After a year in Vietnam the Army transferred Leland to Germany, where he collected intelligence information about the Russian military. It was during this time he began questioning America's foreign policy. He watched as billions of dollars were given to other nations while homeless people in the United States lived on the city streets. He believed the government could do more for the suffering people of his own country if it wasn't preoccupied with helping the other nations of the world.

Leland was forty-six years old, and his military commander knew he could successfully complete any task

26 D'ONOFRIO

assigned to him. During several discussions with his commander, he explained he was becoming more frustrated by the inaction and inability's of the American President and government. He believed the government had to change to become more responsive to people's needs. He became discouraged when he realized that a single military officer could not change the bureaucracy.

"All right, let's get started," Barnes told the group after Vazques sat at the table with Trembulak and his other men. "We're going to review every detail of the plan so you'll all know what you're supposed to be doing during the operation. During the past four months we've met with each of you several times and discussed the parts of the plan that directly affect you. Now its time to tie all the pieces together."

"I have a copy of the complete plan for each of you. You can follow through them as we discuss the different elements," explained Leland as he handed each man a thick computer printout.

"Are you going to tell us which government we will be attacking, or don't you trust us with that information yet Barnes?" asked Trembulak sarcastically. "You told me this was an ambitious plan to overthrow a government, but I was never privileged to know which government I will be destroying!"

"If you shut your fucking mouth for two minutes, I'll tell you, Trembulak. The objective of this operation is the simultaneous military overthrow of the governments of the United States and Russia."

"This is ridiculous!" protested Trembulak as he stood and threw his attack plan onto the table. "You must think we're stupid and will believe these lies you're telling to conceal the true purpose of this attack."

Barnes looked at Leland and laughed as he shook his head. "This fucking asshole thinks I'm kidding."

"He's telling you the truth," Leland tried to reassure Trembulak. "Our targets are the governments of the United States and Russia."

"You're both insane," Trembulak shouted at Barnes as he backed away from the table, "either that or you're too confident and don't realize the dangers associated

JOURNEY THROUGH A LONG WINTER'S NIGHT   27

with such an attack! You told me this was a dangerous plan when we met in Paris, but what you're proposing seems impossible and overwhelming. You would need millions of men to attack both nations. We have only a handful."

Barnes appeared to be infuriated by Trembulak's contemptuous remarks and he replied with hatred and rage in his voice. "I didn't tell you destroying a government was going to be an easy task, Trembulak!"

"If I had known this plan was so ridiculous I would never have agreed to be part of it. This plan has no chance of success. None!" he shouted as he made a fist with one hand and pointed at Barnes with the other.

"Why don't you calm down and listen to what we have to say, Trembulak," suggested Leland who attempted to be the mediator between the two men who disliked each other intensely. "If you don't like what you hear, or don't think we can succeed, you can walk out of here!"

"All right, I'll listen. Tell us the details of your plan, Barnes. I know the overthrow of even one of those two governments is impossible."

"If you sit down and shut up I'll explain how we're going to pull this off, Trembulak," said Barnes as he placed his fingers on a red circle drawn around the state of Rhode Island on a map he opened. "Our President Rockwell is flying to Rhode Island Thursday afternoon, that's three days from today. He's going up there to attend a graduation ceremony at the Naval War College, in Newport."

"What is this Naval War College?" interrupted Trembulak, obviously disturbing Barnes with his impertinent question. "You've never mentioned a Naval base during any of our meetings. I don't want people you consider inconsequential to become our deadly adversaries in the next few days."

"The War College is a school that teaches tactics to our naval officers. There's no weapons there for you to worry about, Trembulak! They have a few computers, some asshole instructors and programmers, and some communications equipment. We described the facility in

28 D'ONOFRIO

your attack plan and included a map with the positions of all the buildings on the base. It's nothing for you to fucking worry about, nothing," shouted Barnes as he became upset with Trembulak's insignificant concerns.

Barnes pointed at a blue circle drawn on another map inside the red one around Rhode Island. "The President will be staying in a hotel on this island in Newport. This is Goat Island. It's less than half a mile long and two hundred yards wide. The hotel, some condominium buildings, a large marina, and a few small stores are all on the island. This is where you're going to take the President of the United States hostage!"

"How are we going to kidnap your President while he's being guarded by the Secret Service?" asked Vazques as he looked up from the map. "How can my men get close to him when his guards are always watching over him?"

"Eliminating his Secret Service protection and the police inside the hotel is my part of the operation." said Leland as he stepped forward and opened a folder. "A group of my men are already in the hotel as part of the President's one hundred and forty member advance team. The Secret Service is going to check the hotel for explosives tomorrow afternoon. After they've completed that task my men will put canisters of a fast acting nerve gas into the building's ventilation shafts. The gas will knock out everyone in the hotel when its released so you can get to the President without any problems."

"I don't like this part of the attack," confessed Vazques as he thought about the risks involved. "How will you release the gas inside the hotel? I don't want my men rushing into a building where the police and Secret Service might be waiting for them."

"American technology has a lot to do with this part of the attack. An electronic signal we'll transmit will open the valves on the gas canisters just before the attack begins."

"That's good, Vazques. Your men will be able to get into the hotel without any resistance," Trembulak told Vazques as he studied the map of the island. "How many men are you bringing onto the island with you?"

"I've selected and trained three hundred of my best

JOURNEY THROUGH A LONG WINTER'S NIGHT   29

combat troops for this attack. They're all experienced and confident they can easily defeat any American forces that might challenge them after the attack begins. They left from Havana on Barnes' yachts six days ago with their equipment."

"Those yachts will dock at this marina on Goat Island tomorrow morning," Barnes told the group as he pointed at a large map of the island. "Vazques' men will remain on the yachts and out of sight until early Sunday morning. When the attack begins they'll secure the hotel, the condominium buildings, and the marina."

"Where did you find the men to pilot those yachts to Newport?" Trembulak asked as though he was questioning Barnes' ability to get Vazques' men to Rhode Island before the attack. "Are they reliable? Can they be trusted?"

"They're a lot more fucking reliable than you are!" Barnes bluntly told Trembulak as he was becoming increasingly upset with the nature of the questions. "My men hijacked the yachts in the Caribbean a month ago and killed the people they found on them. The yachts are ideal for moving the men to the island without arousing any suspicion. Don't forget Vazques, after the attack begins we've got to convince everyone your men are Russian soldiers."

"We've already supplied his men with Russian Army uniforms, weapons, and equipment," Vechesloff told the group as he leaned against the yellowing wall with his arms folded. "Your men must look like they're Russian combat soldiers or this attack will fail, we'll all die on that island! There are so many different nationalities in the Soviet Union no one will be able to tell your men are really Cuban soldiers."

Leland wanted to impress Trembulak with more details of the plan he considered brilliant and unequaled in the military history of the world. "We're even supplying Vazques' men with American made Stinger missiles. We don't want anyone to get near the island after the President is our hostage, and those missiles will keep them away. The shoulder launched missiles are technological marvels that can track and destroy a jet fighter. We can show Vazques' men how to use them in an hour."

30   D'ONOFRIO

"How are you planning to get the missiles and the other supplies onto the island without arousing suspicion?" asked Trembulak who was slowly becoming comfortable with the plan. "We'll need ammunition, explosives, and radios to hold the island."

"Most of the supplies we'll need are aboard the yachts. Three hours before the attack begins my men will drive three trucks pulling supply trailers onto Goat Island. We're using one trailer to move the Stingers onto the island. Another trailer is a communication center we've fitted with radios so we can maintain contact with Vazques' men on the island, and our men in Washington. The third trailer contains a plutonium bomb. Our weapons specialists modified so it can't be disarmed after we activate it. They've rigged the case so it's impenetrable, and have even attached a seismograph trigger to the bomb. If our military attacks the island with conventional bombs and we're all killed the seismograph trigger will still detonate the bomb."

"I'm not sure I understand this part of the plan," confessed Trembulak as he nervously slid his fingers across the map until they were resting on Goat Island. "You said we're going to put the bomb inside the hotel garage so it will be protected from conventional bombing. I still don't understand what we'll accomplish by having the bomb on the island with us?"

"Having the bomb on the island won't accomplish anything, Trembulak. But after you detonate it every nation of the world is going to stop and realize just how vulnerable they are!" replied Barnes who was angry and upset the terrorist who claimed to be an outstanding military strategist could not understand the overall plan. "We want a large part of the northeastern United States to disappear in a mushroom cloud."

"You expect us to detonate that bomb while we're on that island! You must think we're stupid or suicidal!" Trembulak screamed as he stood again and pointed at Barnes. The thought of dying upset Trembulak and he felt his chest suddenly tighten. He often woke wet with perspiration after suffering through a nightmare where he was laying on a city street, slowly dying as a victim of

JOURNEY THROUGH A LONG WINTER'S NIGHT   31

one of his own terrorist attacks. He knew dying in a nuclear explosion would be much different. He wouldn't have time to contemplate his death, he would be alive one second and dead a moment later.

"No I don't think you're suicidal, but I'm beginning to think you're a dumb fucking asshole, Trembulak. Vechesloff, Leland, and I, will be on that island with you. We'll detonate it after we're all safely off the island."

Barnes paused and swore silently at the terrorist when he saw the puzzled look on Trembulak's face. "You still don't understand why we're going through all this trouble to move the bomb onto the island, do you, Trembulak?"

"No, I don't, and I don't know why I was asked to participate, or what my role in it will accomplish? My military background doesn't compare to yours and I have nothing of value to add to the attack."

"You have something we don't Trembulak, you have a face no one knows. No one outside your organization knows what you look like. We have the plan, but you have the face and the personality we need to impersonate a Russian general."

"I will be impersonating a General?" asked the shocked Trembulak. "You told me I would have a large part in the attack, but I never imagined it would be anything like this."

"We couldn't use any of my men, or Vechesloff's men, so you're going to impersonate the Russian general with orders directly from the Kremlin. We're going to hold our President hostage for one week, long enough for the Russian government to emphatically deny you and your men are part of their military forces. That's going to create a lot of fucking confusion in both Washington and Moscow, especially when you tell the world you have a bomb on the island. Both nations' governments will come apart as they accuse each other of allowing this to happen." Barnes looked over at Leland and Vechesloff, and both men nodded their approval.

"Then, on the following Sunday afternoon, you're going to drag the President and his family out of the hotel so the reporters in the city can see them. Then

32   D'ONOFRIO

you're going to kill them very slowly. We don't want you to kill them with a single bullet. We want you to make them suffer so the reporters can hear them screaming while they're dying. After they're dead we'll bring another large group of hostages outside the building and kill them, too. That'll add to the confusion and anger that'll be building in this country during the week."

Barnes enjoyed this portion of the plan and he pictured the President's daughter lying on the ground. He smiled as he watched her screaming in agony while he made deep cuts in the soft skin of her arms and legs with his bayonet. He fantasized about raping the beautiful woman as she slowly bleed to death under him and he immediately had a large erection.

"How will we get off the island before you detonate the nuclear bomb?" Vazques asked as he studied the map of Newport Harbor, and the open ocean beyond it. "Won't your Coast Guard and Navy vessels have a blockade set up across the harbor?"

"They probably will, but those ships will be gone by Sunday night because they'll be expecting a nuclear explosion. At ten o'clock Sunday night we'll move your men onto the yachts. We should be able to get clear of the area in four hours. When the bomb detonates it'll signal the beginning of another phase of the operation."

"What do you mean another phase?" asked Trembulak as he sat at the table again and opened the attack plan. "I still don't understand why we're killing your President in such a dramatic manner outside the hotel. Why not just cut his throat and let him die inside the hotel?"

"That's not the way it's going to be done." Vechesloff suddenly warned Trembulak as he stepped away from the wall. "If you allow the President to die that way I'll kill you myself! The President's dramatic execution as you refer to it, will signal my men to begin their part of the attack in Moscow."

"Your men in Moscow? Russian soldiers are involved in this attack too?"

"My men will be dressed as American commandos when they parachute into the Kremlin an hour after

JOURNEY THROUGH A LONG WINTER'S NIGHT   33

you kill the President. They'll attack the Parliament building where the government officials will be meeting to discuss the situation. It will appear as if American soldiers killed everyone they found inside the building, claiming it is in reprisal for the killing of their President. All members of the Russian government, including President Barakov, will be dead within two hours, even if we have to hunt them down to kill them. Without opposition my leaders will easily take control of the government."

"How do you plan to seize control of the United States' government after your President is dead?" asked Vazques who was knowledgeable about the American system of government. "Won't your vice-president be in control of the government after everyone sees us kill your President?"

"That's what we're hoping will happen." laughed Leland who leaned back on the rusting metal kitchen chair. He planned the final portion of the attack and was proud of how efficiently it would be executed. "We expect the vice-president to be in the White House watching what's happening on television as he consults with his advisors. A team of our men will fire a missile carrying a thousand pound plastic explosive warhead from a base in Maryland after the attack in Moscow. The missile will be programmed to be twenty feet over the White House, or wherever the vice-president is meeting with his advisors, when the warhead explodes. The explosion will level every building within a three mile radius. We'll tell the reporters a Russian submarine fired the missile in retaliation for the killing of the government officials in Moscow. In the confusion immediately after the reporters announce the vice-president's death on the radio and television, our men will declare martial law and mobilize all the Army units across the United States. The military will then temporarily take control of our nation's government, but it will never be relinquished!"

"How can you be sure your vice-president will be in the White House? He may be hiding at some location where you won't have the opportunity to kill him."

34 D'ONOFRIO

Barnes laughed at the comment and shook his head as he looked down at the table. "If we can't kill the asshole in the White House, then we'll eliminate him where ever he's hiding. Two of the military officers on his security staff are working with us. We'll still destroy the White House next Sunday night, and if Benson isn't in it we'll get a message to our men and they'll kill him."

"Aren't you concerned your Marines or Air Force may intervene and try to stop you from toppling your government?"

Barnes laughed as he swatted at a large group of flies which seemed attracted to the perspiration wetting most of his shirt. "I'm not worried about those shit heads. We spent months coming up with a plan designed to prevent that from happening. A few minutes after we declare martial law, a group of our men will kill the commanding officers of the Marines and Air Force in the Pentagon. That'll leave those forces confused and without anyone to issue orders. By the time those assholes realize what's happening our Army units will have their bases surrounded, then we'll disarm them. When things settle down we'll negotiate with their new commanders and ask if they want to join us. If they don't they're all dead."

"Why aren't you using Russian troops to attack Goat Island?" Trembulak asked Barnes. "Why do we need Cuban soldiers disguised as Russian soldiers to attack the island?"

Vechesloff raised his hand and calmed Barnes who immediately became upset after the naive question. "The men who support our cause in Moscow will kill the officials of my government there. Any movement of combat troops from my country right now might arouse unneeded suspicion. American soldiers attempting to impersonate Russian soldiers would be too obvious. That is why Cuban soldiers are needed to impersonate Russian soldiers on the island."

"This is a very impressive and well thought out attack plan," commented Vazques as he turned several pages. "You still haven't explained how you plan to isolate Goat Island from the rest of the city."

JOURNEY THROUGH A LONG WINTER'S NIGHT   35

Barnes found a photograph that showed a bridge suspended ten feet above a wide channel of water, and he pointed at the different features as he spoke. "We have a Special Forces underwater demolition team on the yachts. Their task is to attach plastic explosives to the wooden beams that support the island's only access bridge before the attack begins. When we detonate the explosives the bridge will collapse, and we'll have the island cut off from the rest of the fucking city."

"What'll we do if your Marines try to make an amphibious landing on the island? We'll never be able to stop them from overrunning our positions," added Vazques as he studied the outline of Goat Island on the map, and the photograph. "The island can easily be attacked from all sides simultaneously."

"Immediately after we destroy the access bridge our demolition team will start placing mines in the water around Goat Island," explained Leland as he opened his briefcase and pulled out a folder of papers. "One mine cluster placed on the seabed releases six mines into the water above it. It'll take two divers about four hours to mine all the water around the island. There's going to be so much confusion in those first few hours that no one is going to try to get near the island while they're mining the water."

"That's where you come into play, Trembulak, and if you fuck it up we're all as good as dead!" warned Barnes as he stared at Trembulak. "You're our mouth piece, and you've got to keep everyone as confused as you can while we're getting the equipment ready to defend the island. After you tell the local officials about the nuclear bomb, I'm sure they won't come near the island until they get some guidance from Washington. Everything we want you to tell the local and government officials is in that attack plan, so study it, because our fucking lives depend on it." Barnes was concerned about Trembulak's ability to impersonate a general while remaining emotionally stable under the pressure of the attack.

Barnes' attitude of success convinced Trembulak the plan was viable, and he assured himself several times

36 D'ONOFRIO

he would not have a problem impersonating a Russian general. "Don't forget, Barnes, I'm a military planner and strategist in the Palestine Liberation Organization. My experience will be a benefit to you during the attack," Trembulak conceitedly reminded everyone as he looked around the table. Trembulak was thankful someone more experienced with military tactics developed the details for such a large and complex attack. He realized he could never have planned such an enormous undertaking.

"Your plan seems to have no obvious flaws. How long did it take to develop?" asked Vazques as he studied maps of Newport in the white pages of the thick attack plan.

"We've been working on this plan for the past eight months. We've even run it through our combat tactics and simulation computers a couple of times. There's nothing that can happen, nothing unforeseen, that can cause this plan to fail. We've anticipated and planned for every contingency and outside factor we could think of. We'll pull this off with no fucking problem."

"Very impressive," Vazques added as he nodded at Leland. "It must have taken thousands of man hours to create such a large attack plan."

"Are you kidding? We put together most of the plan with our computers," laughed Barnes as he opened a folder and displayed a computer generated report on green lined paper. "We could never have considered an attack of this magnitude unless we had access to all the government and military computers in the country. We even stole god damn information from the Federal Bureau of Investigation and the Secret Service computers. We used all the classified information we could get our hands on." Barnes was proud of the attack plan since he helped develop it, but he seemed embarrassed by Vazques' compliments.

"If you consider us such integral parts of your plan, then why didn't we have the details of the entire attack to study before this meeting?" Trembulak suddenly and sarcastically confronted Barnes.

Barnes became furious with Trembulak's com

JOURNEY THROUGH A LONG WINTER'S NIGHT 37

ments, and the veins in his neck almost pushed though the skin as his face became a brilliant shade of red. He shocked even Leland when he suddenly pulled a handgun from his shirt and pointed it at Trembulak's face. "I really hate your fucking guts, you arrogant piece of shit. You're a fucking coward who uses car bombs to kill people on city streets. As far as I'm concerned, you're fucking dirt, and I wouldn't mind killing you to rid the world of shit like you. How about if I put a bullet in your fucking head right now? Then you won't have to worry why we didn't give you the details of the plan before now, and I won't have to listen to anymore shit coming out of your fucking mouth."

Barnes' uncontrollable anger was one of several psychological problems he was never able to overcome. That, and his intense and cruel hatred of women. After being sexually and mentally abused by his divorced mother for the first ten years of his life, Barnes now hated and despised all women. It was his childhood abuse that fostered an intense rage that sometimes manifested itself during tense situations. During his career the mutilated and dismembered bodies of savagely murdered young women were found in the towns around the military bases where Barnes was stationed. The police never solved the vicious killings, and never connected the murders to the psychotic military officer.

Barnes' anger now seemed even more uncontrollable because of his intense hatred of Trembulak. He believed the terrorist leader was responsible for the bombing of the Marine barracks in Beirut, but he could not prove it. He often referred to Trembulak as a Rag Head, and promised his men he would kill the terrorist after the attack.

Trembulak's face became pale as he stared at the handgun pointed between his eyes, and as he slowly stood his attack plan fell onto the floor. The others were unsure of what would happen next, and Leland held his breathe because he had seen Barnes kill other men when his rage was uncontrollable.

"I'm just saying it would have been better to know all the details of the plan before today, Barnes. Then we

38 D'ONOFRIO

could have looked for areas to improve it."

"There's no fucking need to improve it, Trembulak. Just do your fucking job and we'll be just fine!" said Barnes as he slowly lowered the weapon and then placed it on the table.

"It's difficult for me to believe an Army major and a colonel have planned how to destroy the United States' government alone," said Trembulak as he sat and lifted the attack plan off the floor. "You are two insignificant officers in your nation's military. Who is pulling your chains as you Americans say?" he laughed as he looked at Barnes.

Barnes became furious as he stared at his handgun and contemplated whether or not to kill Trembulak, then his uncontrollable anger caused him to make a critical mistake. "If Murtagh didn't need your fucking face I'd kill you right now, you bastard." Barnes shouted before he realized what he revealed.

Barnes regretted his outburst, and the secret information he divulged to men he couldn't trust. He immediately looked at Leland who was now standing with a panicked look on his face. Vazques recognized the name that Barnes shouted and he looked at Trembulak. "General Murtagh is the commander of the United States Army. His name appears in all of our intelligence reports."

"Now that we know who is controlling the America part of this operation, tell us Major Vechesloff, which military officer are you loyal to in your nation?" asked Trembulak nervously as his body still trembled from his near fatal confrontation with Barnes.

"Tell the fucking bastard what he wants to know, Vechesloff," Barnes told the Russian officer leaning against the wall. "He'll find out who they are in a couple of days anyway."

"My allegiance is with General Chchenkoff, Admiral Koschgen, and General Konovnitzine. They have their own plan to save my nation, and my men and I agreed to help them."

"A formidable group of cutthroats to organize the overthrow of your government," said Trembulak who recognized all of the names. "I'm not familiar with any

JOURNEY THROUGH A LONG WINTER'S NIGHT 39

of their backgrounds. Can you tell us something about them, Major?"

"General Vladimer Chchenkoff is the commander of the Russian Army, and the inspiration for the Russian portion of this attack plan. The general is sixty-five years old, and veteran of both the Second World War and Afghanistan. He was firmly opposed to dismantling the Berlin Wall, and the uniting of East and West Germany into a single nation. He disagreed when Communism was abolished in the Soviet Union, and tried to prevent the eradication of the KGB, our secret police. Chchenkoff plans to crush the democratic movement in Russia with military force. Then he will take the country back to authoritarian communist rule. He realizes the military knows what is essential for the people's survival, and that military officers should be in charge of the nation. After the failed coup to eliminate President Barakov in 1991, Chchenkoff began planning how he and others could gain control of my country's government."

"How did the military officers of two nations who were mortal enemies suddenly become allies?" Vazques asked Vechesloff.

"President Borakov and United States' President Rockwell met in Moscow last November with the military leaders of both nations. During that meeting the two Presidents announced plans to reduce the size of their respective military forces."

"The Russian government doesn't have the money to fund their military anymore," complained Vazques as he shook his head. "That's why they stopped giving us military supplies and financial aide for our people."

"Exactly," replied Barnes who seemed pleased Vazques understood the situation.

"The Russian government is out of money and believes democracy will help their economy. Borakov has already eliminated the KGB and the Communist Central Committee. During the past few months he's even dismantled the country and allowed the smaller republics to become self governing. The largest and most feared military power on this planet is quickly being reduced

40   D'ONOFRIO

to handfuls of confused soldiers scattered across a dozen new and struggling nations."

"You tell them the rest of it. You developed most of the Russian portion of this plan," Barnes then told Vechesloff. "You should be proud that you're trying to save your nation while your leaders are letting it go to hell."

"General Chchenkoff still commands the Russian Army, and the divisions of his troops now stranded in the republics are still loyal to him. One week after this attack begins, Chchenkoff, Koschgen, and Konovnitzine will assume military control of Russia and will reunite the break away republics into a single nation again."

"Which of the three men will control your government?" asked Vazques, who hoped his nation would benefit monetarily from the reuniting of the nation.

"Instead of one man making all the decisions that affect our nation, the three men will form a triad of military commanders. The commander of the Air Force will then be asked to join the new government. If he refuses we will eliminate him and General Chchenkoff will place one of his staff officers into that command position."

"What do you have to gain from the political overthrow of your nation?" asked Trembulak, who was skeptical of Vechesloff's statements. "I've learned never to believe anything the Russian government or its military tells me. But tell me, why are you doing this?"

"I only want to help the people of my country. I have nothing more to gain from this. The people of my nation have just suffered through a terrible winter, as has my family. President Borakov believes he can sit back and do nothing while a free market economy establishes itself in our nation. Food and gasoline have not become plentiful as he expected, and the food prices are rising so rapidly the people can't feed their families."

"I can see this is a personal battle for you," commented Vazques somberly after listing to Vechesloff. "I wish we could help you, but we have our own problems to deal with in my nation."

Vechesloff suddenly thought about his parents and sister. "My family stands in food lines for hours, but they're usually turned away because of shortages. I re-

JOURNEY THROUGH A LONG WINTER'S NIGHT   41

member watching them huddled around the single electrical heater in their one bedroom apartment in Moscow before I left. I want more than that for my family and people, and I'm going to help them get it." Vechesloff, the thirty-four-year-old son of a poor Russian laborer was an idealist. He wanted the very best for his county, but he was watching it slowly deteriorate.

"Am I to assume that Murtagh and Chchenkoff met at the arms talks in Moscow and discussed this plan?" Trembulak asked Barnes as he slapped at the flies that landed on the maps spread across the table.

Barnes nodded his head in agreement, "They can see what's happening in both countries, and neither has any use for the untrained men who control their nation's government. Someone with guts and foresight has to prevent the politicians from destroying this nation, and General Murtagh is that man. The General is preparing to assume control of the United States' government one week after this plan becomes operational."

"You told me your new government would help the Palestinians after we overthrow both nations. What will Murtagh do to help us?" asked Trembulak as he stood and nervously paced around the kitchen. He thought about the hopeless situation of his homeless people, and the oppression they were facing at the hands of the Israeli military.

"Two months after we've gained control of the Russian and United States' governments, we'll form a combined military force of Russian and American Special Forces. It'll include thirty divisions of tanks and attack helicopters. The coalition force will decimate the Israeli military forces, and the settlers on the occupied Golan Heights and Gaza Strip will be forced off that land. Then the combined force will destroy the nation of Israel and the people will be forced into exile. That land and all the buildings on it will be given to the Palestinians so they can form their own nation."

Trembulak sat back in his chair and smiled at Vazques after Barnes completed his explanation.

"Excellent. After that, all of the Palestinian people

42 D'ONOFRIO

will look to me as their leader. The leaders of my organization have grown complacent with the Israelis' meaningless peace talks and concessions. They don't consider violence as a method of securing a homeland for us anymore. I will prove them wrong, and show them how we should have originally taken the land from the Israelis."

"What will Murtagh do for my country?" asked Vazques who hoped his nation would benefit after the attack. "My people also stand in long lines waiting for food and gasoline. We desperately need food. I've heard rumors there isn't a cat left alive in my nation. The people have eaten them because they are starving and suffering from malnutrition. We also need medical supplies because the Russian government refuses to give us any more aide."

"General Murtagh plans to give Castro the financial aid that is currently given to the Israeli government every year. Since your men are critical to the success of this attack, your nation should receive largest benefits from the new United States' military government. Your people will be taken care of after this is over Vazques, you have my word." Both Trembulak and Vazques appeared satisfied with their compensation for assisting with the attack.

"How many other men in the United States' military are involved in this plan to overthrow your government?" Vazques asked Leland.

"Sixty of the highest ranking officers in our military support this plan, along with four hundred enlisted men. Another group of military officers are evaluating Murtagh's plan, and they'll decide which way to go after the President is our hostage. If they decide not to go with us they're useless to us, and we're better off if we kill them." Leland was reluctant to give many details about the other men involved in the plot. If the attack failed he didn't want to jeopardize the military officers helping him. Leland hoped they would attempt to over throw the government again at an opportune time in the future.

Barnes briefly thought about the President and the other members of the government he hated as he pic-

JOURNEY THROUGH A LONG WINTER'S NIGHT   43

tured the United States' capital in his mind's eye. "Two weeks from today the government of the United States will be out of business, and our military will be running the nation. That's the way it should have been back in 1776. The military had the ability to free this nation from England, and it has always had the leadership and vision to protect and guide it."

Leland agreed with Barnes' comments and looked at his watch. "We've got to get moving, our plane leaves in two hours."

"How are we getting into your country?" Vazques asked Leland as he packed his attack plan into a leather briefcase. "We don't have passports and we'll be stopped as soon as we step off a passenger plane."

"You're flying to Miami aboard one of our helicopters from Guantanamo Bay," Leland laughed after the comment. "You're going with us as United States' intelligence agents. We have a private military jet waiting in Miami to fly us to Rhode Island tonight. We'll get to Newport a few days early, and have time to look around and make some notes. I've been to the city five times while we were planning the attack, but we want to give you some time to see the area too."

Trembulak began packing his own attack plan into a plastic carrying case as he spoke to Barnes. "My people are still dying even after the concessions made by the Israeli government during the peace talks initiated by your government. The Israelis are giving us small pieces of land, but nothing we can call our homeland. The Israelis will soon find themselves without a country as we did many years ago. My people will finally have a nation." Twenty minutes later the group walked out of the apartment building into the sweltering sun. Then they drove to Guantanamo Naval Base.

Chapter Three

At six o'clock the following morning, General Murtagh and Colonel Alfred Vorden walked together in the light of a spectacular sunrise. The scattered clouds appeared a brilliant red hue against the deep blue sky. Murtagh flew to Fort Meade in Maryland the previous night with six of his men. As his men stood on a dusty gravel road and watched for approaching military vehicles, Murtagh and Vorden walked across a deserted rifle range.

"Well, what do you think of my plans for resurrecting our great nation?" Murtagh asked Vorden. Murtagh momentarily smiled and looked to the right when he heard birds singing in the tall pine trees that lined both sides of the mile long rifle range. "I'm planning to change the face of the world during the next few days Colonel. The working people of our nation will benefit from my plans, not just the wealthy and the influential!"

Vorden was a fifty-one-year-old career Army officer, an intellectual who graduated from West Point and later received his Masters degree in Business from Harvard University. The balding, overweight, and seemingly frail military officer was a brilliant financial analyst. His staff's recommendations were the basis for the Army's world wide budget. Vorden, whose office was in a desolate portion of the Pentagon's basement, was honored when a general of Murtagh's stature approached him with a proposal to organize a new government in the United States.

"I analyzed both your preliminary plans and your objectives very thoroughly, General. You do seem to have prepared for every contingency that may arise," Vorden complimented Murtagh as they walked across the dew covered grass that wet their highly polished black shoes. "I'm impressed by what you hope to accomplish General. I often experience the same feelings of frustration that you've described to me as the basis for your radical ideas, but I honestly don't know if you're going to succeed."

"Don't worry, my plan is flawless Colonel," Murtagh

JOURNEY THROUGH A LONG WINTER'S NIGHT   45

confidently reassured Vorden as they stepped over a deep trench used by soldiers at the rifle range. "If we can't make my plan work, and the politicians continue to run the government as they do today, our nation will be in shambles ten years from now. It is my firm belief that if everything remains as it is today, the government as we know it now will be out of business within twenty years. If that occurs, I believe each state will become an autonomous and independent nation struggling to survive in a sea of economic turmoil. Our nation will fall the same way the Soviet Union did."

"I'm not in a position to judge whether or not your ideas are the correct solution to the problems facing our nation today, General," Vorden told Murtagh as the financial planner removed his silver wire rim glasses and began cleaning them. "Why do you want to replace our nation's government? Why don't you present a plan to the President to restructure our present government? Suggest he allow the military to work more closely with the government and private sector manufacturers as a business partner. That would give the military a much higher profile position while it helps the nation deal with its problems."

As Murtagh studied a tall wooden observation tower he slowly became upset. He realized Vorden was overlooking the theories and philosophies, which were the basis of his personal ideas, which he considered revolutionary. "In the first place Colonel, none of the damn politicians are going to listen to the ideas of a military man they consider subservient. Maybe you don't realize it tucked away safely in your little office Vorden, but Rockwell and the other politicians don't have any idea how to use our military's resources to help the nation. Unless there's a conflict somewhere in the world they want us to get involved in, the damn politicians want us to stay on our bases like good little soldiers and not express our opinions. Well, Colonel, I'm tired of watching the politicians destroy this great nation, and now its time to act!"

"If you believe so strongly a military man should be President, why don't you retire and run for office your

46 D'ONOFRIO

self, General? You're young, and I believe the ideas you've expressed could benefit our nation. Why don't you consider running for a vacancy in the Senate, and maybe the Presidency in six years?"

"You want me to become a politician! One of the people I detest? The politicians don't give a damn about the people, not like I do Colonel. If I were the leader of this nation my decision and directions would be based solely on the welfare of the people. They wouldn't be influenced by a need to get myself re-elected. My main concern would be this nation, not myself!" Murtagh seemed enraged by Vorden's suggestion, and as he screamed angrily at the meek and reserved officer, his hands flew in the air in a wild and animated manner.

"I'm convinced certain aspects of your plan are extremely risky, General. Events such as those you're proposing appear in our intelligence reports about other nation's governments everyday. I never thought it might happen in our own nation."

"Of course, it's risky, Vorden. All the great achievements in history have been a risk undertaken by men who wanted change. I've already assembled a large team of Army professionals willing to risk both their careers and their lives to save our nation. I'm asking you to become a valuable part of our team. I know you're highly skilled in the areas of finance and economics, and this nation can use your experience to lead it out of the recession."

Vorden stared at the ground as he walked, and he kicked several brass bullet casings he saw laying on the grass reflecting the morning sunlight. "Do you really believe you can save our nation General?"

Murtagh laughed as he watched three rabbits hopping across the wet grass fifty feet ahead. "They've asked the same thing about other historic men Vorden, men who had vision and dreams of glory. My plan is greater than the heroic feats of Alexander the Great, or Hannibal, and my leadership skills are vastly superior to those men. During the past thirty years, the politicians have allowed the United States to fall from its position as the world's mightiest military force. Now they're allowing

JOURNEY THROUGH A LONG WINTER'S NIGHT 47

the same thing to happen to American business and industry. They're not concerned about providing the unemployed people with jobs, or protecting American businesses from foreign imports. Rockwell promises tax cuts for the people, and protection for American businesses from foreign manufacturers, and then he can't persuade Congress to support his plans."

"The President has already announced some new legislation he believes will help the nation, General. Now it's the Congress that's opposing his ideas for reform," said Vorden, who was trying to justify the government's slow reaction to nation's problems.

"The members of Congress are a mindless bunch of publicity seekers. They veto the President's plans to help the nation and then present their own ingenious ideas to make themselves look good, which Rockwell ultimately vetoes. The people don't benefit from this back and forth bickering bull shit. They voted the politicians into office out of desperation, and now they see nothing but bickering and name calling while nothing is happening to improve their situation. They're becoming disgusted with the American government and its officials, and many of them aren't even voting anymore."

"You should give the President and Congress more time to work out their differences, General. Public opinion is quickly changing and the people are demanding more accountability from our government officials every day. But, even with this new public awareness, you still can't expect the government to react to every new problem it faces with a simultaneous solution."

Murtagh made a fist and punched the supports of another tall observation tower, startling Vorden who was watching the overhead clouds change to white hue as the sun rose higher. "The government has had years to deal with the problems facing us today, but the politicians haven't done a thing to alleviate them until they've become crisis situations. Then they tell us they need more money to correct the problems and are planning to raise our taxes again."

"How would you change things if you assumed control of the government?" Vorden asked as he tried to get

48 D'ONOFRIO

an insight into the General's mind. "Your plan doesn't describe what you're going to do after you install your new government in Washington."

Murtagh eyes flashed with excitement after the question. He reached down and picked up a stick as they walked along the tall pine trees gently bending in the breeze. "During the past five years I've put together a plan to alleviate our nation's problems. The people are looking for a new and dynamic leader to guide them through the difficult times ahead. I have only one problem I can't easily overcome. I can't wait to get myself elected by the people. Instead, I'll have to destroy our entire government with military force, and then announce my ideas and plans to save the nation."

"I must admit, that portion of your plan does disturb me, General. A large concentration of innocent people could get hurt during the initial phases of your operation."

"That's to be expected," laughed Murtagh, oblivious to Vorden's troubled concerns. "A few obscure people won't be missed. People always die when we're trying to free a nation from its repressive government. Look at what happened in Grenada and Panama. Civilians always get killed during the uprising that topples a government."

"That's very true, General. Although I don't like it I'll have to agree some people may die while you change our current form of government. How do you plan to help the rest of the people as a military man leading the government?"

"My first official act will be to kick the slimeball congressmen and representatives out of office," Murtagh told Vorden with a vengeance in his voice. "Then I'll select my most competent and trusted military officers and place them into those positions. Under my direction, they'll dismantle each state's government, and install military officers into the positions of governors, mayors, and local officials. From those positions my military men will direct the local activities of both business and the community. They'll provide military expertise in the fields of finance, manufacturing, commu-

JOURNEY THROUGH A LONG WINTER'S NIGHT 49

nications, medical, logistics, quality control, with a myriad of other knowledge that can be shared with American businesses."

"How can you be so confident that knowledge will help the nation, General? You're suggesting we use soldiers trained to kill in combat to help rebuild our nation? How can these soldiers help the people?"

"They may be trained to kill, but they have other skills just as vital to this nation. There's a debate raging in Congress over a national health care program right now, when I already have a plan to alleviate that problem. We have Army, Marine, Navy, Coast Guard, and Air Force bases located across this country. I propose opening up all the hospitals on those bases so the people can get free medical care there. We're already paying those doctors and nurses to do their jobs, so why not let the people of our nation benefit from both their medical knowledge and skills. I plan to move our mobile surgical units into the rural areas of the nation where there are no doctors to help the people. I want to use the advanced medical facilities at Walter Reed Army Hospital, and the Bethesda Naval Hospital to help fight Cancer, AIDS, Alzheimer's, and a multitude of other deadly and debilitating diseases. The politicians don't give a damn about the people with those diseases, and those people can't wait for a cure."

"I'll agree, those trained medical personnel can help the people, General," commented Vorden as the short man struggled to keep up with the fast walking Murtagh. "How can you use your combat units to help the nation?"

"I can use all the units of the military to rebuild this nation. Our combat engineering battalions across the nation practice building bridges every day because there's nothing else for them to do. Lets move them off their bases, and use their skills and heavy equipment to repair and expand our nation's infrastructure. They should be in California right now helping to rebuild the Los Angeles freeway system. I also want to use them to build housing for the homeless. Allowing people to sleep on the streets and in city parks is ludicrous, and I won't

50   D'ONOFRIO

tolerate it. We've got to help the people who depend on the government for assistance."

"The homeless situation is intolerable, General. It's placing an unfair financial strain on the cities and states because the federal government won't intervene and help with the problem."

"I want to establish programs that will help feed all of the people, not just the homeless. There's no reason in the world why any child or adult should go to bed hungry in this country. I'll use the engineering and combat battalions, and their heavy equipment, to work all the farm land across this nation. We'll even plant food in the national forests if we need it to feed everyone. Paying farmers not to plant crops in their fields so the prices will remain artificially higher is a national disgrace, and I'll end that subsidy immediately."

Murtagh watched a flock of geese flying in the distance, and he paused for several seconds. "We have military police units, counter terrorist units, and Special Forces teams sitting idle today. I plan to use them to crush the drug dealers with military force. We'll kill the bastards if we have to, to stop the flow of drugs into this nation that's poisoning our people. I plan to do the same thing with the street gangs. Kids carrying guns on the streets has to stop, one way or another. If they won't surrender their weapons then we'll send our troops out and eliminate the problem with force. I don't care how many of them we have to kill to stop the senseless violence escalating across the country. We'll use the engineering battalions to build prisons out in the middle of desert, well away from the populated areas. Then we'll end the practice of releasing repeat offenders because the bleeding hearts think our prison system is overcrowded. Those prisoners can rot in concrete prisons for all I care. We're going to make the city streets safe for the public again, and they won't be afraid to go out after dark anymore."

Murtagh pointed into the air ahead with the stick as though he was reading the items on a blackboard. "I have a plan to use our military instructors to the utmost by having them assist our public school teach-

JOURNEY THROUGH A LONG WINTER'S NIGHT 51

ers. I want to teach our children mathematics, foreign languages, and the sciences, so they can be prepared for the future. Eventually our time will be over, Colonel, and the strong nation we're going to build will be theirs. They must be educated so they can nurture and cultivate the thriving businesses and industries of the future."

"What about the other branches of the military, General? Are you going to use them, or eliminate them?"

"Use them, of course! I have plans for the Air Force. I want Doppler radar at all airports across the nation within a year. The government has been working on that project for ten years, and the politicians haven't done shit. The I want the Air Force to work with the aerospace companies. I want larger and safer jetliners, and I want them to help NASA into space. I also want them to begin working on solar powered electrical generation so we can provide electricity to the people free of charge."

"What about the Navy, General?"

"I have a plan for them to produce food in the oceans of the world to feed the hungry, especially in Africa. I want them mining minerals within one year, and oil from the ocean's floor within twelve months. Then I want them producing electricity, cheap electricity, from the ocean."

"Your plans have a solid and logical basis, General, but the American people and business executives may not appreciate or tolerate what they consider military interference. How will you deal with that problem?"

"The people in this country have never received any direct help from the military. They don't even know what types of assistance we can provide to them, and neither do the piss ant politicians running the government. I'm sure the people will appreciate what we can offer and will gladly accept our assistance."

"The American work force doesn't seem able to compete with the foreigner competitors in today's market, General." Vorden shook his head as he thought about the foreign cars and electronics flooding into the nation, "and maybe they'll feel the military is really interfering in their everyday work. "

"There's nothing inherently wrong with the Ameri

52 D'ONOFRIO

can workers, they just need some damn guidance and some technical assistance. The government has ignored them for so long they really believe they can't compete in the world marketplace. They need someone like me to show them the path to excellence, and instill a feeling of superiority as the United States again becomes an industrial giant."

"How will you handle the labor unions if they resist the help you want to give the nation's businesses, General? They may not appreciate it when you start telling them how they can improve the quality of their products or their productivity. That may be enough to cause your plan to fail."

"If they resist, the piss ant unions and the people who run them are out, disbanded, abolished. I don't have time for the petty shit they pull with their damn strikes and senseless walkouts. The workers of this country have to unite and start moving ahead or the other nations of the world are going to bury us economically. Look at what the Japs are doing to us right now. We rebuilt their nation after we destroyed it during the war, and taught them how to work with electronics. Now they're taking money out of American worker's hands with their damn electronic imports."

"I don't know, General. The very nature of your plan can be considered traitorous. You told me, you, your father, and your grandfather served this nation's military for years. How can you propose such a radical change to the government you serve?"

"Don't compare me to my family, damn it. My grandfather and father commanded in times much less difficult than the ones we're facing now. Their job was to fight the Germans, Japanese, and the Russians. They didn't have internal problems destroying their nation while they were fighting on the other side of the world."

"Of course they did, General. They had the Depression to contend with," replied Vorden as he shaded his eyes from the rising sun, and saw the two Jeeps that carried the men to the remote firing range.

"They had wars and the safety of their men to worry about, Colonel. They couldn't be concerned about the

JOURNEY THROUGH A LONG WINTER'S NIGHT 53

problems affecting this country. We had Korea, Vietnam, and Iraq, and now we're in the middle of a worsening depression with no enemies in sight. We should have the intelligence to use the professional military men who normally would be fighting a war to help us find solutions to our nation's problems today."

"Tell me, General, what did the politicians do to make you despise them so much? Did one incident make you this bitter toward the government, or was it an accumulation of problems over the years?"

"When we were in Vietnam, the politicians held us back and wouldn't let us finish the job there. Then they did the same god damn thing in Iraq. They always hold back the military. Then, after we've risked our lives so they can get rich in their god damn offices in Washington, the politicians come up with a plan to save money by firing us. I'd like to see all the gutless politicians stretched out in caskets. Half of them are closet homosexuals who won't be around too much longer after they get AIDS anyway. I've always said the only good politician is one who's lying in a casket."

"You're starting to sound like Hitler. What's next, a master plan to take over the world after you've built a new government in this nation?" Vorden suddenly asked sarcastically.

"No, and if you think that Vorden, you've missed the point of why I'm risking everything to do this. I'm proposing a way to help this nation become the strongest economic force in the world. I'm a superb military commander, a strong leader of men, and an articulate statesman. Some people think I'm opinionated and overbearing, but they can't see the great potential in my ideas, or they fear them. There are times I feel so powerful and full of ideas that I believe I'm the reincarnation of the Julius Caesar. I've studied the ideas and principles written by the famous philosophers such as Socrates and Plato, and I'll use them to lead the nation back to strength. I know where the mistakes occurred in history. I won't make the same mistakes, or allow anyone else to. I'm so convinced I can help the nation, I can feel it in my mind and body."

54   D'ONOFRIO

Murtagh led Vorden to the Jeep as they discussed more details of the plan. "Well, Colonel, now you know everything that's on my mind, my hopes and aspirations. Has that knowledge helped you decide whether you will become part of the emerging government charged with rebuilding our mighty nation?"

Vorden watched the sunlight as it slowly moved across the pine trees and bushes on a mountain in the distance. "I've got to consider the well being of my wife and my family, General. I'm privileged that you think I can help the nation. But, after carefully considering your plan, I don't feel I'm qualified to be part of your attack force, I have no combat experience. If your plan succeeds and you require additional people to help you run your new government, then I'll gladly give you all the assistance I can."

Murtagh became angry after Vorden's comments and he looked away while rubbing his hands together for several seconds. "You sound just like the piss ant politicians I've come to detest Vorden. You're a gutless little bastard who's indecisive and afraid to take the risks that might make this nation great again. You're no better than the god damn President!"

"That's not true, General," protested Vorden as he pointed at Murtagh and stepped toward him. "I've served this country just as much as you have in the military."

"No, you serve the politicians, Colonel. I don't want any spineless bastards like you who don't share my vision serving under me." Murtagh immediately turned toward his men and took a deep breath. "I was wrong, I thought he'd see we're trying to save the nation. Kill him!"

"No, no, lets discuss this some more, General," Vorden shouted after hearing Murtagh's order. "I'm not going to say anything about your plan, you can trust me." Those were Vorden's last words before three bullets struck his chest and killed him. The sounds of the gunshots echoed across the wooded countryside and startled the birds, causing them to fly from the trees in a large group.

Murtagh watched the birds with a smile, then stared down at the blood running from Vorden's body as it lay

JOURNEY THROUGH A LONG WINTER'S NIGHT 55

on the dusty gravel road. "What a damn waste of a great military man's mind. The task ahead of us is greater than the building of the pyramids, and he could have been part of it. Now I pray to God I have the strength to succeed. Dig a hole and bury this piece of garbage. This'll all be over before anyone starts looking for him."

At 11:00 A.M., Thursday morning, the President's jet landed at the Quonset Point Naval Air Station in Rhode Island. The President and his family were not expecting the huge crowds waiting to see them at the military airport as they walked off the jet. Fifty-five minutes later, their motorcade was traveling on Newport's historic streets where the President saw the massive crowds of vacationers waiting to see him. As the limousines traveled over the Goat Island access bridge, the President saw his helicopter parked on a large grassy field beside a hotel parking lot. The limousine stopped at the Sheraton Hotel's ornate front entrance, where the President and his family stepped from the car. They stopped to wave to the large crowd of cheering spectators and reporters who stood behind the police barricades on the long, wide driveway.

Neither the President nor the Secret Service could know Barnes and several of his men were in the crowd, standing in the hot sun and oppressive humidity, dressed as tourists. As perspiration ran down their faces, they watched the Secret Service guards survey the area for potential problems. Barnes inconspicuously elbowed one of his men and nodded to the left. Then he wiped the perspiration off his forehead and shaded his eyes with his hand from the blazing sun. "I count ten Secret Service agents watching the crowd from the hotel roof. These guys are professionals, and look like they're well trained, but they'll be no match for us," he told his men with a wide smile. "This is going to be a piece of cake!"

When the President and his family walked into the hotel's ornate lobby crowded with excited people taking pictures of them, they saw their friends Ervin Peterson and his wife. The lobby's marble tiled floors along with a rose colored wallpaper and soft lighting gave the warm feeling of security one experiences in their own home.

56   D'ONOFRIO

"It's good to see you again, Erv, Debra," the President told his friends as he smiled and extended his hand. "You're both looking good."

"It's good to have you here, Joe," replied Ervin Peterson, as his wife and Melanie Rockwell hugged each other. "Come on, we'll take you up to your suite and you can relax," he said as he led the Rockwell family into an elevator. The elevator quickly rose to the hotel's top floor. When the polished metal doors opened, the four Secret Service agents standing in the hallway immediately stepped aside when they saw the President. Ervin Peterson opened a suite's double wooden doors and led the President and his family into it. The President and his family were delighted when they saw the lavish interior of the large suite where they would be spending the weekend.

Three hours later, as he and his family sat talking to the Petersons, the President looked at his watch when he heard a knock on the suite's door. Sharon Lingard, the President's Event Secretary, and several of her staff walked in after a Secret Service agent opened the door.

"We've got to leave, Mister President," Lingard told Rockwell. "The Fort Adams dedication ceremony begins in less than an hour."

"Why don't you come with us?" Rockwell asked the Petersons as he pulled on his jacket. "You can ride in the limousine with us." It was an offer eagerly accepted by the Petersons.

A police escort met the President's motorcade after it crossed the Goat Island access bridge. It led the limousines through the crowds of spectators that lined both sides of the city streets in the oppressive heat. Twenty minutes later the limousines stopped beside the huge fort's main entrance. The fort's two hundred foot high walls constructed of huge gray stones towered above the limousines and the wooden platform built for the dedication ceremony. Huddled around the platform was a crowd of eight thousand people who sat on the grass in the blazing sun as they waited to see the President and his family.

Rockwell's staff introduced him to the city and state officials on the large platform decorated with red, white,

JOURNEY THROUGH A LONG WINTER'S NIGHT 57

and blue streamers. He briefly discussed the fort's restoration project with them as they stood in the sun and ninety four degree temperature. Thirty minutes later the dedication ceremony began. The Governor of Rhode Island was the first speaker and his shirt appeared soaked with perspiration as he stepped to the microphone. He briefly explained the highlights of the fort's restoration project to the spectators before he introduced the President.

The President stepped to the microphone and waited for the applause to subside, then began his speech. "We're here today to rededicate this fort, which was first dedicated on July 4, 1799, and took its name from my predecessor, President John Adams. Fort Adams was designed to defend Newport against attacks from both the land and sea early in our nation's history. Our government also used this fort to defend our nation against its enemies during the Second World War. Many courageous men have stood on these stone walls, braving the weather to protect this nation's people from its enemies. After the interior is completely restored, this fort will serve as a reminder of what sacrifices our great nation endured to be free. It'll be a tribute to the men and women who fought and died to keep it free. Thank you."

As the crowd applauded the President's speech, Leland and Vechesloff stood among the unsuspecting spectators, shading their eyes from the sun as they watched the people on the podium. After the Secret Service agents led the officials into the fort for a tour, Leland and Vechesloff walked to the edge of the water. Goat Island was only three hundred yards away across the harbor, surrounded by the deep blue ocean water that relentlessly crashed onto the shore. Hundreds of power and sail boats floated gently on the waters of Newport Harbor and in the marina slips on Goat Island. The mix of historic and newer buildings in the resort city formed the background to the scene, and with the seagulls floating in the deep blue cloudless sky, it gave a picturesque feeling of peace and serenity.

"The people of your country are soft and weak," laughed Vechesloff as he watched the huge crowd of

58 D'ONOFRIO

relaxed and happy vacationers walking to their cars in the parking lot. "Vazques' men won't have any problems dealing with them. Your people are feeble and pacified, and are not expecting an attack from within their own nation."

Then he turned and looked at Leland who was watching the seagulls bobbing on the ocean water a few yards from shore. "Doesn't it upset you that we'll have to kill many of these innocent people before the end of the week?" Vechesloff asked Leland coldly.

"People always die during a revolution, Vechesloff," Leland replied without apparent emotion as he stared at a peaceful seagull, although the thought greatly upset him. Then he suddenly turned and stared at Vechesloff. "Don't be fooled by what you see around here Vechesloff. We're getting ready to start a war to rescue our nation from the government trying to destroy it with empathy and inaction."

"I know what we want to achieve, but we won't be killing innocent civilians in my nation, only the politicians." Vechesloff laughed as he admired the body of an attractive young woman dressed in tight fitting orange shorts. "These people are going to suffer and die before we're done here."

Leland suddenly became angry with himself, and with Vechesloff's comments. "Back off and watch what you say here Vechesloff. You're just as dirty as we are, so don't tell me how fucking disgusted you are because we have to kill the people you think are innocent victims. You're the one who came up with the fucking plan to kill all the members of your own government."

Vechesloff stared at the large yachts in the harbor, and those docked at the marina, and immediately thought about the poor people starving in his native country. "You're right Leland. These people have to die if we are to save both nations. I wish there was some other way to do this, but we don't have any other options." He could see the anger in Leland's face and he immediately ended his verbal assault.

"You're starting to sound like you're getting soft." Leland told Vechesloff after he thought about the Rus-

JOURNEY THROUGH A LONG WINTER'S NIGHT   59

sian soldier's remarks. Then he stepped forward and angrily whispered, "The lives of these people mean nothing to me, nothing, and their deaths shouldn't even concern you."

Vechesloff laughed at Leland's comment as he stepped away and looked around to see if anyone in the crowd walking past them heard the comment. "What if I am having problems dealing with what we're going to do here? What are you going to do about it? Report me to that psychopath Barnes?"

"I won't have to tell Barnes, I'll kill you myself if I think you're getting to be a risk, Vechesloff." Leland's reply shocked the callous Russian military officer whose emotions were hardened after three years of combat in Afghanistan. Vechesloff knew he could no longer trust Leland as he stared into the soldier's distant eyes. He knew they were not comrades in arms, nor friends, but were still enemies.

"Nothing is going to stop us from helping my nation, Vechesloff. Not you, not anyone else in this fucking country," added Leland as he looked at the city. "It's unfortunate this city has to be destroyed, but we've got to do it if we're going to save our nation. Now lets get out of here and find my men."

When the President and his family returned to the hotel, they discussed their schedules for the following day. The President's schedule included a meeting with the members of the state's political party at a fund raising luncheon in one of the city's historic mansions. At the same time the President's wife and daughter were to tour another historic mansion in the city. There they would attend a luncheon given by the mayor's wife. They were pleased with the reception they already received from the crowds of people they met, and were confident the weekend would be very enjoyable.

Chapter Four

At eight thirty Friday night, Trembulak and Fasha Partyski slowly walked around the Sheraton Hotel on Goat Island. They held hands and watched the ocean waves crashing onto the rocks that surrounded the island. Several other couples watched the bright orange sunset in the western sky as they walked hand in hand. Another couple sat together on the wide cement seawall that protected the island from the ocean waves and kissed as they watched the sun sinking into the ocean.

"Isn't this island beautiful?" Partyski asked her lover as she held his hand and spun around playfully while they walked on an access road that led to the hotel's rear parking lot. Trembulak watched her jet black hair flying in the air, and smiled at the woman who appeared oblivious to what was about to happen on the island.

Partyski was born in Poland and had joined Trembulak's organization three years earlier. She quickly became his traveling companion and mistress. The twenty-seven-year-old woman was extremely attractive and made her body available to Trembulak whenever he wanted it.

During difficult times when his men unsuccessfully attacked their targets, or died during the attacks, Trembulak would beat her unmercifully until her face was bleeding. At other times he was passionate and loving with her. A true masochist, Partyski lived for the excitement of seeing buildings destroyed by massive explosions and innocent people dying.

Trembulak looked to his left when one of the hotel's rear access doors opened. He watched Andres Vazques quickly run across the grass lit by floodlights on the hotel roof, oblivious to the beauty and tranquility of the ocean and the sunset. "I just finished talking to Barnes! He's still telling me his three trailers of equipment will be here before midnight, but I'm worried they won't get here in time!"

"Everything is happening exactly as Barnes said it would. Relax Vazques, or you will be exhausted before

JOURNEY THROUGH A LONG WINTER'S NIGHT 61

the attack begins," warned Trembulak when he saw how tense the Cuban soldier had become during the past two hours. "Have you been to the yachts to check on your men yet?"

"I walked to the marina an hour ago and spoke to all of them. They're getting jittery sitting around on those boats! They're anxious to attack."

"You knew this was going to happen Vazques! We all have to wait, but not much longer. Warn your men not to do anything foolish that might give us away!"

"You're right, they're my best men. How about you Casimir? Are you ready for the attack?"

"We're ready, and I'm confident we'll be successful!" He replied with a smile as he looked at the lit buildings and streets along the water in the city. "I'm sure I can convince the Americans we are really Russian soldiers! I know I can do this!"

"The feeling of anticipation just before the attack is wonderful, better than that of sex. Isn't it my dear?" laughed Partyski as she rubbed Trembulak's neck with her hand. Then she crushed her lips against his while forcing her tongue into his mouth. She pulled her lips away quickly and stared at Trembulak with an evil smile. "All the people on this island will soon be your prisoners my love! Think of the power you'll have over their lives! The power to decide who will live and who will die slowly as we watch!"

At midnight, Vazques stood in his hotel room window and watched as the three long silver supply trailers Barnes promised crossed the Goat Island access bridge. He watched the drivers carefully maneuver the trailers into a large parking lot filled with cars beside the hotel. They parked the trailers near the four foot high cement sea wall that protected the cars from large ocean waves. Vazques smiled when he realized everything was happening as Barnes had promised.

At one thirty Saturday morning, Barnes walked into one of the hotel's lounges and found Vazques, Leland, and Vechesloff standing at the bar. They were watching several couples dance seductively to the blaring music of a live band as red, blue, and green lights colored the

62   D'ONOFRIO

wooden dance floor and the lounge's white walls. "I think its time to get the party started," Barnes told them, then they walked out of the hotel and turned toward the parking lot. As they walked between the cars in the lit parking lot, Leland looked at the stars and white wispy clouds in the night sky.

Barnes unlocked the door to the trailer that would serve as their communications center and turned on several dim red lights after everyone was inside. The trailer was originally a camping trailer nine feet wide and twenty three feet long. Murtagh's combat engineers removed the trailer's cabinets, beds, toilet, and kitchen facilities. Then they installed new interior walls made of wood veneer and covered them with white paint. This gave the impression the trailer's interior was much larger and roomier. They positioned several metal desks at the rear of the trailer and mounted twelve military radios on a long metal shelf mounted to a wall. Several other tables and chairs, along with cardboard and wooden boxes of supplies filled the rest of the trailer.

The heat inside the windowless trailer was oppressive. Barnes quickly pulled off his blue shirt, and exposed his muscular shoulders and the streams of perspiration trickling down his skin. "We're about an hour from beginning the attack. Are your commanders and their men ready to go?" he asked Vazques.

"Every one of my men knows what he has to do when the attack begins! They won't disappoint you!"

"Good, our divers from the yachts are already in the water mining the access bridge." Barnes and the others carefully read their computer generated timetables, and the immense attack plan in black notebooks on the desks. Barnes became agitated when he realized he would be captured on the island if the attack failed. He knew he would spend the rest of his life in prison for treason and he briefly thought about suicide as an alternative if captured.

At 2:15 A.M., Barnes told the group, "Ok Vazques, contact your men and tell them to start moving into position on the island. Tell them to get rid of any police or Secret Service agents they find on the island!"

JOURNEY THROUGH A LONG WINTER'S NIGHT 63

"Don't worry, they'll eliminate every one they find while they're moving into position!" Vazques replied confidently as he lifted a radio microphone, then gave instructions to his men on the yachts.

The Cuban troops dressed in Russian Army uniforms were aboard the yachts Last Chance, Pale Horse, Princess Ieasha, Second Wave, Daddy's Pride, and Persevere. They impatiently waited in the cramped quarters for Vazques' signal to move onto Goat Island. Each soldier carried a machine gun, hand grenades, a gas mask, and hundreds of bullets.

"My men are moving off the yachts and onto the docks right now," Vazques told the group as he listened to radio reports from his squad leaders. "They'll have the marina walkways secured within the minute so none of the people will be able to get off their boats."

As Vazques' men were moving onto the island, one of his squad leaders used a handgun equipped with a silencer to kill a security guard monitoring traffic into the condominium building's parking lot. As the soldiers quietly moved through the hotel parking lot they heard noises inside a van, and a group quickly huddled around it. A man and women who met in the hotel lounge were inside making love, unconcerned that someone might hear them. They were startled when the Cubans suddenly pulled open the van's doors. The woman began screaming after the Cubans shot her lover in the chest several times, spattering her white blouse with blood. Another soldier covered the woman's mouth with his hand as he cut her throat with a bayonet and left her to die.

Fifteen tense minutes later, Vazques listened to a radio report as he wiped perspiration off his forehead. "My men are in position across the island and around the hotel. They killed thirty two security guards and police they found on the island!"

"That's thirty two assholes we don't have to worry about anymore!" Laughed Barnes with a sadistic tone in his voice as he watched Leland carefully open a silver metal case the size of a briefcase. Then he told Vazques, "Tell your men around the hotel to put on their gas

64 D'ONOFRIO

masks. We're going to release the nerve gas into the building's ventilation system."

Leland's heartbeat increased and his fingers trembled as he slowly turned several switches on a black panel inside the case. Then he watched as six small red lights slowly change color to green. "The gas should be filling the hotel right now! It's going to knock everyone on their ass!"

As the strategically placed blue nerve gas canisters released their contents into the ventilation system, the hotel's night shift employees began collapsing onto the floor. As the odorless gas quickly filled the building, hotel guests still awake in their rooms collapsed onto the floor. Those who were already asleep fell into a deeper sleep as the gas numbed their minds. The fast acting gas also filled the hotel's penthouse suites, and it wasn't long before the unsuspecting Secret Service agents and the President's family were overcome.

"Damn, this is a god damn long twenty minutes to wait!" commented Barnes impatiently as he stared at a digital clock. He fumbled with his pen while he waited for the nerve gas to dissipate harmlessly into the air. Barnes stood during the last minute and when the clock finally changed he said, "All right Vazques, tell your men its safe for them to enter the fucking hotel! They've got forty five minutes to secure the complex before those people start to recover from the gas."

The Cuban soldiers massed in the shadows around the building quickly moved into the hotel. They ran through the building's front lobby doors, and the rear access doors that opened into the large room that surrounded the hotel's indoor swimming pool.

They rushed in through the convention center's elegant glass foyer, the building's rear loading dock doors, and all of the hotel's other access doors. A group of twenty soldiers stepped over the bodies of the hotel workers laying on the lobby's marble floor and crowded into an elevator. When they reached the hotel's top floor they quickly disarmed the unconscious Secret Service agents they found laying on the floor and carried their bodies to a restaurant on the first floor.

JOURNEY THROUGH A LONG WINTER'S NIGHT   65

Trembulak and Partyski cautiously pushed opened the door of the President's bedroom and turned on a light. They smiled when they saw the unconscious man and woman laying on the king size white lace canopy bed, covered with a large embroidered red satin quilt. Partyski used a pair of handcuffs to secure the President's wrist to his wife's wrist. She then ran into their daughter's bedroom and placed handcuffs around the young woman's wrists.

Trembulak looked around at the lavish furnishings in the suite and sat on an antique wooden chair covered with red velvet fabric. He raised a portable radio to his mouth and said, "Barnes, this is Trembulak. Vazques' men have captured your President and his family! Everyone on this floor was unconscious and we didn't have any problems!"

"Good, now stay calm and do the fucking job, Trembulak," Barnes immediately radioed back. "Use your head and don't deviate from the fucking attack plan!"

As Vazques' men moved around, the suite the effects of the nerve gas began to wear off. The President and his wife began to awaken when they heard voices in their bedroom and men shouting in the hotel hallway. They slowly opened their eyes and immediately sensed something was wrong when they tried to move their arms. As the President's vision cleared, he suddenly became alarmed when he saw armed men dressed in camouflaged clothing standing around his bed.

"You'll feel the effects of the nerve gas for a few more minutes," commented Trembulak as he sat on the chair on the other side of the bedroom. "You'll also have a headache, but that shouldn't last too long!"

"What, what the hell is going on in here?" shouted the startled President as he tried to sit up and saw the handcuffs around his wrist and that of his wife. "Who the hell do you think you are coming in here like this?"

"Mary, what have they done with Mary?" screamed the President's wife when she realized her daughter was still in the suite's other bedroom.

"Your daughter will not be harmed! She will be brought from her room when she is conscious. Right

66 D'ONOFRIO

now, Mister President, I think it would be better if you are out of bed before we discuss the situation!" Trembulak nodded at the Cuban soldiers, and they pulled back the covers before dragging the President and his wife from their bed, ignoring the couple's cries and protests.

"I don't understand what's going on here! Who are you?" Rockwell asked before he frantically looked around the bedroom and recognized the armed men's uniforms. "You're god damn Russian soldiers! What the hell are you doing in Rhode Island?"

"I'm General Peskov of the Russian Army, Mister President, and you are now a prisoner of the Russian government!" said Trembulak as he walked out of the bedroom. The shocked President and his wife were then roughly pushed into the suite's living room dressed only in their pajamas.

Mary Rockwell began screaming when she opened her eyes and saw soldiers in her bedroom. The Cubans pulled the young woman from the bed and dragged her into the living room with her parents. "What are these soldiers doing in our room, Dad? What do they want with us?" the terrified young woman asked as she stood behind her father dressed only in a long white shirt.

"I don't know yet, Mary! Try to stay calm so I can find out what's going on here!"

Trembulak suddenly started speaking as he looked through a window at the lit city streets on the other side of the island's access bridge, interrupting the conversation between Rockwell and his daughter. "As I said before, Mister President, you and your family are now prisoners of the Russian government!"

"Prisoners? What do you mean we're prisoners? How did you get onto this island? Who let you into our room? I don't understand who sent you here, or why you're here!"

"President Borakov and the other leaders of my government personally ordered us to this island, Mister President!"

"Borakov sent you here to take me prisoner? I don't believe it! What possible reason could he have for send-

JOURNEY THROUGH A LONG WINTER'S NIGHT   67

ing armed soldiers here to take me prisoner in my own country?"

"Our mission is to hold you as our hostage until your government submits to our demands for humanitarian assistance! You ignored President Borakov's initial requests for aide, so our government has sent us here to force your nation to help us care for our people!"

The President shook his head and appeared confused by what Trembulak told him as the terrorist impersonated the Russian military officer flawlessly. "Hold us prisoner! I spoke to Borakov yesterday and he didn't tell me anything was troubling him, or that he was upset by my policies! I don't understand why he sent you here or what he hopes to achieve by this blatant aggression!"

"President Borakov asked you for humanitarian aide several times during the previous year, but you ignored his pleas! Now your nation will be forced to help our suffering people, or it will suffer the consequences!"

"Borakov and his advisors obviously haven't considered what's going to happen when my government finds out about this attack! They're not going to get any help for his nation this way! Don't you know my nation's military forces are going to overrun this island, and you and your men are going to be killed?"

"My men and I are professional soldiers, Mister President, and dying is a regrettable part of our job. We accept the fact we're all expendable, and that acceptance gives us the advantage over your military forces! There will be no dramatic military attacks of this island, or attempted rescues, Mister President! We've already seen to that!"

Rockwell quickly thought about the situation and he believed he might be able to negotiate with the Russian officer. "You can't hold the innocent people on this island because of differences in our government's philosophies! Please, I'm begging you, put down your weapons and let me talk to Borakov! I'm sure we can work out this problem together. Then we can consider this entire incident just a misunderstanding!"

"I'm sorry, Mister President, but this continued con-

68   D'ONOFRIO

versation is senseless, and a waste of my time! I have very specific orders and I plan to follow them until President Borakov recalls us! You and your family must now be confined to your bedroom while I supervise the next phase of the operation."

"Just wait a damn minute! Let's talk about this before you do something drastic that pushes our nations into a nuclear war!" shouted Rockwell as four soldiers pushed him and his terrified family into their bedroom. The President and his wife and daughter stood huddled together in the bedroom with six Cuban guards. Both Mary and Melanie Rockwell began to cry after Trembulak slammed the bedroom door shut. The President wrapped his arms around them as he tried to understand the confusing situation.

"How did it go in there?" Barnes asked anxiously when he and Vechesloff met Trembulak in the wide hallway outside the suite. "Were you able to convince the President you and your men are really Russian soldiers?"

"He believes it," replied Trembulak as his body trembled from the tension of the confrontation. "I can convince anyone I'm a Russian general here to get aide for my nation!"

"Yes, I knew we could do it!" shouted an elated Barnes as he made a fist and punched Vechesloff's shoulder. "I knew Murtagh's plan would work! He was damn smart having his psychological warfare staff review it. This is fantastic, we've just taken the President of the United States' hostage! We've just done something that's never even been tried before!"

The three men rode to the hotel lobby in an elevator and found Vazques giving instructions to a group of his soldiers. "The attack is going much better and faster than we expected! I'm proud of what my men did here!" Vazques enthusiastically told Barnes. "We've already started moving the people in the hotel to the ballrooms where my men can guard them! The people on the boats in the marina and those in the condominium buildings will soon be hostages, too. We'll control the entire island within the hour."

"Nice fucking job, Vazques!" said Barnes as he looked

JOURNEY THROUGH A LONG WINTER'S NIGHT 69

at his watch and was pleased by how much work had already been accomplished. "Just don't let your men get too fucking confident! We've still got a shit load of work to get done before six!"

"Have your divers finished putting the mines into the water around the island?"

"They're working in the water right now! Lets get the trailers unloaded and the equipment set up! It'll be dawn before we know it!"

During the next two hours Barnes, Vazques, Leland, and Vechesloff supervised the activities of the Cuban soldiers working across Goat Island. A group of soldiers began unloading a silver supply trailer filled with weapons and ammunition. The Cuban soldiers carefully carried long green metal cases from the trailer, each of which contained a sophisticated Stinger missile. They stacked fifteen of the dark green metal cases beside the small lighthouse at the northern end of Goat Island. Then piled another ten more missiles beside the seawall at the rear of the hotel. After they placed a third group of missiles on the ground near the high rise condominium buildings Barnes' men began preparing them to defend the island.

Leland led a group of six Cubans down a cement staircase and into a large and brightly lit electrical utility room in the hotel's basement. The deafening sound and vibrations of ten huge air exchangers forcing fresh air through the building's ventilation ducts distracted Leland as he studied the blueprints the Secret Service brought to the island.

Ten minutes later, he found the island's telephone junction box in a smaller utility room in another area of the basement. All the telephone lines from the hotel and the other buildings on the island passed through the large gray box. After Leland inspected the multicolored wires and their identification numbers he stepped back and pointed at the box. He watched as a Cuban soldier easily chopped through the mass of multi-colored wires with a fire axe, severing all communications with the mainland.

Vazques led another large group of his men into the

70 D'ONOFRIO

hotel's underground garage. They used the valet parking attendant's keys to drive the guest's automobiles out of the garage. Vazques then told the soldiers to block two of the garage's three large entrances with several large automobiles.

Vazques and his men saw the eastern sky beginning to brighten as they ran to the third supply trailer. There they opened the specially constructed doors at the rear of the trailer. As they pulled a metal ramp out of the trailer, another soldier stepped inside and started a four wheel drive, all terrain vehicle. He twisted the throttle, and the vehicle started slowly moving forward. As gasoline fumes and engine noise filled the trailer, the vehicle slowly rolled down the ramp, pulling a long gray box mounted on eight rubber wheels. Ten minutes later, the vehicle pulled the American made plutonium bomb into the safety of the hotel garage, then the Cubans blocked the garage entrance with another automobile.

The four wheel drive vehicle's engine noise echoed through the rough cement walled structure as it pulled the bomb to the center of the garage. After the vehicle was unfastened from the bomb and moved out of the area four Cubans carefully removed six access panels screwed onto the exterior of the bomb's metal case. Three of Barnes' men ran into the garage with a padded black metal box covered with red warning stripes and lettering which contained the bomb's cylindrical detonator.

As one man read from an instruction manual, the others set the bomb's internal switches. They carefully inserted the electronic detonator into its specially designed receptacle and then bolted it into place. After they set several switches, two rows of small red and blue lights inside the bomb's case began flashing. Then a ten inch circular black disk marked with several long white lines began turning as a visual warning the bomb was armed. The men sealed the case after pulling six long black wires from inside the bomb which they placed on the garage's cement floor. Then they used an electric drill to make six, four inch deep holes in the garage's concrete floor. They carefully inserted electronic vibration sensors into the holes after the black wires pulled

JOURNEY THROUGH A LONG WINTER'S NIGHT   71

from the bomb's case were attached to the devices. If the sensors detected the vibrations of large explosions on the island they would detonate the bomb.

Several hours later, Trembulak walked into the President's bedroom and found him sitting on the bed with his wife and daughter. He allowed them to change into the clothing they wore during their trip to Newport the previous day. Then he said, "I think you should step into the living room with me, Mister President. I want you to see what's about to happen!"

"What are you going to do now?" asked Rockwell as he followed Trembulak to the suite's wide balcony door and stood beside him. The sun was already well above the horizon, and Rockwell could easily see the buildings in the city and people out for their early morning walks. He frowned when he looked down at the streets on the island and did not see any people walking, or any cars moving on the roads.

"At exactly six o'clock the world will know Russian soldiers have landed on this island!" Trembulak told Rockwell as he glanced at his watch, and then looked at the bridge. "The destruction of that bridge will signal the world my men and I are here from Moscow!"

The President raised his hand and shaded his eyes from the glare of the bright morning sunlight streaming through the open balcony door. As he looked at the large group of people standing on the two lane cement bridge lined with decorative black streetlights he asked, "What do you mean the destruction of that bridge? There's innocent people fishing on that bridge! They don't know what's going on in here! At least warn them and give them time to get off that bridge before you do anything to it!"

"I'm not concerned about thirty people who should be home in bed at this hour of the morning." Trembulak laughed as he looked at his watch and felt his body tense with anticipation.

"Look at all those people fishing on that damn bridge!" commented a shocked Leland as he stood in another suite with a black electronic detonator the size

72 D'ONOFRIO

of a calculator in his hand. "I thought the damn bridge would be deserted at this time of the morning!"

Barnes stared at his watch and snickered when he heard Leland's concerns. "Fuck the people, I don't give a fucking shit about those assholes! Get that damn detonator ready, we've got ten seconds until we blow the bridge!"

"We can't knock out that bridge with all those people on it Barnes! We'll kill all of those people when it's not necessary!"

"Five, four, three, two, one, now! Do it now damn you!" Barnes shouted as he turned and saw Leland staring out the window. "Do it now, god damn it!"

"I can't kill all those innocent people Barnes! There's kids on that bridge!"

"I don't give a fuck if God is standing on that fucking bridge," shouted Barnes as he suddenly ripped the detonator from Leland's hand and pressed the button. "I still wonder why the hell Murtagh picked you for this part of the fucking mission? You're too god damn soft!"

The President stepped backward and shaded his face with his hand when the access bridge suddenly disappeared in a blinding flash of bright light, and a cloud of gray and white smoke. The concussion of the detonating plastic explosives shook all the buildings on Goat Island as the noise rolled across the city like the sound of thunder. Windows of nearby houses were shattered by both the concussion and pieces of the bridge's concrete structure thrown three hundred yards by the tremendous explosion.

All the people standing on the access bridge died instantly. Dismembered parts of human bodies flew into the air with pieces of the shattered concrete roadbed. Bloody pieces of bodies fell in the blue ocean water and many large body pieces landed on the rocks that surrounded Goat Island. A huge surge of ocean water crashed onto the shores of Goat Island after two thirds of the heavy concrete bridge crashed into the harbor. Another large wave crashed against the city's concrete dock and rose sixty feet into the air before crashing down and flooding the deserted city streets.

When the smoke cleared, the President realized the

JOURNEY THROUGH A LONG WINTER'S NIGHT   73

severity of the predicament he found himself in. His body trembled with fear and rage as he thought about the desperate situation and the senseless killings he just witnessed. "If these soldiers risked their lives and world peace to get help for their people, then I've truly underestimated the severity of their nation's problems. I can't let them hurt any more people on this island because my advisors and ambassador neglected to realize the Russian people need more help! I've got to do something to stop this madness before anyone else gets hurt or killed!"

"Tell me what I can do to end this situation, Peskov, and I'll contact Washington with instructions right now!" The President pleaded with Trembulak.

"There's nothing you can do now, Mister President! Your government's actions and response to this situation will dictate what will happen next on this island. Now, you are only an observer!" Trembulak raised a pair of binoculars and watched as police cruisers, fire trucks, and ambulances began arriving at the Newport side of the destroyed access bridge with their sirens blaring and their lights flashing.

Several Cubans quickly assembled two large green United States' Army public address loudspeakers on the Goat Island side of the destroyed bridge and attached them to a radio receiver. Trembulak slid open the balcony's glass door and listened to the wailing sirens in the city as emergency vehicles continued arriving at the destroyed bridge. He smiled as he watched the growing crowd of frantic police officials, firemen and paramedics, and curious residents and vacationers. They stood together helplessly and pointed at the dead bodies floating on the calm ocean water, and the blood covered body parts scattered across the rocks around Goat island.

When Trembulak saw eight members of the fire department frantically pulling an aluminum boat from a truck, everyone suddenly heard, "Attention, attention at the Newport side of the bridge! Raise your hands if you can hear me!" Trembulak's voice bellowed across the calm harbor water from the public address speakers. Many of the shocked people looked at one another

74 D'ONOFRIO

as others pointed at the island and attempted to locate where the resonate voice originated.

Trembulak watched several surprised police officers slowly raised their arms after the other startled people stopped talking. "Do not attempt to reach this island by boat! Any attempt to do so will result in the deaths of the hostages I am holding on this island! Now, I want to speak to the Mayor!"

The Chief of the Newport Police was dressed in the jeans and a knit shirt he threw on after receiving a frantic telephone call from his office informing him of the disaster. He didn't fully understand what was happening, but immediately lifted a portable telephone. Fifteen minutes later, a speeding police cruiser carrying Mayor Schmitt came to a screeching halt at the Newport side of the destroyed access bridge.

Schmitt was shaken when he saw the bodies floating on the blue ocean water between Goat Island and the city. "What happened to that bridge?" he asked the police chief as he pointed at the one hundred foot long section of the bridge destroyed by the explosives.

After the police chief told the Mayor about the mysterious voice he heard on the island Schmitt said, "He must be crazy! Call the State Police and tell them we need some help while I try to talk to this guy!" Schmitt then raised a megaphone to his mouth as he studied the sunlight bathing the buildings on Goat Island in a warm yellow glow. "I'm Mayor Schmitt, what do you want?"

"Sit in the police cruiser and we'll use the radio to continue our conversation!" were the only words that echoed across the water. Trembulak adjusted several dials on the military radio Barnes provided as he lifted the microphone. "Now, Mister Mayor, we can continue this conversation in private!"

"Are you responsible for destroying that bridge?" asked an angry Schmitt as he watched a man's upper torso floating face up in the water. "Who the hell are you, and what do you want?"

"I am General Peskov of the 413th Russian Para-

JOURNEY THROUGH A LONG WINTER'S NIGHT   75

troopers. My men are here on a mission sanctioned by President Barakov, and the members of my government in Moscow!" Trembulak had memorized exactly what Murtagh wanted him to tell the Mayor, and he recited it without referring to his notes while President Rockwell watched him.

"Russian paratroopers in Rhode Island! Who are you trying to kid? Do you know how many people you just killed? The State Police will be here any minute to deal with you!" The sixty-four-year-old Schmitt was horrified when he saw a bloody human leg floating on the ocean water. He leaned his head forward slowly and rested his forehead on the car's steering wheel as he listened to Trembulak.

"It's too late to be concerned about those people Schmitt, they're dead! You should be worried about the people I am now holding on this island! Now listen very closely to what I am about to tell you."

"Don't tell me what to do, you lunatic! Tell me who you really are, and what you're doing on the that island! I don't believe you're a Russian soldier!"

"Shut up, Schmitt! What you choose to believe is of no concern to me, but you are wasting my valuable time with your inane comments! My paratroopers have secured this entire island and all the people on it are now our hostages! The President of your United States is now my prisoner!"

"You're holding the President on that island?" replied Schmitt with panic in his voice as he frantically motioned the other city officials to the car. "What happened to his Secret Service escort? Where are they? Tell us what we have to do so you'll free the President and the other hostages you're holding."

"As I said, my men and I are here on a mission sanctioned by my government. Our people are in desperate need of help, and this is the only way we can be guaranteed your nation will assist us!"

"What do you want from me? What can I do?"

"Tell your government officials that President Borakov demands shipments of food from European nations begin arriving in Russian ports within three

76 D'ONOFRIO

days, or I will begin killing my hostages! Shipments of medical supplies from the United States must begin arriving within seventy-two hours by plane. My nation also demands a ransom of twenty billion dollars in exchange for the hostages I now hold on this island!"

"What?" shouted Rockwell after hearing Trembulak's demand for ransom. "Twenty billion dollars! Where do you think my nation is going to get that kind of money?"

"You must be insane!" Schmitt naively told Trembulak as he wrote notes on a map he found in the police car. "Our military forces are going to attack that island and kill you and your men! I'll bet you didn't think about that before you attacked that island!" Schmitt added bravely.

"I am not one to be intimidated by threats of military force Schmitt! If your military does attack us, we will detonate a nuclear bomb we have moved onto this island!"

"You have a nuclear bomb on that island? You must be joking."

"This is not a joke. It is a request for humanitarian aid your government will not ignore! Warn your government officials, if our demands are not met your President and his family will be executed! Twelve hours after their execution the nuclear bomb we have on this island will be detonated! Then both nations will be forced to rebuild from rubble with the stronger ruling the world!"

"Why are you doing this to us?" asked Schmitt who was almost in tears after a female spectator screamed and pointed at the bloody body of a young girl floating on the water. "Please, please don't hurt any more people."

"No one else will be harmed if the electrical and water supplies to this island are not disrupted! No one is to approach this island without my permission! We have shoulder launched missiles on the island which will destroy any aircraft or surface ships we consider a threat! If you attempt to overwhelm us with false targets or attack this island, we will detonate our nuclear bomb after we use our last missile to defend ourselves! Do you

JOURNEY THROUGH A LONG WINTER'S NIGHT 77

understand everything I've told you Schmitt?"

"Yes, I've written down everything you've said! How do we know the President is still alive? How do we know you haven't already killed him?"

"He's standing beside me right now, and you may briefly speak to him." Trembulak handed the microphone to the frightened President with the warning, "Impress upon him the severity of this situation, Mister President! Convince him of the danger your nation faces!"

"This is President Rockwell! Can you hear me Schmitt?"

"Mister President, are you all right? Can we do anything to help you?"

"The only thing you can do right now is relay the General's message to Washington. Add to it, I do not want this nation to negotiate for my release, or to succumb to the demands of this fanatical Russian General or his government!"

"I understand, Mister President. I'll call the governor's office and tell him what happened right now!"

Trembulak angrily pulled the microphone from the President's hand and said, "Relay my demands and warnings to the proper authorities in your government Schmitt! I will speak with the officials of your government who wish to contact me by radio tomorrow morning. Until then, there will be no further contact with this island. Remember, no one is to approach this island or we will kill the hostages."

While Trembulak was explaining his demands to the Mayor, Vazques and his soldiers used a security guard's keys and opened the two high rise condominium buildings' front glass doors. Then they used a megaphone and issued the warning, "Stay in your homes and do not move into the hallways. Anyone seen in the hallways will be shot! We've taken twenty women from each building and if anyone tries to escape we will cut their throats and you will be responsible for their deaths." Vazques positioned six of his soldiers on each floor with orders to kill anyone they saw walking in the hallways.

78 D'ONOFRIO

Another group of Cubans dragged the shocked residents from a long row of thirty, two story condominium town houses. The soldiers entered the homes by breaking down the front doors of each town house. After the Cubans forced all the terrified people from their homes, another team of Vazques' soldiers herded them toward the hotel where they were to be guarded.

A group of fifty Cubans began moving the vacationers from their boats docked in the marina. "Everyone out of your boats and onto the marina walkways," shouted the Cubans as they banged the boats with their weapons and fired them into the air. "Anyone found hiding in the boats will be shot!" The frightened vacationers, many still dressed in their night wear, slowly walked toward the hotel on the island's main road as the Cubans aimed their weapons at them.

"My men have secured all the buildings on the island!" Vazques proudly told Trembulak, Barnes, and Leland when he met them in the hotel lobby an hour later. "They're setting up defensive positions around the perimeter right now. We have more than two thousand hostages in our confinement areas!"

"That's what I wanted to hear," replied Barnes, then he turned and watched a group of hostages pleading with Vazques men as they were moved through the hotel lobby. "I knew this attack was going to be a piece of cake after all the planning we put into it! It won't take long for Washington to find out about this attack, so we better transmit that radio message my staff prepared."

"I don't understand what transmitting that message will accomplished," Vazques told Barnes as they walked into the bright sunlight. Barnes and Leland pulled black masks from their pockets and placed them over their heads to protect their identities. Then they walked to the communication trailer with Vazques. "We've already secured the island, and the people on it are our hostages. Why do you want to involve someone else in this attack?"

"We're not really involving anyone else, we're using them. The intelligence organizations in Washington monitor all radio transmissions because they don't

JOURNEY THROUGH A LONG WINTER'S NIGHT   79

trust one another! The message you're going to send will be transmitted on the frequency reserved for the Central Intelligence Agency. The other intelligence agencies will intercept it and think someone inside the Central Intelligence Agency is working with Russians on this island, maybe providing them with intelligence information and assistance. Those intelligence ass holes won't trust each other and they won't work together to find a way to get the Russians off this island! It'll give us a little more room to work," laughed Barnes when he thought himself smarter than the government intelligence agencies he wanted to abolish.

"Won't those same intelligence agencies intercept your radio messages when you talk to your men in Washington?" asked Vazques after he told his men to transmit the message.

"No, we've got that covered too! We're scrambling our radio signals and using one of our own military communications satellites to transmit voice messages back and forth to Washington. Just to be safe we're also bouncing our signals off a commercial communications satellite to confuse everyone. Trust me, no one is going to hear what we're saying."

Barnes quickly looked at his watch and saw it was already seven o'clock. "I've got to send a status report to General Murtagh. I think I can report everything is going exactly as he expected it would! His computer projections were fucking perfect, and I'm sure he'll want to contact Chchenkoff and tell him how we're doing!"

Vazques' men continued with their task of removing the hotel guests from their rooms. The Cubans led the frightened people to one of several containment locations inside the hotel. One area Barnes personally selected was a glass walled hotel restaurant that faced Newport. The restaurant's exterior wall resembled a greenhouse's glass enclosure. The Cubans forced the hostages to sit on the cold tiled floor with their backs pressed against the tinted glass walls. The Cubans also placed large groups of hostages into each of three enormous ballrooms in the hotel's sprawling convention center. The Cuban soldiers stood guard over the terrified people as they lay face down on the carpeted floor and wooden dance floors with their hands tied behind their backs. What began for many as the vacation of a lifetime in an island resort hotel, was quickly becoming a nightmare for all of them.

Chapter Five

At one o'clock Saturday afternoon, a large group of government and military officials met in a concrete walled strategy room built beneath the sprawling Pentagon building in Washington. The government planners designed the facility so military commanders could direct their forces anywhere in the world. A large circular wooden conference table filled the center of the room and provided seating for seventy people. Two telephones mounted under the table beside each chair provided a scrambled voice communications link with any military facility in the world. Individual overhead track lighting allowed a person seated at the table to read documents and see the other people. The other areas of the strategy room remained darkened so military commanders could study the electronic maps attached to the towering dark gray cement walls. Color computer monitors installed in the table top, and covered with clear glass panels allowed military commanders and their staff to display military combat status information, strategy maps, and printed communications with keyboards mounted under the table.

The strategy room's walls were one hundred feet high and suspended from them were seven huge colored electronic maps that depicted the different continents of the world, and the political boundaries of the nations located on them. Four other panels could display color images of the Earth's surface transmitted from various military surveillance satellites. Displayed on one panel with remarkable clearness was a satellite's image of Newport showing a series of city streets and buildings located beside the blue ocean water. Displayed on another panel was a satellite's computer enhanced overhead image of Goat Island showing the buildings and streets on it, surrounded by the dark ocean water. A flashing red circle on the electronic image highlighted the destroyed section of the island's access bridge.

A thick glass panel separated the strategy room's command and control center from an adjacent compu-

82   D'ONOFRIO

ter and communications room. Located inside the room were various types of communication equipment, computers, terminals, and printers, installed for battlefield assessment and for intelligence gathering prior to and during an attack.

With Vice-President Benson still on the west coast, Curtis Wilcox reluctantly presided over the hastily called meeting. When President Rockwell appointed Wilcox Secretary of State, Curtis, the sixty-seven-year-old gray haired, elder statesman, never imagined he would be confronted with such a threatening and potentially disastrous situation. As he watched forty frantic men and women sitting around the table he could see the confusion, frustration, and tension on all their faces.

If nuclear missiles were flying toward the United States, or a hurricane decimated an area of the nation, Wilcox knew the same military and civilian personnel would be adhering to the strategic policies developed to deal with the situations during peacetime. The group never discussed or imagined the alarming situation now paralyzing the government. Contingency plans and strategic policies to deal with such an unbelievable situation did not exist to guide the government officials through the crisis. The contingency plan with the closest affiliation to the crisis dealt with the death of the President, either by assassination or natural causes. A contingency plan to deal with the kidnapping of the President while traveling abroad was still in the draft stages, awaiting more input from the nation's intelligence organizations. The government leaders considered the idea of another nation's military holding the President hostage inside the United States highly implausible. They ignored White House recommendations to develop a plan to deal with the situation years ago.

Now each branch of the military and all of the intelligence organizations were frantically attempting to gather information about the situation on Goat Island, and the Russian soldiers holding the President hostage. Wilcox sat back and watched as both military staff officers and civilian personnel ran around the room delivery reports to their respective commanders and super-

JOURNEY THROUGH A LONG WINTER'S NIGHT   83

visors. Piles of paper a foot high rested on the table in front of some people who spoke frantically into their telephones. A few staff workers shouted information across the room to their supervisors who immediately wrote the information on pieces of paper. As one shouting person tried to be heard over another the noise became deafening and irritating as more people quickly flooded into the strategy room.

"Gentlemen and ladies, please, if I can interrupt for one minute," Wilcox said as he stood dressed in suit pants and a white shirt, and waited impatiently for the others to stop speaking. "What we're doing here isn't accomplishing anything! Lets stop for a few minutes and discuss how we should be dealing with a situation I consider incredible, and extremely threatening. Each of us has our staff members frantically chasing information, and we may be duplicating work that someone else has already completed. We must organize our resources and determine how to best deal with a situation that appears to have caught all of us off guard! We've got to assimilate all the information we can before Vice-President Benson arrives back in Washington."

"When is he due back in the city?" asked the Strategic Air Command's General Sorano as he read a report from the Air Force's Intelligence group.

"The vice-president canceled his trip to California immediately after his aides informed him Russian soldiers came ashore in Rhode Island. He's already on his way back to Washington aboard Air Force Two with additional Secret Service protection. The Secret Service developed a scenario where the Russians may try to kidnap the vice-president in another part of the country now that they're holding the President hostage in Rhode Island."

"That's ridiculous!" commented Colonel Buynicki of the National Reconnaissance Office nonchalantly as he read a report, then he laughed to himself. "What the hell could the Russians possibly get for Benson? We'd all be better off if they kill him!"

"The situation we're facing here isn't a joke Colonel, and I won't tolerate any more comments of that nature

84 D'ONOFRIO

from anyone in this room!" Wilcox angrily told the group after the other men and women began laughing after the demeaning comment. "The vice-president may soon be the leader of this nation, so I suggest you all change your attitudes about the man before he arrives back here! I've already suggested the vice-president assume the powers of the Presidency while he's flying back to Washington. His personal aide informed me he will not assume the office until he's fully briefed about the situation, and has our recommendations."

"How's the Secret Service getting the Vice-President back to Washington?" asked Marilyn Zimmer, one of President Rockwell's aides. She was thankful she remained in Washington to complete a special project for the President, but was now extremely concerned about Rockwell and his family.

"The Vice-President's plane should be landing at Andrews Air Force Base in three hours. His motorcade will then be escorted here by the Secret Service and an armed military convoy. The Secret Service said they couldn't guarantee the Vice-President's helicopter would be safe from a Russian anti-aircraft missile, so they put together the motorcade to get him here!"

"Why would the Russians want to kill the Vice-President?" asked Patrick DeCaulp, one of the Vice-President's more experienced aides who appeared confused by Wilcox's remarks. "I don't understand what they'd have to gain by killing him when our government is already in chaos!"

"The Russians may feel his death will further undermine the United States' government as it's coping with the realization the President is a hostage! I'm not really sure how the Secret Service came up with that scenario. But right now, I think we should use the time before the Vice-President arrives here to formulate a statement he can read to the reporters. We've got to explain the situation to the people of the nation, and hope they remain calm when they learn the President is a hostage of the Russian military. Within the next few hours the television networks will be carrying live pictures of that island, with detailed descriptions of how

JOURNEY THROUGH A LONG WINTER'S NIGHT 85

the Russian military attacked our nation. We better come up with a story that has a calming effect on the people, or we're going to see them panicking in the streets before dark." During the next three hours Wilcox met with Andrew Raymond, the White House Director of Communications, and his staff of writers. The group of thirty people then collaborated to write a three page press release they hoped would adequately explain the situation in Newport, while calming the public's fears.

Immediately after the Vice-President's motorcade arrived at the Pentagon, Kennith Dunnells and a large group of his advisors met Benson in a hallway. They escorted Benson as he walked into the strategy room wearing a blue jump suit and a heavy bullet proof vest.

"How was your trip back to Washington, Mister Vice-President?" Wilcox asked as he helped Benson remove his protective vest.

Benson frowned and felt overwhelmed with apprehension as he looked around at the people working frantically in the strategy room. "Harrowing, tiring, and extremely upsetting! I was having a wonderful time in California until the Russians made my life a living nightmare!" Benson then pulled off the blue jump suit and adjusted his tie as an aide placed a cup of coffee and several briefing folders on the table for him.

Wilcox was irritated by Benson's inappropriate comments, and his apparent lack of concern for the President and the other hostages on Goat Island. "We've gathered everyone here to meet with you, Mister Vice-President. We have the directors of Central Intelligence, Defense Intelligence, and National Security Agencies. We have representatives here from the Army, Navy, Air Force, Marine Intelligence, the Central Imagery, and the Nation Reconnaissance Offices, the Federal Bureau of Investigation, and State Department. The Joint Chiefs of Staff are here and most members of the National Security Council. The Director of the Treasury Department is also here to answer any questions we might have about the President's Secret Service escorts. Have you been fully briefed about your interim responsibilities Mister Vice-President?"

86　D'ONOFRIO

"Yes, yes, an Air Force officer already explained the electronic codes I need to launch our nuclear missiles," replied an irate Benson. The thought of initiating a nuclear war terrified Benson and he sighed heavily as he looked up at the satellite image of Goat Island. He wanted to be remembered as the President who helped the nation out of the recession, not the President who initiated the world's first global nuclear war. The frantic military and civilian technicians he saw working around the strategy room table seemed to add to the anxiety he was experiencing.

"You should be the one to begin this meeting, Mister Vice-President," suggested Benson's advisor Kennith Dunnels as he led him aside. "Take charge of this group and demand they provide you with some pertinent information and solutions to the crisis. You're here only to guide them to the solution, not come up with one yourself! Make them do the work. They're supposed experts in their fields, that's what they're getting paid to do!"

Benson nodded and walked back to the table. "Well, ladies and gentlemen, I'd like your assessments of the situation in Rhode Island." Benson sat at the table with his advisors sitting on both sides of him.

"It's not looking too good right now, Mister Vice-President," Wilcox told Benson as he sat at the table while scanning a status report. "Confusing and perilous are the words I can think of to describe the situation facing us right now!"

"Have we determined how Russian soldiers managed to infiltrate this country without our military forces detecting them?"

"No sir, we haven't. The Air Force reviewed its logs and there were no unknown aircraft detected by radar in the Rhode Island area before the attack. It wasn't an airborne assault of the island."

"Could they have reached the island by boat? Maybe a submarine transported them to the island?"

"That's an unlikely scenario, Mister Vice-President. Satellite images of the ocean before the attack do not show any unidentified surface vessels. They might have come off a submarine, but we can't be sure of that."

JOURNEY THROUGH A LONG WINTER'S NIGHT 87

"What are we sure of, Wilcox? What have all of you been doing in here while I was flying back from California?"

"We've been gathering information about the situation," Wilcox explained as he attempted to justify the work performed in the strategy room.

"I would think you would have enough information by now to draft a plan designed to end the situation peacefully. If not peacefully, I would hope you have a military option designed and ready to review so we can attempt to rescue the President and the other hostages on that island."

"We don't have a firm action plan established yet, Mister Vice-President. The Federal Bureau of Investigation, the Secret Service, and the Central Intelligence Agency already have their teams in Newport. They're collecting information and we're using that data to put together a list of possible options we can discuss and consider," reported Wilcox as the leaders of those organizations nodded their heads in agreement.

"Is the information those men are gathering in the city being given to our military leaders so they can plan an assault of the island?" Benson's fear, nervousness, and lack of experience were immediately apparent to the group.

"We're not considering a military attack of the island right now, Mister Vice-President. We don't have enough information about the Russian attack force, or that island, to even consider that option yet!" replied General Roberts of the Defense Intelligence Agency as he closed a folder filled with information about Newport.

"Based on General Roberts' statement, can I assume we haven't confirmed the report I heard about the Russians having a nuclear bomb being on the island?"

"That assumption is correct, Mister Vice-President," Wilcox told Benson. "The sophisticated equipment needed to confirm the presence of a Russian bomb on the island was in *Arizona* this morning. The equipment is already aboard an Air Force C5-A, and on its way to Rhode Island as we sit here."

"Have your agents in Newport reported anything we

88   D'ONOFRIO

might be able to use to end the situation peacefully?"

"We've had reports of vehicle movement and a few sightings of hostages on the island. One report described how the Russians shot a man and woman as they attempted to escape from a condominium building. We've also received a report that described the killing of a man and pregnant woman on the rocks that surround the island!"

"The Russians are killing their hostages on the island?" a frantic Benson asked Roberts as he nervously twisted on his chair and clasped his hands together tightly. "You're telling me Russian soldiers are killing people on that island while we're sitting here deciding what to do. This is incredible, and I find it difficult to believe. I'd like to know how Russian soldiers on that island got past the President's Secret Service escort?"

"I truthfully can't answer that question, Mister Vice-President," confessed James Reynolds from the Treasury Department's Secret Service. "Not until I have more information about what's going on up there." Then Reynolds looked at his supervisor Charles Macsuga for assistance.

"We haven't been able to figure out how the Russians got into the country, let alone how they got onto that island!" added Macsuga as he rubbed his unshaven face with his hand. "I don't have any idea what happened on that island during their attack, or how our people with the President screwed up and allowed him to be captured."

"What do you mean you don't have any idea what happened Macsuga? You and Reynolds are responsible for preventing these types of incidents from happening. This entire affair is your department's fault! It's apparent to me you and Reynolds haven't been doing your jobs or we wouldn't be in this predicament right now!" Everyone seated around the table immediately looked at one another after Benson's impertinent accusations.

"There's no way anyone could've seen this coming, Mister Vice-President!" commented General Roberts as he flipped through his organization's intelligence reports. Benson's remarks angered Roberts and he refrained from

JOURNEY THROUGH A LONG WINTER'S NIGHT 89

criticizing the Vice-President's handling of the meeting. "We all know this nation's relations with Moscow have never been better than right now! This attack is a shock to everyone in this room!"

"It must be a very big shock to those of you who should've anticipated it happening, General." Benson pointed at the satellite image of Goat Island displayed on a large screen, and insinuated the other government officials were not performing their jobs adequately. "Although you all permitted this event to occur by not performing your jobs adequately, I'm now forced to use your knowledge and skills to develop a plan to end this situation."

Herbert Spencer, the Director of the National Security Agency, drummed his fingers nervously on the table top before he spoke. "I think you should consider getting President Borakov on the telephone right now, Mister Vice-President. Ask him why he sent his men to attack that island, and what he wants in return for releasing the hostages and withdrawing his men peacefully!"

"This group hasn't given me enough information to make that call, Spencer. I'm not comfortable with that idea and I'll sound ridiculous if I contact Borakov without having some facts in front of me."

"That may give you the edge, Mister Vice-President," added Spencer as he looked at the others seated around the table. "Ask him what's going on and see what he knows! Did his government really send those soldiers to Goat Island, or is this situation a covert military operation he knows nothing about?"

"I'll decide what we'll do here, Spencer, and I'll put off making that call until we have more information about what's going on in Rhode Island!" replied Benson angrily as he looked away from Spencer and ignored his comments. "What about establishing a dialogue with the Russian General on the island? Maybe the State Department can negotiate some kind of a deal with him to release his hostages."

"My hostage negotiation teams are already trying to contact General Peskov by radio, Mister Vice-President," explained Robert Coleman, the Director of the Federal Bureau of Investigation. "They haven't been able to get

90   D'ONOFRIO

a response from anyone on the island. It looks like the Russians have cut all the telephone lines that lead to the island, too!"

Benson angrily shook his head after hearing the report. "Every idea I have for ending this confrontation is stalemated for one reason or another! What about our military forces? What's their status right now in case more Russian troops attempt to enter the country?" Benson's questions pertaining to the military made him sound ridiculous, and caused a few of the military commanders to smile.

General Roberts flipped through a thick report and found the information he needed. "As of eighteen hundred hours Zulu, which is the Greenwich Mean Time, ninety percent of our world wide military units reported their forces on alert. We're ready for a possible ground, air, and naval confrontation with the Russian forces. Ten percent of the military units are still locating their people on leave, but they should be combat ready by twenty four hundred Zulu. Our military forces with missile launch capabilities are on a Stage Three alert right now."

"Stage Three?" questioned Benson as he looked at one of his aides with a frown. Benson quickly thought about the military intelligence reports Rockwell's secretary's placed onto his desk every week. He considered reading the reports the most trivial part of his job as Vice-President, and ignored the information he thought he would never use.

"Stage Three is two stages from the actual launch of our land, sea, and air based nuclear missiles, Mister Vice-President," Benson's aide whispered to him. "Stage Two sends a scrambled message informing the military units with launch capabilities to prepare their missiles for an imminent attack. Stage One is the actual launch of the missiles."

"I don't want anyone moving our military forces from Stage Three without my expressed approval," Benson warned as he looked each man and women in the face. "Do we know what the Russian military forces are doing right now, or do we have to wait for that information too?"

JOURNEY THROUGH A LONG WINTER'S NIGHT   91

"Our intelligence satellite images and intercepted radio communications show some of the military forces that report to Moscow are already on an alert status," explained Roberts as he stood and pointed at a large computer generated map of Russia. "The red tanks and artillery pieces on this electronic map represent the military units we know are ready for combat. The red submarines on the world map are the current locations of their underwater missile launching fleet. Right now, Mister Vice-President, both nations are ready for a sustained nuclear confrontation."

"What about those military forces our intelligence organizations reported staging near the southern border of Russia? Do they have anything to do with this situation?"

"It doesn't appear that way, Mister Vice-President," explained Wilcox. "Barakov says he moved those forces south to prevent an escalation in the fighting when the United Nations' cease fire was violated in Bosnia. Our original thoughts were correct about that situation."

"What about our NATO allies?" Benson asked the group after Kennith Dunnells wrote several notes on a pad and pushed it in front of the Vice President. "Are they prepared to help us force the Russian government to withdraw its forces?"

One of General Murtagh's staff officers immediately opened a bright red folder and handed it to him. "All NATO forces are currently on an alert status. Tank, attack helicopter units, and mobile missile launcher teams, both conventional and nuclear, are ready to move forward into Russia if needed. All Airborne and ground troops units in Europe are also reporting they're ready to attack if we need them."

"Well, where do we go from here? I'm open to any and all suggestions and recommendations," said the confused Vice-President, who desperately wanted someone to suggest a plan of action to help him. "What do we do next? I need something, anything, to go on from here!"

"I don't think we can give you anything to work with right now, Mister Vice-President. We really need more time to meet with our staff and come up with some

92   D'ONOFRIO

ideas," replied Jamison as he looked at his watch. "Most of my staff is still in shock over this thing!"

"I don't care how shocked any of you or your staff members are right now. You're all responsible for letting this happen, and now I need some solid recommendations from all of you for ending this intolerable situation peacefully." Benson paused for several seconds and attempted to stop his hands from shaking as he lifted his coffee cup. "All right, here's what I suggest we do. Take the next several hours to meet with your staff and discuss the situation and our options. We'll meet back here in five hours to review what you've come up with." The group was angry after Benson's comments and insinuations, and they quickly walked out of the strategy room and left him sitting alone with his staff.

After watching several hours of live television news broadcasts from Newport with his staff, Benson sat with his staff and advisors in a large Pentagon conference room. Benson admitted to the group he was not prepared for the pressures associated with the crisis. Then he informed the group he was depending on them to supply him with the critical information and advice he required to maintain control of the government.

At seven thirty that evening Benson met the government officials in the strategy room. Many more of the military commander's staff officers were present at the meeting. When militatry leaders conducted other meetings in the strategy room there were usually many empty seats. During this meeting every chair was sat on, and nearly forty military officers and civilian personnel stood along the room's outer walls. "What's the latest report from Newport?" Benson asked the group as he sat at the table.

"Our spotters are reporting that everything appears to be quiet on the island," said Wilcox, "but there's a lot of activity in the hotel that we can't identify."

"Activity we can't identify," Benson repeated skeptically as he looked at his aides. "Other than that informative report, do we have any new information about the situation?"

"Nothing has changed since the last meeting, Mis-

JOURNEY THROUGH A LONG WINTER'S NIGHT   93

ter Vice-President. We're still unable to contact General Peskov by radio. We've even used loudspeakers to blast messages across the harbor to him, pleading with Peskov to negotiate with us, but they've gone unanswered."

"I can see we're no further along than we were at the end of the last meeting Curtis. Well, my advisors have put together a check list of items they consider critical, so lets go over them one by one. What are we doing in Newport to prepare for the crowds of curious people that might converge on the city to get a look at Goat Island?"

"The state and local police have the task of crowd control. Several nearby Army and National Guard units should arrive in the city before midnight to establish roadblocks. We'll reinforce those troops with a division of Marines in the next few days. Ships from the Newport Naval Base and the Coast Guard have already established a blockade across the mouth of Newport."

"Good, we don't want anyone getting close enough to that island to provoke the Russians into a confrontation!" Benson told the group as he studied a satellite image of the island. "Do we have any historical or background information about the Russian general on Goat Island?"

The anxiety and tension in the room seemed to increase after an ominous disclosure from Edward Jamison of the Central Intelligence Agency. "I don't understand this, Mister Vice-President, but none of my agency's computers contain information about General Peskov. We've never heard of him before this incident!"

"What do you mean you've never heard of him?" asked an angry Benson, becoming nervous when he realized the group still did not have a solution to the crisis. "Isn't your organization supposed to have files of information about all the Russian military commanders for use in situations like this? Why are we pumping billions of dollars into your organization if your information about the Russian military isn't current?"

"Peskov could be anyone from an Army private who decided to promote himself to general, to an actual general using a false name to mislead us, Mister Vice-Presi-

94 D'ONOFRIO

dent! He could even be a Russian paramilitary fanatic here with his followers! Contrary to what you might think, Mister Vice-President, we don't have a historical background about every god damn person living in Russia!"

"That's a very disturbing statement to hear during this time of crisis, Jamison! I'm sure the President would be greatly encouraged and comforted on that island if he could hear you justifying your agency's inadequacies to all of us right now."

Jamison looked around the room at the other men and women with an embarrassed look of guilt on his face. "Maybe one of the other intelligence organizations has some information about Peskov in their files!"

Benson became angry when the other men and women shook their heads somberly and did not look at him. "So, this General Peskov is a mystery to all of you who should know about him." Benson suddenly began shouting at the group instead of giving them constructive ideas. "What about the intelligence organizations of our allies? Maybe they can provide the so called intelligence organizations of our nation with information about the Russian General!"

"None of the allies, or large number of nations that contacted us to offer their assistance have information about Peskov, Mister Vice-President," replied General Roberts who was quickly becoming disgusted with Benson's attitude. "You can bust our ass all you want, and accuse us of not doing our job, but it's not going to help the situation right now! We need some more time with this one, that's all there is to it!"

"Take it easy, General," cautioned Wilcox when he realized Roberts was furious with Benson, as he himself was. "Everyone in this room is under an enormous amount of pressure right now! Lets not say anything to jeopardize the cooperation we're getting from everyone right now!"

"You're right, Curtis, this is a difficult, as well as a physical and mentally exhausting situation. Why doesn't the Vice-President back off and allow us some more time to do our jobs? Right now we don't know if this damn General Peskov is legitimate, or if he's even a fucking

JOURNEY THROUGH A LONG WINTER'S NIGHT 95

Russian citizen," Robert shouted as he angrily sat back in his chair and threw his pen onto the desk.

Benson seemed intimidated by Roberts' remarks and profanity, and he immediately became unsure of himself again. "All right, all right, take more time, but you've got to get me something concrete to work with! Contact our allies and see if they can help you do your jobs!"

"Speaking of our allies, Mister Vice-President, how much do you want to tell those governments and their intelligence organization about this situation?" Jamison posed the question he knew Benson would have difficulty answering, because he wanted to stop the Vice-President from badgering the men in the room.

Benson felt overwhelmed by the increasing tension in the strategy room, and the unexpected question. He immediately looked to Susan Franklin, one of his senior aides, for help. "I recommend that Secretary of State Wilcox contact our allies and provide all the details of the situation to them, in a manner so as not to alarm them. We want them to know the United States' government is functioning normally during this exceptionally difficult time with Vice-President Benson firmly at the helm. The Vice-President's schedule during the next few days will unfortunately preclude him from speaking to, or meeting with, the leaders of the allied nations."

"Let's not have the entire world think this nation or its government is falling apart because the Russians have kidnapped President Rockwell," added Benson as he wrote a note on his pad. "As it is I'm very concerned how the people of our nation are perceiving this entire situation, and our lackluster response to it."

"You can be sure the people are very concerned by what they're seeing on their televisions, and hearing on their radios," Wilcox warned everyone in the strategy room. "We're receiving thousands of phone calls every hour at the White House, the Capital, and the State Department. The people are frightened and extremely concerned about how we're going to respond to the Russian aggression!"

"I was afraid that was going to happen. I'm going to need a convincing speech to calm the people and as-

96 D'ONOFRIO

sure them we're dealing with this monumental problem. I want a toned down speech so we calm the people," Benson told his aides, then he sat back and looked around the table as though pleading for suggestions from the military and government officials. "You've been very quiet tonight, Admiral Andrews. You're the Chairman of the Joint Chiefs of Staff! Do you have any thoughts you'd like to present to the group?"

"Well, Mister Vice-President, I've been thinking about the situation while I was studying the photographs of Goat Island taken by our reconnaissance satellite. I can't believe the Russians have already mined all the water around Goat Island in such a short period of time. Maybe the Russians only mined the water between the island and the city hoping we would assume they mined completely around the island," explained Admiral Ralph Andrews, who was also the Chief of Naval Operations.

"What do you propose we do, Admiral?" asked an elated Benson after hearing an idea he might use. "Tell us what's on your mind!"

"I'd like to put two divers from the Newport Naval Base into the water near the city side of the destroyed access bridge. We'll do it after dark so they won't be seen by the Russians on the island. I want them to search for an underwater access route to the island that's free of mines. If they can find a way to the island we'll move our SEAL teams onto the island later tonight. They'll move into the buildings and neutralize the Russian soldiers, then they'll free the President and the other hostages!"

"That's an excellent idea, Admiral!" said an ecstatic Benson as he stood and began walking around the room. "That's what I need from the rest of you, more ideas like the Admiral's."

Several of Andrews' staff officers sitting behind him immediately looked at one another and frowned after Benson's enthusiastic comments. They knew Andrews based all of his ideas and recommendations on the antiquated principles and tactics he learned during the Second World War. Many politicians and military officers believed the seventy-year-old Andrews should have

JOURNEY THROUGH A LONG WINTER'S NIGHT   97

retired ten years ago, and that the chain smoking admiral retained his position only for the prestige associated with it. He was often insolent and intolerant with his staff officers and frequently questioned their competence when they could not rectify the problems he created. Andrews always professed a superior knowledge of the Navy, and believed he was able to make better decisions than any of his staff members.

Andrews was confident of his decision and he turned to his staff officers standing behind him. "Get the Newport Naval Base commander on a scrambled communications line. Tell him to personally select two of his best and most qualified divers. I want them to begin a systematic search of the island's defenses after dark. Tell Dupont I want a progress report from his divers every fifteen minutes after they're in the water!"

At 10:00 P.M. Admiral Dupont, the Newport Naval Base commander, arrived at the destroyed Goat Island Bridge. As he climbed out of an open military Jeep he glanced at the large crowds of people standing under the bright street lights behind the military and police barricades. Many of the people were still attempting to take pictures of the island even in the darkness. Dupont studied the lit buildings on the island as he walked to where two divers already dressed in their wet suits were strapping air tanks onto their backs. "Watch yourselves down there! We don't know what types of mines the Russians may have put in the water. They could be using magnetic or the new motion triggered model we've heard about. Just watch your asses."

Using the lights on Goat Island that reflected off the ocean waves, Dupont watched the divers slowly wade into the water beside the town dock and sink below the surface. He saw the divers' air bubbles break the water's surface as tiny circular spheres reflecting the lights on Goat Island. He could see the bright beams of light projected from the diver's powerful flashlights, but they disappeared as the divers swam deeper into the water. Dupont wiped the perspiration from his forehead in the sweltering heat and swatted away the annoying mosquitoes as he walked back to his Jeep.

98 D'ONOFRIO

Several seconds later, a thunderous explosion that catapulted ocean water seventy feet into the air, shattered the harbor's tranquillity. As startled spectators began screaming, Dupont ran to the end of the island's destroyed access bridge. He watched for his divers to surface as two more loud explosions sent ocean water hurtling a hundred feet into the air. As the ocean water fell onto the bridge it saturated Dupont's clothing as thirty of his men ran beside him and searched for the divers.

Several minutes later, Dupont walked back to his Jeep and used a radio to contact his staff at the naval base. "Get the Pentagon on a secure line and tell Andrews the damn mines killed our divers!" After hearing the report the officials in the Pentagon's strategy room agreed there would be no additional probing operations of the water around Goat Island.

"That was a good attempt to get our men onto the island, but it just didn't work out! What other options do we have available to us?" Benson asked the group as he appeared unconcerned by the deaths of the two divers.

"The most viable option is payment of the ransom to the Russian government," said a solemn Jamison. "We can begin shipping food and medical supplies to Russia within forty-eight hours, that's not going to be a problem. Raising the twenty billion dollar ransom is going to be tough, and it may mean borrowing money from some other nations!"

"I'm sure we can arrange to borrow from other nations if we get the Federal Reserve and the Treasury officials involved in our planning," Dunnells told the group.

Spencer suddenly suggested the only two choices available to the government to alleviate the situation. "We either pay the ransom now and negotiate with the Russians for its return after they release the President, or we consider an all out military assault of Russia in retaliation for their attack in Rhode Island."

Wilcox didn't approve of Jamison's idea to pay the ransom and he abruptly commented about it. "If this nation submits to the Russian demand for ransom, we

JOURNEY THROUGH A LONG WINTER'S NIGHT 99

may be fostering other attempts to kidnap officials of our government! Who knows what other nation might kidnap a senator or representative to get money for their people?"

During the next two hours, the group discussed the paying of the ransom to the Russian government. After a short break several members of the Joint Chiefs of Staff suggested preliminary plans to use the nation's military forces to attack the island. "We've put together seven preliminary attack plans for a military assault of the island," General Murtagh told the others as he stood and handed each man and woman a folder. "We can't let the Russians execute the President and the other hostages on that island!"

"Maybe the Russians will free the President and the others after we pay the ransom and begin shipping supplies to their nation," speculated Benson. "They said that's all they want."

"How do we know that's all they want, Mister Vice-President? Once they see we've caved in and are complying to their demands, who knows what the Russians may want next. This situation may continue for months as they make more demands on us."

"I didn't think of that, General Murtagh, but you may be right."

"Of course I'm right, Mister Vice-President. We may be forced to use military force, even if it risks the President being killed during an attack. A military strike will give the impression the United State's government refuses to submit to the demands and aggression of the Russian government and military!"

Murtagh felt a sense of accomplishment when he saw the confusion and tension his suggestions created in the conference room. His suggestion that the group should not be concerned about killing the President during a military operation added to the anxiety in everyone's mind. None of the government or military officials wanted to be responsible for the President's death.

Richard Shackleford was a thirty-seven-year-old analyst from the Defense Department, and he pointed out several obstacles to a military attack of the island.

100   D'ONOFRIO

"What'll happen if Peskov detonates his plutonium bomb while our military forces are attacking the island, General? The explosion will decimate our entire attack force, and it'll create destruction more devastating than that seen in Hiroshima. Before we can consider a military response to end this crisis, we'll have to plan for the evacuation of the entire state of Rhode Island, and maybe portions of surrounding states."

Everyone knew Shackleford's reputation of being a brilliant intelligence analyst, and his concerns and fears seemed to frighten the group. He slowly removed his thick glasses and rubbed his tired eyes as he added, "Without some additional information and computer projections we don't know how far the explosion's radiation might be carried by the wind! Can our submarine base in Connecticut be contaminated by the radiation if it drifts south? Can the Naval facilities in Boston and Maine be contaminated? We don't know how many people might be killed if the wind carries the plutonium radiation over Connecticut, Massachusetts, and New York. What'll happen if it drifts into Canada?"

"I've already anticipated this discussion," interrupted Andrews as he pointed at a man seated beside him. The Naval officer stepped forward from the darkened area and appeared solemn and extremely pensive as he stood. "This is Captain John Stockholm. He's an expert in the field of nuclear medicine. During the past thirteen years, the Captain has been treating military personnel exposed to nuclear materials and radiation. I asked him here to provide us with more details about the plutonium bomb's effects."

Stockholm appeared extremely nervous and agitated as he stood in front of the group in a starched military uniform. "If the Russians do have a plutonium based bomb on that island, we must do everything we can to prevent them from detonating the device! If the active ingredient in the bomb is Plutonium two thirty nine, then the effects of the explosion and its radiation will be devastating! I can't impress this upon you enough! The half-life of plutonium two thirty nine is roughly twenty-four thousand years. That means Rhode Island and any

JOURNEY THROUGH A LONG WINTER'S NIGHT 101

other areas contaminated by radiation will be uninhabitable for thousands of years!"

"What makes this type of bomb so deadly, Captain?" asked Andrews as he lit another cigarette and sat back in a cloud of blue gray smoke which slowly rose to the overhead lighting.

"When a plutonium based bomb detonates it emits a high concentration of alpha particles which creates the radioactive fallout. Plutonium compounds produced during the explosion and contained in the radioactive fallout concentrate in the spleen, and on the bones, of all living organisms. These are the areas where the body creates blood cells. The radiation stops the production of the blood cells and causes the established cells to become mutated. This means the body can not get an adequate supply of oxygen and nutrients. The result is a slow and horrible death." Everyone appeared upset by the report, and during the next two hours Stockholm answered detailed questions about the effects of exposure to plutonium radiation.

After hearing about the destructive capabilities of the bomb, Andrews lifted a telephone under the strategy room table and contacted Admiral Dupont at the Newport Naval Base. "I want a detailed report from your Damage and Assessment Research Group in my hands by tomorrow morning! Use your computers to simulate what might happen to the surrounding areas if the Russians detonate their nuclear bomb on Goat Island. You're only a few miles from the site so you're the most qualified group to perform this research. Get started Admiral, I want that information as soon as you have it ready!"

Vice-President Benson was not satisfied with the progress of the meeting, although he did not contribute any ideas and actually added to the confusion and apprehension. Several hours later he could see the men and women seated in the strategy room appear exhausted, and he saw it was already 2:00 A.M. when he looked at his watch. He stood and motioned to his aides it was time to leave as he gave the military and government leaders a somber warning. "I don't know about any of you, but I'm not encouraged by what we've ac-

102 D'ONOFRIO

complished here today. I hope you'll all have more to contribute tomorrow morning! Arrange the next meeting for the morning Wilcox, and then call my staff with the time. Have a good evening everyone," he said as he walked from the room with his staff.

Chapter Six

At four o'clock Sunday morning, Secret Service agents drove Vice-President Benson to the Pentagon in a dismal, heavy rain. Benson spent the night at a remote military installation outside Washington, where fifty Secret Service agents and a company of Marines guarded he and his wife. Normally Benson and his wife lived at the Vice-President's official residence on the grounds of the Naval Observatory in Washington. The Secret Service told the Vice-President the official residence lacked the security provisions to adequately protect him during the crisis. Reynolds and his director Macsuga recommended the Vice-President spend every night in a different location until the crisis could be resolved.

Wilcox anxiously met Benson's limousine on a restricted lower level of the Pentagon's sprawling underground concrete parking facility. Positioned inside the garage were two hundred heavily armed soldiers eerily lit by the glowing overhead fluorescent lights. They huddled beside the garage's walls in teams with their weapons readied as though they were expecting an imminent attack. "How are you this morning, Mister Vice-President?" Wilcox asked as he extended his hand and helped Benson out of the black limousine covered with raindrops.

"I'm exhausted!" replied Benson angrily as he adjusted his jacket and looked around at the soldiers nervously. "My aides kept waking me all night! I didn't expect to see all of these combat soldiers here this morning! Do they think I'm in danger even in here, Curtis?"

"No, no, this is just a precaution to ensure your safety!" replied Wilcox as he and Benson sat on the back of an electrically powered cart. As a Marine officer drove the cart through two thick steel doors Wilcox explained a decision he made during the night. "I advised all of the senators and representatives to return to their home states earlier this morning. I told them to use radio broadcasts, television interviews, and personal contact to assure their constituents the government is dealing

104   D'ONOFRIO

with this crisis appropriately."

"That's a very good idea," Benson praised Wilcox as he studied the yellow walls of the long tunnel the cart was moving through. "It's a shame the other men in positions of responsibility in our government don't have your initiative. If they did, this situation would already be solved and our lives would be back to normal!"

"Everyone is trying, Mister Vice-President. It's just a very confusing and intimidating situation, and none of us wants to suggest a course of action that might put the people of our nation at risk."

"We're relying on our foremost government officials to make the difficult decisions here, Curtis, and they're not doing it. We're paying those people for their ideas, but they're not doing their jobs."

"We're all trying, Mister Vice-President. Give them some more time and they'll have the solutions you need."

"Are they all here to meet with me this morning?"

"Yes, sir, everyone is already here. They're waiting for you in the strategy room."

"Good, they better have some ideas for me this morning if they want to keep their jobs!" said Benson as the cart stopped and several Secret Service agents helped him step off it. Benson and Wilcox walked through another set of polished metal doors, and then through a long wide tunnel with painted blue walls which eventually opened into the underground strategy room.

Everyone at the table stood and greeted Benson, and when he sat an aide placed an agenda and a cup of coffee in front of him. "Well, I hope you've all had time to meet with your staff, and I hope you managed to get at least a little sleep. Let's get started and see if we can be a little more productive than we were yesterday! I see you're first on the agenda this morning, Curtis."

"My office received several messages from Foreign Minister Gagarin in Moscow during the night, Mister Vice-President," Wilcox told the group as he sat at the table and reviewed the printed communications. "Gagarin is adamantly saying neither his country's military forces, nor President Borakov, have anything to do with the soldiers claiming to be Russian paratroopers

JOURNEY THROUGH A LONG WINTER'S NIGHT   105

on Goat Island. I'm getting the impression he's telling me the truth about this, Mister Vice-President!"

"Well, we're not here to base our decisions or actions on your gut feelings, Curtis," Benson responded, angering many of the men and women with his condescending comment.

"You said you want our ideas and opinions, Mister Vice-President. Well, I've known Gagarin for many years and I trust him! He told me Borakov and the leaders of the other republics are already meeting in Moscow to discuss our accusations Russian soldiers kidnapped the President. They're all denying they sent their troops to the United States, and I believe what Gagarin is telling me!"

"I don't think we can trust any of the god damn bastards in Moscow right now," General Curtis Abrahams suddenly told the group, "and neither should you, Curtis! They're up to their old tricks again, and this attack proves it!"

"I don't agree with you, General! Borakov took time to meet with foreign reporters this morning to answer their questions about our accusations he's responsible for this attack! The Russian ambassador in Washington has even volunteered to meet with the members of our government to answer any and all of their questions. He wants to assure us his government has nothing to do with this situation! Those don't sound like the actions of a government that just sent its troops to kidnap our President!"

"Those generous actions could just be a ploy to mislead us," Jamison of the Central Intelligence cautioned Wilcox. "Borakov and his government can lead us on with rhetoric indefinitely while their military continues to hold the President for ransom!"

"I don't agree with either of you! The Russian military reported they can account for all the nuclear weapons in their arsenal. That should make us question Peskov's claim he has a nuclear bomb on Goat Island, and should be telling us something is wrong here!"

"I just don't trust the Russian military leaders," Benson told the group as he looked up at an electronic map. He squinted at the map when he saw the large

106   D'ONOFRIO

number of red tanks and artillery pieces near the Russian borders. Then, without further explanation he asked, "What's the status of our military forces?"

"All of our active military units are at one hundred percent combat readiness, Mister Vice-President. We've notified the National Guard and Reserve units to contact their troops and prepare them for possible combat," explained General Abrahams as he read from a thick status report. "I contacted the commander of the Third Special Forces Group after our last meeting. I'm moving that group from their home base of Fort Bragg to the Quonset Point Naval Air Station. We've spent years training the members of Blue Light to deal with terrorists and handle hostage situations. They'll be in the area and available if we need them."

"I've already moved the Eighth and Tenth Special Force Groups and their equipment to a location outside the city," added Murtagh as he read the information from another report. "They're watching the island and searching for a way to get onto it. We'll need their information if we decide the only way to end the situation is with a military strike of the island."

"What about the spotters we already have in Newport? Have they seen anything we can use? Maybe the Russians withdrew from the island after they saw our military forces and the spotters just don't know it yet!"

A few men snickered after Benson's naive comments. "I doubt that's going to happen, Mister Vice-President!" replied Abrahams after he sipped his coffee. "We've already received reports this morning describing the defensive positions the Russians are establishing across the island. It appears they're here to stay."

Benson could feel small beads of perspiration forming on his forehead as his body temperature slowly rose from his nervousness. He knew he needed something to give the impression he was in control of the meeting, then he remembered his conversation with the President earlier in the week. "Have all of our Strategic Air Command bomber wings been reactivated? I told the President it was a bad idea to moth ball them!" Benson's chest tightened when he pictured huge mush-

JOURNEY THROUGH A LONG WINTER'S NIGHT   107

room clouds rising into the blue sky over Washington in his mind.

"All of our bombers have been airborne for the past six hours, Mister Vice-President," reported General Bittner, the Air Force Chief of Staff. "We've contacted our missile launch crews in the underground silos and alerted them for a possible showdown with the Russians. The Navy contacted all the submarine commanders and notified them we may send the missile launch codes if the situation escalates into a nuclear confrontation."

"Ladies and gentlemen, I suggest we slow down here, and not recommend anything that we might regret a few hours from now," General Murtagh warned the officials seated around the table as he leaned forward in his chair and looked around the strategy room. He was concerned the conversation was moving toward recommending a nuclear strike on Russian territory in reprisal for the President's kidnapping. Murtagh stood and walked to a long table covered with many varieties of pastries, coffee, and other beverages. He ignored the coffee he believed was an addictive fluid and selected a bottle of cold tonic water as he gave the others a warning. "I realize this is a tense, confrontational situation, but let's not do or say something that might jeopardize the people of our nation, or the entire world!" Murtagh knew he had to say something to defuse the situation, he didn't want to assume control of a nation decimated by a nuclear war.

"Are you so blind that you can't see the Russians are stalling right now by disavowing the soldiers on that island are part of their military!" Benson shouted at Murtagh angrily as he pointed at him. "What's wrong with you, General, that fact is apparent to everyone else in this room but you!"

Murtagh struggled to control his anger and rage after the remarks from the man he hated, and he made a tight fist after he sat at the table. "Let's use our damn heads and not do anything until we can talk to the Russian general on that island! Peskov hasn't said anything since yesterday morning and he may want to start ne-

108 D'ONOFRIO

gotiating with us today!" replied Murtagh as he struggled to appear outwardly calm and collected.

"That's a long shot, and it could be very costly for this nation if you're wrong, General! If something goes wrong it's on your head, General Murtagh!"

Murtagh suddenly wanted to strangle Benson, but he concealed his emotions well and ignored the Vice-President's threatening remarks. "I do have an idea that we might want to consider this morning, Mister Vice-President. I think we should establish a forward command center on the grounds of the Newport Naval Base. Some of us should be in the city where we can see what's going on first hand, and can relay information and opinions back here. We can use the Naval Base's communications center to send information back here, or to any military installation in the world."

All of the men acknowledged the importance of Murtagh's idea and began speaking with their aides. "That idea does have merit, Mister Vice-President," agreed Andrews as he studied an infra-red image of Goat Island taken two hours earlier by a satellite. "I think the Central Intelligence Agency and the Federal Bureau of Investigation should be part of the command center we set up in Newport. That way they'll be closer to the situation."

"That sounds like a very good idea. The rest of us will remain back here in Washington. We can coordinate the activities of the intelligence organizations, civil defense organizations, and the military," said Benson as he sat back in his chair with a smile. Benson quickly agreed with Murtagh's suggestion as he attempted to give the impression he was in charge.

"Are you going to address the nation again today, Mister Vice-President?" Wilcox asked Benson as he read his own list of suggestions.

Benson immediately looked at one of his advisors nervously, and the woman nodded at him slowly. "I'll schedule another news conference for later this morning after I have a new speech that explains any new developments in Newport. I need a speech," he repeated as he looked at the Director of the White House Communications Office, Andrew Raymond. Raymond nod-

JOURNEY THROUGH A LONG WINTER'S NIGHT   109

ded at Benson and then wrote a note to himself in his appointment book.

"Are you going to assume the office of the President today?" asked Reynolds who appeared distracted when one of Benson's aides held up a red folder so the Vice-President could see it.

"I'll make that decision later Reynolds! Right now I have something else I want to discuss with everyone," Benson said nervously as he stood and began pacing while rubbing his clammy hands together. "I read a troubling report prepared by the Defense Intelligence Organization earlier this morning. It said the Russian soldiers on Goat Island sent a scrambled radio message to the Central Intelligence Agency's communication center in Langley immediately after they attacked Goat Island. Can you tell me why the Russians contacted your organization after they took the President hostage, Jamison?"

Edward Jamison, the Director of the Central Intelligence Agency, placed his pen on the table and leaned back disgustedly as he prepared to defend his agency. "That's true, Mister Vice-President, we did receive the coded radio transmission. But I don't know why the Russians transmitted the message on our reserved frequency. I questioned my directors about it last night, but we can't figure out why the Russians sent the message to our communications center or what it means. The message is in some new type of code structure we haven't been able to decipher." The fifty-one-year-old former ambassador to India assumed responsibility of the intelligence gathering agency three years earlier. It was during a time when people were questioning the loyalty of the agency's staff, and whether the country truly needed the organization's services.

Benson immediately sensed his power over the officials as he watched Jamison struggling for an answer. "You expect me to stand here and believe you don't know why the Russians on Goat Island sent you a coded message? Your organization doesn't have anything to do with this incident, do they Ed?" asked Benson as he seemed to smile at his aides.

110   D'ONOFRIO

"I object to that statement, Mister Vice-President! Who the hell do you think you are asking something like that about my organization?"

"I'm the chief executive right now Jamison, and don't you forget that!"

"Well, you're coming across as one hell of a leader right now, Mister Vice-President! My people are loyal to this country no matter what you or your aides want to believe!" Jamison knew his organization's prior covert operations and disclosures of wrongdoing were almost self incriminating in this situation.

"I wish I could believe you without feeling a bit uneasy, Ed, but I know your people can't be trusted! I'm putting three of my people into your office to watch your staff until we can resolve the situation in Newport! I better not find out that you or anyone else in this room is involved in this incident!" Becoming angry, everyone immediately looked down at their notes after the Vice-President's comments.

Admiral Herbert Spencer, the Director of the National Security Agency, slowly unwrapped one of his long cigars as he stared across the table at Benson. "I think I'll fly up to Newport with some of my staff, Mister Vice-President. I'd like to get a look at the city and see what the island looks like."

The former President, defeated by Rockwell in the previous election, appointed Spencer to the position of Director of the National Security Agency. Spencer's prior performance and accomplishments so impressed Rockwell he chose to leave him as the intelligence agency's director. Rockwell ignored both his advisor's objections and his advisor's politically biased suggestions to replace Spencer with a more prominent and articulate candidate. Rockwell then publicly reaffirmed his confidence in the sixty-three-year-old retired Navy admiral, who commanded destroyers during his long Naval career. After retiring from the Navy the veteran of World War Two and Korea spent five years in Vietnam working for the National Security Agency. The fifty civilians who worked under Spencer in Saigon functioned as an intelligence gathering unit and planned military opera-

JOURNEY THROUGH A LONG WINTER'S NIGHT   111

tions in Laos and North Vietnam.

After the group thoroughly discussed each item on the agenda, they concluded the meeting after agreeing they all had research work to perform. As the men and women walked out of the strategy room a statuesque and extremely attractive woman met Spencer in a Pentagon hallway as she juggled an armful of manila folders. "How did everything go during the meeting, Admiral? Are the Russians going to withdraw their forces from Goat Island?"

"I don't think so, Mahoney!" Spencer replied to the unexpected question as he took a group of folders from the woman's arms and then walked beside her in the well lit and wide corridor. "The Russians would be disappointed they didn't take control of the entire country if they knew how little we've accomplished during the past twenty four hours. None of us has any idea how we should be dealing with this situation, or what our correct response to it should be. Do we negotiate, pay the ransom, go to war? No one is really sure what to do in this situation and we're no closer to finding a solution to this problem than we were yesterday morning!"

"Does everyone else feel that way, Admiral?" asked a concerned Mahoney as she turned and pushed open a thick wooden door with her hip. Then she led Spencer into a large lounge filled with brown leather furniture.

"They won't admit it, but I can tell they feel just as helpless and unsure of their actions as I do! I can see it on their faces, but they don't want to say anything," replied Spencer as he poured coffee into two of the Pentagon's fine white china cups. "Benson and his aides aren't helping the situation either. Their lack of experience is a detriment to solving the situation. We're going to need something, or someone, to pull this together."

"Too bad that Green Beret, the Tactical Operations Officer from San Francisco, went home last month," commented an exhausted Mahoney as she lay back on a long leather couch. She raised her long legs and placed her black high heel shoes up on the couch's arm, unconcerned she was laying on her long curled blonde hair. "I can't think of that guy's name. I thought he was a

112   D'ONOFRIO

great planning coordinator!"

Spencer stared at the floor as he thought about Mahoney's comments. "You mean Major Rosner," he said several seconds later as he smiled with satisfaction after remembering the man's name.

"That's the one! The one who couldn't remember how many times he got shot in Panama!" she laughed as she pointed at Spencer. "Imagine getting shot so many times you lose count, and you still live!"

A frown appeared on Spencer's face when he suddenly had the sensation he was standing in a room with white walls and a ceiling decorated with sculptured plaster reliefs. In his mind, he stood beside a large open window and watched the heavy rain falling onto the crowded city streets below. He could feel the oppressive heat and humidity as he watched the crowds, and he looked up when several low flying helicopters passed over the building. In his mind, Spencer slowly turned and saw a room filled with tables covered with papers, and maps and charts on easels. It was a scene set against a black backdrop. Then he saw men moving in slow motion as they leaned over the maps and pointed at the features, and he slowly studied each man's face.

Spencer was startled, and the image of everything except one man's face suddenly faded from his mind when he heard, "Admiral, are you all right?" Mahoney immediately sat upright on the couch, unconcerned that her gray skirt slid up on her long slender legs.

"I'm fine," said Spencer as he sat beside her. "For a second I was back in Saigon after you mentioned being shot. Evelyn, I need you to find some information for me this morning. I want you to find a Major Robert Van Horne. I know he resigned from the Third Special Forces about a year ago, but I don't know where he's living today."

"Who is he, Admiral?" asked Mahoney as she wrote a note in her book.

"Someone I've known since Vietnam, but lost contact with after Desert Storm. I don't have any idea where he is today, or if he's even still alive."

"I'll find him, Admiral, but I've got something else to tell you first. One of our units reported another

JOURNEY THROUGH A LONG WINTER'S NIGHT   113

scrambled radio transmission was broadcast from the Newport area earlier this morning! Our people couldn't locate the source, and they still can't decipher the messages!"

"Tell them to keep listening! I want to know if those messages are coming from a transmitter on Goat Island, or one in the city."

As Murtagh walked back to his lavish office in the Pentagon, he was both pleased and confident after what he saw and heard in the strategy room. His planning was flawless and everything was proceeding exactly as he knew it would. He knew that within a few days he would be the leader of the nation's new government. He laughed to himself when he thought about the government's response to the unprecedented situation. Murtagh knew the officials didn't have any idea how to proceed. He considered them weak and indecisive, and that was imperative for his plan to succeed. "Before anyone realizes what's really going on, Rockwell is going to be dead and Benson will be out of the way! Then I'll put together the new government charged with rebuilding our great nation."

When he walked into his large inner office, Murtagh found fifteen of his staff officers listening to a conversation between the Secretary of State, Wilcox, and the Russian Secretary of State, Gagarin.

"That was a good idea tapping the hot line between Moscow and Washington gentlemen," Murtagh complimented his men as he sat at his large desk covered with memorabilia. "Now we'll have some idea about what the leaders of both nations are planning to do so we can stop them! We'll wait twenty four hours, then we'll start moving our men into position tomorrow afternoon. You're listening to the rebirth of this nation on that radio. I don't know about any of you, but I'm damn proud to be part of it! I hope all of you feel the excitement and satisfaction as much as I do."

Murtagh stared at his reflection in a strategically placed mirror hanging on the office wall. He admired his thick graying hair and trim body. He wondered how he would look on national television when he announced he was declaring martial law across the nation after his men killed Benson. He hoped the people would perceive him as a strong and dynamic leader. A man with the talent and ability to lead the nation into the future with innovative ideas and a compassionate, guiding hand.

Chapter Seven

At nine o'clock that morning, a thirty-six-foot long cabincruiser sailed toward Newport Harbor on a calm blue sea. Fourteen people who lived on nearby Block Island were aboard the boat. Some of the excited people stood on the deck in the bright sunlight. They pointed at the hotel on Goat Island, the condominium buildings, and the boats docked at the marina, now seven miles ahead. They were disappointed when they and hundreds of other curious boaters were turned away from the harbor entrance by a blockade of fourteen Coast Guard cutters and Navy war ships.

The men on the boat's bridge were experienced fisherman familiar with the area. They carefully maneuvered the large boat through a narrow, unused channel, and into the harbor three miles beyond the patrol boats. As the power boat slowly sailed toward Goat Island, the Cuban soldiers waited until it was two miles from them before they fired a Stinger missile. Grayish white smoke trailed from the fast flying missile and created a streak across the deep blue sky as it flew toward the boat.

The missile exploded when it struck the boat's white wooden hull, filling the interior with flames and killing four people preparing breakfast in the galley. Another large explosion moments later destroyed the entire boat and killed the people standing on the deck. The explosions propelled flaming fragments of the shattered wooden boat five hundred feet into the sky and covered the calm ocean water with burning fuel. Crowds of horrified spectators on the docks and city streets in Newport stopped talking as they watched clouds of thick black smoke rising from the flames.

"Let that be a warning to everyone to stay away from this island," laughed Vazques as he watched three bodies floating in the raging flames through his binoculars.

Barnes stood beside Trembulak in a hotel room and watched the burning debris floating on the water with a wide grin. "We couldn't have planned anything fucking better than that. That'll show our government and mili-

116 D'ONOFRIO

tary commander we're not fucking around here, and that we're going to destroy any boat that comes near this island. Now they know we're fucking real."

At nine thirty, Spencer received a report of the boat's destruction and the news seemed to depress him even more. As he stared through his office window at the wet city streets in Washington he thought about submitting his resignation to Vice-President Benson. "Maybe someone else who's stronger than I am in this position can help those people. I honestly don't know if I can right now." Mahoney interrupted Spencer's thoughts when she walked into the office and unfolded a large map on his desk.

"I found the address of the man you're looking for, Admiral. Van Horne is living in northern Virginia, in a town called Saint Stephens Church. After he retired from the Army he went into business for himself. He owns some kind of a farm, but the computer didn't give the specifics. The town is right here on the map."

"Good work, Mahoney, I knew you'd be able to find him. Do you think we can get my helicopter off the ground this morning?"

"The storm front is already clearing from the south and I saw blue sky in the distance. I'll contact your pilots and tell them you're on the way. I'll pick the closest base we have to that town and I'll have a car waiting to pick you up there."

"You know where I'll be if you need me. I don't want anyone else to know where I'm going."

"Good luck, Admiral," said Mahoney as she rushed out of the office to coordinate Spencer's trip. "Mahoney," she knew that was the name Spencer called her when he was either upset, or deeply concerned about a situation. She knew he was now troubled by both. Evelyn Mahoney was Spencer's trusted and conscientious personal assistant. The thirty-one-year-old mother of two young daughters began her career with the National Security agency after graduating from Vassar seven years earlier. It was her brilliant recommendations during Operation Desert Storm that made her superiors aware of her performance. The woman many believed could

JOURNEY THROUGH A LONG WINTER'S NIGHT   117

be a model was married to a computer salesman, and they owned a home in Virginia.

Twenty minutes later, Spencer's limousine stopped beside a black Bell Jet Ranger helicopter on the wet grass behind the National Security Agency building. The sky was still overcast as the helicopter flew southwest from the city, passing into the sunlight after flying under the trailing edge of the storm front. An hour later it landed on a deserted military runway at Camp A.P. Hill, Virginia.

Spencer climbed into a waiting limousine as the driver checked his maps, and forty minutes later they drove into the town of Saint Stephens Church. Several miles beyond the center of town they found a wooden sign hanging from a large oak tree beside a driveway that read, "Van Horne & Schultz Tree Farm."

The limousine turned onto a dirt driveway lined by towering oak trees that snaked between seemingly endless fields planted with rows of evergreen trees. Spencer smiled when he saw the small trees planted in the dirt and the tall oak trees that formed a border around each enormous field. A large white colonial style house came into view when the limousine rounded a corner. Behind the house were eight huge warehouses and several pieces of large earth-moving machinery. A group of forty men was unloading pallets of tree seedlings from several flatbed trucks in the sweltering heat. They immediately stopped working, and watched as the limousine parked and Spencer stepped from it. Spencer shaded his eyes from the bright sun as he walked across the large dirt parking lot. "Good morning, I'm looking for Robert Van Horne."

"He's not here. What can we do for you?" asked an older man with unshaven face carrying a machete ominously. Spencer immediately became alarmed when the man started walking towards him. A deep laugh from the front porch of the house suddenly broke the tension and Spencer turned to see a large man sitting on the railing in the shade. Spencer shook his head and grinned when he saw Van Horne jump to the ground and walk toward him with a wide smile. Van Horne wasn't wearing a shirt and his deeply tanned skin was covered with

118 D'ONOFRIO

dark brown hair. Spencer could see several deep and painful wounds Van Horne received during his long military career.

"I can still see where that Viet Cong sapper shot you in the shoulder," commented Spencer when he met the large man on the dirt driveway.

Van Horne didn't comment but instead raised his large hand to the man whom he still considered more than just his military commander. "It's been a long time Admiral. How've you been?"

"Fine, fine, my boy, and you're right, it has been too long," said Spencer as Van Horne led him under the shade of a nearby tree, where they felt a gentle breeze blowing across the fields. "It looks like you have a good size operation here, Robert. It's quiet out here, quiet and very peaceful. I miss that in my life sometimes."

"I bought this place from a friend's father," explained Van Horne as he pointed at twenty long greenhouses in a clearing below the house. "I have sixty men working for me, and we have about ninety thousand trees in the ground. I enjoy the hard work. You know that, Admiral," laughed Van Horne as he looked around proudly at what he accomplished. Spencer remembered Van Horne's compassion for animals and he smiled when he pictured the large man feeding the fragile deer and squirrels by hand in the nearby woods.

"I see you're still keeping yourself in good shape, Robert," commented Spencer as he looked at Van Horne's muscular, six foot, two inch, two hundred pound body. "You're still spending hours lifting weights to work out the problems in your mind, aren't you my boy?"

"The demons we created in combat seem to die slowly, Admiral. A few of them are always trying to take over your mind," Van Horne reminded Spencer as the handsome man ran his hand through his short dark brown hair. Then he and Spencer began walking on a dirt road that led to a large lake in the center of a nearby field. "Are you still with the National Security Agency, or are you working somewhere else in the government, Admiral?"

"I'm still with the Agency, but right now I'm not too proud if it. You must have heard about what's going on

JOURNEY THROUGH A LONG WINTER'S NIGHT 119

in Newport by now, Robert. I feel like my people are responsible for allowing the Russian soldiers to come ashore, but I just can't figure out what we did wrong."

"I saw the report on the national news. Why the hell would the Russians send a task force to attack this country? Why would they want to take the President hostage? It doesn't make any sense to me."

"I don't understand it either, but they're here, Robert. It looks like there's an entire company of Russian paratroopers on that island."

"Have you been able to locate any information about their unit? Their home base of operations? Their training? Anything that might give you something to go on?" asked Van Horne as he knelt and carefully piled dirt around a small tree with his hands.

"We don't know anything about them. We can't even find any information about the Russian general in charge on that island." Spencer confessed to Van Horne as he looked out over a deep ravine and saw a large lake in the distance.

"A no name general leading this kind of attack? Wouldn't you want your most combat experienced officer to lead an attack force like that?" Van Horne suddenly stopped walking and looked at Spencer with a puzzled look on his face. "Why are you here, Admiral? Why aren't you in Washington or Rhode Island?"

Spencer didn't reply as he continued walking, looking down at the coating of brown dirt that now covered his black shoes. The sunlight filtering through the tall trees beside the road made designs on the dirt, and Spencer studied them like the pieces of a puzzle. "I have to tell you the truth, Robert, I can't lie to you. I came here to ask you for help. I want you to work with me for a few days." As he looked at Van Horne's face he could immediately see the shock in his dark brown eyes.

"No, I'm sorry, Admiral, I can't do that," replied Van Horne as he suddenly seemed to walk faster with Spencer trailing behind. "I retired because of the bull shit politics in the military. Why would I want to put myself back in that same situation again? I won't get caught up in the politics, indecisiveness, and back stabbing

120 D'ONOFRIO

that's going on in Washington right now. I don't see how you can deal with what must be going on there now."

"What choice do I have, Robert? I allowed the President to be captured by the Russians because my organization didn't see this coming. It's my fault he's a prisoner on that island."

"That's ridiculous, Admiral. How the hell could you have known the Russians were going to attack that damn island."

"My organization should have known about it or seen it coming, Robert. We're charged with gathering that type of critical information. The only thing I can do now is try to help the President, and prevent any other hostages from dying on that island."

"What are you talking about?" asked Van Horne with an extremely concerned look on his face. "What hostages are dying on the island?"

"The Russians have already killed some of the hostages they're holding on that island, Robert."

"How many people do you think the Russians are holding, Admiral?"

"The hotel's reservation computer shows somewhere around two thousand guests. There were three hundred employees working the morning the Russians took the island. We figure about twelve hundred people in the condominium buildings, and maybe eight hundred on the boats in the marina. That gives the Russians about forty three hundred hostages."

Spencer's revelation shocked Van Horne and he took a deep breath. "Why would Russian combat soldiers kill unarmed civilians? What could they possibly gain by killing those innocent people when they know the world will condemn them?"

"What do they care what the world thinks, Robert? They're probably killing them as a sign they mean business."

"No, I don't think you're right about that, Admiral," said Van Horne as he lifted a stone and threw it toward the lake.

"Now you see what I'm up against, Robert. Nothing is happening the way it should with this one, and I need

JOURNEY THROUGH A LONG WINTER'S NIGHT 121

help from someone I can trust. I need some ideas for stopping the Russians, and I need your help today."

Van Horne was angry and he lifted a large rock and threw it off the road. "What the hell can I do to stop what's going on in Newport, Admiral? I'm not one of your agents, I'm not even in the damn military anymore. What the hell do you think one man can do up there?"

"You can come to Newport with me as my advisor. Look around the city and give me some idea of what I should do. That's all I'm asking, Robert. I need your ideas and I need you with me for a few days."

"Why me, Admiral?" Van Horne asked as he looked at Spencer and saw the gray haired man was exhausted. "We don't see each other for eight years. Then you come out of nowhere and tell me I'm the only one who can do something to end a situation I don't even understand. You have thousands of advisors and strategy people in your organization. What the hell do you think I'm going to be able to tell you that you're not going to get from your own people?"

"You're right, Robert, I already have hundreds of people working on this crisis. My problem is they all go by the damn book, and ninety five percent of them have never been in combat. That's the only way we can operate in Washington today. But you, I know how you operate. You've survived the hell of combat, and you've been in more than your share of life and death struggles. They're the basis of your radical ideas, and you're damn dangerous because you're so unpredictable. You're not afraid to express your opinion either even if it's different from mine. I've seen you do it a hundred times, sometimes you did it just to aggravate me. That's your nature and that's why you're so god damn good Robert."

Van Horne laughed at Spencer's statement as he rubbed brown dirt off his jeans. "Is that a compliment, Admiral? If it is you're going to have to do a lot better than that if you want to convince me to go with you." Van Horne thought about the situation for several minutes as they walked silently on the dirt road and listened to the birds singing in the trees. Van Horne looked at the wispy blue clouds in the clear sky, and then at a

122   D'ONOFRIO

large field of tree seedlings as he made his decision. "I don't know what the hell you think I'll see if I go to Newport with you, Admiral."

"You'll see the situation through your eyes, Robert, with the background of an experienced combat soldier. Then maybe you can give me some idea what to do. What'd you say? I know I'm asking you to drop everything to come with me, but you know I wouldn't be here unless I was in trouble, Robert."

Van Horne took another deep breath and pictured the lush green jungles of Vietnam in his mind, and the beautiful countryside. "I owe you a lot for helping me get through Vietnam, Admiral. You took care of me like a father when we were there, and I still appreciate that today. I'll go with you, but you have to agree to a few things first."

"Anything, what are they?" asked an elated and somewhat relieved Spencer as he looked at the tall trees with a slight feeling of relief.

"We're going to need some men we can trust in Newport with us. I'll give you a list of men and you get them there without any questions asked."

"No problem, what else?" Spencer asked as he brushed away several bugs flying near his face and pulled a cigar from his pocket.

"I don't want anyone to know who I am when we get to Newport. We'll say I'm an advisor from your Washington office."

"I understand, Robert, and I don't have a problem with that." Spencer looked at his watch and became anxious when he saw it was already ten thirty. "We've got to get out of here, Robert. My private jet is waiting in Washington to take us to Rhode Island."

At eleven fifteen, Spencer's helicopter took off with Van Horne aboard. "I'll read the reports you brought with you before we get to Washington," said Van Horne as he felt the helicopter's familiar vibrations while they flew over the treetops. "They'll give me some idea what you already know about the situation before we get to Newport."

At four o'clock that afternoon, Spencer and Van

JOURNEY THROUGH A LONG WINTER'S NIGHT   123

Horne arrived at the Newport end of the destroyed access bridge that once linked the city to Goat Island. "I thought this would attract a large crowd, but I'm surprised to see so many people already in the city," commented Van Horne when he saw the huge crowds filling the streets and ignoring the traffic as they walked toward the harbor. "There must be two hundred thousand people in the city."

Spencer's driver parked beside a State Police roadblock preventing the crowds of curious spectators from walking onto the portions of the access bridge not destroyed by the explosion. The heat and humidity seemed more oppressive than in Virginia. After Spencer removed his suit jacket, the two men walked to the end of the destroyed bridge with binoculars. In the background, a few of the spectators shouted profanities at the Russian soldiers in the island. The sun was shinning directly into Spencer and Van Horne's eyes as they looked west, toward Goat Island. They shaded their eyes with their hands as they studied the island and the buildings on it.

"Check the Russian soldiers sitting on those pieces of concrete on the bridge. They're sitting there smoking cigarettes and talking to one another. They're not even concerned about the crowds. I'm really surprised to see that," commented Van Horne as he held the binoculars with one hand and shaded the lens with his other hand. He made a mental note of what he saw around the hotel as perspiration ran down his forehead and neck while he stood in the sun. Then he slowly scanned the rest of the island and watched armed sentries walking at different locations.

Spencer was anxiously waiting for Van Horne's reaction and comments, but Van Horne didn't say anything as he lowered his binoculars and stared at the island. "What do you think, Robert?"

"I think you've got a big problem here, Admiral. I can see Russian combat soldiers all over that damn island, and I'm sure they have more men inside the buildings. If this was my operation I'd have most of my men hidden inside the buildings watching the water around

124   D'ONOFRIO

the island with machine guns and rocket launchers. I wouldn't want the military forces of the nation I just invaded to know how many men I really have on that island. That Russian general is good, very good!" If Van Horne suggested such an elusive tactic, Spencer knew the Russians were probably using it to give a false impression of the size of their force.

"I've got to find a hotel here in the city, Admiral," Van Horne explained as they walked back to the limousine. "I want to be as close to this island as I can, so I can watch it day or night without attracting a lot of attention."

"Why don't you stay on the Newport Naval Base with me? There's plenty of room there and we've got an open mess serving hot food around the clock."

"No, I'm not comfortable with that idea, Admiral. Someone may get suspicious about who I am when they see me wandering around."

"How about if I use some influence and get you a room in the Marriott Hotel?" asked Spencer as he pointed at a large building near the harbor several blocks away. "We'll put some pressure on the manager and see if we can get you a suite facing the harbor on the hotel's top floor."

Thirty minutes later, the two men walked into the air conditioned comfort of a large suite on the Marriott Hotel's top floor. They carried Van Horne's suitcase, his large canvas travel bag, and his briefcase. Spencer walked onto the suite's large balcony and stood beside a metal railing where he had an unobstructed view of Goat Island in the afternoon sunlight. "This is a great location for watching the island," he told Van Horne. "It's only about three hundred yards from here to the island. You'll be able to see everything that's happening on it."

Van Horne looked at Spencer when they heard a knock on the suite's door. "It's all right, Robert, it's probably some of my people." Spencer opened the door as Van Horne held the handgun he had hidden in a holster under his shirt. Spencer nodded when Mahoney walked into the suite dressed in red shorts and a white lace top, with a large blue duffel bag pulled over her shoulder. "Van Horne, this is Mahoney. She's the one

JOURNEY THROUGH A LONG WINTER'S NIGHT   125

who found you for me."

Mahoney raised her hand to Van Horne as he caught himself staring at the beautiful woman's slender legs. "Hi, I'm glad to meet you. You were easy to find for the Admiral. You have quite a military record."

Van Horne was immediately embarrassed by the beautiful woman's compliment and he seemed to blush as Spencer told him, "I asked her to bring some equipment you might be able to use, Robert. Binoculars, a night vision scope, and a camera and some film. If you need anything else Mahoney can get it for you."

"I could really use a good-looking hooker in this high priced suite you got for me, Admiral. Do you think you can take care of that too?" asked Van Horne as he pulled an address book from his briefcase and sat at the suite's wooden desk. His comments brought a strange look to Mahoney's face as Spencer smiled, and then almost laughed.

"I'm going to need some credentials that show I work for your organization, Admiral. I want to look around the city without attracting any attention, so I'm going to need a nonmilitary Jeep and a portable telephone."

"That won't be a problem, Admiral," said Mahoney as she wrote notes in a book. "I can have those things for him in a couple of hours."

"What are you writing on that pad?" Spencer asked Van Horne as he opened a bottle of whiskey on the suite's long wooden bar and poured himself and Mahoney a drink. "How about you, Robert, can I get you a scotch?"

Van Horne nodded as he wrote on the pad. "This is a list of forty men I want you to contact today, Admiral. Tell them I'm already here and that I want them to meet me here. Mention the word Tabasco, that's my code for trouble and they all know what it means. If they agree to come you've got to have them here by tomorrow night at the latest. Let them bring anything they want with them, legal or not."

"Do this outside the normal channels, Mahoney," cautioned Spencer after he swallowed the whiskey and looked at his watch. "No one is to know these men are in the city. I've got to get over to the Naval Base and find

126 D'ONOFRIO

my temporary office, and the other officials who are already here. I'll meet you back here later tonight, Robert."

After Spencer and Mahoney left the suite, Van Horne sat on a white metal chair on the balcony in the bright sun with the binoculars and a pad. He began writing notes as he watched the activity on Goat Island. He thought about serving under Spencer in Vietnam and remembered meeting with him one morning after a night patrol at Fire Base Danger. He remembered being dressed in only his underwear as he spooned chocolate ice cream from a half gallon container for breakfast while Spencer paced angrily in front of him. "I specifically told you not to get involved in anything out there last night, Van Horne. I sent you out there on a damn reconnaissance mission. But what did you do? You went out there and took on a god damn company of irregulars during that fire fight."

"What was I going to do, Admiral, let them breach the wire on the north wall? They were ready to overrun the perimeter when we hit the bastards."

"Look, I know your team's success and your reputation are based on your own strategies and planning. I keep telling you that you can't take on the whole god damn North Vietnamese Army by yourself. The only reason you're all still alive is because your ideas for attacking the enemy are so god damn unorthodox and unconventional. They never know what the hell you're going to throw at them next, and neither do I."

"Keeping my men safe and getting the job done are the two things most important to me, Admiral. But keeping my men safe always comes first, you know that."

"You're giving me more god damn gray hair, Van Horne. You did a great job out there last night, just watch your ass a little more."

"I didn't have a choice, Admiral." Van Horne smiled, then he stuck a spoon of ice cream into his mouth. The image quickly faded from his mind and a frown formed on his face when he saw a pickup truck quickly moving across the island.

"Where the heck did you meet that wacko, Admiral?" Mahoney asked as Spencer opened the limousine

JOURNEY THROUGH A LONG WINTER'S NIGHT   127

door for her. "He sounds like a real winner with those comments he made."

Spencer laughed at Mahoney's observations as he switched on a small television in the air conditioned limousine and searched for a local news report. "Van Horne and I first met in 1969, when he was just a nineteen year old soldier in Vietnam. He was a member of the Airborne Ranger unit I used in Laos for special operations."

"I'm sorry, Admiral. I shouldn't have made those comments about him," Mahoney immediately apologized as she slipped off her shoes and enjoyed the sensation of the limousine's cool red carpet under her feet. "I didn't realize you two knew each other for such a long time. I didn't mean to judge one of your friends that way. I'm really sorry."

"Don't worry about it, Evelyn. At first I was leery about him too. I really got to know Van Horne after he decided to stay in Vietnam for a second tour."

"I read that in his military folder, Admiral. Why did he re-enlist in the combat zone when everyone else was trying to get out?" she asked as Spencer continued changing the channels on the television.

"I never really figured why he stayed there so long. I know he never considered himself a patriot or a hero. He just wanted to help the people of Vietnam, and the men in his combat team. He's an excellent military planner and an outstanding leader."

"How much time did he spend in Vietnam, Admiral? He doesn't look old enough to have done everything that was in his military folder."

"He was there for thirty-seven months, but he got careless and got shot during an ambush. After the Army doctors patched him up they shipped him home. He retired from the Army because of those injuries, but after a year of physical therapy he re-enlisted in the Third Special Forces Group."

"He was with Blue Light?" asked Mahoney as she adjusted the air conditioner vent and enjoyed the cool air blowing on her face and shoulders.

Spencer nodded as he watched a woman pushing a baby stroller on the city street with two twin girls in it.

128 D'ONOFRIO

"Van Horne was in charge of tactical operations planning for Blue Light. I think that after Desert Storm was over he realized there was more to life than just the military and he decided to try it as a civilian."

"I thought my husband was tough to figure out. This guy's a lot tougher to read without knowing him. I thought he was serious when he made that comment about the hooker in the hotel room. I thought he was talking about me."

"No, no, he would never say anything like that about you, Evelyn. It's his dry sense of humor and subdued personality that give people the impression he's dangerous and someone to be feared, but that's entirely wrong. Don't get me wrong, you wouldn't want to meet him in a dark alley, or in combat. Special Forces trained him to work with weapons and explosives, and then cross trained him in communications. I don't understand why, but he always functions better under extreme pressure."

"The perfect combat soldier?"

"No, hardly. I had to bail him out of trouble at least two dozen times while we were in Vietnam. He has a dark side you never want to see Evelyn, and that's his intense temper and anger. He struggles to control both, all the time. He can never let his anger override his logic or someone might really get hurt."

Mahoney brushed back her blonde hair and crossed her long legs as she tried to relax for a few minutes. "How did you talk him into coming to Newport with you, Admiral? I'm surprised he wants to be back in the center of the action again."

Spencer stared through the limousine's tinted window for several seconds before he replied. "Van Horne has never able to accept the deaths of the men who served under him in Vietnam. I think those deaths still upset him every day of his life. He thinks he allowed them to die while he should have been watching over them more closely. I think that's why he's really here, Evelyn. He's trying to help as many people as he can before he dies to make up for letting his men die in combat."

"I don't like the sounds of that, Admiral. I hope he

JOURNEY THROUGH A LONG WINTER'S NIGHT   129

didn't come here to get himself killed trying to help the people on that island. I don't want anything happening to you because he's taking too many risks."

"That's not even a concern, Evelyn. Believe me, he's not here to die. I think the thought of dying scares Van Horne. I remember he was never religious and he always thought death would be the end of his new experiences. Believe me, he didn't come all this way to die here." Neither Spencer nor Mahoney spoke during the remainder of the trip as they thought about the emotions Van Horne was still experiencing, even after all the years since Vietnam.

When Spencer arrived at the Newport Naval Base, his staff told him a tele-conferencing meeting between the officials in Newport, and those who remained behind in Washington, was already in progress. Spencer walked into a large conference room in the base's communications building equipped with four large television monitors. One monitor displayed the person speaking at a podium in the Pentagon's strategy room, while the others displayed the people seated around the circular table. Several cameras mounted in the conference room where Spencer and the other officials were seated displayed their images on a large monitor hanging from the Pentagon's strategy room walls.

Spencer listened as Admiral Andrews described a new plan with the aide of diagrams and pictures of Goat Island on the television monitor. "We feel we can easily guide a remotely controlled submarine into the harbor to get some pictures of the underwater mines. Using the pictures as reference points my divers might still be able to find a safe underwater route to the island. The pictures might provide our intelligence agencies and ordinance groups with some new information about the mines. Maybe they can find a way to disarm them."

After a brief discussion of Andrew's plan, Vice-President Benson stood and addressed the group. "General Peskov spoke by radio with Ed Jamison and General Roberts earlier this afternoon. He adamantly restated his demand for payment of the ransom he says his government demands. He also refused to discuss withdraw-

130   D'ONOFRIO

ing his men from the island, or our suggestion he free a group of women and children." Benson appeared upset by the report, and the strain was apparent on his face as he read his notes and infrequently looked at the men he was depending on for solutions.

"He's probably afraid to withdraw his men because he thinks we'll take him into custody after they're off the island," speculated Coleman of the Federal Bureau of Investigation.

"Maybe we can offer Peskov and his men written amnesty if they'll release all the hostages," Spencer suggested to the group. "Maybe we can convince him to pull out if we guarantee him safe passage out of the country. It can't hurt to try." The officials then extensively discussed that idea, and others, to end the negotiating impasse.

At six o'clock, Spencer walked into the evening sunlight. He wore slacks and a light shirt because the heat and humidity seemed more oppressive. He wasn't expecting to see Van Horne studying a map in an open dark brown Jeep with a black roll bar. "Mahoney told me you'd be here. Let's take a ride around the city."

"What are you looking for?" Spencer asked as Van Horne weaved the Jeep through the crowds of people that filled the city streets.

"I'd like to get a look at the buildings on Goat Island from different angles. I want to get some perspective of where the buildings are located on the island. This is where I want to be, Fort Adams," he said as he studied the map after stopping the Jeep because thousands of spectators filled the city street. Twenty minutes later, they parked the Jeep in a large dirt field beside the fort, where thousands of curious and excited spectators were watching the island. Van Horne pulled a pad from his pocket and wrote several notes as he and Spencer stood in the jeep and studied the island with binoculars.

"What do you think so far, Robert? Can you see any way to get onto that island?" asked Spencer after he watched five Russian soldiers escorting two frantic female hostages across a parking lot.

"I haven't found anything that even comes close to

JOURNEY THROUGH A LONG WINTER'S NIGHT   131

a flaw in their tactics, Admiral. Someone developed a damn good plan to attack that island and cut if off from the rest of the world. They must have spent months planning and training for this one. Then they pulled it off when we weren't expecting it." Van Horne turned and looked at the fort's towering stone walls, and the green moss and grass growing in the dirt deposited by the wind between the huge stones. He studied the rusting iron bars in the windows and looked up when a large flock of squawking sea gulls flew overhead.

Spencer turned and looked at the fort, and then back at Van Horne. "What are you thinking about, Robert?"

"I'd like to look around inside this fort. We might be able to use this place during the next few days."

"Use it for what?" laughed Spencer as he looked around at the heavy equipment and large piles of construction supplies that were to be used for the fort's renovation. "This place is a dump. They just started renovating it."

"A dump with built in camouflage," laughed Van Horne as they stepped out of the Jeep and walked toward a construction office trailer near the heavy equipment. Inside they found a man and a woman frantically packing the folders contained in gray filing cabinets into cardboard boxes. "I'm Admiral Herbert Spencer, of the National Security Agency," said Spencer as he raised his identification cards. "Who's in charge here?"

"I'm Sam Johnson. I'm the director of the fort's restoration project," replied the man as he stood and walked across the trailer filled with blueprints and construction work orders.

"I'm Robert Van Horne. We're considering using your fort as a command center for the next few days. What's the inside of it look like?"

"Most of the fort is in shambles because nothing was done to preserve it," replied Jamison who was a historian. "We renovated a few areas for official ceremonies a couple of years ago. We have some small rooms that can be used as private offices and four large con-

132 D'ONOFRIO

ference rooms. There's even an area where fifty to sixty men slept and showered before official ceremonies."

"Is that area clean?" asked Spencer. "Or would we have to clean it before it could be used?"

"Its not too dirty in the renovated areas. Its been abandoned for the past couple of years, and it'll take a few hours to clean it up. No longer than that."

"I was wrong, Robert. This might be a good location for you to set up a command center." Spencer told Van Horne as he studied a large map of the city fastened to the trailer's wall. "It's away from the Naval base and the city, yet you still have a perfect view of the island from here."

Van Horne bent forward and watched the buildings on Goat Island in the distance through a dirty trailer window. "We have a better view of Goat Island from here than we did anywhere else in the city. We'd be stupid not to use this place."

"We're going to need your fort for a few days, Mister Johnson. I'd like to keep our presence here as confidential as we can," cautioned Spencer as he pulled a piece of paper from his pocket and wrote several notes on it.

"I'm glad we can be of some help. Do you know why the Russians attacked that island? Why Rhode Island and not California or Florida?" Neither Van Horne nor Spencer replied to the question as they studied the map. "I've already sent the work crew home so you'll be alone in the fort. Let me show you around the inside and then I'll give you the keys to the padlocks." As Johnson led the men quickly through the fort's interior he explained it was built to house five-thousand colonial troops. The fort's two hundred foot high stone walls surrounded a twenty-seven acre center courtyard.

Spencer arrived back at the Newport Naval Base several hours later, and found the building where his staff set up temporary offices. He saw James Reynolds of the Secret Service in a hallway accompanying another man dressed in military fatigues. Reynolds wore jeans and a sweatshirt, and a shoulder holster. The thirty-nine-year-old Reynolds was in good physical shape, as were all of his agents. "Admiral Spencer, I'd

JOURNEY THROUGH A LONG WINTER'S NIGHT   133

like to introduce you to Commander Thomas Holloway, of the Navy's Nuclear Weapons Team. His group flew in from their base in California this afternoon."

"It's a pleasure meeting you Commander," said Spencer as the two men shook hands. "I'm glad you're here to help us."

"I hope we can be of some assistance, Admiral," commented Holloway as a large group of military officers rushed past them. "The situation doesn't look too good right now."

"What's your team's specialty?" asked Spencer as Mahoney stepped beside him and handed him a folder.

"Our tactical training deals primarily with the placing and detonating of offensive and defense nuclear weapons during ground combat operations. We also have expertise disarming tactical nuclear weapons." The two men talked for several minutes and Spencer discovered the thirty-four-year-old Navy officer was a SEAL; Sea, Air, Land, the equivalent to the Army's Special Forces. Spencer was impressed by Holloway's background and the special training his team received.

At nine o'clock that night, Barnes, Vazques, and Leland stood in the communications trailer and watched Trembulak transmit a prepared message to Washington using a short wave radio. Eight of Vazques' men sat at the other radios in the trailer checking on the status of their men across the island. "Not only are they hearing this message in Washington, we're transmitting on a frequency short wave radio operators around the world can monitor. They'll hear the message and report it to their radio and television stations so everyone will know just how critical this situation is becoming."

Trembulak slowly read the statement's final paragraph as his hands trembled while he held the microphone. "The people of the United States' now have six days left to deliver the food and medical aide the Russian government demands. If we do not receive the aide or the ransom we demand, the President and his family will be executed. Then we will detonate our plutonium bomb. Our demands and warning should not be ignored by the United States' government."

134   D'ONOFRIO

"Good, that should scare the shit out of everyone," commented Barnes as he took the microphone from Trembulak and turned off the radio.

"Do you think the attack is proceeding as your General Murtagh expected?" Trembulak asked Leland as he turned in the chair.

"It's going better than any of us could have imagined. Our government and the Russian government are already beginning to fall apart because of this. The tension and accusations are escalating and now the internal fear and anxiety in both nations is beginning to take its toll on the people and the government officials."

"What about your military commanders in Washington? Do you think they may try to attack this island without you knowing about it? We'll all die here if that happens."

"Don't fucking worry about it, Trembulak, you're going to die someday, one way or another," replied Barnes as he immediately became upset with the terrorist's cowardice. "Murtagh will persuade the other military leaders it's too dangerous to attack the island, so you don't have to worry about it."

"Do you think your military might be planning how to attack us?" Vazques asked Leland, because he knew he would receive a logical answer from him, unlike the sarcastic and belittling replies he received from Barnes.

"I'm sure they're working on a dozen different attack plans right now. We have the technology to destroy the mines around the island in a second, but the threat of detonating a nuclear bomb is too much of a deterrent. They won't risk destroying part of the United States during a surprise military strike. If they knew we're going to blow the bomb Sunday night, I'm sure they'd have second thoughts about attacking us today."

At eleven o'clock that evening, Mahoney and Spencer sat in Van Horne's hotel suite with him and read the surveillance reports compiled by the various intelligence organizations. Van Horne immediately looked up and asked them, "Does anyone know you two are here?" after someone knocked on the door. After they shook their heads, Van Horne pulled the handgun from under his

JOURNEY THROUGH A LONG WINTER'S NIGHT 135

shirt and held it behind his back as he cautiously opened the door.

"How the hell are you, Major?" asked Jim Owen as he led six men carrying luggage and golf club bags into the suite. "We came as soon as we got your message."

"It's good to see all of you. You all remember Admiral Spencer, don't you?" asked Van Horne after he shook each man's hand. "Admiral, Mahoney, this is Jim Owen, Harvey Taylor, Robert Willey, Howard Nielson, Gene Depietro, Donald Shaw, and Michael Kearns."

"How are you doing, Major?" asked Taylor as he carefully placed a golf club bag that contained two rifles onto the carpeted floor. "We lost contact with each other when you retired after Desert Storm."

"I'm fine, Harvey. Come on, lets sit down." During the next hour, Van Horne explained the situation to the men, and what he had already seen on the island. Then he turned off the suite's lights and led the group onto the balcony, which was dimly lit by the city lights. The island was well lit by the lights inside the buildings, streetlights, and the lights on the marina docks. "That's it. If you use the binoculars and the night vision scope you can see all the details. They keep it well lit at night, but I still haven't figure out why they're doing that."

"Maybe they're doing it to throw the whole thing in our faces," speculated Kearns as he focused the binoculars on six Cuban soldiers walking on the island's deserted main road. "We can see them, but we can't do anything to stop them."

"Psychological warfare?" Van Horne asked himself, then he pointed into the distance. "If you look beyond the left end of the island you'll see a large lit stone structure across the harbor. That's Fort Adams. That's where we're going to set up our command center. We'll make a list of the equipment we'll need and the Admiral will get it for us from the Naval Base."

During the next two hours, as they ate dinner delivered by the hotel's room service, they compiled a list of the equipment they would need to assemble a command center. Van Horne and the others were members of the first military units moved into Saudi Arabia after

136   D'ONOFRIO

Iraq invaded Kuwait. The experiences learned while hastily establishing a command center under those extreme conditions allowed them to easily compile an extensive list of equipment.

"We'll have everything at the fort in the morning, Robert," said Spencer after he and Mahoney discussed the items on the handwritten list. "Why do you want such advanced communications equipment?"

"We'll try to locate the frequency the Russians are using to communicate with their troops on the island," explained Jim Owen as he stood and threw a can of soda to Taylor, then opened one for himself. "We might be able to get some information if we can eavesdrop on their conversations."

"They may even be sending and receiving intelligence reports to a Russian submarine. It might be submerged somewhere off the coast," speculated Taylor as he watched the alternating white and red light from a lighthouse beacon in the distance. "They've got to be getting their information from somewhere."

Fatigue and anxiety soon tired the men and they decided to stop for a few hours of sleep. Spencer arranged for separate rooms for each man in the hotel, and Mahoney gave them keys. Then she and Spencer drove to their quarters on the Newport Naval Base.

Van Horne woke at five o'clock Monday morning and felt exhausted as he sat on the edge of his bed. He pulled back the drapes across his balcony's sliding glass door and saw puffy white clouds floating in the placid deep blue sky over the bay. He walked onto the balcony with his binoculars and watched the Russian soldiers on Goat Island for several minutes, then he walked back into his suite and showered.

Thirty minutes later, Van Horne dressed in brown shorts and a red shirt, knocked on the door of Jim Owen's room. While Owen finished dressing, Van Horne quickly cleaned the nine millimeter handgun he was carrying in a holster under his shirt. "I want you to be the executive officer while we're here, Jim. You and I have always worked well together and we know how each other operates. We both put our men first."

JOURNEY THROUGH A LONG WINTER'S NIGHT   137

"Just tell me what has to be done, Major," replied Owen who was pleased with Van Horne's confidence in him as he pulled on a brightly colored blue and green shirt. "How involved are we going to get in this hostage deal? I thought the government and the military would be coordinating everything that's going on here. Why are they letting us look around?"

"They don't know we're here," laughed Van Horne as he pushed the full ammunition magazine into the handgun. "I asked you here to help develop some ideas for getting men onto Goat Island for the Admiral to present to the military. If we can't come up with anything then we'll get the hell out of here in a few days. If we do come up with a plan, we'll give it to Spencer and then blow out of here before the shooting starts."

Owen accepted Van Horne's explanation because he trusted the man he served under in Vietnam. Owen was the forty-one-year-old father of four children who became a real estate agent in Orlando, Florida, after retiring from the Army. Owen brushed back his short blonde hair and remembered being a member of Van Horne's combat team in Vietnam, where he served as a captain for two years. After Owen finished his second tour of Vietnam, his mother and father pleaded with him to return to the safety of the United States. Although he wanted to stay and help the Vietnamese people, he knew his family was more important and asked to be transferred home.

This battle was personal for Owen who now wanted to protect his wife and children from the Russians invading his own nation. He talked with his wife for several hours and explained his reasons for asking for a leave of absence from his employer, and his plans to travel to Newport. He explained he might be able to help find a solution to the problem because of his background in military tactics, and the fact he and Van Horne worked closely together in Vietnam. He couldn't tell her he always regretted leaving Van Horne and the other men in Vietnam while he retreated to the safety of the United States. It was something that still troubled him when he thought about the war, but now he had the chance

138   D'ONOFRIO

to make up for something he considered a mistake.

Van Horne and his men met for a quick breakfast in a hotel restaurant filled with excited tourists. After they finished they drove to Fort Adams in the Jeep. They were dressed like the thousands of other spectators crowded into the city to see the Russian soldiers on Goat Island, and they didn't attract any attention. As Van Horne unlocked the padlock and pulled open the fort's rusting black steel gates, he told Owen, "When the others get here, I want guards on this entrance around the clock. No one gets in unless you or I say so."

When the group walked into the fort they could smell the musty dampness that seemed to permeate throughout the interior of the stone structure. In some areas of the neglected fort, the weeds were three feet tall, and animal droppings could be seen in many of the stone hallways constructed with arched ceilings. In many areas the stone hallways had collapsed with age, and bright green moss was growing on the rocks as sunlight streamed in through the holes. Van Horne led the men into the area where the offices and conference rooms built with huge stones were painted white. The paint was now peeling and flaking away because of the dampness in the fort.

One hour later, as the men were moving a wooden desk and chairs covered with mildew out of a conference room, Mahoney drove a large truck into the fort filled with supplies. They used the cleaning supplies and quickly washed the offices. Then they began assembling the equipment packed into Mahoney's truck.

At ten o'clock, Spencer walked into the fort with more of Van Horne's men, and they found him assembling a radio. "It's starting to take shape, Robert," commented Spencer as he lit a cigar and watched the men working around him.

"Anything new happening on that island this morning, Admiral?"

"I just got off the phone with Jamison of Central Intelligence. He told me his intelligence sources deep inside the Russian military have never heard of General Peskov. Jamison should know what's going on in-

JOURNEY THROUGH A LONG WINTER'S NIGHT   139

side the Russian military establishment, yet he keeps insisting he doesn't have any information about that general."

"Do you think he has anything to do with this attack? I know he's your friend, but do you think he has anything to gain from this?"

"No, I don't think so, Robert. I've known him for twenty years and this doesn't seem like something he'd be involved in. On the other hand, anything is possible, so I've got some of my men watching him."

"Have you considered Peskov might be a paramilitary clown, who thinks he's can save Russia by attacking the United States with his followers?"

"I might have thought that at first, Robert, but not after what I've seen on that island. Look at how much planning and logistical work went into this attack. Peskov needed intelligence information about the local police, Coast Guard patrols, Navy picket ships, and even the President's personal schedule. Look at all the military equipment they have on that island. No, I don't think you're right about that, Robert."

The tension made Spencer feel exhausted and he sat on a chair beside Van Horne. "Anything I can do for you in here, Robert? I feel useless just sitting around here while everyone else is working."

"You just sit there and take it easy, Admiral. I've got some men setting up more radios in a room down the hall, and some others are setting up the smaller offices. We'll use this large room as our main conference room," said Van Horne as it was suddenly lit by forty construction lights with yellow plastic protective covers his men fastened to the room's stone ceiling.

Van Horne looked at the door when the statuesque Mahoney led fourteen more men into the conference room. An hour later, another group of men arrived at the fort and Van Horne asked everyone to find seats in the conference room. "Lets go over what we already know about the situation. Then we'll move on from there and discuss what we want to accomplish in the next few days." During the next hour, Van Horne told the men what the government knew about the situation.

140   D'ONOFRIO

"Where do you want to start our part of the operation, Major?" asked James Neville whose specialty was planning ambushes.

"We're going to need some pictures of Goat Island to work with during our planning sessions, so some of you get that assignment. There's cameras and film in the boxes at the back of the room."

"We have some good Long Range Reconnaissance men in the group," said Owen as he turned on a metal chair and pointed at several of his friends. "They can watch the island and look for weaknesses."

"Good, I want to watch the Russians on that island day and night. We need to know if they're doing anything on a routine basis. Are they rotating their guards at the same time of day? Do they meet at specific locations on the island to talk? Are they eating together in a central location? Use the same tactics we used in Vietnam and Iraq. The Russian paratroopers on that island are just as deadly as the enemies we've faced before, maybe more so."

"Lets get some teams into the city so we can get pictures of the island from all sides," suggested Donald Shaw as he drew the outline of the island on a pad. Then he drew a diagram of the mainland with six arrows pointing toward the island. "I saw a few parks in the city we can use as a platform for taking pictures. We'll blend in with the crowd dressed like this," he said as he pointed at his blue summer shirt, "and it'll give us all a chance to look around."

"When you're in the city don't forget you're spectators and nothing more than that. Admiral Spencer said all of our intelligence agencies have people in the city, and there's agents here from England, France, Germany, Japan, and all the NATO nations. Try to keep a low profile out there."

"How about getting the blueprints and floor plans of the hotel and the other buildings on the island?" asked Bob Jarvis as he wrote notes on a small pad. "We should have them so we can get an idea what the interiors of the buildings look like."

"Good idea, Jarvis. You get with the Admiral and

JOURNEY THROUGH A LONG WINTER'S NIGHT 141

see what you can find in the town hall. The government agents, and the press, may be after the same information, so watch your step."

"How about weapons, Major?" asked David White after he pulled a large handgun from a holster behind his back. "Should we carry these or leave them here?"

"You better carry them with you. Don't trust anyone and don't get involved in anything that might put us all in jeopardy. Admiral Spencer has identification cards that show you work for his organization and I want you to carry them with you. All right, lets get started. Lets say we meet back here in six hours and go over what we've found."

Van Horne drove Spencer and Mahoney to the Newport Naval Base in the scorching midday sun so the Admiral could check for new information about the Russians. While they were in the communications center they met Commander Holloway. "I'd like to introduce you to one of my men Commander. This is Robert Van Horne."

"It's a pleasure. Are you here from Washington, too?" Holloway asked Van Horne as he closed a thick folder that described the technical specifications of Russian nuclear weapons.

Van Horne briefly looked at Spencer, then attempted to sound panicky as he replied. "I'm only here for a few days to look for solutions. Then I'm out of here before the end of the week. Aren't you worried about being this close to that bomb?"

"I am, but I've got to give an assessment of the damage we can expect if the Russians detonate the bomb on that island."

"What can we expect, Commander?" asked Spencer as he pulled a cigar from his pocket. Mahoney handed him a book of matches before she walked into a nearby communications room.

"Total destruction of that island, the city, this base, and everything else with a thirty to forty mile radius. The land around here will be contaminated for thousands of years by the plutonium radiation, and this part of the country will become a wasteland. No people, no

142 D'ONOFRIO

animals, no birds, and anything that accidentally wanders into the area will be dead within days."

Mahoney suddenly ran into the hallway with her long blonde hair bouncing behind her and she grasped Spencer's arm. "Admiral, General Peskov is broadcasting a message from the island now." She led the group into the communications center and they listened to the message on a radio loudspeaker.

"The United States' government now has five days left to deliver the ransom my government demands for the release of the hostages. I wish to prove to the United States' government that I do have a nuclear weapon on this island. Therefore, I will allow five people to tour Goat Island today. I also want them to see President Rockwell so they can assure the world he's still alive. If you wish to accept my offer the five people may board a boat that will dock in Newport at exactly two o'clock this afternoon. My soldiers are not to be taken into custody. If they are, fifty of the hostages will be executed for every one of my men that does not return to the island. This is all I have to say."

"I've got to find the other officials and discuss this message with them," Spencer frantically told Van Horne as he backed out of the room. "I want to accept Peskov's offer and get onto that island." Peskov's message troubled Van Horne. He walked to the Jeep and studied the map as he tried to understand why the Russians wanted visitors on the island they controlled.

Spencer and the other officials met in the teleconferencing room five minutes later, linked electronically to those in Washington. "I think we should send a group of men to Goat Island," Spencer explained to the others as he looked at his watch nervously. "This'll give us a chance to get a good look at the equipment the Russians have on that island. We can also check on the condition of the President and the other hostages."

"That's a ridiculous and dangerous idea, Spencer," protested Coleman of the Federal Bureau of Investigation. "I'm totally opposed to sending anyone to that island. This offer may be a trick to lure more hostages, more prestigious hostages, onto the island."

JOURNEY THROUGH A LONG WINTER'S NIGHT   143

"Then why the hell did we come to Newport, Coleman?" Spencer said angrily as he stared across the table at him. "Did we come here to watch that island and wonder what the hell is going on out there? We don't even know how many Russian soldiers are on the island. This is a good way to find out what's going on out there and do some quick reconnaissance work at the same time."

"I think Spencer is right, we should send some men to the island," commented General Murtagh in the Pentagon's strategy room as he sat back in his chair. "Who knows what they'll be able to tell us when they get back."

Murtagh wanted the men to see what was taking place on Goat Island, and he didn't want anyone to prevent it from happening. When the group reported the Russians did have a nuclear bomb on the island, he knew his government and the people of the world would be enraged by the Russian's aggression. It was this anger and rage he hoped to foster as he prepared the people for what was to follow later in the week.

"I can see that discussing this idea with you is a waste of my time," Spencer bluntly told the others as he looked at his watch and then stacked his intelligence reports into a pile. "I'm going onto that island with some of my staff. I don't care what the rest of you do. I didn't come to Newport just to become a god damn spectator because I'm worried about taking risks."

Holloway stood as Spencer walked toward the conference room door. "Wait a minute, Admiral, I should go to that island with you. I should try to get a look at the Russian's bomb."

"Don't be ridiculous, Commander," shouted Admiral Adams as he immediately stood and walked behind the men seated around the table in the Pentagon's strategy room. "What if the Russians take you hostage after you're on that island?"

"That's a risk I've got to take, Admiral. No one else in this room can tell you if that bomb is real or a sophisticated dummy. You've got to let me go with Admiral Spencer."

Adams knew Holloway's concerns and comments

144 D'ONOFRIO

were valid and he immediately stopped protesting. "All right, Commander, I see your point. You may accompany Spencer to the island."

"I'm going with them too," an exhausted Governor Winston suddenly told the others as he stood. "A lot of the hostages on that island are my constituents and I'm concerned about their welfare." Winston looked at Mayor Schmitt as he arranged his papers, as though he was waiting for him to volunteer.

"I can't do it, Peter," Schmitt suddenly burst out as he buried his face in his hands and began to cry. "I can't go to that island. I'm too afraid. Too afraid of dying after seeing what they did to the people on that bridge."

Winston didn't look at the others as he replied, but instead stared down at the wooden tabletop. "I understand. I'm scared as hell, too, but I have to know what's happening to the people on that island."

"I'm letting those people down by not going out there, I know I am."

"No, you're not."

"I am, I'm sending you out there alone to do the job I should be doing."

"Don't worry, Schmitt, they're not going alone. I'm going with them," said Reynolds as he stood with several of his staff analysts. "Maybe I can find out what happened to my men who were guarding the President."

Fifteen minutes later, Spencer walked out of the building with Holloway and Reynolds, and saw Van Horne waiting in the Jeep parked in the shade under a large tree. Spencer introduced Reynolds to Van Horne, then told him about their plan to go to Goat Island.

"If you're going to that damn island, then I'm going with you," Van Horne told Spencer without giving him a chance to protest. "You're not going out there alone."

The comments surprised Holloway, who initially saw Van Horne as a large, timid man, afraid of the bomb only a short time before.

An hour later, Van Horne stood on the town's concrete dock in the blazing sun with Spencer, Holloway, Governor Winston, Reynolds, almost thirty members of their staff. News camera crews from more than sixty

JOURNEY THROUGH A LONG WINTER'S NIGHT 145

stations and forty nations filmed them, while the state and local police held back the curious crowds.

Van Horne watched a large white Boston Whaler slowly sail across the calm blue ocean water that separated the island from the city. "Look at how that boat is zig-zaging through the water. They must have put their mines into the water in a pattern," he told Spencer.

The crowd shouted loud profanities and other statements of displeasure at the soldiers on the boat as it pulled beside the dock. The crowd's comments became louder and angrier after three heavily armed Cubans climbed out of it.

"Each of you must be searched before you get onto the boat," said one of the soldiers. Several minutes later, two Cuban soldiers guarded the men while the third piloted the boat back to Goat Island.

Twenty Cuban soldiers met the boat when it docked at a wooden pier beside the Sheraton Hotel. Vazques waited to meet the men dressed in a green camouflaged Russian Army combat uniform. "I'm Colonel Rubelnesk, of the Russian Paratroopers. I hope my men weren't too rough when they searched you. As you can see, all my men carry automatic weapons, radios, and hand grenades. We've already constructed fortified positions so any attack of this island by your military forces will be futile. We can kill all of our hostages before your first landing craft reaches the island."

"We've also saturated the waters around the island with mines," Vazques told the group as he led them across the lush green grass that separated the hotel building from the blue ocean waves. He pointed at the water as he said, "The mines are sensitive to metal and vibrations in the water. They're what killed your divers. Sending those men into the water was a foolish act of stupidity by your government and military forces. This island is impenetrable."

Van Horne and the others studied the large number of Vazques' men dressed like Russian soldiers as they walked across the parking lot behind the hotel in the bright sun. They stopped beside one of the hotel's two rear garage entrances, where Vazques's men prevented

146 D'ONOFRIO

them from walking into the concrete structure. "That is our nuclear bomb," he said as he pointed at a gray metal box measuring four feet wide, four feet deep, and six feet long in the center of the garage. "My government has given me explicit instructions to detonate that bomb if your military attacks this island."

"I'd like to take a closer look at that device," said Holloway as he strained to get a better look at the bomb. Then he shaded his eyes from the glare of the overhead sun. "I'd like to verify it's real."

Vazques replied immediately, hoping to upset the group by not giving Holloway the information he desperately wanted. "Let me assure you that bomb is very real. Do not be so naive to think that combat hardened Russian paratroopers would attack this island with only idle threats."

"I need something to take back with me to prove the bomb is real," explained Holloway angrily. "Something to tell my commanders."

"Tell them this," laughed Vazques as he pointed at the bomb. "If you attack the island that bomb can be detonated by a small transmitter General Peskov carries with him. Before your military forces can get close to him, he can destroy your nation with that device. If you look beside the bomb you will see vibration detecting sensors we set into the garage's concrete floor. If they detect the vibrations of large explosions on the island they'll signal the bomb to detonate. I hope you understand that using conventional bombs to destroy this device will be futile and will only result in its detonation."

Vazques led the group beside the cement seawall located along the harbor side of the island. "You are not prepared for war with your enemies. If you were, you would not be standing here on an island controlled by Russian paratroopers."

"That's because we're not at war with any nation," said Reynolds sarcastically. "Your government told us the Cold War is over, and we believed you."

Vazques ignored the indignant comment with a wave of his hand and a laugh. "None of my men were injured

JOURNEY THROUGH A LONG WINTER'S NIGHT   147

when we secured this island. Some of our hostages refused to cooperate with us. Their actions forced us to use them as examples for the others."

"What are you telling us, Colonel?" Governor Winston asked as he quickly became nervous and distraught in the oppressive heat that was upsetting him. "What did you do to those people?"

"If the people follow our instructions and listen to our warnings they will not be harmed." Vazques leaned forward and proudly pointed at the rocks on the other side of the thick cement seawall with a wide grin. "These are the people who did not heed our warnings."

Van Horne closed his eyes after he looked over the wide seawall and saw an ocean wave momentarily cover the fifty dead bodies laying on the rocks. "You tied their hands behind their backs before you shot them in the head," he said angrily as he turned toward Vazques.

"I haven't seen anything like this since Auschwitz!" commented Spencer, who was sickened when he saw several bloated bodies covered with flies as they lay on the rocks in the hot sun. "How could you kill those defenseless people? You call yourselves paratroopers, yet you kill people who couldn't possibly be a threat to you."

"You're murdering innocent people on this island," Winston screamed at Vazques as his eyes seemed to fill with tears. "How can you justify allowing combat soldiers to kill unarmed civilians?"

Vazques laughed at Winston's comments, as did his men. "These bodies will remind the others they will die if they do not follow our instructions. Whether the other hostages live or die means nothing to us. If they're dead, it's less my men must be concerned about."

"I know what you mean," Van Horne suddenly commented as he stared into Vazques' eyes coldly. "At Khe Sahn we had so many dead enemy bodies we didn't know what to do with them. We dug a hole with a bulldozer, and threw them into the bottom of it. While they were pushing the dirt over those bodies with the bulldozer my partner and I drank from a bottle of scotch and then spit on the fucking grave!"

148   D'ONOFRIO

Spencer watched Vazques as he tried not to appear upset by Van Horne's comments, but he could see the unexpected and brutal statement startled him. Vazques immediately walked away, leading the group across the two lane access road behind the hotel and the green grass. As they walked toward the building's rear access doors, Van Horne carefully studied the Russian soldiers escorting them, and the equipment they carried.

Van Horne quickly looked to his left, toward the end of the island three hundred feet away. He saw Cuban military equipment stacked on the island's lush grass, and the camouflaged tarp that covered it. He stared at the canvas as he walked and was briefly able to look under an open end, where he saw something that looked strikingly familiar.

Several minutes later, as the group was standing in the air conditioned coolness of a hotel suite, Trembulak nervously walked in dressed in a camouflaged military uniform. "I am General Peskov of the Russian Army. I'm pleased your government allowed you to come here, and I hope my men have given you a satisfactory tour of the island. I assume you will tell your military leaders that we do have a bomb on this island, as I claimed. As you will soon see, I have not killed your President or his family."

A soldier opened the suite's bedroom door, and everyone watched as President Rockwell and his family were pushed into the living room by six soldiers. They appeared exhausted and Van Horne saw the bruises on the President's face, which he received during a recent beating.

"As you can see, the President and his family are still alive. That can change based on the actions of your government. If my nation does not receive the ransom it demands, they will be executed."

"Don't negotiate with these damn Russians," the President suddenly shouted at the group. "Reynolds, Spencer, attack this island and kill all of them. Don't give in to their demands."

"That will be enough from you," Trembulak told Rockwell as Vazques' men forced the shouting man back

JOURNEY THROUGH A LONG WINTER'S NIGHT   149

into the bedroom with his crying wife and daughter. "I will transmit a radio message tomorrow morning, instructing your government where I want the ransom delivered. If you do not deliver it, I will bring your nation to its knees when I detonate the plutonium bomb."

"Can't we negotiate a peaceful ending to this situation?" Spencer pleaded with Peskov, knowing this might be his only chance for a face to face discussion with the Russian general. "Can't we sit down and figure out a way to end this situation without anyone else getting hurt?"

"The only way to end this unfortunate situation is to send food and medical aide to my nation. Tell your government officials what you've seen on this island. Warn them about the seriousness of the situation and the consequences if they ignore my demands."

"What'll it prove if you kill yourself when you detonate that bomb?" Spencer suddenly asked as he tried to gain insight into the Russian General's mind.

"Neither I nor my men are afraid to die for our nation," replied Trembulak as he remembered the portion of the attack plan.

Murtagh wrote that dealt with his response to that very question. "If we are going to die, then let it be while we are trying to help our people." Without waiting for a reaction from Spencer, Trembulak told Vazques, "Take them back to Newport, now."

"Where are the Secret Service agents who were guarding the President?" Reynolds suddenly asked Trembulak as he walked toward the door.

The unexpected question made Trembulak and Vazques look at one another momentarily. Then Vazques laughed as he replied, "They're already dead. They were first to be killed."

"You rotten bastard," shouted Reynolds as he stepped toward Vazques with his fists clenched. Van Horne quickly stepped to the side and pushed Reynolds backward as the Cuban soldiers nervously aimed their automatic weapons at them. "I should tear off your fucking balls and stuff them up your ass," he shouted at Vazques over Van Horne's shoulder.

150   D'ONOFRIO

"Take it easy, Reynolds," warned Van Horne so all the men in the room could hear him. "That asshole is nothing more than an errand boy dressed in a fucking clown's outfit. That's the fucking cockroach you want to kill," he said as he turned and pointed at Trembulak. "He's the one you want to see laying face down in a pool of blood."

Trembulak appeared panicked by the verbal confrontation, and after Van Horne's brutal remarks. He wasn't expecting such an assault and wasn't prepared to deal with it. "This is not how American officials should speak to a superior Russian military man, a Russian general!"

"Maybe you underestimated us, General," Van Horne told Trembulak as he suddenly appeared calm and collected. It was a tactic Spencer had seen Van Horne use before in other fierce confrontations.

"Don't you realize, I can have my men kill right here?" Trembulak screamed at Van Horne. "I… I can have you held on this island as my prisoner if I wish."

"No, I don't think you're going to do that," said Van Horne as he briefly and sarcastically smiled at Trembulak, unnerving the terrorist. "You want the publicity of allowing American officials to tour the island! It won't look good if you hold one of us here and release the rest. You don't want to hold me on this island as your hostage, Peskov. I'd find a way to get free, then I'd cut your fucking throat from ear to ear and watch you drown in your own blood. Then I'd find this fucking asshole and do the same to him," added Van Horne as he looked at Vazques.

"All right, we're leaving," Spencer told the group as he began pushing Van Horne and Reynolds toward the door, hoping to avoid another confrontation.

Van Horne meticulously studied the Russian soldiers standing on either side of the suite's door as Spencer pushed him toward it. "These aren't the elite soldiers I'd want to pull off such a complex attack like this. They look like the dregs of the Russian Army." Van Horne suddenly saw something that startled him. His eyes widened for a second, then he immediately tried to con-

JOURNEY THROUGH A LONG WINTER'S NIGHT   151

ceal his shock after seeing a piece of equipment hanging from a Russian soldier's belt. Vazques watched Van Horne and he immediately panicked when he saw the mistake made by one of his own men.

"What were those questions they were asking, and those threats?" a confused and shaken Trembulak asked Barnes. Barnes stood in the shade on the suite's balcony with Leland and Vechesloff, watching the boat sailing back to the dock in Newport. "You never told me they would question me that way. Who were those men who just threatened us?"

"Shut the fuck up and let me think, Trembulak." Barnes lowered his binoculars and watched the men as crowds of reporters shouted questions to them when they stepped off the boat and onto the dock.

Vazques frantically ran into the suite and began screaming at one of his men, and Barnes and the others immediately looked into the suite when they heard the commotion. "Look at this," Vazques shouted as he frantically pulled a gas mask off a soldier's belt and angrily threw it onto the carpeted floor. "Look at this, you stupid, brainless, fool. You're still wearing one of the special American gas masks from the night of the attack. You're standing in this room dressed as a Russian soldier and you're carrying an American gas mask. Do you know what you've just done?"

"Maybe they didn't see its one of our nerve gas masks," Leland told Barnes as he immediately thought about the implications of the mistake. "Even if they did, they seemed pretty shook up, and maybe they won't put it together."

"I was watching the insolent one who called me an errand boy. He saw it," Vazques shouted at Barnes, "and he knows something is wrong. I saw it in his eyes. That arrogant one must die."

"Vazques is probably right. Contact our men in the city and give them his description," Barnes told Leland as he thought about the gas mask Van Horne saw. "Tell them to get rid of that bastard as soon as they can. I don't want anyone to find his body. This is just a minor

152 D'ONOFRIO

problem we can take care of, nothing more than that."

Spencer and the others stood on the dock and watched the boat slowly return to Goat Island. As it did the Cuban soldiers threw more mines into the deep blue ocean water. Van Horne thought about what he saw on the island, and in the hotel suite, as he shaded his eyes from the bright overhead sun with his hand.

"They're scared, I've seen it before."

"What the hell was that stunt you two pulled in there with Peskov?" Spencer angrily asked Van Horne and Reynolds. "You could have both gotten yourselves killed."

"I'm sorry I got mad, Admiral. I guess I lost it up there," Reynolds apologized to Spencer, fully aware if it wasn't for Van Horne he would be dead. "Thanks for jumping on me, Van Horne."

Van Horne continued watching the island as he replied. "When Peskov was giving his speech he looked like a pompous jerk reading from a script. As soon as we confronted him, and put the pressure on him, he fell apart. He's nervous about something, but I don't know what it is."

"You're right, now that I think about it," agreed Reynolds as he turned and looked at the news camera crews that were already filming them with the boat in the background.

"Come and find me after your meeting," Van Horne told Spencer as he backed toward the military road-block holding back the surging crowd of spectators. He ignored the questions the nearby reporters were already shouting at him. "I've got to talk to you as soon as you're free."

"Why, what's going on? What did you see on that island, Robert?"

"Just find me as soon as you can. I'll talk to you when I see you there," shouted Van Horne as he stepped between the police department's orange barricades. Then he quickly disappeared in the crowd as the reporters and their cameramen chased after him for an interview.

Spencer, Holloway, Governor Winston, and Reynolds were driven to the Newport Naval Base for a debriefing session with the officials in Newport and Washington.

JOURNEY THROUGH A LONG WINTER'S NIGHT   153

The group was questioned about what they saw on the island, and the condition of the President and his family. Holloway reported the bomb appeared to be genuine from what he could see of it.

"Your observations are absolutely correct, Commander," Adams somberly told the group after he read a report placed in front of him by a staff officer. "We have a Nest team in the city and their equipment found stray neutrons in the atmosphere. That confirms the Russians do have a bomb on the island."

"What's a Nest team?" asked one of Benson's aides after she flipped through her booklet of government agencies but was unable to locate the acronym.

"Nest stands for Nuclear Emergency Search Team. Even small nuclear weapons emit a spectrum of telltale radiation, and this agency has the equipment needed to locate it. They've already found minute traces of residual radiation over Newport Harbor. We can consider this a confirmation the Russian bomb on that island is a threat."

After the debriefing concluded, Army officers in Washington and Newport handed each official several maps of Rhode Island, as Jamison of the Central Intelligence Agency stepped to the podium. "We'll use these maps to coordinate the evacuation of the people from around Newport. The shaded area of the maps represents a fifty mile radius around Newport. All the people living in this area must be evacuated and moved to shelters."

"Who's going to coordinate the evacuation of these areas?" asked a concerned Governor Winston. "I want my office to be heavily involved in an evacuation operation of this magnitude."

"You will be, Governor. All direction will be passed through your office for approval. General Murtagh is activating all the Army, National Guard, and Army Reserve units in the New England states, New York, Pennsylvania, and Delaware. They'll evacuate the people and then provide security in the area. Looting and vandalism will not be tolerated in the evacuated area. We're going to use radio messages to warn potential looters

154 D'ONOFRIO

we're going to shoot to kill."

Activating the Army units in the eastern United States was the first part of Murtagh's plan to use military force to help him gain control of the government. Immediately after the bomb exploded on Goat Island, he planned to activate all the Army units across the nation and use them to calm the people. After the Army units were patrolling the city and rural streets across the country to maintain law and order, he planned to declare martial law and immediately assume control of the government. The troops would then be used to eliminate the people who resisted his new government.

At five o'clock the meeting ended, and the officials scheduled another for eleven o'clock that night. Thirty minutes later, an upset Spencer walked into Van Horne's hotel suite. There he saw five shirtless men wearing shorts sitting on the balcony watching Goat Island with binoculars in the blazing afternoon sunlight. "Ok, what did you see on that island?" he impatiently asked Van Horne, who was sitting at a table with Owen.

"When is the last time our military inventoried its supply of Stinger Missiles?" asked Van Horne as he put his pen down and rubbed his fatigued eyes with his hands.

"I can't answer that question, Robert, that's not my area. Why should I even care about that right now?"

"I think the missiles the Russians have on Goat Island are Stingers. I may be wrong, but when we were walking behind the hotel I saw some green metal cases. They look just like the ones we used to ship Stingers to Saudi Arabia."

Spencer suddenly became concerned and he frowned when he thought about Van Horne's statement. "We don't even give those missiles to our allies. How the hell could the Russians have gotten their hands on them?"

"That's a damn good question, Admiral. Where did they get them? I saw something else when we were in that hotel room with Peskov. One of his men had an American made gas mask hanging from his belt."

Van Horne's comment shocked Spencer and he immediately questioned the observation. "Are you sure

JOURNEY THROUGH A LONG WINTER'S NIGHT 155

about that, Robert? Are you sure it just didn't look like a piece of our equipment?"

"I'm sure of what I saw, Admiral. I don't make mistakes like that. It even had a red and green symbol on the carrying case to designate it for use against nerve gas."

"You're saying the Russians have Stinger missiles on that island, and that they're using American made equipment. If another person made those observations I'd be skeptical, but now I'm concerned by what you saw, Robert."

"Did you notice the Russian soldiers never spoke to one another while we were on that island? The only ones who spoke were the ones in that boat, and the colonel and general, and that was in English."

"You're right, I didn't realize that until you mentioned it. No one spoke in a Russian dialect, not even a comment from one soldier to another."

Van Horne stood and opened a can of soda as he watched his men on the balcony. "I don't want you to tell anyone about what I saw on the island, Admiral. Not until we have a better idea of what's going on here."

Van Horne and Spencer drove to Fort Adams thirty minutes later, to check on the progress of his men there. As they walked through the cool and damp interior of the stone fort they found the men monitoring various radio channels for messages transmitted by the Russians. "We still haven't been able to locate the frequency they're using, Major," explained Malin as he moved the black electrical cables snaked across the floor out of the way. "But we're here for the duration and we'll keep listening."

Van Horne and Spencer sat in the conference room where the yellow construction lights were hanging from the ceiling and read several reports written by the men. "Damn it, they all say the same thing. It doesn't look like there's anyway to get onto the island. Come on, I need some air," said Van Horne disappointedly thirty minutes later.

They walked into the fort's massive center courtyard and trampled down the waist high green weeds as

156 D'ONOFRIO

they walked through them. Spencer saw a wide stone staircase that led to the fort's roof and they carefully walked up it. "This is a very pretty area," commented Van Horne as he studied the buildings in the city and the surrounding coastline in the orange glow of the evening sunset. The ocean waves were crashing onto the rocks near the fort and the full moon was already a bright orange sphere low in the eastern sky.

"I always enjoyed staying at these seacoast towns when my wife was alive. She would have enjoyed staying in that hotel on Goat Island. She was kind of a military history buff, and she would have enjoyed seeing the island," replied Spencer, as he stared at the condominium buildings on Goat Island.

"Why that island, Admiral? I thought they built the island so they could put the hotel on it."

"No, no, Goat Island is a natural formation. It was the site of the Navy's first torpedo manufacturing plant. I read about it in a report my staff prepared for me yesterday afternoon. They couldn't find any information about the island in our computers, so they searched through the National Archives and found something for me."

"There was a manufacturing plant on that small island? I guess I'm not getting a good perspective of how large that island really is from here."

"The Navy manufactured torpedoes on that island until they shut down the plant and gave the island to the city. They built the hotel and the condominiums in the years after."

"What are the chances of your staff finding the officer who was in charge of that manufacturing plant?"

"My people might be able to find a name in the old Navy records. Why do you want that?"

"You never know what he might be able to tell us about the island."

The two men walked into the fort and Spencer drove to the Naval base and relayed Van Horne's request to his staff. Spencer walked outside the office complex alone and watched the island as he lit a cigar. "I didn't use my organization or people well enough to prevent the Russians from capturing the President and the other peo-

JOURNEY THROUGH A LONG WINTER'S NIGHT 157

ple on that island, My people are responsible for gathering intelligence information about other nations while they maintain the security of this nation. If the Russians planned the attack and were able to get into the United States without them knowing about it, then my organization isn't functioning properly. Or, someone in my organization is a traitor."

Chapter Eight

At seven o'clock Tuesday morning, the officials at the Newport Naval Base, and those in Washington, began another arduous meeting. Vice-President Benson paced nervously around the Pentagon's strategy room and was the first to speak at the podium. "After meeting with Kennith Dunnells and his staff, I've decided to postpone assuming the Presidency until tomorrow morning at the earliest. I need more time to decide what's best for the nation during this time of unprecedented crisis."

"Why are you waiting so long to assume control of our government, Mister Vice-President?" asked a shocked Wilcox, as he removed his reading glasses. "The people of our nation are becoming more concerned and alarmed as they watch the situation developing in Rhode Island, and realize we're not taking firm action to end it. The people need to see you're stepping in to lead the government through the difficult decisions that must be made during this time of turmoil. I personally feel it would be beneficial if you take control of the nation today, and then relinquish the office after the Russians release the President."

"Your personal feelings have no bearing on this situation or its resolution, Curtis Don't you see what's really going on here? In my opinion, the Russian soldiers on that island are there only to prove a point, and will withdraw by the end of the week. They only want to show us how vulnerable we are to attack if we don't help them in the future. I'm sure they're hoping this exhibition of force and the fear associated with it will coerce us into helping them feed and care for their people."

"I still think it would send a positive message to the people."

"I don't agree. Why should I create more public fear and anxiety by assuming the President's office? It will appear we know the President is either dead, or he's going to die on the island. What kind of message will that send to the people?"

None of the men looked at Benson after he abruptly

JOURNEY THROUGH A LONG WINTER'S NIGHT 159

sat and glanced at his staff with a nod. The military and government leaders appeared outwardly disgusted with Benson's decision. Everyone realized it was based on his personal fears and inability to lead the nation while dealing with the rapidly escalating crisis.

Admiral Adams slowly stood in the strategy room and opened a thick folder. "My various offensive weapons planning staff have put together the rough draft of a plan I'd like to discuss with all of you. They've developed a plan to destroy the Russian plutonium bomb on Goat Island using one of our conventional nuclear devices dropped from a Stealth bomber." The announcement shocked the seventy people seated in the room and many of them began whispering to one another.

"I hope we can find a more suitable way of ending this situation, Admiral," the horrified Vice-President told Adams, as he nervously fumbled with a pencil. "What you're proposing should be our final option, after we've exhausted all of our other options. We should be discussing raising the ransom money, not ways of destroying our nation."

"I don't understand what we'll gain by destroying the island with a conventional nuclear bomb," said Holloway while he watched a monitor displaying the Pentagon's strategy room. "Besides the island, you'll incinerate everything else within a thirty to fifty mile radius. The electromagnetic pulse that'll accompany the detonation of our bomb will destroy every computer microchip from here to Baltimore, in everything from personal computers to microwave ovens and irons. Then we're going to have the problem of dealing with the area contaminated by the radiate fallout."

Adams became angry and defensive after others in the group immediately challenged the viability of his plan. "Didn't the Russians tell you they have sensors attached to the garage floor to detect explosions on the island, Commander?" he angrily asked Holloway as he pointed at the television camera. "Even if we use the force of one thousand pound bombs to destroy that hotel garage, those sensors might still detect the explosions and detonate that plutonium bomb before it can

160 D'ONOFRIO

be destroyed. Am I right, Commander?"

"Your plan to use one nuclear explosion to neutralize another nuclear warhead is an unproved theory, Admiral. That's a purely hypothetical concept developed forty years ago. It's never been tested or proved."

"Answer my question before you dispute the ideas of the experts, Commander. Am I right about those sensors detecting the vibrations of a conventional bomb's explosion in the garage floor?"

"You're right, Admiral. There's always the possibility those sensors may detonate the bomb."

"Now, do you have any better ideas or recommendations for destroying a Russian bomb encased in a cement garage built under a hotel? If you do, I'd like you to share them with the group right now, Commander!" Adams shouted as he held up the black folder which contained the specifics of his staff's attack plan. "If you don't have a better idea, then this is the only plan we have to work with right now. So instead of criticizing it, I think you should look at the idea and think about making it work."

"I don't have anything ready to present yet, Admiral."

"All right then, hear me out. Assuming the plutonium bomb can be destroyed in the heat and concussion of a conventional thermonuclear explosion, my experts believe the land areas contaminated by radiation might be safe for resettlement in ten to twelve thousand years. This is far less than the twenty five thousand years the area may be unhabitable after if its contaminated with plutonium radiation. We'll have to build a thick concrete wall twenty feet high topped with barbed wire around the contaminated land area to prevent people and animals from wandering into it. Then we'll have to restrict people from living within fifty miles of that wall."

"I don't know if I can approve that plan, Admiral," confessed Benson as he tightened his grip on his pencil nervously. "How will we ever compensate the people when we destroy their life's work, their homes and businesses? I would hope we can find a better solu-

JOURNEY THROUGH A LONG WINTER'S NIGHT   161

tion to this problem than approving the use of nuclear weapons."

At the same time that meeting was taking place, Leland and Vechesloff walked into an elegant lounge in the hotel on Goat Island. They saw Vazques' men had destroyed the interior of the lounge during a party the previous night. The Cubans smashed all of the wooden tables and chairs, and threw the pieces through the lounge's ornate windows. Using the table legs they shattered the decorative mirrors behind the long liquor bar. The wall's white textured wallpaper was stained where the Cubans smashed their empty liquor bottles against it. In some areas long red streaks of dried blood covered the walls. The smell of liquor and urine were almost overpowering, and both men shook their heads disgustedly when they found the naked bodies of six women the Cubans repeatedly raped and then murdered.

Leland tapped Vechesloff on the shoulder when he saw Barnes reading beside a window the Cubans smashed. An empty scotch bottle lay beside Barnes on a wooden window seat as he stood in the bright sunlight streaming through the window.

"Isn't it a little early to be drinking, Barnes?" Leland laughed as he looked around at the empty bottles laying on the wooden dance floor.

"Vazques' men drank this place dry last night. I came in here because I wanted a quiet place to read this morning's status report from Washington. In a few days, this country and mother Russia will be part of the new world order."

"Good, good," replied an elated Vechesloff as he violently kicked a broken table leg that landed on a naked woman's lifeless body. "My government will soon be under military rule and we will move back to communism and rebuild the nation. I hope my family will have enough food to survive until the military forms a new government to help them."

The three men suddenly looked at one another, and then crowded beside the window, after they heard a low flying helicopter pass over the island. They frantically ran out of the lounge when they believed the hotel was

162   D'ONOFRIO

under attack. They ran through the lobby's front glass doors and into the bright sun shining on the hotel driveway. Barnes ran to a large decorative concrete planter built in the driveway to control the flow of traffic, and he jumped onto its four foot high wall. From there he could see a news helicopter hovering over the western end of the island. A cameraman aboard the helicopter videotaped the hotel complex and the soldiers standing near the dead bodies scattered across the rocks.

"Shoot that fucking thing down," Barnes screamed after he jumped off the planter and ran toward a group of Cuban soldiers pointing at the helicopter. For a brief moment his anger made him forget the black hood he and Leland both carried in their pockets to conceal their identify from the news camera crews. Barnes quickly pulled the black cloth sack over his head as he ran toward the Cubans.

The helicopter suddenly turned and flew toward the city after the pilot saw the soldiers running toward the equipment. Moments later, a Stinger missile struck the helicopter and it exploded in a huge ball of flames near the tall steeple of Saint John's Church. Thousands of spectators on the city streets below ran in terror, but the twisted wreckage covered with flames fell onto a large crowd. Seventy five people died in the inferno as thousands of other spectators watched in horror.

Spencer was discouraged by the lack of progress made during the meeting just adjourned as he walked from the communications building on the Naval base. Instead of riding in his limousine he walked across several roads and grassy fields on the way to his temporary office on the base. "Why would the Russians risk global nuclear war with a stupid stunt like this? They knew our response to this situation would be a nuclear showdown. Or, did they know that we're not strong enough to use our nuclear arsenal?"

Spencer walked into a building where almost three hundred members of his organization were working. He locked his private office door and removed several thick folders from his briefcase. The folders contained the military backgrounds of the men Van Horne asked to

JOURNEY THROUGH A LONG WINTER'S NIGHT   163

Newport. Then he sat on a red leather couch and read a short history of each man:

Howard Nielson, two tours of Vietnam with the Airborne Rangers. Thirty-seven years old, and the father of two. Now working as a plumber in Seattle.

Angel Nieves, seventeen month tour of Vietnam. Forty years old, single. Working as a teacher's aide in Florida.

Robert Willey, two tours of Vietnam with the Green Berets. Forty-six years old, married with no children. Working as a bartender in Missouri.

Harvey Taylor, two tours of Vietnam with the Rangers. Thirty-nine years old and divorced. Working as mason in Florida.

Charles Gatting, three tours of Vietnam as a Green Beret. Forty-one years old, working as a policeman in Texas.

Douglas Guay, two tours of Vietnam as an Airborne Ranger. Forty-three years old, divorced. Now working as a car mechanic in California.

John Grogan, Airborne Ranger. Thirty-one years old, married and the father of four. Working as a security guard in South Carolina.

John Walsh, Green Beret. Twenty-nine years old, married with one child. Working on college degree in New Hampshire.

David White, two tours of Vietnam as a Green Beret. Forty-five years old, now working as a welder.

Scott Willet, Airborne Ranger. Thirty-one years old, single. Working as an electrician in Connecticut.

Gene DePietro, two tours of Vietnam with the Green Berets. Forty-three years old, widowed. Works as a policeman in Phoenix.

Michael Kearns, three tours of Vietnam as a Green Beret. Married with three children, now works as a newscaster in Austin, Texas.

Stephen Shepard, Airborne Ranger. Thirty-eight years old, engaged with three children from previous marriage. Works as an air conditioning service man.

Donald Shaw, three tours of Vietnam as a Green Beret. Forty-six years old, divorced. Now working as an

164 D'ONOFRIO

air traffic controller.

Gerald Sharpe, Airborne Ranger. Personal history incomplete. Graduated from law school and is now a practicing attorney.

John Foran, two tours of Vietnam as a Green Beret. Forty-three years old, married with family of three. Now operates his own house remodeling company.

Paul Fuller, Green Beret. Thirty-four years old, married with two daughters. Started a company to manufacture wooden pallets and skids in Minneapolis.

Edward Gallo, two tours of Vietnam as an Airborne Ranger. Forty-three years old, works a physician's assistant in New Jersey.

James Howard, a Green Beret. Thirty-two years old. Works for a tree service in South Dakota. Married and divorced, supports two children.

Bruce James, two tours of Vietnam as an Airborne Ranger. Forty years old, working as a programmer in Massachusetts.

Bob Jarvis, four tours of Vietnam as a Green Beret. Forty-five years old, widowed, with three daughters and four grandchildren. Vice-President of corporate planning for one of the largest insurance companies in the nation.

Raymond Lee, a Green Beret. Thirty-four years old. Works as a furniture salesman in New Jersey.

Edward Long, two tours of Vietnam as an Airborne Ranger. Forty years old. Married with one son. Works as a private detective in Chicago. Recalled to active duty by the Army during Operation Desert Storm.

Robert Mahoney, a Ranger. Thirty-two years old, works as a bank teller in Dallas. Recalled to active duty by the Army during Operation Desert Storm.

George Malin, two tours of Vietnam as an Airborne Ranger. Forty-one years old, owns a sandwich shop in Pittsburgh.

Joseph Manley, Airborne Ranger. Thirty-two years old, contractor in Sarasota, Florida.

James Neville, two tours of Vietnam as an Airborne Ranger. Forty-three years old, and recently divorced. Works as an electrical contractor in Memphis. Recalled

JOURNEY THROUGH A LONG WINTER'S NIGHT 165

to active duty during Operation Desert Storm.

Martin Hourigan, Airborne Ranger. Took part in Desert Storm ground offensive. Working as a baker in Seattle Washington.

James Owen, two tours of Vietnam as a Green Beret. No personal history available. Employment history not available.

Kevin Ryan, two tours of Vietnam as an Airborne Ranger. No personal history available. Working as mortgage consultant with a bank in Fresno, California.

Frank Morrisroe, one tour of Vietnam with Green Berets. Retired after being shot several times. Working as a professor at Notre Dame University.

Robert Preston, Green Beret. Thirty-two years old, working in a public relations firm in North Dakota.

Spencer closed the folder and opened the door when he heard Mahoney calling to him from the outer office. "I'm sorry to disturb you, Admiral. We just found the names of the two men in charge of the Navy facility on Goat Island," she explained as she handed him a folder with a triumphant smile on her face. "You're not going to like part of it."

Fifteen minutes later, Spencer walked into Fort Adams and found Van Horne sitting in the conference room. "How's everything going, Robert?" Spencer asked as he watched a few men working around a large map of Rhode Island.

"It's a slow process getting everything organized and everyone working together, Admiral. Our teams watching the island and have already provided us with some good information. What are you doing here so early? It's a beautiful morning and I thought you'd still be asleep."

"We had a meeting at the base earlier this morning, but we didn't get anything accomplished. My staff did locate the men who commanded the Goat Island Torpedo Station for you. Commander Keith Robinson was in charge of the manufacturing equipment and building maintenance. He died six months ago of lung cancer."

"That's too bad. How about the other one?"

"Admiral William Sullivan was in charge of the torpedo manufacturing personnel and testing. The last

166 D'ONOFRIO

known address we have for him is his daughter's house in Connecticut. He's ninety-three years old if my math is right here."

Van Horne stopped writing on his pad and took the report from Spence's hand. "He's still alive?"

"I don't know what shape he's in today, but this report says he's still alive."

"There's nothing much going on here, Admiral. Want to take a ride this morning and see if we can find him? Maybe he can tell us something about that island."

"I'll have a helicopter ready at the base in an hour, Robert. I'll tell Mahoney to call Sullivan's family and ask if we can meet with him. Who knows, he may have had a stroke and can't talk to us."

At nine o'clock, a helicopter flew from the Newport Naval Base with Van Horne and Spencer aboard it. Fifty minutes later it landed in a large field at the Groton Submarine Base in Connecticut. The two men climbed in a waiting car and Van Horne drove as Spencer studied a map. When they reached the center of Groton, Van Horne turned onto a winding road, and several minutes later they parked in front of a house in a residential section of the city.

Spencer and Van Horne carefully stepped around a child's red tricycle and other toys scattered across the lawn as they walked to the front door and rang the doorbell. "Can I help you?" asked a woman who appeared to be about thirty years old.

Spencer raised his identification card and held it so the woman could read it. "I'm Admiral Herbert Spencer, of the National Security Agency. This is Major Robert Van Horne. We're here to see Admiral Sullivan."

"Please come in," said the woman as she lifted a young child with bright blonde hair dressed in blue jean overalls. "A woman from your agency called earlier this morning and said you were coming. I'm Janet Gionfrido," she laughed as she juggled her son in her arms and raised her hand to the two men. "This bundle of energy is my son Jonathan. My grandfather is William Sullivan. He really got excited when I told him a government agent asked to speak with him."

JOURNEY THROUGH A LONG WINTER'S NIGHT   167

The woman led Spencer and Van Horne through the house and into a library in a small spare bedroom. The gray haired and fragile looking Admiral Sullivan sat behind a wooden desk as he read from an old book. Arthritis and age had weakened his body, but he slowly stood and walked across the room to greet Van Horne and Spencer as he steadied himself with a cane.

"It's a pleasure to meet you, Admiral Sullivan," said Spencer as he carefully shook hands with the frail man. Spencer knew he was going to like the old man even before he spoke a single word. "I'm Admiral Herbert Spencer, Director of the National Security Agency. This is Major Robert Van Horne. Thank you for taking the time to talk to us this morning."

"It's my pleasure. Please, make yourself comfortable," said Sullivan in a low voice as he pointed at several chairs while steadying himself with the cane. "I was surprised when my granddaughter said you were coming to see me. What can an old Navy man like myself possibly do for two young men from the government?" he added as he eyes appeared to be filled with vitality after he sat beside them.

Spencer slowly and thoroughly described the details of the situation in Newport to Sullivan, intentionally disclosing information the government considered classified. He carefully described every aspect of the hostage crisis in great detail so Sullivan would fully understand what was happening on the island. Sullivan frowned after he learned the Russians were killing people on the island and frowned again after Spencer told him about the Russian's ransom demands.

"The Navy records show you were one of two men who supervised the production of torpedoes in the manufacturing plant located on Goat Island," said Spencer after he pulled a small notebook from his jacket pocket. "We need to know everything you can remember about that plant. Where the buildings were located, how the plant was run, and how many people worked there. We need to know anything you can remember about that facility and the island."

Sullivan stood and slowly walked to a large wooden

168 D'ONOFRIO

bookcase where he studied several tattered volumes as Van Horne asked, "How long were you stationed on Goat Island, Admiral?"

Sullivan meticulously selected several old books and carefully placed them on a wooden coffee table in front of Spencer and Van Horne. "I was on the island for twelve years my boy. I really wanted to be doing my part on a fighting ship in the Atlantic or Pacific during the war, but the Navy told me my skills were needed at the plant. I can use these books to give you some background about the island," he said slowly as he sat and read from a reference book. "The Navy began using Goat Island in 1870, right after the end of the American Revolution. They used the island for experimenting with explosives and torpedoes. The first buildings were put up on the island sometime in the early nineteen hundreds."

Sullivan slowly browsed through the book's yellow pages and turned it toward the two men after he found an old picture of Goat Island. "This is what the island looked like during the Second World War. More than thirteen thousand people worked in a hundred buildings crowded onto the island. My wife and I, and a few other Navy officers, lived in cottages at the western end of the island. We lived there so we'd be close to the plant if there was a problem."

"When was the plant closed down, Admiral?" asked Spencer as he leaned forward and studied the photograph. "Why did the Navy shut it down?"

"The government built a new manufacturing plant on the Newport Naval Base sometime during the early fifties. We moved all the people working on the island to the new plant because our manufacturing equipment was obsolete. We couldn't use it to build the more sophisticated torpedoes the modern Navy ships needed. Instead of retooling our plant, the Navy went ahead and built a new one."

There was a knock on the library door, and Sullivan's granddaughter walked into the room with a tray of coffee and cups. Her young son followed behind her. As she poured coffee for the three men and handed each of them a cup, the young boy walked to Van Horne and smiled at him. The child steadied himself as he held

JOURNEY THROUGH A LONG WINTER'S NIGHT 169

onto Van Horne's leg, an action that immediately brought a smile to Van Horne's face.

"I don't understand how my grandfather can help you after all the years he's been retired."

"Your grandfather might remember some information that's no longer in the Navy records," explained Spencer as he took a cup from the woman's hands. "Even the smallest detail he can tell us may be useful."

"We're looking for any information we can use to free the hostages on the island," explained Van Horne as he lifted the boy and sat him on his leg. "The Russians have the island isolated and so well defended we can't find a way to get onto it." Van Horne studied the picture in Sullivan's book as the child playfully wrapped his arms around his neck. "I can see railroad tracks in this war time picture of the island, Admiral. Did you use a train to take the torpedoes off the island?"

"We had to build a trestle that stretched from the city to the island for that train. Supplies came in to us on the train almost every day, and we shipped torpedoes off the island once a week."

"Were all the materials you needed to manufacture the torpedoes stored on the island?" asked Spencer as he studied the photograph.

"We stored all of our supplies and raw materials in these large warehouses at the far end of the island. We needed the materials on the island because we were manufacturing around the clock. Everyone worked for the war effort, and no one complained about the hours or the hard work like they do today."

"Where did you store the torpedoes you assembled while you were waiting for the train to take them off the island, Admiral? In these buildings that look like large warehouses?" asked Van Horne as he pointed at a picture and the child reached for his hand playfully before his mother carried him out of the room.

Sullivan chuckled at Van Horne's question as he sipped his coffee. "No, we assembled our torpedoes in those large buildings. We never stored the torpedoes on Goat Island."

Van Horne was confused by Sullivan's statement

170 D'ONOFRIO

and he looked down at the photograph again. "I thought you said you moved the torpedoes off the island on a train once a week. What did you do with them until the train got there? Did you keep them in warehouses in the city?"

"No, security would have been a problem if we stored the torpedoes in the city, or even on the Naval Base my boy. The Navy and our coastal watchers spotted enemy submarines off New England. It would have been too easy for saboteurs to destroy the warehouses with explosives."

Spencer was puzzled by the old man's evasiveness. "Then where did you store the torpedoes, Admiral?"

Sullivan laughed when he saw the frustration on Spencer's face, and he slowly leaned back in the brown upholstered chair. "The Navy must have destroyed the plant's blueprints after they gave the island to the city, or you wouldn't be asking these questions. You've both got to think like you are in the middle of a World War, and remember our concerns at that time. We were afraid someone would destroy the torpedoes if we stored them on the mainland, or at the plant, so we did the only thing we could with them. We buried them under Goat Island."

Van Horne and Spencer immediately looked at one another with disbelieving and troubled looks on their faces. Sullivan picked up his coffee cup and smiled at the two men with a devilish grin that reminded them of a young child with a secret.

"What do you mean you buried them under Goat Island?" asked Spencer who was becoming upset with Sullivan. "You're telling us you dug holes and buried those torpedoes in the dirt?"

Sullivan appeared pleased he remembered information his country lost in its sophisticated computer systems and extensive microfilm libraries. "Let me explain what we did to safeguard our torpedoes. Robinson knew a Japanese or German airplane could destroy the entire island if it dropped even a single bomb onto a warehouse. One explosion might have triggered a series of explosions that could have leveled all the buildings on

JOURNEY THROUGH A LONG WINTER'S NIGHT 171

the island, and killed everyone in them. That would have left our carrier based attack planes, submarines, and PT boats without torpedoes, and we would never have won the war."

"How did you work around that problem?" asked Spencer as he placed his cup on the wooden table and sat back in his chair. "Tell us how you stored the torpedoes so they would be safe."

"After taking some core samples on the island, Robinson came up with an idea to cut tunnels into the bedrock under Goat Island and Newport Harbor. It was a plan he called Project Blindsight. He knew the ocean water would dissipate the explosions of falling bombs or naval artillery shells, and the torpedoes stored in the tunnels below would be safe. Even if an explosion destroyed the entire island the worst that might happen is the tunnels would flood with ocean water. If that happened divers could always remove the torpedoes from the water and they could still be used."

"You cut tunnels into the rock under Goat Island?" asked a skeptical Van Horne as he looked at Sullivan. "That sounds like it would be a major undertaking."

"I know everything I've said must sound like the ramblings of a senile old man, but those tunnels did exist, my boy. The Navy approved Robinson's plan after a defense contractor proved the tunnel walls could be waterproofed. Robinson knew salt water leaking into the tunnels might rust the torpedoes and make them unreliable when they were fired. He insisted the tunnel walls had to be waterproofed before the torpedoes were stored under the island."

"Were the tunnels cut into the rock by hand, Admiral?" asked Van Horne as he tried to determine whether the tunnels Sullivan was describing existed, or were something the old man envisioned in the years after he retired.

"No, that was too big a job to be done by hand, my boy. We cut the rock away with specially designed mining machines. We moved the crushed rock and other debris to the surface in carts pulled by a small steam engine on rails, like the ones they used in the Virginia

172 D'ONOFRIO

coal mines. Then we loaded the rock onto barges and dumped into the ocean at night so there'd be no large piles around to make anyone suspicious. We knew there were enemy intelligence agents in the city even before the war, and we had to be very careful."

"The tunnels never collapsed under the weight of the water above them?" Spencer asked as he pictured a four foot high, two foot wide, poorly lit tunnel in his mind. "There must have been tons of rock and water on top of them."

"After we cut a section of the tunnel into the rock, our construction crews braced up the ceilings and walls with metal beams and welded supports. Then we waterproofed the walls, floors, and ceilings."

"How long did it take to cut all the tunnels into the rock?" asked Van Horne, knowing the answer to his question would give him some indication if the tunnels really existed. If Sullivan said it took only days to cut the tunnels he could be sure they didn't exist. Sullivan's answer seemed to trouble Van Horne even more.

"I seem to remember it took us eight or nine months to finish the tunnels. Then Robinson needed another month to select the sixty sailors he stationed in the underwater complex as caretakers. He even tunneled out an area in the center of the complex and built them a barracks with bedrooms, a kitchen, and a dinning room. Robinson was a dreamer, too far ahead of the rest of us for his time."

Sullivan placed a sheet of white paper on the wooden coffee table in front of him and slowly began drawing on it with a pencil. "We built the complex with the main storage tunnel under the island, and five separate tunnels that projected out under the harbor from it."

Van Horne pictured the early morning sunlight shining onto the buildings on Goat Island, while staring at Sullivan's drawing. "How did you get the torpedoes into the tunnels from the plant?"

"We cut a narrow opening into the tunnel ceiling in our main assembly building. It was just wide enough for a conveyor belt to pass through it. We put the assembled torpedoes on the conveyor belt and it carried them down

JOURNEY THROUGH A LONG WINTER'S NIGHT 173

into the storage area. We reversed the process when the train arrived for the torpedoes. We used the conveyor belt to get the torpedoes out of the tunnels."

"How big were the tunnels?" asked Spencer as he pictured the narrow dark tunnels dug by the Vietcong for their command centers and storage areas. "Can you remember how wide and how high were they?"

"I seem to remember they were about twelve feet high. Maybe twenty feet wide. In some places they may have been fifty feet wide. I can't really remember, I'm sorry."

"Don't apologize, Admiral," Van Horne immediately told Sullivan as he smiled at him. "You've already given us an enormous amount of information. Did you spend a lot of time in the tunnels?"

"No, I always thought they were like a lit crypt and they gave me the willies. I didn't enjoy being down there like Robinson did." The reply made both Spencer and Van Horne laugh.

Sullivan looked very tired and Van Horne was hesitant about asking any other questions, but he needed more information. "Were there ever any accidents in the tunnels? Any explosions, or large water leaks in the walls or ceiling?"

"I guess we were very lucky. We never had any problem, thanks to Robinson's planning. He was always worried something like that might happen down there, so he gave his boys a way to get out just in case it did. He really took care of those boys, buying them food, magazines, candy, anything to make them feel like they were living in a house."

"Wait a minute. Wait a minute. What did you just say Admiral? He gave them a way out?" asked Van Horne who frowned as he impatiently sat forward on his chair. "How could those men get out of the tunnels?"

"Robinson changed his original tunnel plans as we were finishing the project. He cut a couple of escape tunnels into the rock for his men. He didn't tell the Navy about them until after they were done. He felt obligated to give his men a way out of the tunnels if they collapsed, or filled with water."

"Where did Robinson cut those escape tunnels?"

174   D'ONOFRIO

asked Van Horne, who was now getting excited. "Did they open onto Goat Island?" His sudden sense of urgency seemed to intimidate Sullivan. Spencer placed his hand onto Van Horne's arm and motioned him back in his chair with a subtle movement of his head.

"I remember we cut one tunnel into the foundation of a War College building," said Sullivan as he opened a book and slowly flipped through the brittle yellow pages. Then he suddenly smiled and pointed at a building in a picture. "Now I remember. We cut an escape tunnel in the basement of this building."

Spencer leaned forward and read the caption under the picture in the book. "Luce Hall. That building is still standing on the base today. I drove by it this morning."

"Do those tunnels still exist, or did you collapse them when the plant was deactivated?" asked Van Horne who suddenly became agitated and rubbed his leg nervously.

"The tunnels weren't destroyed when we closed the plant. I seem to remember we covered all the openings with thick steel plates and sealed them with an air tight compound. I think we built a cement wall over the tunnel in the basement of the War College building. I remember we attached vacuum pumps to fittings in the steel plates and removed all the air from the tunnels."

Van Horne looked through several old photographs of Goat Island that Sullivan slowly pulled from between another book's pages. "If it's all right with you, Admiral, I'd like to take some of these pictures with me. I'll return them to you as soon as we're done with them."

Sullivan smiled and nodded at Van Horne, then motioned toward his bookcase as though he was the man's grandfather. "You may take anything you wish from my library, my boy. Please, look through my other books and reference materials and take anything you feel might be helpful." Sullivan was ecstatic he could still help the government with its problems.

Thirty minutes later, Spencer and Van Horne thanked Sullivan and his granddaughter and walked to their car. "I think we should get some military police units to guard this house until the Russians are out of

JOURNEY THROUGH A LONG WINTER'S NIGHT 175

Newport." Van Horne told Spencer as he pulled his holster and handgun from under his shirt and placed it on the automobile seat before he climbed in.

"Why? Who would want to hurt these people? Sullivan isn't a threat to anyone."

"What do you think will happen if the Russians followed us here? They'd probably torture Sullivan's family to make the old man talk, and even then I don't know if he would tell them everything he just told us."

"You're right, Robert. I'll get someone over here to watch the house." Fifteen minutes later, three military police cars and two local police cars parked in front of Sullivan's house.

Spencer called his office at the Newport Naval Base from the car and wrote notes as he spoke to Mahoney. Then he told Van Horne what he learned. "My people reported the Russians executed twenty more hostages this morning. Adams is planning to send his robot submarine into the harbor tonight to get some pictures of the underwater mines."

"I don't know who the real enemy is anymore, the Russians or that nit wit, Adams," replied Van Horne sarcastically as he interrupted Spencer, then both men began laughing.

"Peskov transmitted another radio message from Goat Island a few hours ago. He said he wants the ransom money delivered to some obscure airstrip outside Moscow. Then the Russian government warned Curtis Wilcox we'd be violating their air space if we try to land an aircraft at that airstrip. Mahoney told me a god damn television network wants to do a live interview with Peskov on Goat Island to get his side of the story. Now they want to make the murdering bastard a hero."

Van Horne was already thinking about the tunnels Sullivan described to him as he stared at the buildings ahead in Groton, and wasn't really listening to Spencer's comments. "We've got to find the escape tunnel in the War College building that Sullivan told us about. If we can find it, and the tunnels can still be used, then maybe we can do something with them."

The two men boarded the helicopter at the Groton

176 D'ONOFRIO

Submarine Base and flew back to Newport. Van Horne's men gathered around them when they arrived at Fort Adams. There they explained what Sullivan told them about the island, and the tunnels. "These pictures are fifty years old and show the manufacturing plant that was on Goat Island during World War Two. I want you to compare them to the pictures we've already taken and see if you can find anything we can use."

A telephone in the conference room began ringing, and several seconds later David White answered it. "Major!" He excitedly shouted to Van Horne. "The spotters on the roof see three men walking toward the fort. They're in the restricted grassy area near the Navy housing behind us!"

Van Horne quickly looked around the room and found three men who functioned as snipers during the Iraqi ground offensive. "Long, Manley, and Neville, get your rifles and get up on the roof. Don't do anything unless I raise my hands over my head. The rest of you watch the other entrances. Jim and I are going to drive behind the fort in the Jeep."

"Got ya'h covered, Major," shouted Long, as he opened a golf bag and pulled out a rifle.

As they ran from the fort, Van Horne checked his handgun and pushed it back into the holster, then he and Owen climbed into the Jeep. Several minutes later, they drove onto a large field covered with tall weeds and pink wild flowers behind the fort. Then they slowly drove toward the three men dressed in jeans and light shirts, all of whom were wearing backpacks. "Lets watch our step out here, Jim. We'll show these three guys the way out if they're lost. If they're not, then we may have a big problem on our hands."

Owen drove across the bumpy ground, pushing down the tall green weeds and grass. He stopped the Jeep beside the three men in the sweltering sunlight and humidity. "Are you guys lost out here?" he asked as if he was joking with them. "This is Navy property and it's off limits to civilians."

"We didn't know that," replied one of the men cynically as he quickly looked around the area. "We're just

JOURNEY THROUGH A LONG WINTER'S NIGHT   177

looking for a place to do some surf casting." Van Horne saw the men's large backpacks were filled with supplies. One of them had pieces of pipe in his backpack and Van Horne saw none of them were carrying fishing poles, or bait buckets.

"The beach is back that way," said Owen as he pointed behind the three men. They looked behind them and when they turned back to Owen and Van Horne, each of them was holding a handgun equipped with a silencer.

"Get out of the Jeep, nice and slow," said one of the men as he pointed his handgun at Owen's chest. "You're gonna take a walk to that beach with us. It'll be your last walk. Now raise your fucking hands."

"Is this the right one?" one of the men asked the others as he pointed his handgun at Van Horne's head. "Is he the one we're looking for?"

"He's the one. Now let's get out of here before anyone sees us standing here jerking off. We'll use the boat and dump their bodies a few miles out at sea. We'll be out of here before anyone finds what's left of them."

"Who the hell are you?" asked a shocked Van Horne when he realized their mission was to kill him. "Who sent you here after me?"

"That's no concern of yours," laughed one of the men. "You're both going to be fish food in a couple of minutes."

Van Horne knew he wouldn't get any answers from the men and he slowly raised his hands above his head. When he and Owen heard the first rifle shot echo across the field behind them, they immediately fell onto the ground. One of the men was violently knocked to the ground when a single bullet stuck his chest and ripped through his body. The other confused men raised their handguns as they frantically looked around for the sniper. Moments later, bullets violently knocked them to the ground.

Van Horne and Owen clawed through the tall weeds to the three wounded men and discovered two were already dead. The third died as Van Horne attempted to stop the blood pouring from his chest. "We're not going

178   D'ONOFRIO

to get any answers from these three." Van Horne told Owen as he stood and wiped the warm red blood off his hands with a rag he took from the Jeep.

Several minutes later, twenty men stood around the bodies. "Nice shooting, you three just saved our lives," Van Horne told the snipers. "Lets move these bodies into the fort before anyone sees them."

"I don't understand what's going on, Robert," said a visibly shaken Spencer as he stared at the bodies.

"I don't know either, Admiral."

Spencer suddenly seemed to realize how vulnerable Van Horne and his men were as they walked back to the fort. "They've compromised your security here, Robert, they know where you are. Why don't we move your command center out of the fort and into a hotel? When these three don't return to where ever they came from, they may send others after you."

"We're not going anywhere damn it," replied Van Horne angrily, as they walked around the fort and saw the crowds of spectators watching the island from the fort's parking lot. "We're damn lucky none of those people heard the gunshots."

"I still think you should move your men out of here."

"We're staying right here where we can see who's coming after us. I won't make it easy for them to kill us by moving into a hotel."

"Do you have any idea why they would want to kill you and Owen?" Spencer asked Van Horne, as they watched his men open the three backpacks in the fort's center courtyard.

"They didn't want to kill us, Admiral," said Owen nervously, as he accented the word, us. "They were here to get the Major. I was just unlucky enough to be with him."

"Why would they single you out from the rest of us who went to that island, Robert? Why should they want you dead and not the rest of us?"

"They must think I saw something I shouldn't have on that island. Something I haven't told anybody about yet. Well, now we know they have more men in Newport, and that's something we didn't count on."

JOURNEY THROUGH A LONG WINTER'S NIGHT   179

Spencer was shocked when he saw the men pull three long mortar shells from a backpack. "These are Russian made ninety one millimeter mortar rounds," Michael Kearns told the others, as they stood around him. "This is Russian lettering on these shells. They're probably filled with nerve gas."

Owen lifted one of the dead men's handguns and studied it. "These are Russian made handguns, Major. These guys are straight from the Kremlin."

"Have we misread the situation on that island, Robert?" asked Spencer, as he thought about the military equipment. "Maybe we're really up against the Russian military, but just don't realize it."

"I don't have any idea what's going on right now, Admiral, I thought I had this entire situation worked out in my mind, but right now I'm not sure what the hell is happening."

While Van Horne gathered his men together in the fort's conference room, Spencer met with Mahoney and asked her to locate information about Project Blindsight. Then he told her he wanted the three bodies flown to Washington and put into deep freeze.

At nine o'clock that evening, Marine General Hutchinson stepped beside the podium in the Pentagon's strategy room. Then he began another simultaneous meeting between the Pentagon and the Newport Naval Base. "My tactical operations staff is currently putting together the details for an airborne assault of Goat Island. They're planning to use a team of specially trained Marines who will parachute from a transport plane eight miles from Goat Island after dark. They'll be using a new type of wing parachute that will allow them to fly to the island and land in the building's shadows. After the team is on the island they'll move into the hotel where they'll neutralize the Russian soldiers they find as they attempt to rescue the President."

"I'm sorry, General, but I don't agree with using your men to attack the island," Reynolds told Hutchinson after his hearing more details of the plan. "What'll happen if the Russians fire their missiles and machine guns at those men as they hang from their

180   D'ONOFRIO

parachutes? We won't be able to help them while they're being slaughtered."

"My tactical staff has already considered that possibility, and that's a risk we've got to assume, Reynolds. We can't allow the Russians to hold the President without attempting some type of military rescue operation. This airborne attack is the only plan we can come up with given the intelligence information known about the Russian soldiers on that island."

"I know how frustrating this is for everyone, General," confessed Spencer who didn't approve of the Marine's plan, "but I don't think it's wise to risk the lives of your men on a mission that could end in disaster."

Forty minutes later, Spencer and the others watched the television pictures transmitted from a five foot long remotely piloted submarine as it slowly moved along the harbor floor. The submarine's lights illuminated a shiny object on the seabed and the group quickly identified it as a large plastic box with thin wires extended from it toward the surface. The submarine began a slow ascent and found a black circular mine eight inches in diameter and two inches thick attached to a wire. The submarine slowly inched forward as it took pictures of the mine, and as it did, the mine began moving toward the submarine's metal hull. The pilot immediately pulled back on his remote controls, but the mine touched the nose of the submarine that housed the camera. A blinding flash of light momentarily filled the room, then the television screen faded to black.

Spencer suddenly heard Adams' dejected voice as his image appeared on the monitors in the teleconferencing room. "I think we can all agree that finding an underwater route to the island is impossible. Those mines have already killed two of my divers, and now they've destroyed one of our most sophisticated probing submarines."

After the meeting concluded, Spencer drove to Van Horne's hotel and walked to his suite. He and Van Horne sat and talked in the suite's living room as six men sat on the balcony watching Goat Island in the darkness with night vision equipment. "You know you

JOURNEY THROUGH A LONG WINTER'S NIGHT   181

can't tell anybody what Sullivan told us today," warned Van Horne as he poured two glasses of whiskey and handed one to Spencer. "We've got to get into that War College building so we can find the escape tunnel in the basement. If we find it, then we can decide what to do with the information."

"They'll probably hang me for this one, Robert. When do you want to do it?"

"Tonight, we've got to got do it tonight. We're running out of time and we can't wait any longer."

"What time do you want to get started?"

"I'll meet you in front of the building at two. See if you can get the equipment on this list," replied Van Horne as he handed a piece of paper to Spencer.

"I'll be there. Don't keep me waiting."

Chapter Nine

After Spencer left for the Newport Naval Base, Van Horne drove to Fort Adams. He enjoyed the breeze blowing on his face in the open Jeep. It was a pleasant break in the heat and humidity that did not diminish after dark. Inside the fort he opened a can of soda and sat beside a large group of his men gathered in the conference room. They were comparing the details in their photographs to the pictures Van Horne borrowed from Sullivan. "That story Sullivan told us about the tunnels under the harbor has been on my mind all afternoon. It sounds too crazy to be real, and I just don't know what to believe."

"Sullivan might have become senile after he retired from the Navy, Major," Manley warned Van Horne. "He may have dreamed up those tunnels as he got older and sat around with nothing to do. You know what that can do to a person's mind."

"He's right," added David White, whose father was sick with Alzheimer Disease before recently dying. "Even though we don't like to think about our parents getting older, the man is in his nineties. He may not know what's reality and what's fantasy anymore."

"I know what you're both saying. We've got to find out if those tunnels are real before we do anything else. The only way to do it is to break into that War College building and check the basement. Owen, Malin, White, and Preston, you're with me tonight. The rest of you keep watching the island."

At 1:50 A.M. on Wednesday, the sky was clear and the stars were bright specs of light set against a black background. Van Horne drove his men to the Newport Naval Base and parked the Jeep beside Luce Hall. Each of the men pulled on a shoulder holster as they studied the well lit Goat Island only two miles from them. Then they walked across the building's dimly lit front lawn and met a group of men waiting for them.

Van Horne studied the exterior of the four story brownstone building constructed with ornate arches and pillars. "How the hell could anyone have cut a tunnel

JOURNEY THROUGH A LONG WINTER'S NIGHT   183

into the rock under this building?" he asked himself. "I think I'm chasing an old man's fantasy, and the worst part is, I'm getting excited about it."

"It's after two o'clock," said Spencer when Van Horne stopped beside him. "My staff can't find anything about Sullivan's Project Blindsight, and I've been standing here wondering if his tunnel even exists."

"I was just wondering the same thing, Admiral," laughed Van Horne as he rubbed his burning eyes.

"When is the last time you had some sleep, Robert? You look like you're exhausted, even in this light."

"I got a couple of hours back at the fort. I don't feel too bad right now."

When they walked to Spencer's truck, Van Horne saw Mahoney dressed in blue shorts and a yellow tee shirt handing supplies to the men. The twelve men, and Mahoney, then carried the tools and eight large duffel bags to the buildings' front doors. As the others watched for security patrols, Mahoney pulled keys from her tight fitting shorts and unlocked the building's doors.

Van Horne and Spencer led the group into the building dimly lit by numerous red exit signs. Brown veined marble blocks were used to construct the building's walls, floor, and towering four story high central foyer. The group carefully walked down a wide marble staircase that led to the building's basement. Van Horne turned on the long fluorescent lights hanging from the huge exposed wooden beams that supported the floor above. A wide corridor filled the center of the basement constructed with a ten foot high ceiling. Thirty offices and eight storage areas filled with personnel files and desks lined both sides of the central corridor. Several large stone pillars in the central corridor supported the building above, and their brownstone color was a contrast to the basement's painted white walls.

"They covered the foundation with walls," said a surprised Spencer, after he pulled a the cigar from his mouth. "They covered the god damn foundation stones with drywall and painted it."

"I knew finding this tunnel wasn't going to be easy," laughed Owen as the real estate agent studied the con-

184   D'ONOFRIO

struction materials. "They did a damn good job building those walls too."

"Sullivan couldn't remember where they cut the escape tunnel down here," commented Van Horne as he switched on all the overhead fluorescent lights. "If they cut the tunnel from the island they probably did it in a straight line, so we'll start with the foundation wall that faces the harbor. If we don't find it in there we'll try another wall."

The building's foundation was almost three hundred feet long and Van Horne knew the task was going to be difficult. "This is going to take hours, so lets split up into groups and work in different areas." The sounds of breaking plasterboard soon filled the basement as the men tore down pieces of the walls.

One hour later, Owen and White exposed a sixty foot long section of the building's foundation after a section of wall they were hitting with sledge hammers unexpectedly collapsed. The entire foundation was constructed of rough brown stones that measured eight to ten feet in length, and four feet in thickness. Everyone was discouraged when they found the foundation wall was intact in that area of the building.

Outside the building dense clouds of fog began rolling onto the land from over the water. As they listened to fog horns in the distance, three men concealed in the mist slowly rowed an inflatable boat across the harbor and ran it aground on the shore in front of Luce Hall. The men quietly pulled the boat onto the grass and then fell beside it as they checked their automatic weapons. Then the three men began crawling across the wet grass, toward the front doors of the Luce Hall, which were now almost totally obscured by the dense fog.

At four thirty, Van Horne and the others were examining the huge foundation stones behind long sections of the walls ripped down in four offices. "Look at this," said an excited Preston as he knelt on the floor beside a large foundation stone. "This area of the stone is a different color." Everyone huddled around him and the others saw a slight color variation in the stones above where Preston was kneeling.

JOURNEY THROUGH A LONG WINTER'S NIGHT 185

"This could be what we're looking for," said an excited Van Horne, after he pulled a wire brush from a duffel bag and handed it to Preston.

"Beautiful," was Owen's only comment several minutes later, after Preston brushed away the years of filth on a rough concrete patch.

"Let's move our equipment in here and find out what's behind that patch," Van Horne said as his enthusiasm began to excite the others. "Maybe Sullivan was right, maybe his tunnel is real."

As the others worked in the basement, two of Spencer's men guarded the building's front doors. As they huddled in the building's dimly lit doorway in the damp fog, a Cuban soldier slowly crawled forward on the wet grass until he was fifteen feet from them. His handgun's silencer prevented any sounds from escaping from the weapon, and seconds later, Spencer's men lay dead on a concrete sidewalk. The Cubans ran to the doorway and dragged the bodies into the building, motioning to one another when they heard voices. They quietly moved through the darkened building and cautiously walked down the stairs that led to the basement, as they listened to the men talking below.

As Van Horne and the others were gathering their supplies the sounds of three machine guns suddenly filled the basement with a deafening noise, startling them. When Van Horne heard the Russian made AK-47 machine guns they immediately brought back the memories of combat he tried to forget. The helpless and powerless sensation of walking into an ambush filled his mind as he looked to his right and saw the three men crouching on the steps. He momentarily panicked, but then quickly regained his composure.

As bullets shattered the fluorescent lights above him into thousands of pieces, Van Horne pushed Spencer into an office and fell onto the floor with him. As more bullets ripped apart the wall beside where he was laying Van Horne thought, "Those bastards are going to kill us as soon as we're out of ammunition. Why the hell didn't I bring some of our men for security." Then he reached around the door frame and fired his handgun

186   D'ONOFRIO

at the end of the building as the machine gun's noise echoed through the basement.

Owen knelt behind a stone support column as bullets struck it, and he frantically looked around for something to distract the gunmen. Most of the supplies lay on the floor beside him, and when he emptied the contents of a brown duffel bag onto the white tiled floor he saw two small propane gas tanks. As bullets struck the front of the stone pillar he knelt beside, Owen placed the two gas tanks and a clean white rag between his legs. Then he frantically wrapped electrical tape around them. Owen searched for a plastic bottle of concrete cleaning solvent and poured its contents over the rag wrapped around the propane tanks.

"Hit the deck," Owen screamed as he touched his cigarette lighter's flame to the rag and watched it burst into flames. As bullets shattered the ceiling lights near him, Owen threw the hastily constructed device around the stone column, toward the Cubans fifty feet from him.

A bone jarring explosion and concussion filled the basement after the burning rag caused the gas in the propane tanks to expand and ignite. The explosion created a fireball eight feet in diameter that filled the end of the basement from the floor to ceiling. The concussion in the confined area shattered ceiling lights and violently blew out basement windows.

The shrieking of fire alarms replaced the gunfire as Van Horne slowly stood, stunned by the explosion. He looked around and found the handgun knocked from his hand by the concussion. When he looked around the corner he saw two of the Cubans laying motionless on the floor. Then he looked past the flames and smoke of several burning desks, and watched the third man crawling up the stairs that led to the building's first floor.

Van Horne stumbled toward the stairs and cautiously followed the trail of blood up the steps until he reached the first floor doors. He stepped over Spencer's dead men and violently pushed the doors open with his shoulder, then he staggered out of the building. He looked around, still dazed by the explosion, and even-

JOURNEY THROUGH A LONG WINTER'S NIGHT   187

tually saw a man dressed in black pants and shirt hobbling painfully into the dense fog.

"Hold it," Van Horne shouted, as he chased the man into the fog and aimed his handgun with his shaking hands. The limping Cuban suddenly stopped, and as he turned he raised his machine gun. The sound of gunfire echoed across the Naval base as two bullets from Van Horne's handgun shattered the bones in the Cuban's hip and upper thigh. As the wounded man fell to the side he began firing his machine gun, and Van Horne fired three more bullets that ripped through the Cuban's chest.

Van Horne ran to the dead man and began searching his clothing, hoping to find something that might provide him with information about the man's identity. "Damn it, he isn't carrying any identification. He's only a kid," thought Van Horne as he studied the dead man's face in the dim light. "They sent a kid to kill me." Van Horne stood and grasped the dead man's ankle. He quickly dragged the body across the wet grass and left it beside the bodies of Spencer's men inside the building.

The flashing lights and sirens of approaching military police cars and fire engines pierced the early morning fog. As Van Horne was checking the condition of Spencer's men, three military police men suddenly ran into the building. "Freeze," shouted one of them as they all pointed their handguns at him. "Move an inch and you're dead."

"I'm Van Horne of the National Security Agency. Check the identification card in my back pocket. Do it, or some of our men are going to die if we don't get them some help."

A police officer removed the identification card and quickly verified Van Horne's identity. "We've got some wounded men downstairs. Call an ambulance," he shouted, as six firemen rushed into the building and he led them into the basement. As the firemen extinguished the flames the paramedics arrived and attempted to save the lives of the two wounded Cuban soldiers. When the propane gas tanks exploded they projected metal frag-

188 D'ONOFRIO

ments outward like a grenade's shrapnel, fatally wounding both men.

Van Horne nervously searched for his men and checked to ensure none of them was hurt during the attack. "I thought you said there wasn't going to be any shooting, Major," said an obviously shaken Owen as he sat on the floor and lit a cigarette. "I don't think we're taking this seriously enough," Owen then motioned behind Van Horne, and he cursed when he saw Spencer kneeling beside the body of Mahoney and another of his men, both of whom were dead.

Van Horne walked to Spencer and wondered how he could comfort his friend as the reality of the hostage situation became more apparent to everyone. "I know this is difficult, but we didn't have any idea this was going to happen. You can't blame yourself for what just happened, Admiral."

"What am I going to tell her husband and daughters, Robert? What can I possibly say to them so that they'll understand why this woman had to die in a place like this? She died with no one even to hold her hand and comfort her. How am I ever going to tell them what happened to her?" Van Horne didn't reply, as he studied the beautiful woman's long blond hair and the red blood that saturated her yellow shirt. "How did they know we were here, Robert? How did those bastards know we were going to be in this building at this time of night?"

"I honestly don't know, Admiral. I don't have an answer for anything that's going on here."

Van Horne stood and his anger flared when he realized Spencer's agents died while they were trying to help him. He suddenly lifted a sledge hammer and threw it against the foundation wall. "That's what they died for, a piece of cement. They should have been asleep in their homes, with their families, but instead they were here with me. They died for a piece of worthless god damn cement."

"Spencer was right, Major," said White dejectedly, as he lay on a desk and held his bruised ribs. "How did they know we'd be working down here? We didn't tell anybody outside our group that we'd be in here."

JOURNEY THROUGH A LONG WINTER'S NIGHT 189

As Van Horne thought about the question, he suddenly looked up when he heard the sounds of men running into the building on the floor above. The Newport Naval Base Commander, Admiral Dupont, and eight of his staff officers quickly ran down the stairs and into the basement with several military police officers. "What in the name of God is going on in here?" shouted a stunned Dupont when he saw the walls damaged by both the explosion and Van Horne's work crews. "Look at the damage down here."

"I'll explain everything to you," confessed Dupont's old friend Spencer, as he slowly stood and turned toward him. The two men met while they were apprentice seamen in the Navy and they developed a strong friendship that lasted throughout their careers. Spencer knew he needed Dupont's help to determine what was behind the wall.

"Herbert, what in the world are you doing down here?" Then he saw his medical team carrying Mahoney's body out on a stretcher. "What happened in here?"

"Four of my best people were just killed in an ambush, Stephen."

"What are you doing in my building at this time of night?"

"My staff has been doing some research work about Goat Island, Stephen. I flew to Connecticut yesterday and met with the Navy officer who was in charge of the Newport Torpedo Station. That was an installation located on Goat Island during the Second World War. He described the facility and an area where he claims the Navy stored the torpedoes ready to be shipped to our combat ships during the war."

"What does that have to do with you being in this building at this hour, and your people getting killed?" Dupont asked as he stepped over shattered pieces of walls and wooden furniture destroyed by the explosion.

"This is what we were here to find," said Spencer as he rubbed his hand over the reddish area of the foundation wall. "If you look at this section of the foundation you'll see its redder than the rock around it. We think someone tried to hide something behind this concrete patch."

190   D'ONOFRIO

"What could possibly be hidden back there, Herbert? Those are the building's foundation stones, and there's nothing but dirt behind them."

"That's what someone may want us to believe, Stephen. Look at it closely, it's almost the shape of a doorway six feet high and three feet wide. This cement work could be covering the entrance to some tunnels built by our government before the Second World War."

"You're down here looking for a tunnel?" asked a skeptical Dupont, as he looked at his staff. "I've never heard about any underground storage areas in the four years I've been the base commander."

"We're talking about a Navy facility built more than fifty years ago, Stephen. After the Navy demolished the plant they may have forgotten about the tunnels. There's only one way to know if our information is accurate, we've got to tear down this wall and see what's behind it."

"Why haven't you told anyone else what you think is in this building? Why are you chasing this mysterious tunnel without telling anyone else about it?"

"I don't know who to trust anymore, Stephen. Adams didn't tell you there's a possibility someone in our own intelligence organizations may be working with the Russians on Goat Island. I don't know who I can trust except you, and my men."

Dupont thought about the situation and realized Spencer would not be risking his life, and those of his men, unless he was confident the tunnels existed. The mysterious gunman who attempted to kill Spencer also troubled Dupont. "I can see why you didn't tell anyone about what you know, Herbert."

Dupont suddenly became concerned about security inside and around Luce Hall, and he immediately turned to his staff officers. "I want three light weapons teams inside this building watching all the entrances. Get them here on the double. I want four fully armed teams positioned around the building within the hour. I don't want word of anything that happened in here to leak out, so talk to the firemen and the medics and tell them to keep quiet. Call Marlowe, and tell him I want him and his men over here with all their equipment."

JOURNEY THROUGH A LONG WINTER'S NIGHT   191

"All right, Herbert, lets see what you've found," said Dupont who realized he forgot to lace his boots when he rushed from his residence, and began to do so. "What'd you want to do first?"

"We've got to move the debris away from this wall so we'll have a place to work." The men immediately began stacking the pieces of drywall and other wreckage they found scattered across the floor in a far corner of the basement.

Forty minutes later, Captain Thomas Marlowe and his men walked into the basement dressed in green fatigues and saw Dupont speaking to several of his security team leaders. "I'm glad your team isn't scheduled for evacuation until tomorrow, Thomas. I've got a problem here and I'm going to need your help."

"What happened down here, Admiral?" asked Marlowe, as he looked at the shattered walls and broken fluorescent light fixtures hanging from the ceiling. "I heard the fire trucks and ambulances, but I didn't pay any attention to them."

"The head of the National Security Agency seems to think the Navy dug some tunnels under Goat Island during the Second World War. His sources told him the entrance to those tunnels is down here."

"Can't we contact Washington and check out the story, Admiral?"

"That might not be wise right now. Based on what happened in here, I think we may already have a security leak."

Marlowe shook his head as he listened to Dupont's concerns, then he saw the wet red blood streaked on the tiled floor by the men's shoes. "Where did all this blood come from?"

"Three men with automatic weapons tried to kill Spencer and his group while they were looking for their tunnel. That adds some credibility to their story, don't you think?"

"Do you know who the gunmen are, or how they got past our security and onto the base?"

"Spencer's men killed them, so we'll never know who they are or where they came from."

192   D'ONOFRIO

"Killed them!"

"Yeah. Come on, I'll introduce you to, Spencer."

Captain Thomas Marlowe was a career Navy officer who served under Dupont during the previous four years. Marlowe and his twenty man Seabee team were skilled construction and demolition specialists, who completed many of the heavy construction jobs at the Newport Naval Base. Their expertise could be used anywhere in the world; and their accomplishments included everything from building hospitals to destroying bridges. The thirty-seven year old Marlowe operated his team like a construction crew with him acting as the foreman. The tall, muscular man, who enjoyed hard work and the challenge of finishing jobs others considered impossible, was well liked and respected by his men.

"Someone went to a lot of trouble to cover this part of the wall with concrete," Marlowe told Van Horne, as he felt the texture of the other foundation stones, and then the discolored reddish area itself. "They even colored the concrete when they mixed it to match the foundation stones around the patch. If you weren't looking for this you probably wouldn't have noticed it."

"Do you think we can drill a hole through this patch so we can see what's on the other side? I want to be sure there's a tunnel back there before we knock down the wall."

"I don't think that'll be a problem," replied Marlowe, then he discussed the task with his men. Three of them began preparing a large electric drill equipped with a diamond tipped, one inch diameter drill. Four other men assembled large floodlights beside the foundation. They attached long gray electrical cables to the building's electrical box and used them to power the bright floodlights and the drill.

When the drill and other equipment were ready, Marlowe told three of his men to pull on their gloves and safety goggles. Then he turned to Dupont and the other people in the basement. "I'd feel better if all of you move back to the other end of the basement until after we've finished drilling through the wall."

As the others stepped back, Van Horne told Marlowe,

JOURNEY THROUGH A LONG WINTER'S NIGHT 193

"I'm staying here with you. I want to watch what's going to happen while you're drilling."

Marlowe smiled and handed Van Horne a pair of goggles. The men started the drill and several seconds later the diamond tip penetrated the reddish patch over the foundation stone. As they pushed the drill deeper into the wall Marlowe pointed at debris accumulating under the hole when silvery metal flakes began to mix with cement dust. They were an indication some type of metal object was located behind the concrete. Ten minutes later, the drill suddenly slid into a hollow area behind the discolored area of the wall. The Seabees slowly pulled the drill out of the hole after they pushed eight inches of the shaft into the stone.

After the electric drill's powerful motor stopped turning, the men could hear a whistling, high pitched sound, but none of them could locate the source. Van Horne knelt on the floor and held his breathe. "I don't believe this. Where is this air going? What the hell is behind this wall?"

The Seabees then moved sophisticated electronic equipment beside the foundation wall. Marlowe placed a small black and white television monitor on a desk his men moved beside the foundation. Then he connected the long black wires that extended from an electronic relay box to the monitor. Marlowe knelt beside the drill hole with another large black box and carefully attached a long cable to it as he explained its purpose to Van Horne. "This is a fiber optic cable with a lens attached to the end of it that we use when we have to inspect inaccessible areas. The fibers carry an image to a stationary video camera mounted inside this box. We should be able to see what's behind this wall on the television monitor after I push this through the drill hole."

Dupont and the others crowded forward and watched Marlowe as he carefully inserted the cable into the drill hole, then slowly began pushing it forward. Marlowe carefully pushed several inches of the cable into the drill hole before he switched on a powerful light source in the black box. The fiber optic filaments in the outer edge of the cable carried the light to a

194 D'ONOFRIO

special lens at the cable's tip. The television monitor suddenly brightened, and after Marlowe's man focused the picture, everyone could see the smooth interior of the circular drill hole.

Van Horne held his breath when the picture suddenly darkened, and Marlowe stopped pushing the cable forward and focused the monitor again. Darkness covered the monitor until Marlowe twisted the fiber optic cable, and the end pointed in a different direction. The bright light at the end of the cable momentarily illuminated a flat surface, and Marlowe twisted the cable again as he tried unsuccessfully to display the object. He twisted the cable and pulled back on it slightly. Everyone appeared shocked when they saw the side wall and roof of a wide tunnel on the monitor.

Van Horne became excited as he knelt beside the monitor and slowly ran his fingers over the details displayed on the screen. "Look at that, it looks like there is a tunnel behind the wall." Marlowe twisted the cable so the tip was pointing toward the floor and Van Horne became more excited. "Look at how that floor drops away. This is it, this is the escape tunnel Sullivan told us about that leads to the underground storage area."

Van Horne looked at Spencer and smiled as he stood and thought about what they accomplished. "We've just found something everyone in the Navy has forgotten about since the end of the war. Now we've got to get through this wall and find out where that tunnel leads to."

"I don't think I want to risk tearing down that wall by hand," Marlowe told Dupont, as he stood and stared at the image on the monitor. "Judging from the sound of the air flowing into that drill hole, I'd guess there's a huge vacuum behind that wall. The whole wall might implode if we try to cut through it with jackhammers. I think we're going to need some explosive charges to get through it."

"I don't like the idea of using explosives in here," said a concerned Dupont, as he studied the reddish patch. After he thought about the situation he added, "Do whatever it takes, Thomas. I want to know what's

JOURNEY THROUGH A LONG WINTER'S NIGHT 195

behind that wall within an hour."

During the next thirty minutes, the Seabees carefully attached small explosives around the perimeter of the reddish discolored area, and then attached another charge to the center of it. "I think it would be safer if you move everyone out of the building while we detonate the explosives, Admiral," Marlowe warned Dupont as his men stretched black detonator wires across the basement floor. "We're staying in here just in case we start a fire."

Dupont thought about the unexpected death of his divers in Newport Harbor and immediately told the other men to move out of the building. The Seabees dragged their detonator wires to the far end of the basement and into the building's furnace room. The thick concrete blocks that protected the building from a boiler fire would protect the men from the explosion. As a Seabee finished attaching the wires to a detonator, Van Horne watched him wrap his hand around the small black plastic handle. As he remembered his years in Vietnam, and the battles in Iraq, Van Horne's body tensed as he anticipated a bone jarring shock. He immediately remembered the signal to find shelter because an explosion was imminent. He shouted the words in his mind as the Seabee twisted the detonator's handle, "Fire in the hole."

Van Horne's body shuddered and his eyes tightened when a deafening noise filled the basement. The explosion shattered most of the ceiling lights, and the sound of wind filled the darkened end of the basement as air was violently drawn into the large hole in the foundation. Van Horne suddenly realized he was having difficulty breathing as the oxygen was sucked out of the furnace room. He watched as debris was pulled past the furnace room door by the force of the rushing air.

Van Horne and the Seabees waited in the furnace room for ten minutes until the wind's force slowly subsided. "I can't stand around in here any more. I've got to know what we've found behind that wall," Van Horne told Marlowe impatiently, as he looked at his watch. The two men walked out of the furnace room together and stared into the darkness at the far end of the base-

196   D'ONOFRIO

ment, but they were not able to see the foundation. Marlowe found two flashlights in an equipment bag and handed one to Van Horne. The flashlight's beams pierced the darkness as the men walked toward the sound of rushing air that reminded them of huge ocean waves crashing on the beach. As they moved the flashlight beams over the foundation stones they saw the explosives destroyed the entire patch over a stone doorway.

"Lets move our floodlights up to the wall and get them powered up," Marlowe shouted to his men after they walked out of the furnace room and stood behind him cautiously.

Dupont led the other men into the basement and everyone stared at the hole in the foundation, which was occasionally lit by the two moving flashlight beams. "We've got to find out where this tunnel leads to," Van Horne shouted to Spencer as the group cautiously stepped forward. "Its dark as hell in there and we're going to need some flashlights and radios, just in case we get into trouble. Can you get your hands on some equipment for us?"

Fifteen minutes later, fresh air was still being drawn into the tunnel, but the intensity had substantially decreased. Immediately after they switched on the floodlights, Marlowe and three of his men began working in the tunnel entrance. As the Seabees stood on a narrow black metal scaffolding they removed several access plates from a steel conduit fastened to the ridged stone ceiling. They studied the mass of blue, red, yellow, gray, and orange wires they found inside.

Several minutes later, three of Spencer's men ran into the basement carrying five military radios and large flashlights. Van Horne and Owen immediately began checking the equipment. "I'll take one radio, you take another, Jim. We'll leave one here in the basement just in case we get into trouble and have to call for help."

Van Horne impatiently looked at his watch and then at Marlowe and his men working in the tunnel entrance. "We'll use our flashlights while you're working with that wiring. We're wasting a lot of time standing around here."

"Is there anything else you need, Robert?" asked

JOURNEY THROUGH A LONG WINTER'S NIGHT 197

Spencer as he stared apprehensively at the hole in the foundation.

"I wish we had a few more men to take with us. We don't know what we're going to find."

Dupont didn't respond to Van Horne's statement for several seconds. He stared at the tunnel and thought about the morning he was standing on the deck of the battleship *Arizona*, while it was tied to the dock at Pearl Harbor. He remembered his feelings as Japanese planes flew overhead and torpedoes struck his ship. He wanted to fight back and kill the Japanese attackers. Instead, he found himself fighting for his life as tried to avoid the raging flames on the water after the ship lurched and threw him from the deck.

Now Dupont was experiencing the same feelings after the Russians' surprise attack of an island only two miles from his base. He realized the tunnel might provide him a way to defeat the Russian attackers, and he felt compelled to do anything he could to help Spencer. "What's your feeling about exploring in that tunnel with them, Thomas? You don't know how dangerous its going to be."

"We helped Van Horne find his tunnel, Admiral, and now I'd like to see what's at the end of it. We'll just have to watch our step until we're sure its safe down there."

"All right, take some of your men and go with them, but be careful. I don't need any more of my men getting hurt."

"I'll lead the first group into the tunnel," Van Horne told Marlowe and Owen. "Marlowe, you take the second group in five minutes after us. Owen you move in five minutes later. If anyone has a problem use the radio and call for help. Keep your eyes open in there, we don't know if they left any booby traps when they sealed the tunnels."

Van Horne and his men carefully stepped around the Seabees working on the scaffolding, and into the coolness and darkness that immediately surrounded them in the tunnel. The beam from their quartz flashlights pierced the darkness as the men walked into the isolation and silence of the tunnel. Van Horne estimated the

198   D'ONOFRIO

tunnel to be four feet wide and seven feet high, and the floor was smooth so walking was not difficult or dangerous. He studied the stone walls and felt the small ridges evenly spaced one inch apart on both walls and ceiling.

The quiet in the tunnel caused Van Horne's ears to ring and the silence soon became deafening as he walked further into the darkness. After the group walked forward for ten minutes, Van Horne stopped and looked behind the group. He could see the brightly lit tunnel entrance in Luce Hall in the darkness, along with the beams of the flashlights Marlowe's men carried in the second group. Van Horne's group continued walking forward in the eerie darkness, and they realized the narrow tunnel had ended and they were now inside a much wider tunnel.

"I don't like it down here, Major," Malin confessed, as he shuddered in the darkness. "I don't like being down here at all. I feel like I'm walking in my own grave."

Van Horne and the others were startled when the loud metallic sounds of the radio's external speaker shattered the silence in the darkened tunnel. "Trojan Guide, this is Midway Barber. What's your current position? Over."

"I'll bet Spencer hasn't used that Midway Barber designator since he was in Saigon," Van Horne laughed as he searched for the microphone of the radio strapped to Malin's back. "Midway Barber this is Trojan Guide. We've been walking forward in a straight line since we left Luce Hall. The floor began a steep descent about a hundred feet from the opening in the foundation. The tunnel has widened and we're on a flat stone floor now. Over."

"Roger, Trojan Guide. Contact me if you need anything. Midway Barber, out." Spencer was thrilled by Van Horne's report, but he knew something was troubling Dupont when he looked at him. "What's wrong, Stephen, is Trojan Guide bothering you?"

Dupont nodded with a frown as he sat on the edge of a desk when one of his staff gave him a cup of black coffee. "I don't understand what it means."

"Trojan Guide is the designation Van Horne used in Vietnam, and probably while he was in Iraq. It's based on Greek mythology."

JOURNEY THROUGH A LONG WINTER'S NIGHT   199

"How did he ever come up with that."

"I've had to tell the story a hundred times, so I know it well. Do you remember when the Greeks attacked the City of Troy during the Trojan War? They finally managed to capture the city after some of their warriors slipped past the gates hidden inside the wooden horse. Only a few people escaped from the city, and one of them was a guide who led a few survivors to Italy. Van Horne believes Trojan Guide means the leader and protector of the survivors."

"I'm not sure I like what I'm hearing. I think that would worry me if his team was ever in trouble. He may feel he's invincible, and that may get him and his team killed."

Spencer carefully sipped a cup of coffee that had been handed to him, as he shook his head in disagreement. "Don't take my explanation the wrong way. I'll have to admit there have been times when I've believed he really was that guide in another life. He always takes care of his men, and he instinctively protects and watches over everyone he considers close to him. Not that many people ever get that close to him."

"He does seem to intimidate everyone. I don't know if it's his voice, or his mannerisms, but something about him makes me nervous."

Spencer smiled after Dupont's comments, they were the usual reaction to Van Horne's personality. "He doesn't do that intentionally Stephen, believe me. He's a good man with a big heart, but he thinks he became something evil while he was in Vietnam."

"That's why he doesn't let anyone close to him now?"

"That's it. He's an outstanding battlefield commander, and if you're in trouble you can depend on him to get you out of it. He's the best I've ever commanded, Stephen. He's imaginative, resourceful, and relentless. If he's after you, you're as good as dead."

Dupont appeared relieved by Spencer's further explanation, and he listened to a radio conversation between Marlowe and Van Horne.

"We must be under the harbor by now," Van Horne told his men as they walked forward on the flat stone floor.

200   D'ONOFRIO

"What was that?" asked a shocked Preston after an arc of light seemed to fill the tunnel like lightening. The group immediately stopped walking when the ceiling lights suddenly flickered in the darkness for a moment again.

"Marlowe's men must be trying to connect the wires they found in that conduit to the electricity in Luce Hall," said Van Horne as the dim lights struggled to life again, and remained lit seconds later. Circular gray light fixtures attached to the tunnel's stone ceiling every eight feet held large bulbs. A series of silver metal conduits which contained the tunnel's electrical wiring and communication system snaked across the rock ceiling.

A dim yellow light filled the entire tunnel, and Van Horne and his men looked around the area with shocked expressions. They stood in a forty foot wide tunnel with a ceiling twelve feet high, cut into solid gray rock. Van Horne saw a set of railroad tracks along the tunnel's left wall. "They must have used a train to move the torpedoes through this central shaft. Look at those smaller tunnels that branch out to the left and right of this tunnel up ahead. Those green metal racks bolted to tunnel walls must be where they stored the torpedoes down here."

"Look at the size of this place," said a shocked Malin as the group continued walking forward, and he pictured the blue water that surrounded Goat Island above in his mind. "I can't believe we're standing under the harbor."

"That must be the barracks where the men lived down here," speculated Van Horne when he saw a large building with a blue clapboard exterior in the tunnel's central shaft. The barracks was constructed with windows and doors, and Van Horne speculated kept the living area warm when he realized the temperature in the tunnels was about sixty degrees.

"They cooked meals and slept down here to avoid detection by enemy agents they thought were in the city," Van Horne told the men as he led them into the barracks. They found furnished sleeping areas, dinning areas, and storage rooms that contained the supplies

JOURNEY THROUGH A LONG WINTER'S NIGHT   201

abandoned when the Navy deactivated the facility. All the items they found were from the 1930s and 1940s, and the absence of air and light in the tunnels stopped the aging process and preserved everything. The group examined many of the items they found, but were hesitant to touch anything in the area that now resembled a museum. The group separated and explored the living quarters, then met in the dining area as Marlowe's team, and then Owen's team, walked into the barracks.

"If I remember Sullivan's drawing correctly, we're almost under Goat Island," Van Horne told the three groups, as they walked forward together. "Lets find out where this tunnel ends."

The group eventually found a red steel ladder bolted to the tunnel's rock wall. "This might be another escape tunnel," said Van Horne as he climbed the cold metal ladder while his men pointed their flashlights into a ten foot wide circular shaft cut into the tunnel's ceiling. At the top of the ladder he found a thick steel plate welded to a massive metal frame covering the tunnel. Van Horne examined the plate for several seconds and then climbed down the ladder.

The group continued walking forward and the tunnel began to narrow to a width that reminded everyone of the tunnel entrance in Luce Hall. The tunnel abruptly ended and the men found another vertical shaft cut into the stone ceiling, and another red metal ladder. A metal sign fastened to the tunnel's rock wall indicated the ladder led to an emergency exit.

As Van Horne slowly climbed the ladder, he realized this tunnel was different from the first vertical shaft they located. Instead of finding a heavy steel plate covering the top of the tunnel, he discovered a thinner piece of metal covered this tunnel. Van Horne hung on the ladder with one hand and pressed his ear to the metal plate. He froze and stopped breathing when he heard sounds on the other side of it. He listened for several seconds before climbing down the ladder and motioning the group away from the end of the tunnel. "I heard voices on the other side of that plate. I think, I heard men talking and laughing."

202 D'ONOFRIO

Everyone agreed the complex was watertight and appeared to be safe after more investigation and exploration of each tunnel. Owen and Van Horne walked together as they led the group toward Luce Hall. "We may have just found a way to get some men onto Goat Island. The Russians won't even know their security has been breached until it's too late for them to do anything about it," said an excited Van Horne. At noon the group walked out of the tunnel and into the basement of Luce Hall.

"How did it go in there?" Spencer asked Van Horne as he looked at his watch. "I was beginning to worry about you."

"Everything looks good down there. We found the torpedo storage area and the barracks Sullivan told us about. I think we may have found two more escape tunnels too."

Spencer smiled when he heard the news, and Van Horne appeared distracted when a heavily armed sailor walked past him. "Dupont thought it might be wise to move more of his security forces into the building, Robert. He thinks this tunnel is as important as we do, and he doesn't want to take a chance of anyone destroying it," Spencer studied Van Horne's face, and the solid facial features and dark brown eyes that sometimes frightened people. "You really look like you're exhausted, Robert. You've been pushing yourself for more than a day."

"You're right, Admiral, I'm beat," he replied as he turned to Owen. "Take the men back to the hotel and get something to eat and some sleep. Call me at seven to wake me up." Then Van Horne, Dupont, and Spencer walked out of the building and into the hot sun and humidity that accompanied a blue, cloudless sky.

Van Horne shaded his eyes from the sun's glare so he could look at the exterior of the building. He saw sailors dressed in camouflaged clothing guarding the rear of the building, while others hid on a nearby grassy hill, and in the dense brush that lined the building's access road. "I'm glad your men are watching the building, Admiral. I still don't understand how those three knew we'd be in this building this morning."

JOURNEY THROUGH A LONG WINTER'S NIGHT   203

"I didn't tell anyone I was coming here except Mahoney," confessed Spencer as he became upset when he pictured her laying on the floor as blood wet her shirt. "I read your list of supplies to her while she was sitting in my office here on the base. I told her to have everything here at two this morning."

Van Horne turned to Spencer with a look of panic on his face. "You read her that list of supplies over the phone."

Spencer suddenly looked into Van Horne's cold eyes, "Someone tapped the telephone in my office, haven't they? I told them exactly where we were going to be working. I'm responsible for getting my own people killed."

"You can't blame yourself, Admiral. Even if we're right, there's no way you could have expected this to happen on one of own your military installations."

"That means someone on this base, either military or civilian, is working with the Russians on that island. Now I really don't know who to trust."

"I'll have my base maintenance personnel check the telephone wires in the office you're using, Herbert," said Dupont, as he pointed at one of his aides. "Every time you use a telephone you've got to assume its tapped and someone is listening to your conversation."

"You're right. We've scheduled our next tele-conferencing meeting with Washington for five o'clock this afternoon, Stephen. I don't want to say anything about what we've found here until we've had more time to check it out."

"Good idea. It's safer for all of us if no one knows about it."

"I'm heading back to the hotel to get a few hours of sleep, and something to eat." Van Horne told the others as he checked his handgun and pushed it back into the holster. "I'll meet you back at the fort after your meeting, Admiral."

Van Horne drove to the hotel and fell onto his bed, where he quickly fell asleep. After Owen called him at seven o'clock to wake him, Van Horne took a hot shower, dressed, and then met a few of his men in the hotel lobby. They walked into the city and found a small Ital-

204 D'ONOFRIO

ian restaurant that was not overly crowded with spectators. His lack of sleep did not leave him with much of an appetite, but he knew he had to eat. After they finished they drove to Fort Adams.

Spencer sat uncomfortable and waited for the teleconferencing meeting to begin as he contemplated the fact he couldn't trust any of the men seated in the room with him except Dupont. Vice-President Benson began the meeting with the startling announcement that neither he nor his staff had anything new to report, placing more pressure on the others to find a solution to the crisis.

Central Intelligence Director Edward Jamison was the next speaker and he stood uncomfortably at the podium in the Pentagon's Strategy room. "My nuclear weapons specialists have been working closely with Admiral Adam's planning team. They're working to determine the optimum size of the nuclear device we'll need to detonate over Goat Island to incinerate the Russian bomb. Our computer projections indicate our device will completely vaporize the plutonium device in the moments before the vibration sensors in the hotel garage can detonate it. We won't need a Stealth bomber to deliver the warhead to the island as we first thought. We'll use a Cruise missile to fly the warhead into the hotel moments before its detonated. We proved we can deliver a payload with pinpoint accuracy in Iraq."

"When that bomb detonates it's going to destroy everything on that island," thought Spencer as he ignored Jamison's continued narrative. "All the evidence that might show us who in our government or military is working with the Russians. If I didn't know better I'd say Jamison is trying to get rid of everything that might link him to this situation." Now Spencer wondered if Jamison, or someone else in the Central Intelligence Agency, was involved in the kidnapping of the President after hearing his ideas for destroying the island.

Jamison concluded his report with a comment that upset many of the other officials. "Whether we like it or not, we've all got to start accepting the fact that the President and the other hostages on that island cannot be saved. We can't do anything to help those people,

JOURNEY THROUGH A LONG WINTER'S NIGHT   205

and right now our only concern should be finding an efficient way to destroy the Russian bomb. Keeping this nation free from widespread nuclear contamination is much more important than saving the hostages on that island."

"I'd be willing to bet that if you were a hostage on that island right now you wouldn't think your life was so unimportant." Holloway unexpectedly told the group as he stood in the conference room. "If you were a hostage on that island you'd expect your government and military to do everything they could to rescue you. You wouldn't expect them to kill you to eliminate the problem."

"That's enough, Commander," shouted Adams angrily, as he stood at the table in the Pentagon's Strategy room. "I know you must be very tired and frustrated, or you wouldn't be as insubordinate as you are right now. You know there's no other way we can end this confrontation. Peskov is demanding his ransom, while the Russian government is warning us not to deliver it. It's double jeopardy, and the only thing we can do is look for a way to destroy the bomb on that island before it can be detonated."

"Innocent people are on that island with Peskov and his bomb. I can't believe you're willing to sacrifice them on a theory that a nuclear explosion may destroy the Russian bomb. What if the explosion increases the effects of the plutonium? What'll we do then? Say we made a mistake, apologize, and walk away from the destruction we've caused. This is permanent. Once we detonate that bomb there's no way to go back."

"The commander is right, this plan is trash," commented Reynolds with an offended tone in his voice. "We should be negotiating with Peskov right now. Not sitting here discussing how to destroy a portion of our own nation."

"You're all out of line," shouted Jamison as he slammed his folder onto the podium and startled Vice-President Benson.

"Don't tell me I'm out of line because I don't agree with this insane idea of yours," Reynolds shouted back as he pointed at the television camera he knew was

206   D'ONOFRIO

transmitting his picture and voice to Washington. "We've got all the power and technology of the free world at our disposal, and this is how we propose to deal with this problem? We're going to destroy a part of our nation and then leave our future generations with the problem of cleaning up after us. That's being irresponsible."

During the next three hours, all the men and women in the Naval Base conference room, and those in Washington, angrily discussed the options available to them. Some believed other strategies and plans could be developed to rescue the hostages on the island. Others argued that if the military attempted to attack the island the Russians would detonate their bomb immediately after they realized they were under attack.

"I still contend we should attempt to negotiate with the Russian general more forcefully," said General Murtagh as he sat back on his chair. "I'm opposed to any consideration of military or nuclear intervention until we've exhausted all of our other options." Murtagh didn't want to utilize any military personnel he might need to control the civilian population after he assumed control of the government.

After the meeting, Spencer rode to Fort Adams in his limousine, where he sat and talked to Van Horne as the spotters continued watching Goat Island. At eleven o'clock, Van Horne and Spencer heard shouts and whistles coming from the room used as a radio room.

They ran through the stone hallway with an arched ceiling to the isolated room and found eight men congratulating each other. "What's going on in here?" asked Van Horne as he looked around.

"We just recorded a scrambled radio message transmitted from somewhere in the city, Major, probably Goat Island," explained Willey as a tape recording of the intercepted message was playing in the background. "They're using voice scrambling equipment and that's why the message sounds like its overlaid with static and random tones. Now all we've got to do is figure out how to decipher it."

Chapter Ten

At six o'clock Thursday morning, Van Horne met with his men in the fort's conference room after an early breakfast. "We've got three days left to come up with a working attack plan before Peskov kills the President, and World War Three begins! That means we only have a day and a half to finish the plan and document it. That'll give our military a day and a half to study it before they implement it."

Van Horne opened his note book and removed several pages of notes he wrote during breakfast. "Here's what we've got to get done today. We've been using those three personal computers to accumulate the information our spotters gathered. I want all that information combined into a single report we can use to develop a plan. After you're done with that, I want you to start considering how a military force can use the tunnels we found to get onto Goat Island. I know you're all tired, but we've got to keep pushing until we get this finished. They've already killed a lot of innocent people on that island and the others need our help."

Barnes and Leland sat eating a breakfast they prepared in a hotel restaurant on Goat Island as they read the morning status report from Washington. They sat at a chrome and glass table in a restaurant overlooking the calm blue ocean water of Newport Harbor. Barnes sighed heavily and shook his head when he saw Trembulak and Vazques rush into the restaurant.

"What are you two doing in here? How can you sit here and eat like nothing is going on out there?" Trembulak asked nervously as he looked through a large window. "More of your Navy and Coast Guard ships are blocking the entrance to the harbor this morning. I can see several amphibious landing ships that joined the blockade during the night. I didn't expect to see that much military force in the harbor this morning. Your military might be preparing to attack the island while you're sitting here eating. I want you to contact Murtagh and ask him what your military forces are doing out there."

208   D'ONOFRIO

"I'm not going to interrupt the General because you're worried about something that's none of your fucking business," Barnes replied as he stood, angered by Trembulak's lack of confidence in his leadership. "He'll get to me when he has time. Until then, you should be out there doing your fucking job."

"That's not what I want to hear, Barnes. We should know what's going to happen. Our lives depend on knowing that information."

"Listen to me, you fucking asshole," Barnes screamed as he grabbed Trembulak's camouflaged Russian combat jacket and pushed him backward. "You're going to settle down, shut your fucking mouth, and follow that fucking attack plan. You're supposed to be out outside killing fifteen more hostages this morning. Now drag your fucking ass out there and do it."

"Don't try to intimidate me, Barnes," warned Trembulak as he attempted to regain his composure while he adjusted his jacket. "Other men have tried and no one has ever found their bodies."

"Don't you ever fucking threaten me you Palestinian camel jockey! I should blow your fucking head off," shouted Barnes as he put his hand on his handgun's holster. "You could be laying on the rocks next to those other useless hostages if you keep pushing me Trembulak."

Trembulak always thought the American soldier was an unemotional and psychotic killer, and he suddenly wanted to avoid any further confrontation. "I'll follow your precious attack plan, but I want more information about what's going on around us," he shouted at Barnes with hatred in his voice as he backed toward the restaurant door.

A few hours later, Leland walked into the large and lavishly furnished hotel suite Barnes was using for his office. He appeared shocked when he saw an attractive woman with long red hair lying naked on the floor's brown carpet. The woman, whose hands were tied behind her back, endured an hour of abuse by Barnes. He beat her face with his fist, then burned her skin with a cigar before savagely raping her several times. Barnes

JOURNEY THROUGH A LONG WINTER'S NIGHT   209

was buckling his pants as he stood over the hysterical woman, and he turned when Leland walked into the suite, followed by three Cuban soldiers whom he immediately pointed at. "Get her out of here and do whatever you want with her. After you're done kill her and then throw her body on the rocks with the rest of them."

"No, please, you said you wouldn't hurt me anymore," the woman screamed as the laughing soldiers grasped her ankles and painfully dragged her across the carpet on her back. "You promised you wouldn't hurt me," were her last words as the Cubans dragged her onto an elevator.

"What are you doing in here, raping these women and then killing them?" asked a disgusted Leland.

"Why the fuck not? This whole fucking island is going to be a dust cloud Sunday night. No ones going to know what we've done here, so why not have a little fun and fuck'em before we kill them."

"Is this what's going to happen after we're in control of the country? Rape the women and do whatever else we want because we're part of the military running the government? I thought we were doing all of this to help our people, not so you could screw any woman you want on this island to prove how much of a man you are."

Barnes became incensed by Leland's derogatory remarks, and he pulled his handgun from the holster laying on a table. "I should kill you for that comment," he shouted, as he pointed the handgun at Leland's chest. Then he slowly smiled as he regained his composure and lowered the weapon. "If it wasn't for people like me Leland, you wouldn't be standing here right now. What the fuck do you want in here anyway?"

Leland walked to a window and watched the crowds of spectators standing in the city streets, sweltering in the humidity and heat as they took pictures of the island. "I just got off the radio with General Murtagh. His staff and General Chchenkoff's people in Moscow are ready to take control after we kill Rockwell and detonate the bomb. The General wants us to execute another group of hostages this afternoon, and he wants us to kill a few kids this time. He wants it done in an

210   D'ONOFRIO

area where the news people can record the Russians killing the innocent children."

"We'll do it in front of the hotel this time. We've covered the rocks on the harbor side of the island with bodies, but the damn news people can't really get a good shot of them back there. Lets find Vazques and tell him to round up twenty men and women, and six kids. We'll do it near the hotel dock."

Thirty minutes later, Barnes and Leland were standing outside the hotel with a group of frightened hostages in the blazing midday sun. Both Barnes and Leland wore the black knit hoods over their faces to conceal their identities, the same type worn by anti-terrorist units of the military.

As Vazques' men forced the hostages to stand against the hotel's exterior red brick wall, Barnes looked toward the city. He saw the television news crews were following the group with their cameras. Barnes aimed his handgun at a frightened man in his mid twenties dressed in faded jeans and a shirt covered with marijuana plant designs. The man wore his long black hair pulled back in a ponytail that touched his waist.

"Look at this piece of shit. He thinks he's living in the seventies," Barnes told Leland moments before he fired a bullet that ripped through the man's upper leg. The wounded man fell backward against the brick wall screaming. Then he fell onto the ground and screamed loudly as he held his bleeding leg.

"That's good, now scream louder," laughed Barnes as he stood over the wounded man and fired a bullet through his shoulder. Deep red blood covered the screaming man's hands and clothing as he rolled on the ground in agony. When the man became quiet, and was almost unconscious, Barnes fired a bullet through his heart. Then he motioned to two Cuban soldiers who lifted the dead man by his wrists and ankles and carried it to the edge of the island. As the Cubans threw the body onto the rocks the news cameras recorded the sickening event.

Barnes dragged a five year old girl wearing white pajamas decorated with red ribbons away from her

JOURNEY THROUGH A LONG WINTER'S NIGHT   211

screaming mother and the other hostages. "I want my mommy," screamed the terrified child as Barnes dragged her by the wrist. Barnes pulled the child toward him and she fell onto the grass, screaming for her mother. As she was attempting to stand, the child's head seemed to explode after Barnes fired a bullet into the side of her skull near her ear. Warm blood covered the child's pajamas as her small body fell onto the ground. Barnes smiled as he motioned to Vazques' men to throw it onto the rocks with the others.

"Do the same to the rest of them," Barnes told Vazques, as he wiped the child's blood off his hand with a white hotel towel. Then he laughed as he waved the blood stained towel at the child's hysterical mother. "Kill them slowly and make them suffer. It'll really get the people worked up if we torture them before we finish them off."

Barnes and Leland walked toward the communications trailer to send a status report to Murtagh. When they walked around a corner of the hotel building they heard a woman screaming hysterically. They quickly ran across a parking lot and stopped beside a grassy area where they saw thirty of Vazques' men standing in a circle.

After they pushed their way through the soldiers they were surprised by what they saw. Four Cubans were raping two young women on the grass as the others cheered them on. The soldiers found two thick ropes in a boat docked in the marina and tied the ends to the steel guard rails in a parking lot. Then they tied the other end of the ropes around the necks of the helpless women. The rope prevented the women from escaping after one of the Cubans finished raping them, and another took his place. Barnes was pleased when he saw the news cameras pointed toward the group, and he moved the soldiers apart so the cameramen could film the brutal scene. He motioned to Leland and the two men walked to the communications trailer to prepare a status report.

"Have you heard anything from the men we sent to get rid of that group at Fort Adams?" Barnes asked

212 D'ONOFRIO

Leland as he shaded his eyes and looked across the bay at the large stone fort.

"No, I didn't expect to hear from them this soon. I told them to get out of the city as soon as they finished the job. They're probably on their way back to Washington right now and we'll hear from them tomorrow morning. Those three were our best ambush planners, and I'm sure that asshole who came to the island is already dead and buried at sea. If he reported seeing the gas mask Vazques' man was wearing, I'm sure Murtagh would have heard about it by now in one of his meetings. I think we got to him before he said anything about it."

"How about the men Vazques sent to the Newport Naval Base to ambush the group working in that building? Have we heard from them?"

"Our men said they heard a lot of gunfire coming from the base, but they couldn't see anything because the fog was so thick. The police probably got Vazques' men so we'll have to get them released from jail before we pull out Sunday night. We'll threaten to kill more hostages, and you know the gutless wonders that make the decision in Washington will free them."

"Did we ever find out what they were doing in the building? That list of tools they wanted sounded pretty bizarre."

"They could have been digging for buried treasure for all I know. It doesn't matter. Its too late for anyone to stop us now. Anything they did in that building is going to be destroyed Sunday night when we detonate the bomb." laughed Barnes as he walked into the communications trailer.

Spencer stood alone on one of Fort Adams' two hundred foot high stone walls and watched the buildings on Goat Island with binoculars in the bright sunlight. He watched the Cuban soldiers laying in the sun on the decks of the yachts docked at the marina, while others patrolled around the perimeter of the island carrying their rifles. He focused the binoculars on a group of male hostages standing beside the ocean waves crashing onto the island. Then he watched helplessly as the Cubans

JOURNEY THROUGH A LONG WINTER'S NIGHT 213

shot each of them in the head.

"When did you get here, Admiral?" asked Van Horne when he walked onto the roof to check on his spotters. "I didn't see you in the conference room."

"I came up here to be alone and think about what's going on, Robert. We're so close to that island, and we still can't do anything to help those people, or stop them from being killed. I feel helpless, and that aggravates me."

"We all feel that way, Admiral," confessed Van Horne, as he watched the sentries near Barnes' three storage trailers through his binoculars. "If it wasn't for the mines in the water I'd already be on that island killing those bastards myself," Van Horne took several seconds and calmed himself, then he asked, "Have you heard anything new from Peskov?"

Spencer shook his head as he stared at the abandoned pleasure boats moored in the harbor. "No, he cut off all communications with our negotiating teams, and hasn't said a damn word in the past twelve hours. We pleaded with him to release the women and children, but that bastard isn't going to let anyone off that island."

Van Horne squatted down and focused his binoculars on the hundreds of dead bodies laying on the rocks around the island. "Maybe he can't let anyone off that island, Admiral. The women and children may have already seen too much. Maybe they know what's really going on and who's really behind this attack."

"If he can't release the hostages, then how can this situation end peacefully, Robert? Even if he accepts our offer of amnesty to withdraw from the island, he'll still have to kill all the hostages to prevent them from talking if you're right."

Van Horne nodded his head in agreement as he pulled a piece of paper from his pocket and read several notes. "We need a ground position sensor, a camera and film, and an altimeter, delivered to Luce Hall in an hour. Any chance of getting a reconnaissance plane to take some aerial pictures of Goat Island today?"

"Why do you want aerial pictures?"

"We can use them to plot the exact location of where the escape tunnels are after we get the coordinates.

214   D'ONOFRIO

That'll give us a better idea of what those tunnels can do for us."

"I'll get you satellite pictures of the island, the details are much clearer. Don't you think we should tell our military commanders about the tunnels, Robert? I'm beginning to feel guilty about sitting on this information."

"I don't think we should tell anybody about them yet. If the military finds out about them, they may decide to put a nuclear device under the hotel tonight to destroy the island. Wouldn't you rather have a full attack plan in your hands to present to everyone when you announce your discovery?"

"You're right, Robert. I guess I'm getting caught up emotionally in all this, and you're not."

"If you have an attack plan in your hands when you tell them about the tunnels, that'll force everyone to stop and review it. Then, if they think about it, they may see the feasibility of using the tunnels to get some men onto the island."

One hour later, Van Horne, Spencer, and Owen walked into the basement of Luce Hall with Admiral Dupont and Holloway. "This is the entrance to the tunnels I told you about this morning, Commander," Dupont told Holloway as he rubbed his hand over the red foundation stones and the tunnel entrance. A look of amazement spread over Holloway's face as he stared into the lit tunnel. Then he contacted his team and asked them to meet him in the building's basement.

Marlowe and his men walked into the basement as Van Horne strapped a radio onto his back. "We're going to need someone on the radio at this end, Admiral," Van Horne told Dupont, "just in case we get into trouble in there."

"Do you mind monitoring the radio on this end while we're in the tunnels, Thomas?" Dupont asked Marlowe. "Herbert and I would like to look around down there, and I'd feel better if you're here watching over everything."

"No problem, Admiral. I've got all my men in the building so we'll be here if you have a problem."

Van Horne led Spencer, Dupont, Holloway, Owen, and two armed Navy security guards through the stone

JOURNEY THROUGH A LONG WINTER'S NIGHT   215

doorway and into the tunnel lit by the overhead light bulbs. The men appeared amazed by what they saw in the tunnel, and were shocked when they reached the underground barracks. They continued walking, and passed under the first escape tunnel, and then found the second escape tunnel at the end of the complex.

"I heard voices on the other side of this plate yesterday," Van Horne whispered to Spencer as he handed him the radio. "Now we're going to know exactly where this tunnel is located on the island." Van Horne activated the ground position monitor, and Owen recorded the series of red numbers that appeared on the device in his small notebook.

Van Horne climbed to the top of the escape tunnel as he held the small gray altimeter in one hand. He pressed the device against the bottom of the metal plate and studied its white gauge in the yellow glow of the tunnel lights. "The top of the tunnel is twenty feet above sea level," he told the others after he climbed down the ladder. Then he stepped aside while Owen took pictures of the ladder, the tunnel, and the steel plate covering it. The group walked back to the first escape tunnel where they repeated the process. Van Horne told the group the altimeter showed the top of that tunnel was eighteen feet above sea level as Owen took more pictures.

"We should search this entire building before we walk back to Luce Hall," Van Horne told the group as he opened a door and led them into the underground barracks dinning area. "We might find some maps or notes that describe the tunnels, or show where the escape tunnels open onto the island."

"He's right," agreed Spencer as he looked at the white appliances in the barracks' kitchen. He studied the kitchen's white walls and the shelves of cooking utensils left behind when the Navy abandoned the tunnel. The men searched through the barracks for an hour, but didn't find anything of value, and met in the living room.

"There's nothing we can use down here," a depressed Spencer told the group as he sat on a large green chair decorated with embroidered flowers. "I found well preserved newspapers and some canned foods."

216   D'ONOFRIO

Van Horne was discouraged by the group's inability to find anything useful in the barracks, and he leaned back in his chair dejectedly. He closed his eyes and listened to the tunnel's silence ringing in his ears as he pictured the sunlight shining on the buildings on Goat Island above. Suddenly, a faint sound in the tunnel quickly erased the images from his mind and changed the view to black. He immediately sat upright and shocked everyone when he said, "Someone is walking this way in the tunnel. Owen, kill that radio and get rid of it. Admiral, you and Dupont get into a back room and find some cover." Van Horne remembered the ambush in Luce Hall and his feeling of helplessness. Now he was determined it would not happen again.

Van Horne positioned Holloway, Owen, and the two armed guards who accompanied the group. As the sounds of footsteps and voices became louder in the tunnel, the nervous men checked their weapons as they waited for the approaching enemy. Van Horne and Holloway opened two of the barracks green access doors and stood behind them as the other men hid behind couches and chairs.

Van Horne felt his heart pounding in his chest and he stopped breathing when he saw the first man dressed in camouflaged clothing walk past the open door. He waited until the last man in the group walked past the door, then he quickly reached out and wrapped his large hand around the man's face and mouth. Van Horne pulled the struggling man who weighed about one hundred pounds violently backward. As he dragged the tall man through the doorway, Van Horne pressed the barrel of his handgun against his head. "This is for that fucking ambush yesterday morning." he thought as his finger slowly pulled back the weapon's trigger.

Holloway leaped into the hallway and tackled another soldier to the tunnel's rough stone floor. A shocked man rolled onto his back, he looked up and saw Holloway kneeling beside him with a handgun pointed at his chest. "Wait, wait," Holloway suddenly started screaming. "This is my team! Van Horne don't hurt them, this is my team!" Holloway quickly stood and pulled the man he tackled

JOURNEY THROUGH A LONG WINTER'S NIGHT 217

to the tunnel floor to his feet.

When Van Horne heard Holloway shout his warning, he quickly pulled his handgun away from the man's head and released him. He was shocked when the person he believed to be an enemy soldier frantically pulled away from him, and then angrily turned toward him. "What the hell do you think you're doing? You bastard," a startled woman shouted at Van Horne as she pulled off her hat and her long black hair fell onto her shoulders.

Van Horne looked surprised to see the angry woman standing in front of him, and for a moment he didn't know what to say. "I'm sorry, we didn't know you were Holloway's group."

"You just scared the hell out of me you bastard, and you almost shot me," shouted the upset woman after she saw his handgun. As her heart stopped racing and she became calmer, her angry frown slowly changed to a smile when she saw the concerned look on Van Horne's face. She carefully studied his large body and smiled to herself as he pushed his handgun into his shoulder holster. "I'm Lieutenant Margaret Decker, but everyone calls me Maggie," she said as she extended her hand to Van Horne.

"What are all of you doing down here?" Holloway asked as he led his group into the barracks.

"Someone in that building named Marlowe told us to come in here and find you," replied one of the men as he looked at the long wooden dining room table in a nearby room, and the old pictures hanging on the white walls. "Where are we, Commander?"

"Who lived down here?" asked another man as he looked into a sleeping area filled with varnished wooden bed frames. "A house inside a tunnel?" he asked with a startled tone in his voice.

"You can't tell anyone about what you've seen in these tunnels, or the basement of the building you were just in," Holloway warned his group as they looked around.

"We've got everything we need down here. Lets start walking back to Luce Hall," suggested Van Horne who was anxious to get the people out of the tunnel. As they

218 D'ONOFRIO

walked past the green metal storage racks bolted to the rock walls, Van Horne realized he was walking beside Decker. "I'm sorry about what I did to you back there. I hope I didn't hurt you when I pulled you through that doorway."

"I'm fine, really. You shook me up a little, but I'll be fine," she laughed as she adjusted her hat and continued walking.

"I'm surprised to see a woman on Holloway's team. I think that startled me too."

"I can do my job, and I've already proved that to my team and Commander Holloway," she replied to Van Horne's statement with a defensive tone in her voice, as her smile quickly turned to a cold stare. "Don't think I can't deliver when the situations get tough just because I'm a woman."

"I didn't mean that to sound the way it did," Van Horne immediately apologized. "I didn't expect to pull a woman through that door. I was expecting a Russian combat soldier. That's all." The smile slowly formed on Decker's lips again when she realized he was not belittling or harassing her for being a woman in the military. "How did you get to be a member of Holloway's team?"

"My father was a research scientist who spent most of his career helping to design the nuclear power plants for our Navy ships. My mom died when I was just a kid, and I spent a lot of time with my dad after that. I watched him when he was working his equations and formulas, and before I knew it he taught me everything he knew. I was just a bright kid who stayed home a lot," Decker laughed as she looked at the ridges in the tunnel's gray rock walls.

Van Horne smiled as the attractive woman continued explaining her background. "I used everything I learned from my father and went on to college. After I finished graduate school I didn't have a job, and I enlisted in the Navy after I found out they were forming this group. I'm lucky, I'm able to use what my father taught me, and what I learned in college, in this job."

"What are you doing here?" Decker unexpectedly asked Van Horne as she studied the narrow railroad

JOURNEY THROUGH A LONG WINTER'S NIGHT   219

tracks beside the tunnel wall and smiled. "That looks like something from Disney World. Do you work for the government, or are you from one of the intelligence organizations?"

Van Horne was uneasy about answering the question because he still didn't know who he could trust outside his own group. "I'm just here to help an old friend, nothing more than that." He knew his reply made no sense to the woman by the expression on her face. Although he was comfortable and at ease talking to Decker, he knew he couldn't tell her why he was really in Newport.

Thirty minutes later, the group walked into the basement of Luce Hall. Owen handed the camera to Spencer and said, "Can you have someone you trust develop this film, Admiral? We'll need some eight by ten prints of each picture."

Owen and Van Horne stopped for lunch, and then drove back to Fort Adams where they gathered the men together in the large, damp conference room. "We inspected the tunnels again this morning and they're still watertight," Van Horne told the group. "While we were down there we got the coordinates of the two escape tunnels and some pictures of them. Admiral Spencer is having the film developed for us right now. I'd like to hear the attack plan you've come up with so far, so I'll turn the meeting over to Bob Jarvis."

Van Horne asked Jarvis to become the planning coordinator because that was his task during the four years he spent in Vietnam as a Green Beret. Jarvis told Van Horne he was eager to accept the coordinator assignment because he wanted to help defend his nation. But Jarvis had a personal reason for wanting the assignment, a reason he couldn't disclose to anyone. Although the forty-five year old man appeared healthy and strong, his doctors recently discovered he was suffering from inoperable liver cancer, a disease that would take his life within a year. He knew that Newport would be his last battle, and he wanted it to be his greatest.

Spencer walked into the conference room and sat beside Van Horne as Jarvis carried several thick folders

220 D'ONOFRIO

of hand written notes to the front of the room. A floor plan of the hotel was drawn on a chalkboard, several men moved it to the front of the room. "We designed this attack plan with two major objectives in mind," Jarvis began the meeting. "The first is to get some men into the hotel garage to disarm the Russian bomb. The second is to free the President and as many other hostages as possible before the Russians can retaliate."

"To accomplish these objectives we've identified several areas of the island that must be attacked simultaneously. The first is the hotel garage where the Russians have their bomb," explained Jarvis as he turned and pointed at the hotel floor plan on the chalkboard. "The second is the hotel penthouse where we think the Russians are holding the President and his family. The third are the areas of the hotel where the Russians are holding the hostages, and the fourth is the marina and condominium buildings at the far end of the island."

"The first problem we've got to overcome is finding a way to destroy the three trailers the Russians seem to be using as a command and control center. After we destroy their command center we'll have the Russian soldiers isolated from their leaders. Without communications those men are going to be vulnerable in the first minutes of confusion during an attack."

"The sound of the explosions when those trailers are destroyed will give away the element of surprise," Van Horne thought, as he folded his arms across his chest. "The Russians will know an attack force is on their island."

"Our next problem is finding a way to eliminate the Russian soldiers in the hotel garage. We've come up with a plan we think will work. The garage's front entrance is a wide inclined cement ramp that leads from the hotel's front doors. We've worked it out so one team will move around to the back of the hotel and attack the garage through its two rear entrances. This rear attack will occur as another team attacks the garage's front inclined entrance. After they've secured the garage that team will disarm the bomb."

"Every Russian soldier on the island is going to hear

JOURNEY THROUGH A LONG WINTER'S NIGHT   221

the automatic weapons echoing through that garage." thought Van Horne as he shifted uneasily on the chair.

"We can get a team onto the convention center roof if they climb up the balconies at the rear of that three story building. They can get to the main hotel building by walking across the convention center's roof, and the roof over the hotel's indoor swimming pool. There's an inclined roof they can climb that leads directly to the suite where the President and his family were originally staying. That team can destroy the windows when the attack begins and move into the suite to rescue the President. We never considered a plan to fight our way into the hotel on the ground level, and then up eight flights of stairs to find the President. That's a plan we considered suicidal and rejected."

"Risky!" Van Horne thought as he pictured the hotel roof in the mid morning sunlight in his mind. *If the Russians see that team moving across the roof they're as good as dead without cover up there.*

"When the attack begins we plan to send another team into the convention center through the building's rear doors. They'll terminate the Russians they find in the building and free the hostages. Then they'll search for any Russian soldiers that might be hiding in the building that houses the indoor swimming pool."

"Terminate, a polite way for soldiers to say they're going to kill someone. Combat inside a building still scares the shit out of me," Van Horne thought as he remembered searching for snipers in buildings after dark. He remembered the terror and nerve racking sensation of crawling through hallways looking for gunmen, and the idea frightened him. *It's risky in close quarters. Risky, nerve wracking and very dangerous.*

"A fourth team will hit that glass walled restaurant we all call the Greenhouse Restaurant, and free the hostages we can see in there. Then that team can clear the hotel lobby from there. The teams securing the indoor swimming pool building and the Greenhouse Restaurant will then link up and ensure the areas don't fall back into the Russian's hands."

More combat inside the damn building, thought Van

222 D'ONOFRIO

Horne, as he studied the hotel floor plan drawn on the chalkboard. *I don't like this fighting inside the damn hotel, especially if the power gets knocked out and we've got to do it in the dark.*

"A fifth team will use the second escape tunnel to get onto the island. Their mission is to clear the marina before they hit the high rise condominium buildings. Our spotters reported the Russians are using the marina building as a barracks, and that team will have to clear it before they move to the condominiums."

Jarvis walked to a large map taped to the conference room wall and pointed at a red circle. "Our surveillance teams have reported there's always a Russian sentry on the hotel roof with a pair of binoculars and a radio. He's going to be a big problem because he may see the attack force moving into position on the island. We've checked out this church steeple in the city, and it could be used by a sniper with a high powered rifle to get rid of him. Then the sniper can provide some cover fire for the teams as they move across the island during the attack."

This whole plan could collapse if that damn sentry sees one of the teams moving into position, thought Van Horne, as he studied the black board. *No matter how well we plan this, that one bastard can screw up the entire operation if he sees something and radios the others.*

Jarvis closed his notes and looked at Van Horne. "That's what we have so far, Major. It's got to be five separate teams, each an independent Mike Force, all attacking at the same time, after they use the tunnels to move onto the island."

"It's risky, but I don't think there's any other way to do it," said Van Horne as he stood and walked to the front of the room. "Now we need a list of weapons, and a detailed description of how each team will hit their individual target. You've done a great job so far, so lets finish it up so the Admiral can give it to the military, and we can get out of here."

At three o'clock that afternoon, Spencer attended another meeting at the Newport, Naval Base. Adams stood at the podium obviously exhausted as he solemnly

JOURNEY THROUGH A LONG WINTER'S NIGHT   223

spoke to the group. "The Vice-President and I were just trying to figure out why General Peskov suddenly cut off his negotiations with our representatives here in Washington. I'm sorry to tell all of you we've suspended all negotiations between our State Department and the Russian government for the release of the hostages on the island. We have no plans to resume those negotiations in the near future." That news upset the men and women in Washington and Newport who believed the only way to end the situation peacefully was to keep the diplomatic channels of communication open.

"What about the negotiating team the United Nation sent to Moscow? They sent over a hundred ambassadors and representatives to help us work with the Russians to solve this problem. Weren't they able to give us any assistance?" National Security Advisor Peter Komoroski asked Curtis Wilcox.

"Unfortunately, the Russians have been telling those negotiators the same things they've reported to us. They emphatically deny they have any involvement in this situation. The United Nations is insisting the Russians work with us to end the situation, but Barakov and his officials in Moscow still say they can't help us because those aren't their soldiers on the island."

Benson suddenly stood and addressed the group, interrupting Wilcox. "I've taken the initiative and recalled Ambassador Kolbane and his entire staff from Moscow this morning. If the situation changes and the Russians wish to begin negotiating again, then I'll order them back."

"If we've cut off our only channel of negotiations, I don't see how we expect to end this situation without storming that island," commented a concerned Katherine Bardeck, the Assistant Secretary of State. "I just don't see it."

"I don't believe diplomacy or a military attack of that island will end the situation," sighed Benson as he looked around the table. "I've spoken with my advisors and we all agree on that one fact. Because of that, and if we do not see any change in the situation, I will assume the Presidency of the United States at exactly six o'clock Monday morning. The Speaker of the House, Mister

224 D'ONOFRIO

Rusczyk, will assume my office as the Vice-President. Immediately after we complete that formality, I will give the electronic codes needed to destroy Goat Island. That will be done with a Cruise missile carrying a single thermonuclear device. The ensuing explosion will destroy the Russian bomb and much of the northeastern United States. Then we'll all have to deal with the situation together."

"Our NATO allies will be told of our action fifteen minutes before we drop the bomb," Adams explained to the group. "Attacking the Russians after our bomb destroys the island will serve no useful purpose, so our military forces will immediately stand down. After we deal with the mass hysteria that's going to follow the dropping of our bomb, we'll deal with the Russian government."

Murtagh was pleased with the group's reaction to the announcement. The tension was so great that many of the officials began smoking again. Some of the men and women hadn't slept for days as they searched for a peaceful end to the situation, and they now appeared exhausted. Many of them hadn't seen their families since Sunday morning, and Murtagh knew the separation during this type of crisis was deeply affecting them. He was pleased all the events appeared to be occurring exactly as he planned, and he sat back in his chair and read several military reports as he smiled to himself.

Barnes walked through the deserted hotel that afternoon as he searched for Trembulak and Vazques. He immediately became enraged when he found them pouring drinks from a bottle of brandy in a hotel restaurant as sunlight streamed through a shattered window. "Let's not fucking overdue it with that alcohol, Vazques. You've still got a job to do here."

"There's nothing else for us to do on this island Barnes. You've assured us your military forces are not going to attack the island. Your President is safe and confined to his room, and my men are guarding all the hostages. We may as well enjoy ourselves for the few days we have left here."

"This isn't a fucking vacation, you ass hole. You're on this island to command your men, Vazques. I just

JOURNEY THROUGH A LONG WINTER'S NIGHT 225

found ten of them raping some guy outside the building, when they should have been watching that fucking harbor for American ships. They're supposed to be Russian combat soldiers, not drunken bums who haven't had a piece of ass in three years. We have a lot to lose here, so drag your ass out there and straighten out your men."

"Go check on your sentries," Trembulak told Vazques as he took the glass from his hand. "Check all your men and make sure they're doing their jobs. If they want the American women tell them to do it when they are not on duty. This is too important to jeopardize because of liquor and women."

"We need him and his men," Trembulak told Barnes after Vazques adjusted his camouflaged shirt and staggered out of the restaurant without an argument. "We would not have been this successful without him. Ease up on him, he's trying his best."

"He's an officer in the fucking Cuban Army! If that's his best, it's not good enough for me. You keep an eye on him and make sure he doesn't fuck up. If he does, you're both dead!"

Chapter Eleven

After the meeting at the Naval Base concluded, a depressed Spencer drove to Fort Adams. "I hope your men are close to finishing their plan," he told Van Horne after he slowly sat on a chair in the conference room. "I'm exhausted, but I'm going to wait around until its done. I've got to have it in my hand tonight."

"What's your rush, Admiral? We'll give you the plan so you can get it typed tonight, then we'll review it once more in the morning. You should be able to give it to the military brass before noon tomorrow. Then we're all out of here."

"Those tunnels and the plan your men are putting together may be the only way to prevent our government from using a nuclear bomb to end this insanity. We're not working with the Russian government to negotiate an end to this situation anymore. We've also agreed a conventional military strike of the island is out with the Russians threatening to detonate that bomb. Benson and everyone else in a decision making capacity is close to recommending we drop a nuclear bomb on that island. I'm really getting scared about what can happen here."

"Weren't we supposed to deliver the ransom today? Maybe that'll help make a difference and the Russians will start talking again."

"I forgot to tell you what happened with everything else that's on my mind, Robert. The Russian Air Force sent up six squadrons of fighters and threatened to shoot down our transport plane carrying the gold bullion. They forced our transport to turn back, even with its F-15 fighter support."

"I think the Russians are just as much in the dark about this whole situation as you and I are, Admiral."

"I don't know, Robert. I just don't know."

Thirty minutes later, Jarvis began explaining the numbers written on a chalkboard. "We've put together a list of the weapons the attack force will need to attack Goat Island. Each man will be equipped with a nine

JOURNEY THROUGH A LONG WINTER'S NIGHT   227

millimeter handgun equipped with a silencer. Each will carry either a CAR-15 automatic rifle with a ten inch barrel, or the longer M-16A1 version, both of which use ammunition in twenty round magazines. We picked the larger M-16s because they can be fitted with a forty millimeter grenade launcher. Each man will carry a twelve inch bayonet. The attack force will also have five to ten shotguns available. We'll need one hundred and fifty concussion grenades, one hundred white phosphorus grenades, and two hundred fifty regular grenades. We'll also need fifteen AT-4 shoulder launched rockets to destroy the Russian's communications and supply trailers, and the Stinger missiles on Goat Island."

"What about explosives?" asked Van Horne as he stood and remembered his years of combat, and the unexpected situations he encountered. "I wouldn't want to get stuck in the hotel with only hand grenades when I want to knock down a wall."

"Good idea, Major, we'll add some blocks of C-4 plastic explosives and remote detonators to the list. Every man can carry the explosives with him so it won't weigh down one man."

"How about clothing for the team?" asked Spencer. "Will it be black or camouflaged combat clothes?"

"Neither, Major. We're going to have each man dress in jeans and a black shirt. Think about this for a minute. The ambush goes bad and they see the team moving into position. That's going to cause a lot of confusion. Some of the hostages they're holding may even get free. It would be nothing for men dressed in jeans and shirts to blend in with the crowd, but men dressed in fatigues would be easy to find, and shoot."

"You're right, that's good thinking. Now, I want to discuss the problems we still don't have solutions for." Van Horne took the photographs of the steel plates covering the access tunnels from Spencer and studied one. "We still haven't come up with a way to get the plates off the escape tunnels."

"We sure as hell can't suggest the attack force use plastic explosives," warned Owen after he pictured the tunnel's rock walls and ceiling in his mind. "We don't

228 D'ONOFRIO

know how thick the rock ceiling is in that area, and an explosion might bring it down. Those tunnels would be flooded in a minute if that happened."

"There's no way to muffle the explosion, and the Russians would hear it, and know something is going on," added Malin.

"How about using acetylene torches to cut through the metal," suggested Douglas Guay who worked as an automobile mechanic. "I use one to cut through sheet metal car bodies at work. There's no noise, but there could be a lot of sparks."

"It might look like a god damn Roman candle out there in the center of the island." Van Horne commented with a smile, and that made the other men laugh. "I'll get with Marlowe and see what he thinks."

"The ceiling lights in the tunnel are the next problem we've got to consider," Van Horne told his men. "After the steel plate comes down the light from the bulbs attached to the ceiling near the escape tunnel are going to shine through the opening. If its raining, the light may create a halo effect in the raindrops over the hole. That could signal the Russians something is happening."

"If it's too bright in that tunnel where the attack force is waiting, it'll take a few minutes for their eyes to become adjusted to the dark after they climb onto the island," Jarvis warned Van Horne as he thought about the bright lights he saw on the island at night.

"What if we replace the clear light bulbs with red ones?" asked Spencer, as he wrote a note on a pad. "They may have manufactured the light bulbs in that tunnel during the war, and they may have special bases. If they don't, I'll see about getting red replacements."

"If we can't get red bulbs, then you'll have to knock out all the lights around the escape tunnels, Admiral. The darker we keep it in the tunnel, the easier it'll be for the men to see in the dark after they climb onto the island."

"Why don't we recommend killing the electricity to Goat Island just before the attack force moves out of the tunnel?" asked Paul Fuller as he studied a schematic drawing of the power transformers on the island.

JOURNEY THROUGH A LONG WINTER'S NIGHT   229

"The team could use night vision equipment to move into position on the island."

"Good idea, Paul, but I think it would be safer if we don't do anything to alarm the Russians before the attack begins. They won't expect trouble if we leave their routine exactly the way its been during the past few days. If we suddenly kill the electricity and darken the island, I think we'll be telling them something is about to happen."

"You're right, Major."

Van Horne looked to Spencer for advice about his next problem. "If the attack force gets lucky enough to free the President, they'll need a way to get him off the island."

"The Coast Guard or Marines can have a Sea Stallion helicopter ready to take him off the island. Those helicopters are equipped with infra-red systems that lets the pilots fly in the dark. We can have a couple of them hovering in the area, waiting for the attack force to call them to the hotel."

"Good, then we don't have to worry about clearing the mines in the water around the island for a landing craft." Van Horne suddenly realized how tired he was and he looked at his watch. "I think we've all had enough for tonight. Lets leave some guards here and head back to the hotel for some sleep."

At eleven o'clock, Van Horne returned to the hotel and walked into the coolness of his suite. He sat in a comfortable chair and watched Goat Island through the closed balcony door in the darkened suite. "The more I try to understand what's happening on that island, the less I understand what's really going on around me. Why did the Russians wait to grab the President here in the States when he is always overseas? Why didn't they just ask us for more help from the United Nations?"

Van Horne thought about the questions in his mind. Then he stood and pulled off his shirt and jeans before lying on the bed. He could not sleep and he stared at the patterns on the suite's ceiling created by the lights on Goat Island. "I'm not doing enough to help the people on that island. I'm letting them die by not doing

230   D'ONOFRIO

anything to help them, but I don't know what to do." As his frustration increased so did his restlessness, and no matter how much he tried to relax he couldn't fall asleep. He stood and dressed in the dark, then opened the door to his suite and walked into the hotel corridor decorated with maroon and white wallpaper.

Several minutes later, he walked through the hotel's front doors and turned toward a nearby city park. The park was located beside the harbor in the center of the city and contained many varieties of fragrant purple, red, and yellow flowers. Located around the park were ornate wooden and metal benches for the vacationers, who wanted to sit and watch the harbor during more peaceful times. Curious spectators filled the park, and Van Horne eventually found a vacant bench where he sat and watched the lit buildings on Goat Island. The night air was warm and the sound of the ocean waves crashing onto the rocks gave the impression of tranquility. The only distractions were the messages blaring from the police car's public address speakers, warning everyone to be out of the city before ten o'clock the following morning.

"That island is only two hundred yards away and I can't do anything to stop the people from dying out there!" he thought as he watched several soldiers walking across a road on Goat Island.

The bright glow of the full moon lit the ocean water, and made the high clouds look like wispy cotton. The moon's bright glow allowed Van Horne to see the vacationer's boats abandoned in the harbor, and those docked at the marina on Goat Island. He stared at the moon for several minutes and then studied the large crowds of curious people walking through the park as they talked about Goat Island.

Why would you want to bring your kids to see people slaughtered? Van Horne asked himself when he saw a man and woman with six children standing beside the water, pointing at the island. *What's wrong with these people? They're turning the brutal killing of those innocent people into a sightseeing adventure.*

Van Horne studied the people in the park for sev-

JOURNEY THROUGH A LONG WINTER'S NIGHT 231

eral minutes. As he was about to leave he saw a woman waving as she crossed a street and walked toward him. As the woman walked closer he could see it was Maggie Decker dressed in a short denim skirt and a purple cotton blouse. She pulled back her long black hair and rested it on her chest above the low neckline of her blouse. Decker was tall, and Van Horne admired her proportioned breasts and slim waist as she stood in front of him. "Hi, I couldn't get to sleep. It's such a nice night a few of us decided to drive into town and look around. I'm surprised I found you sitting out here with all these people walking around. Do you mind if I sit here with you for a few minutes?"

Van Horne was immediately concerned by Decker's presence in the park. Was it a coincidence she found him in the large crowd of people, or was someone watching him now that they were unable to kill him. He didn't know how she found him among the crowds of people unless someone was watching him. "Sure, I'd enjoy the company right now. I couldn't sleep so I decided to take a walk out here to see what's going on. I didn't think there was going to be a crowd out here watching the island after dark."

Decker was obviously upset the people were making a spectacle of the hostage situation, and she shook her head disgustedly as she sat beside Van Horne. It was the second time he saw her without a hat, and Decker's long dark hair intrigued him. "What are all these people doing here? They must be crazy to be making people's suffering into a family outing. This really upsets me."

"You're right to be upset. They seem oblivious the next world war could start right here."

"I'm really afraid of what might happen," Decker suddenly confessed to Van Horne, as she looked at the lit buildings on the island. "Not only about what's going to happen here if they detonate that bomb. Even though we're trained for something like this, we're all afraid we won't be able to do our jobs if we have to get involved in the attack. I'm really afraid of dying here."

Van Horne heard the same concerns a thousand

232 D'ONOFRIO

times before when he spoke with soldiers prior to combat operations. "You've got to settle down and relax, or you're going to burn out mentally. You've got to get control of your own fears. Try talking them out with someone, and maybe that'll help. How about your family, can you talk to them?"

"I only have my dad, and he's not too good at that kind of thing," she said as she looked at the moon. "How about you, do you have someone you can talk to?"

Van Horne momentarily appeared saddened when he suddenly saw an image of his mother and father standing beside the harbor water together. He wished he could speak to them to discuss his own fears. "No, I'm on my own. Both of my parents are dead and I don't have any other family. I've always had to fight these battles alone."

Decker felt embarrassed about asking her next question and she looked at the brick walkway lit by decorative antique brass street lights. "I've been afraid to ask you this next question. I know you're not wearing a wedding ring, but are you married?"

"No, I'm not. I don't think there's any woman who could put up with having me around all the time."

"That's good," Decker quickly replied, then she suddenly raised her hands to her face as she appeared embarrassed by her comment. "I'm sorry, I didn't mean it to sound that way. I just didn't want to be sitting here with you, pestering you, if you were thinking about your wife."

"I was just thinking how stupid I was to never have taken the time to settle down until a few years ago. I spent my life in the Army, and moved from one battle to the next. I served in Vietnam, Grenada, Iran, and Iraq, and I have the scars to prove it."

"You're lucky, you survived all those conflicts when thousands of others died," she said as she studied his face in the glow of the streetlight. His features suddenly appeared chiseled and cold, and she wondered how he would treat her if they were together in bed.

"I volunteered for those assignments, so I shouldn't be complaining about getting wounded. I asked for eve-

JOURNEY THROUGH A LONG WINTER'S NIGHT   233

rything that happened, and if I had a choice I'd probably do the same things again."

"You've already risked your life so much, and I'm sitting here telling you I'm worried about dying," said Decker as she frowned and looked at the ground. "Is there something wrong with me because I'm so worried about it?"

"Everyone has concerns about dying. No one knows if it's the end of everything, or the start of the next great adventure. I stopped thinking about dying when I was in combat, because if it was going to happen there was no sense in me worrying about it all the time."

"Why did you volunteer for the assignments that could have gotten you killed?"

"Because I really thought I could make a difference in the world. Sometimes you've got to get into the middle of the action before you can do any good. Sometimes it takes years to help, and then you still wonder if you've done anything to make the situation better."

"I've read a lot about Vietnam. That's the best I could do because I was only a kid during the war. Weren't combat tours one year? Did you stay there for more than a year?"

"I stayed for thirty-seven months," replied Van Horne with a disgusted tone in his voice. Then he leaned forward and rested his elbows on his knees when he thought about Saigon. "I was working on my fourth tour when I got shot, then they shipped me home."

"Why did you stay there so long? Didn't you want to come home after you finished your first year?"

"I really wanted to get out of there, but at the end of each tour I thought I had a good reason for staying another year. I watched my friends die because of poor planning by our commanders and intelligence organizations in Saigon. I saw them leave for combat missions and come back in black plastic body bags."

Van Horne paused as the anger and rage he felt in Vietnam slowly began to return. It quickly combined with the frustration he felt after watching the innocent people dying on Goat Island. "I became very good at what I did, and I'm sorry to say that killing

234   D'ONOFRIO

Viet Cong soldiers eventually didn't bother me any-more. I became exactly what I detested, a killer with no remorse or emotion."

Van Horne looked into Decker's eyes and could sense his inner most thoughts and secrets were beginning to frighten her as she stared at him. Then she asked, "Didn't you want to find a woman to spend your life with after you got back to the States?" Decker immedi-ately realized she didn't know if Van Horne was gay, and she regretted asking the question.

"No, I wasn't looking for anyone to be with then. I hated what I'd become and I didn't want to get close to anyone." Van Horne rubbed his neck and sat back while images of fierce battle in the Vietnam jungles suddenly filled his mind. In the distance dying men screamed his name in the dense jungle as huge explosions seemed to surround him. "The day I got wounded we got caught in an ambush fifty miles north of the demilitarized zone. I got shot a couple of times and one of my men carried me two miles to a helicopter. As he was laying me on the helicopter floor he got shot and died. I spent the next six months in an Army hospital and every day I could see that guy screaming as he was dying beside me. My friends died while they were trying to help the people of South Vietnam, while protesters back here called us baby killers. I got out of the Army for a year, but I never got my life going, so I re enlisted with the Special Forces."

"Are you still in the Army?" asked Decker as she watched a Navy patrol boat moving in the harbor. "I've never seen you in a uniform."

"I resigned two years ago. During Desert Storm I was in Saudi Arabia with the Tenth Special Forces Group. We slipped into Iraq two weeks before the ground war began. Then we began destroying Iraqi installations so our forces could go all the way to Baghdad and get rid of Hussien. I got upset when the President stopped the ground offensive and left that clown Hussien in power. I decided it was time to retire so I could find out if there's anything else I'm good at besides killing people."

"I can tell by the way you talk that you don't let too many people get close to you. Do you?"

JOURNEY THROUGH A LONG WINTER'S NIGHT   235

Van Horne quickly became cold and detached, and Decker immediately sensed it in his voice and mannerism. "The people who get close to me usually end up getting hurt. I've killed more people then you'll ever know, and that's still a problem for me."

"You killed those people during a war. You didn't walk down a city street and kill them with an assault rifle."

"Please, don't say that. It doesn't help and you don't have any idea how it feels," he replied as he pictured a Vietcong soldier he choked the life out of with his hands. "Those people are still dead, and I'm responsible for it."

"I don't know how it feels because I've never been in that situation. I'm not condemning you for anything, but I can tell it really upsets you."

"It didn't upset me at first, because if I hadn't killed those people, I would have died. It upsets me now, when I have time to think about what I've done, and realize those men won't be going home to their wives and children. I know what I'm capable of doing, and that's why I'm always worried that the people who get close to me will get hurt."

"I trust you for some reason I can't explain, and I feel like I can tell you anything. You wouldn't hurt me would you?"

"No, I don't go around hurting beautiful women because I find them attractive." Decker laughed at the comment as he gazed into her blue eyes. He decided he told her more than enough about his past, and he wanted to know more about the intriguing woman who sat beside him in the moonlight. He was attracted to the woman's outgoing personality, which was the opposite of his. "How about you, are you married?"

"I was married two years ago, but it didn't work out," she replied nervously as she twisted her long hair. "I met a consultant working at the Pentagon while I was stationed in Washington. We dated for about six months, and the next thing I knew we decided to get married. A few months after we were married my assignments began taking me away from home more often."

"He must have known that was going to happen

236   D'ONOFRIO

with your line of work," said an understanding Van Horne as he remembered his mother's emotional reaction each time he told her he was staying in Vietnam for another year.

"He knew it would happen and he seemed to accept it. But I began to notice he changed a little each time I was away. At first, I thought it was just me, but then I sensed that something was wrong. Whenever I came back from an assignment, I thought he seemed overly concerned about how long I would be home and when I would be leaving again. It got so bad I thought about retiring to save my marriage. My marriage was the most important thing in my life."

"Did your career end your marriage, or was it something else?" "Being away did have a lot to do with ending it," she laughed, but Van Horne didn't see the humor in her remark.

"I got a call from Commander Holloway late one night. He told me the Houston police found a nuclear bomb hidden in a truck by terrorists. We flew to Texas with our equipment, but none of us knew the bomb was really a dummy, or that the whole thing was just a training exercise. Our commanders had microphones hidden inside the truck so they could listen to us working, and they filmed the whole thing with telephoto lenses. Even Holloway thought it was a real bomb. We passed the test and we did an excellent job."

"That should have made everyone on your team very happy."

"It did, and it gave me the confidence to do almost anything. But that's when my life fell apart. The night we flew back to Washington, I was going to call my husband and tell him I was on my way home. Then I thought it would be a nice surprise to walk into our apartment, climb into bed, and make love to him. I didn't call and I drove home after our plane landed at Andrews Air Force Base."

Decker's hands trembled as she spoke, and she stared at the lit buildings on Goat Island so she wouldn't have to look at Van Horne. "I got the surprise of my life when I walked into our bedroom and found him laying

JOURNEY THROUGH A LONG WINTER'S NIGHT   237

beside my best friend. I walked out of the apartment and hired a lawyer the next day, and finalized my divorce four months later. I eventually found out she'd been living in my apartment whenever I was out of town, and that's why he was always so nervous when I was home. I've done all right without him."

"How old are you, Maggie?" asked Van Horne as he reached out and touched her long black hair.

Decker laughed at a question not many other men had the nerve to ask her. "I'm thirty three. I don't have any kids yet, but I want to have two babies someday. I've spent most of my life getting one Masters Degree in Nuclear Physics, and a second degree in Electrical Engineering. Now I want to know what it feels like to be a mother."

"You handle yourself very well," said Van Horne who seemed impressed by the woman's education, and the way she described her failed marriage to a relative stranger. "Are you going out with anyone now?"

"No, there's no one in my life. I didn't want to get hurt again so I put all my energy into my second degree and this job. I had a few affairs after my divorce, but nothing much came of them." Decker stared at the ground as her face flushed with embarrassment after the revelation. She looked at Van Horne after he took her petite hand in his, and she quickly regained her composure. "They were interesting diversions, but nothing more than that. I knew they weren't the right men for me."

Decker watched Van Horne as he looked into the night sky and stared at the full moon. "I don't know why, but you're different from the other men I've met. Most of the men I've met say they're intimidated by my looks, or my brains, and that's why I don't get asked out much."

"If either of those two things intimidates them, then believe me, you don't want to be with them." Van Horne laughed as he imagined how anyone could be threatened by the woman as he studied the smooth skin of her long legs and realized how relaxed he felt beside her.

"When I think I might die in the next few days, I

238 D'ONOFRIO

look back at my life and think about the things I should have, or could have done differently. Do you have any regrets about your life?" Decker asked emotionally.

"Probably that I didn't get married. I sometimes feel disappointed when I look at other men with kids and realize I don't have any. But, there's nothing I can do about that right now."

"I know that feeling. I have the same feeling every time I see a pregnant woman, or one with a baby in her arms. It's as though something is missing in my life. It's just a strange feeling women get." Decker looked around at the people walking around the park bench, then she looked into Van Horne's eyes. "Tell me something I don't have to know. Why are you here risking your life again?"

"I'm not really here by choice. I came here to help out an old commander of mine. Then this thing turned personal, I can't leave until I know there's a way to help the people on that island."

"You're something, Van Horne. You're either the luckiest man I know, or one of the most talented I'll ever know. I'm just not sure which one."

Van Horne laughed as he gently felt Decker's hair with his finger tips. "I wish I'd met you under some different circumstances, any other time than now Maggie. I wish I had more time to get to know you right now."

Decker smiled as she intertwined her small fingers into his. They stood and slowly walked through the center of town hand in hand. They looked into the small shops filled with crowds of excited spectators looking for souvenirs. They discussed their families and the events that influenced both of their lives. Three hours later, they walked into the hotel and Van Horne led her into his suite, then he closed the door quietly behind him.

Chapter Twelve

Van Horne was awakened from a deep sleep at five thirty Friday morning, when the telephone beside his bed suddenly began ringing.

"Hello," he said groggily, as he felt Decker move beside him.

The next voice he heard instantly cleared his head of the sleepy haze that filled it, and caused his body muscles to tighten.

"Van Horne, wake up! Don't say a word, just listen to me. Tabasco! We'll be there in fifteen minutes to pick you up."

When Van Horne heard the code word for trouble he reached over and gently nudged Decker. "Come on Maggie, wake up. You've got to get out of here."

Ten minutes later, Van Horne watched Decker drive from the hotel parking lot as dense gray fog blanketed the city, reminding him of the ambush in Luce Hall. As he stood in the hotel lobby, he saw a blue Chrysler New Yorker speed along the deserted street and suddenly turn into the hotel parking lot. Four of his men stepped from the car holding their handguns when it stopped, as Owen ran to the lobby. "Come on, Major, we've got the area secured." A few hotel guests packing their cars with luggage looked shocked as they watched armed men climbing into the car. Then the automobile sped out of the parking lot and turned toward Fort Adams.

"What's going on Jim?" asked a surprised Van Horne as he pushed his handgun under his shirt. "Where did you get this car?"

"We stole it from another hotel parking lot on the way here Major. We've got a problem back at the fort and we didn't use the Jeep in case we need some speed. No one is following us Angel, hit it." Nieves pressed down the accelerator until the car was weaving through the narrow seaport streets in the dense fog at fifty miles an hour. Ten minutes later the car pulled to a screeching halt in front of the fort and the men ran inside. Then they quickly led Van Horne through the fort's arched corridor toward the radio room.

240   D'ONOFRIO

"What have we got?" Van Horne asked after they walked into a dimly lit windowless room made of huge gray granite stones, where he saw eight more of his men huddled around the communications equipment.

"We finally figured out how the freaking Russians are scrambling the voice messages they're transmitting from Goat Island. We decoded a message we intercepted about an hour ago and we think you better listen to it Major," explained an excited David White, as he handed a pair of black headphones to Van Horne.

Gerald Sharpe started a tape recorder after Van Horn adjusted the headset over his ears, and the men watched the expression on his face as he listened to the conversation. Van Horne was grinding his teeth by the time the conversation finished. As he pulled off the headset he said, "I don't like the sounds of what I just heard. We better get over to the Naval Base and let Spencer hear it. I need a copy of this message on a cassette tape in ten minutes."

Thirty minutes later, Van Horne and six of his men drove onto the Newport Naval Base and slowly cruised the fog shrouded streets as they searched for Spencer's limousine. "He's not in his office damn it," commented Van Horne as the car passed the long building the government officials were using for their temporary offices.

"There's his limo," said Owen when he saw the long black car parked in front of the building that housed Dupont's office. It was another three story brownstone building built around the late eighteen hundreds that resembled Luce Hall.

Van Horne studied the groups of armed guards patrolling around the building. Then he watched hundreds of sailors frantically loading cardboard boxes into ten large military trucks backed onto the building's front lawn. "Lets walk in there like nothing is wrong and find Spencer."

Six heavily armed military police officers stopped the group at the building's front doors and demanded to see their identification cards. "Do you know where Admiral Spencer is right now?" Van Horne asked impatiently, as he stepped aside so a group of frantic sailors could carry boxes to the trucks.

JOURNEY THROUGH A LONG WINTER'S NIGHT   241

"He's probably in Admiral Dupont's office on the third floor. It's the last office on the left."

The group saw hundreds of additional sailors and civilians moving boxes of officials documents inside the large building. As they climbed the building's ornate marble stairs Van Horne told his men, "I want two of you to stay at the top of these stairs. If anyone followed us here they're yours."

Van Horne was again surprised to find forty sailors and civilian employees working in Dupont's large outer office. They were packing the personnel folders and official documents in their metal file cabinets into cardboard boxes. "Is Admiral Spencer in here?" he asked a military policeman he grabbed by the arm and stopped as he was rushing past him.

"He's meeting with Admiral Dupont," shouted another high ranking Naval officer. Then he pointed at a brown wooden door at the far end of the large office filled with nervous, shouting people.

"We work for Spencer and we've got to talk to him. It's urgent."

"Forget it. He's in there with Dupont, and Marlowe and Holloway. They said they weren't to be disturbed for anything, or by anyone." Van Horne ignored the man's warning and immediately began walking toward the office door. "Hey, I just said you can't go in there," shouted the surprised officer. Seconds later, a large group of nervous military personnel surrounded Van Horne and his men.

Van Horne studied the faces of men and women standing in front of him. He could sense they were nervous as they watched the suspicious civilian dressed in jeans and a red shirt. He immediately used their fear to his advantage and unexpectedly lunged forward with all of his strength and weight, knocking eight of them to the brown carpeted floor between the metal desks. Then he pushed two military policemen backward against Dupont's office door, violently pushing it open. When the military policemen fell onto the floor in the office they startled everyone seated inside.

Spencer immediately stood up with the other men when they saw Van Horne step into the office. "What's

242   D'ONOFRIO

going on here, Robert?" he asked when he saw Owen and the others step into the office with their handguns drawn.

"Tell your men to get out of here," Van Horne shouted at Dupont as he aimed his handgun at the floor. "I'm not in any mood to fuck around with them this morning."

"What the hell are your men doing in here, Herbert?" Dupont asked before he realized Spencer was just as confused by what he saw. "All right, everyone out. I'll deal with this myself."

"Should we call base security and get an armed detail over here, Admiral?" a timid young secretary asked Dupont as she briefly stepped into the office. She was obviously frightened by Van Horne's cold stare.

"Don't do anything until I tell you too. Shut that door on your way out."

Van Horne nodded at Owen and he and the others stepped out of the office and closed the door. "You men better have a damn good reason for barging into my office like this," Dupont shouted at Van Horne.

"I need a cassette tape recorder, Admiral," replied Van Horne as he pulled the tape from his pocket and threw it onto Dupont's desk which was covered with stacks of military communications. "I have something I want all of you to hear."

Dupont shook his head angrily as he opened a cabinet and pulled out a tape recorder. "I don't like people barging into my office making demands."

"Why don't you stop bitching for two minutes and listen to this tape, Admiral. Maybe you'll learn something. This is a radio message my men recorded and decoded an hour ago." Van Horne pressed the tape recorders buttons and the men heard static, then metallic voices.

"Black Specter this is Inca Atlas, over," said Barnes as he attempted to contact Murtagh's command center from the communication trailer on Goat Island.

"Inca Atlas this is Black Specter," replied Murtagh as he sat behind his desk in the Pentagon. "How's everything going on the island? Over."

"Everything is proceeding exactly as we planned.

JOURNEY THROUGH A LONG WINTER'S NIGHT 243

I've already started making final arrangements for getting us off this island after we execute the President. I need the exact time the boats will be here to pick us up. I'm going to explode all the underwater mines a few minutes before they reach the marina. I've also got to know what time you want us to detonate the bomb. We've got to give ourselves enough time to get clear of this island before it detonates. I don't want to be anywhere near here when that radiation starts falling out of the sky. Over."

"Roger that Inca Atlas, I'll get those times for you. What about your hostages? What'll we do if they manage to get free and contact the mainland before the bomb detonates? Over."

"That's not going to be a problem, Black Specter. We're going to kill all of them before we leave the island. The explosion will destroy their bodies, so no one will know what happened to them. Over." That response made Dupont, Spencer, Holloway, and Marlowe immediately look at one another with shocked expressions on their faces.

"Killing them will eliminate the risk of them contacting the mainland, that's good planning on your part Inca Atlas. I want you to increase the tension and anxiety today. I want you to hurt the President's wife and daughter in an area where the television camera can film it happening. I want the world to see what the heartless Russian soldiers are doing to their helpless female hostages, irregardless of who they are."

"I'll take care of that myself, Black Sector. What about the men we sent to the War College to ambush that group working in the building? Have you heard from them, or the team we sent out to eliminate the others in that fort?"

"No, I haven't heard reports about either incident," replied Murtagh as he flipped through the pages of a status report. "They must not have found the bodies in the War College building or at the fort yet. I'm sure our men are waiting with the others in the city until Sunday night. Don't be surprised if they break radio silence and contact you as our boats are approaching the island."

244   D'ONOFRIO

"Is there anything else I should know about?"

"The country is coming apart, and I've already started moving our men into position. We've only got a few more days until this is over. Contact me this afternoon with your next status report. This is Black Specter, out."

"That conversation is unbelievable! I can't believe what I just heard," said Spencer as he looked frantically at the others.

"That doesn't start to describe how I feel right now," commented Dupont.

"Who were those men?" asked Marlowe. "Who the heck are Inca Atlas and Black Specter?"

"It sounds like the two men on that tape are Americans. Neither one of them has an accent." Van Horne told the men as he thought about the voices.

"That could be a Russian delegate speaking from his consulate in Washington, Robert," speculated Spencer. "Some of those delegates speak better English than I do. Why do you think they're Americans?"

"It's just a hunch I have after listening to their voices, and tying it together with everything else we know about this situation. The pieces of the puzzle are coming together, but I just can't figure out what they're moving into position for."

"That's a ridiculous supposition for this man to be making, Herbert," Dupont told Spencer as he stood and pointed an accusing finger at him. "Why have you given your staff so much latitude in dealing with this situation?"

Spencer frowned and quickly looked at Van Horne, then back to Dupont. "These men don't work for me Stephen. They're all volunteers I asked to come here to help me."

"They're what?" asked a confused Dupont as he pounded his fist down on his cherry desk. He appeared angered by the thought Spencer deceived him. "What the hell was that story you told me in the basement of Luce Hall the other morning? What are you trying to do here, Herbert?"

"I couldn't trust anyone in Washington or the mili-

JOURNEY THROUGH A LONG WINTER'S NIGHT   245

tary after the Central Intelligence Agency received a message from Goat Island, Stephen. That's why I had to find some men outside my own organization I could work with. These men worked together during Vietnam and Iraq, and I know they can all be trusted."

"Anyone except the men I asked here to Newport could have something to do with this," Van Horne told Dupont as he took the cassette out of the tape recorder and put it into his pocket. "Think about everything you've seen happen here, Admiral. Even the men under your command could be involved in this. You can't trust anyone on this base or in Washington right now."

Dupont reluctantly agreed with Van Horne's assessment of the situation. "You may be right, Van Horne. We checked the office Herbert was using and found someone tapped all the phone lines on the base from a communications building two blocks away. Someone attached a small electronic transmitter to the switchboard and the conversations were being broadcast to a receiver somewhere. It's a sophisticated system, and someone needed the wiring diagram of the entire base to do the work."

Marlowe was extremely upset by Van Horne's comments as he thought about the distressing message. "If we can't trust anyone in our government, then what are you going to do with that tape? Who can we tell what we know?"

"I don't know, Thomas," replied Dupont as he threw his pen onto the desk. "You should have told me the truth about all this from the start, Herbert. You shouldn't have kept me in the dark."

"What difference would it have made, Admiral? What would you have done differently if you knew who I really was?" asked Van Horne who was becoming angry with Dupont's incessant complaining. "He did what he thought was right. It's time for you to stop feeling sorry for yourself and start working with us."

"I'm still shocked by what I just heard on that tape," said Spencer as he thought out loud. "If we wait for them to leave the island, and then move in to disarm the bomb, we'll be sacrificing thousands of hostages, and the President."

246   D'ONOFRIO

"We all know waiting that long isn't the answer," Van Horne told Spencer as he leaned back against Dupont's wooden desk. "Someone has to get onto that island and stop them before they leave."

Spencer stared at the blue carpeting on the office floor as he thought about the problem. Then he looked at the expression on Van Horne's face and knew what he was thinking. "If we can't trust anyone except your men, and a few of my own, then that's all we'll have to work with, Robert."

"What're you talking about, Herbert?" asked Dupont as he walked around his desk and stared at Spencer. "Use them for what? I don't want to hear that you're planning to do something that's not sanctioned by our government leaders, Herbert."

"The only way to save those hostages is for us to get onto that island before those Russians, or whoever they are, pull out," Van Horne replied coldly and with hatred in his voice. Dupont's office contained a large white marble fireplace and Van Horne walked to it and ran his hand over the polished surface for several seconds as he thought about the situation. Then turned to Spencer and said, "We can use the attack plan my men developed as the baseline. We'll just have to improvise everything else as we go."

"This is insane," Dupont told Spencer as he frantically walked around the office with his arms flailing as he spoke. "What you're proposing here isn't only ludicrous, Herbert, it's illegal. You'll be violating countless United State's laws if you attack that island without the proper authorization from Washington. Even if you get approval from Washington, you only have a handful of men here with you. Our military forces have had special training to handle these situations. You have nothing more than a bunch of civilians playing paramilitary soldiers here with you. No, I won't be a part of it, and I don't want anything to do with it." Dupont suddenly walked to a wall covered with awards given to him by the Navy. He stared at them, oblivious to the other men and the conversation for several seconds.

"Don't be deceived by what you think we are, Admi-

JOURNEY THROUGH A LONG WINTER'S NIGHT   247

ral. We're still well trained, and we can handle ourselves very well. If we couldn't, we'd be dead right now after that ambush in Luce Hall."

"You don't know how stupid and irresponsible you sound right now, Van Horne. You're civilians planning to attack combat soldiers on that island. This isn't a game, or a move, and you're not Rambos."

"There's no denying we've all been out of the service for a while. But all of the men I asked to come to Newport dropped everything, their lives, their families, everything, to come here and help us without any questions."

"You're not using your head. You're not soldiers! You're going to get yourself and all your men killed."

"Then tell me how you think we should deal with this, Admiral? Based on what you know right now, what would you do next?" asked Van Horne who was obviously irritated with Dupont's responses. "Call Washington and tell them you know the Russians are going to kill the hostages? Call a news conference and let the press listen to what's on that tape. The minute you do that they're going to execute everyone on that island because they'll know someone breached their security."

"I'm just not convinced we as a group can handle this entire situation. There's a million things that could go wrong. Things that can get you and more of my men killed."

"I'm sorry, Admiral, but I have to agree with Van Horne," said Marlowe as he leaned forward on the chair. "I don't like the idea anymore than you do, but it looks like we're on our own here."

"If you tell your commanders what you heard on that tape," Spencer warned Dupont, "you know there's a chance they'll detonate that bomb to cover their tracks if they're part of this conspiracy. They're not going to leave anything or anyone on that island that might incriminate them if they suspect someone is getting suspicious about a connection to our military or government."

Holloway startled Dupont when he said, "I can't stand around and let that happen, Admiral, even if it means putting my career on the line. I want to be part of whatever Van Horne is going to do on that island. My

248   D'ONOFRIO

team has the expertise to disarm that bomb, and getting them to help us is the only way to prevent it from being detonated."

"I have to agree, Commander, Herbert's concerns do seem to be legitimate. If someone in our government is behind this, it would explain how those Russian soldiers got into this country and onto the island so easily," said Dupont who turned toward the group and reluctantly agreed with the other men's remarks. "I have to agree with all of you, we've got to stop them."

Van Horne was relieved everyone was in agreement. He carefully studied a large map of Newport Harbor fastened to the office's brown paneled wall, then he turned back to the group. "This has to start with Marlowe and his group. You've got to get my men and Holloway's team onto Goat Island. Holloway, you've got to come up with a plan for disarming the bomb. Admiral Dupont, you've got to arrange for an area here on the base where Admiral Spencer can coordinate the attack."

"I've already got the weapons your men wanted, Robert. Some of my men are guarding them in a warehouse at the Quonset Point Air Station," said Spencer as he opened his briefcase and found a folder filled with eight by ten color photographs. "These are satellite images of Goat Island taken yesterday."

"What are these two white circles on the pictures?" asked Van Horne after he handed each man a photograph.

"We superimposed the coordinates of the escape tunnels you took from the ground position monitor onto each picture. One tunnel is in that grassy area near the hotel parking lot in the center of the island. The second tunnel wasn't as easy to find. Your coordinates show it's somewhere under the marina building!"

"That would explain the voices I heard on the other side of the metal plate. That's going to be a problem. Maybe a big problem."

"Did you get the weather forecast for the next forty eight hours?"

"The National Weather Service is predicting a large low pressure ridge and a cool front will move into New

JOURNEY THROUGH A LONG WINTER'S NIGHT   249

England sometime today. They're calling for three to four inches of rain beginning this afternoon."

"Good, we like working in the rain," commented Van Horne as he put the pictures into the folder. "I haven't seen or heard a news report in the past three days. How are the people across the country handling what's happening here, Admiral?"

"Things aren't too good out there, Robert. A lot of people are worried the United States and Russia are moving toward a nuclear confrontation, and that they'll die during the war they're expecting. The people seem so frightened the Federal Reserve decided to close most of the banks across the country. The people were standing in lines for blocks to withdraw their savings. The Federal Reserve had to close the banks because they don't have that much cash available to give out all at once. That started a few large riots in some cities, and the police ended up shooting some people while they were trying to restore order."

"I really feel bad for those poor people. How about the stock market?"

"They had to close the American, New York, and Chicago exchanges two days ago because all three took the largest plunge in history. They'll reopen after we've resolved this situation and the people settle down. We've received a lot of reports that people are trying to sell their gold and jewels on the city streets to raise cash. Most of the supermarkets across the country have sold out of everything because people are hoarding food in case there's a war. People are hoarding gasoline too, and most gas stations have been pumped dry. Gun shops across the country are reporting long lines of people waiting to buy rifles and handguns. They want the weapons to protect themselves from the Russian invasion they're convinced is coming, and to safeguard what they've hoarded after the nuclear war."

"They must be terrified after what they've seen happen here," said Van Horne as he shook his head.

"They are, the people are crowding to the airports trying to get flights out of the country. A lot of them are trying to get to Australia and Greenland to avoid the

250   D'ONOFRIO

nuclear war they're expecting. The people are so angry that a large crowd tried to burn down the Russian embassy in Washington earlier in the week. Parts of Washington are already a ghost town because many people who live and work there think that's the first place that's going to be destroyed by nuclear missiles when the war begins. The looters have ransacked and burned many of the stores, and much of Washington already looks like a war zone. We've even had some unbelievable reports of people committing suicide across the country because they can't deal with the thought of dying in a nuclear confrontation."

"You're kidding," commented a shocked Van Horne. "Why would they do that when they don't even know what's going to happen?"

"Most of the people have already convinced themselves war is inevitable. They've seen the television news reports showing the Russian soldiers executing the hostages on Goat Island all week. They think that if the Russians will kill defenseless people that way, then they won't care about killing millions of others with nuclear weapons."

"I didn't think things were so bad already. I was stupid not to realize this would happen. What's the government doing to help the people deal with the situation?"

"Vice-President Benson has been addressing the nation on the radio and television every six hours for the past three days. He's trying to reassure the people this country is not going to war with Russia, but nothing seems to calm them down. We have psychologists on the television and radio telling people to relax and settle down. Nothing is helping, and as we move closer to Peskov's deadline of Sunday night, the people are getting more frightened and nervous. We don't have any idea what effect all of this tension and anxiety is having on the children."

"I really feel sorry for those people, they must feel helpless. They can't do anything but sit back and wait to see what's going to happen to their country, and the rest of the world."

"A lot of the low lifes think they've got nothing to

JOURNEY THROUGH A LONG WINTER'S NIGHT   251

loose now, and crowds have started looting buildings and robbing stores in a lot of cities. They think the world is going to end in the next few days and they're trying to accumulate as much as they can before it goes. Instead of working together, and helping one another through this crisis, the bastards are out there robbing each other. I read a report about a god damn vigilante group killing Russian immigrants in the Los Angeles area. They think the Russians in this country have something to do with what's happening on Goat Island, and we both know that's bull shit. Those vigilantes are no better than the Russians killing the hostages on Goat Island."

"Have many people driven into Canada and Mexico to wait out the end of the week there?"

"Hundred of thousands have already moved north to Canada, but the Canadian government has warned Washington they may have to close the border. There's just no place to put those people and no way to feed all of them in emergency shelters. Mexico is letting our people into their country for now, but there's no place for them to stay down there either. The situation is becoming critical, and the governments of Canada and Mexico are both expressing their concerns about a United States' nuclear confrontation with Russia. They're worried their land may become contaminated with radiation, or that they may become targets too."

"How are people in the other countries dealing with this situation? Has the tension spilled over there too?"

"It's all coming apart, Robert. If someone wanted to cause mass hysteria around the world with this situation, they should be happy when they see what's going on today. The entire planet seems paralyzed from India, to South Africa, to Japan. Everyone is terrified and expecting the worse."

"Well, we've got to end this shit. Whoever we heard on that radio is using the people's fear to their advantage for something. Its time for us to screw up their plans." Van Horne quickly looked at his watch. "Its already seven thirty. I'm going to stop back at the hotel for a quick shower and to get something to eat. Then I'm heading over to the fort. I'll meet you there."

252 D'ONOFRIO

Forty minutes later, Van Horne and his men drove to Fort Adams and he gathered everyone together in the stone conference room at nine o'clock. He wondered what reaction they would have after he explained his ideas to them. "I have something I want all of you to hear," he told them, then he played the taped conversation and watched the concern on their faces.

After listening to the message several times the stunned men began discussing the conversation. "This blows a hole in all of our government's strategic planning," commented Robert Mahoney as he closed his notebook and sat back in his chair. "Nothing our freaking government officials do or say while they're negotiating with the Russian government will help those hostages. They're all as good as dead."

"What'd you think our options are right now, Major?" asked Joseph Manley as he remembered serving in combat under Van Horne.

Van Horne thought about how he would answer the question as he slowly sat on a long table. He knew attacking the island meant asking the men to risk their lives again, and he wasn't sure how they would react when they heard his idea. "I think the only way we can save the hostages is to hit the island ourselves, without any help from our military. I really don't know who to trust right now except Admiral Spencer, and some of Dupont's staff."

Some of the men seemed shocked to hear Van Horne's reply and they sat back in their chairs and stared at him with surprised expressions on their faces. "During the week I know some of you began to realize our attack plan might be the only way to save the hostages and prevent the Russians from detonating that bomb. I didn't have you develop that plan expecting we'd be the ones to implement it."

Van Horne was trembling as he spoke and he suddenly stood and began pacing. "I want you to remember that none of you have to get involved in this. You're not part of the military anymore. A few years ago we had no choice but to be part of the war in Iraq, but now the situation is different. Whether you get involved here, or walk away from this shit, it has to be your own personal

JOURNEY THROUGH A LONG WINTER'S NIGHT 253

decision without any outside pressure. I can't tell you what to do here, but I can remind you that you might get killed on that damn island. You've got to consider the careers you've worked so hard to establish since you left the military. Your main concern should be your families and what they'll do if something happens to you."

For a reason he couldn't explain, Van Horne suddenly saw an image of his parents standing together on a sandy beach in the bright summer sun when he was a young boy. He thought the image might have appeared because he desperately wanted to talk to them about the fears he was now experiencing. "You've got families, your parents, and many other people who need you today. We still don't know who we're fighting on that damn island, or how well they're trained. If any of you feel that this damn idea of mine is too risky, or has commitments on the outside that are much more important, you know everyone in this room will understand if you want to get out now."

Van Horne let the men think about his warning for several minutes as he studied the huge gray cut stones that formed the conference room walls. He momentarily thought about his father and what advice he might give to his son now. He knew his father would tell him to follow his instincts and do what he thought was right to help the people on the island. Van Horne suddenly thought about the day he was shot during the ambush in Vietnam, and the pain he experienced afterward. The memory caused him to remind the men of the risks they would be taking. "We can all get onto that island without anyone seeing us, and two minutes after the attack begins they can detonate that bomb. No matter how much planning we do, there's always the possibility we won't be able to stop them from detonating the bomb. I want you to think about that when you're deciding what to do here."

David White was sitting at a table at the back of the conference room and he stood after he thought about Van Horne's comment. "What are you going to do, Major? Are you staying or bailing out?"

"You know me well enough by now, Dave. You know

254   D'ONOFRIO

how I feel about innocent people getting hurt. If I walk away from here now, then I'll be deserting those people, and myself."

"Well, while I was flying to Newport it hit me that I might get involved in this with you, Major. If you're going to lead a team onto the island, then I guess I'm going with you."

"I can't stay, Major, I'm sorry," explained Martin Hourigan as he stood and studied the faces of the men seated in the room around him. "I want to stay and help but I can't, I just can't. My daughter is so sick I didn't want to leave her to come here, but I knew you needed me. I've got to be with my wife to see her through this. I'm sorry, I can't let her do it alone."

"That's all right, Martin, your family comes first. That's why we're here discussing this. If you can, I'd like you to stay until we complete the planning phase of the attack. Then we'll get you out of here."

"Sure, that's not a problem, Major," replied Hourigan as he sat down self-consciously. He seemed surprised when the men seated around him expressed their concerns about his daughter's health as they tried to console him.

John Walsh was wounded several times during Operation Desert Storm and he momentarily remembered the pain he experienced each time. The thought frightened him and his fists clenched in desperation, but then he pictured the dead hostages laying on the rocks around the island in the bright sunlight, and his hands slowly relaxed. "I'm in too, Major. I can't leave here and wait to see my country destroyed. We don't know how far the radiation is going to drift, and I can't let people die because I didn't do anything to stop this."

"I'm not going to let all the hostages on that island die, Major," said John Grogan as he thought about his wife and three children. "If my wife and kids were hostages on that island I'd be up here trying to find a way to rescue them right now. I can't just say the hell with those people because they aren't part of my family."

"I'm sorry, I can't stay either, Major," said Frank Morrisroe as he watched his hands trembling. "I know

JOURNEY THROUGH A LONG WINTER'S NIGHT 255

what it's like to get shot, and I can't stand the thought of getting wounded again. I won't be any good to you on that island in this condition. I'm sorry, Major, I just can't handle the pressure anymore." Van Horne didn't know what to say and he only nodded. Then he asked Morrisroe to stay until they completed the attack plan.

Edward Gallo thought about the implications of the attack, and how it might affect the nation. "If they detonate that bomb this country will be paralyzed, and it'll take three generations to rebuild it. We'll be an easy target for other counties the whole time. It's time to say enough, and stop the killing."

"Are you doing this for revenge?" Van Horne cautiously asked Gallo. "Remember what happened to me, I almost got myself killed because I wanted to kill the Viet Cong."

"I guess I am, Major. You all know I work as a physicians assistant in a hospital. My job there is to save lives, so I guess what I'm saying here is a contradiction. I know you don't like hearing that, but I'm staying because I want revenge."

"If you're going to kill for revenge, how many bodies will it take to appease you? Everyone has a limit to the amount of revenge they need."

"I don't know, Major. In this situation, when I think about all the bodies I've seen on the rocks around the island, maybe I'll never reach my limit. I just don't know."

"He's right, Major, I feel the same way. Count me in too," John Foran shouted across the room as he pulled his handgun from his shoulder holster. "If I have to use this again, then I'll have to deal with it myself. For years I've had to deal with what I did in Vietnam. This one is for our own people, and it's right here at home."

Eventually, after the other men thought about the consequences, each told Van Horne he would stay. "I think the best time to hit the island is tonight. If the soldiers on that island are working with someone in our government, they're probably receiving intelligence reports saying none of our military forces are preparing to attack the island. But they won't know about us. For a few minutes we're going to have one hell of an advan-

256 D'ONOFRIO

tage. Ok, lets get the plan and figure out who's going to be doing what when we're on the island." Van Horne and the group discussed the attack plan for the next three hours, during which time the men expressed many concerns, and discussed a few new ideas.

Spencer, Dupont, and Marlowe walked into the fort's conference room at one o'clock that afternoon, and several minutes later, Holloway and his team followed them inside. They saw a large satellite photograph of Goat Island Spencer provided laying on the room's cement floor with brown metal folding chairs arranged around it. Van Horne and three other men stood on several wooden planks suspended over the picture on cinder blocks taken from the piles of construction supplies outside the fort. As they discussed the attack they pointed at the details on the picture below them. When Van Horne looked up and saw Decker they briefly smiled at one another.

"We're just going over some details of our plan," Van Horne told Dupont as he pointed at a red circle drawn around a building in the photograph. "This is Saint John's Church. It's on a street right beside the harbor and directly across from Goat Island. We're going to need a sniper team in this steeple, but we can't spare any of our men. Can we use some of your men, Admiral?"

Dupont did not approve of risking more of his men in the attack, but he wanted to provide Van Horne with as much assistance as he could. "I can find some men to handle that job for you. I'll ask some of my military police, they're all good shots."

"I'd like to use my men if you don't have a problem with that, Admiral," Marlowe suddenly told Dupont after he knelt beside the photograph and studied the church and the details of the buildings on Goat Island. "Some of my men can help Van Horne's men get onto the island, while the others move into this church steeple. We're already involved in this so why bring in someone else we can't trust?"

"I know you're not going to listen to me and leave when we evacuate the rest of the base, Thomas. If I can't talk you into leaving, I may as well give you all the help

JOURNEY THROUGH A LONG WINTER'S NIGHT   257

I can," commented Dupont who was extremely concerned about his junior officer's well being, and that of his men. "All right, that's your part of the operation. Just take care of your men in that steeple."

"We're going to need some plastic explosives to shatter the hotel's plate glass windows," said Van Horne as he quickly flipped through a handful of pictures and handed one to Marlowe. "I want to shatter these windows, but I don't want to hurt anyone who might be inside the rooms."

"That's not a problem. I'll have my men make something for you this afternoon. We'll check the copies of the hotel building plans your men got from the town hall and figure out how thick the windows are, and what we'll need."

"We'd like to get onto the island around midnight and move into position to hit them about two o'clock. That gives everyone about twelve hours to get ready. Does anyone have a problem with that time schedule?"

Spencer suddenly stepped forward with a concerned look on his face. "Why not wait until tomorrow night and give your men some more time to rest and prepare for the attack, Robert? It seems like we're rushing into this."

"We can't wait, Admiral. If we have a problem in the tunnel tonight we can always work out a solution and postpone the attack until tomorrow night. If we wait until tomorrow night and we have a major problem we may never have a chance to pull this off. It's got to be tonight."

"Will your team be ready to move onto the island with us?" Van Horne asked Holloway when he saw all of his team members appeared to be extremely nervous.

Holloway studied his people and realized they looked terrified. Then he realized his body was trembling from fear and anticipation. "We'll have all of our equipment ready. We won't know exactly what we're up against until we see the bomb. I can't promise we'll have it disarmed in ten minutes, but we'll get it done as fast as we can."

"One of our teams will get you to the garage, but you'll have to wait here in the shadows until they secure the area." Van Horne then pointed at a large deck

258   D'ONOFRIO

surrounded by evergreen bushes behind the hotel building in the aerial photograph.

As the group discussed the attack they had no idea Barnes, Trembulak, Vechesloff, and Vazques were watching the President's wife and hysterical daughter being dragged out of the hotel. The women struggled with the soldiers who pushed them to a grassy area where Barnes knew the news reporters could easily record what was about to happen. Barnes pulled on his black knit hood to conceal his identity and walked outside the building. He was upset thick gray clouds obscured the sun and hoped the news cameramen would be able to film the women's faces so they could be identified.

"Get their clothes off," Barnes told Vazques' men as he watched a small crowd of reporters standing in the city on the streets. He was angry the police had already forced all of the spectators and most of the news crews to evacuate the city. "Make this good, its for television," he laughed as he looked at Vazques.

The President's wife stepped in front of her crying daughter as Vazques' men moved toward them. "Stay away from my daughter you bastards," she screamed as she viciously lunged at a soldier who fell to the ground screaming after she savagely kneed him in the groin. "I'm warning you to stay away from her," she shouted as she moved toward another soldier who immediately stepped backward.

"Come on you fucking ass holes," Barnes screamed at Vazques's men as he stepped behind them. "You're letting a woman get the best of you." After Barnes' ridiculing ten soldiers surrounded the two women and quickly overpowered them. As the women pleaded and screamed the soldiers cut their clothing with bayonets and pulled it off their bodies.

"Take the mother," Barnes told Vazques as he pointed at the struggling older woman laying on her back. "I want the daughter for myself!"

"Please, please don't do this to me," the President's naked daughter screamed as the soldiers forced her onto the grass on her back.

"I always wanted to fuck this terrific body of yours

JOURNEY THROUGH A LONG WINTER'S NIGHT   259

when I saw you in the White House!" Barnes laughed as he slowly lowered himself onto the naked woman while the Cuban soldiers stretched her legs painfully apart. "I hope you're going to enjoy this as much as I am!" Barnes quickly pulled the mask off his face, then forced the screaming woman's mouth open with his hand. As she struggled under him he began forcing the black material into her mouth, choking her with it as he penetrated her savagely.

"I'm sorry this had to be done, but we must convince the people of your nation we are still a threat." Trembulak explained as he stood beside the President in the penthouse suite and stared at the low gray clouds hanging over the city. He listened to the two women screaming hysterically through the open balcony door on the grass beside the edge of the island.

The President forced the image of Vazques' men attacking his wife and daughter from his mind as he became enraged. "You had to rape my wife and daughter to prove you're a threat! Killing the other people on this island wasn't enough for you," shouted an exhausted Rockwell. The President quickly lifted a large red lamp off a table and prepared to throw it at Trembulak. A nearby Cuban soldier knocked it from his hand and it shattered into hundreds of pieces when it fell onto a wooden coffee table.

"For that stupid and senseless act I'm going to leave your wife and daughter with my men for a few hours," laughed Trembulak after he composed himself. "I'm sure they can keep two attractive women entertained while you listen to them from up here."

The Cubans pushed the President back into the suite's bedroom where he sat on the unmade bed and buried his face in his hands. "My government has deserted us. I knew Brad wouldn't be able to help us, and now those Russian animals are using my wife and daughter. We're never going to get off this island alive." Then Rockwell began to cry as he lifted a pillow and buried his unshaven face in it.

Several hours later, Vechesloff stood in the lounge located on the hotel's top floor. He stared at the shops

260 D'ONOFRIO

and houses that lined the deserted city streets in the afternoon rain. "It's hard to imagine this city has been here for hundreds of years, and that it's going to be destroyed in just a few days."

"What the hell does that matter to you?" laughed Barnes as he poured himself a full water glass of whiskey, then smashed the empty bottle against a wall. "What the fuck do we care about New England anyway? There's only a bunch of no brain farmers growing fucking potatoes around here."

"But this is a historic city."

"Destroying a city is nothing! I did a lot worse than this in Vietnam! I poisoned a well in North Vietnam one time and then waited around to see what would happen. I got a kick out of watching hundreds of people rolling around on the ground after they drank that water. It took hours for some of them to die. I even fucked a good looking young girl a couple of times while she was dying. She was nice and tight when the poison made her muscles contract. This is no different, and you shouldn't be worrying about this place. You should be worrying about your own people right now."

Vechesloff thought about his sister, and her long brown hair and pretty face. He imagined what he would be feeling if she was a hostage on the island with Barnes. Then Barnes heard Vechesloff recite several lines of poetry:

> 'As a child I walked with my mother
> in the deep snow, On a journey
> through a long winter's night,
> And at the end we found our home,
> Where I felt the warmth of the fire,
> And the tranquility of sleep'

"What the hell was that?" asked Barnes, "Russian poetry?"

"My mother taught me that poem when I was a little boy. I've always associated it with the safety and security of being home with my parents. During the past few days I've felt like the child in that poem. After we're done here everything will return to normal in my nation, and I'll return home to the safety I've always found there."

JOURNEY THROUGH A LONG WINTER'S NIGHT 261

"Philosophy and poetry were never two of my strong points," laughed Barnes in response to the poem, then he swallowed the rest of his drink. "Killing people is what I'm best at. Come on, lets check on our hostages. I saw a good looking redhead in a ballroom confinement area. I know she wants to get to know me intimately this afternoon."

At three thirty that afternoon, Gatting found Van Horne and Marlowe seated at a table discussing how to remove the steel plates that covered both exit tunnels. "The equipment and weapons Admiral Spencer got for us are outside in four trucks, Major. I'm going to need some help getting the boxes into the fort." The men quickly stacked the boxes of various types of ammunition in the fort's wide stone central corridor, and ten men began loading magazines with bullets. Another group began unpacking and inspecting the weapons in the fort's conference room.

At the same time Holloway and his staff met in a smaller conference room with their equipment and manuals. "I want to discuss how we're going to disarm the bomb while we have the time right now. We've got to get it done fast, but we've got to be careful and watch for booby traps. If we discuss what each of us is going to do when we get to the bomb, we may eliminate some confusion when we get into the garage. I'd like to have the device disarmed fifteen minutes after we start working on it."

At five o'clock that afternoon, Van Horne took a break and walked out of the conference room for some fresh air. He was surprised to see Decker sitting on the cool stone floor inside the fort's main doorway as she watched the light rain falling on the buildings on Goat Island.

"Hi, what are you doing out here alone?" he asked as he sat beside her and leaned back against the stone wall.

"I was just thinking about what's going to happen on that island in a few hours," she replied as she grasped his hand. Then she stared at the raindrops making circles in a large puddle outside the door and wondered if she would be alive in twenty four hours.

"Stop worrying, Maggie. Why are you thinking about it so much?"

262   D'ONOFRIO

"I'm worried I'm going to die out there. I do get to do that. I said I would help disarm that bomb, but maybe I'm not strong enough to get through this." Then she suddenly wrapped her arms around his neck and began crying, a combination of the extreme emotional stress and her own fears breaking through her normally calm exterior.

Van Horne was relieved Decker was crying and he held her tightly. He had seen exhausted and frustrated soldiers crying in the foxholes and dirt trenches in Vietnam, and watched as the anxiety unexplainably fade from their minds after their momentary breakdowns. "You're not going to die, Maggie. You've got to believe me."

At six o'clock Friday evening, Marlowe and his men arrived at Fort Adams carrying canvas bags. "The plastic explosives we made to shatter the hotel windows are in these bags. We've filled the other bags with plastic explosives, remote detonators, and the electronic triggering devices your men wanted."

"What's it look like in the tunnels? Do you think we're going to have any problems down there?"

"I really don't think so. I have two teams preparing our equipment in the tunnels right now. One team is mixing the acid paste we're going to use to cut through the first plate. There won't be any sparks or noise, and we shouldn't have a problem getting through the metal. My other team is attaching small plastic explosive charges to the bottom of the plate under the marina. We've already braced up the stone walls and ceiling around that escape tunnel with welded metal supports. There's no chance of the tunnel walls collapsing during the explosion. That plate is going to come off hard and fast."

Van Horne pictured the exterior walls of the yellow two story marina building on Goat Island. "They must have built the marina over the damn escape tunnel without even knowing it was there. Or, if they knew it was there, the Navy may have asked them to cover it. Whatever. What about you and your men?"

"I'll be at the first tunnel when you get there, and my snipers will be in the church steeple while we're cutting through the plate. They'll warn us if they see

JOURNEY THROUGH A LONG WINTER'S NIGHT   263

anything that might be a problem on the island. After we get you onto the island I'll head over to the church and stay with my men."

"Thanks for all your help and ideas," Van Horne told Marlowe with a smile. "Come on, lets take a look around." The two men checked a few of the handguns the group was preparing and then checked on the men sitting on chairs in the stone corridor loading ammunition magazines.

"Everything seems to be going like we planned," said Spencer when he arrived at Fort Adams thirty minutes later and saw the men preparing the weapons.

"We're looking very good, Admiral," replied Van Horne as he lifted a five inch long, forty millimeter rocket propelled grenade, and nonchalantly tossed it toward Spencer. "Everything is going according to schedule."

Spencer fumbled with the grenade as he tried to catch it, then he gently put it back on the table with an upset look on his face. "Its six o'clock, Robert, and I'm ready to serve dinner. Why don't we give everyone a break?"

Van Horne walked to the front of the room and waited until the men stopped talking. "We're going to serve a small dinner, compliments of Admiral Spencer. If you walk into the hallway, and through the last door on the left, I think you'll be as surprised as I was."

The men walked out of the conference room and into a large dining room made of huge granite stones. The cantilevered ceiling gave the impression the room belonged in a medieval fortress in England. Tables and chairs filled the room and fifteen large turkeys lay on platters along with hams, roast beef, steaming bowls of mashed potatoes, hot rolls, and an assortment of other foods. Spencer also provided coffee, milk, and juice for the men. Ten minutes later, Marlowe and his Seabees, and Holloway's group, joined the men serving themselves dinner.

The group finished dinner several hours later, and were talking to one another over their last cups of coffee when Van Horne walked between the tables. "It's nine o'clock, and we've got about three hours before we have to start packing our equipment. I think we should get

264   D'ONOFRIO

some rest until then." Van Horne's men walked to the area where they assembled cots Spencer had delivered to the fort. Holloway and Marlowe moved their teams to different rooms in the fort where they planned to rest.

Van Horne waited beside Spencer as he finished speaking into a portable telephone. "My men just finished installing the red light bulbs in the tunnel, Robert. We've evacuated the Newport Naval Base and the entire city. In fact, we've evacuated almost all of the state. It's up to you now, Robert, you and your men."

The two men walked into the large conference room they used for their planning meetings. Van Horne walked between the chairs until he was standing in front of a large map of Rhode Island. He stared at it for several seconds then asked Spencer, "Are there any aircraft carriers in the area or have they already been moved out to sea?"

"There's nothing around here right now, Robert. We moved all the ships in Maine, Massachusetts, and Connecticut, south and east when we found out about that Russian bomb. Why?"

Van Horne thought about a combat operation in Vietnam when a low flying jet frightened the enemy and saved his life. "We might need some kind of a diversion if things really get hot on the island. I'm sure the noise of an F-14's engines might give us the edge for a few seconds if we're in trouble."

"I might be able to find a few fighters for you, but that'll mean bringing pilots and navigators we don't know into this operation. I don't know if we'll get many volunteers for a mission that's unsanctioned. I'll try to arrange for three jets and a refueling tanker to be airborne near New York City. If you need them they can go supersonic and be here in a couple of minutes."

Van Horne lifted a pad and began writing as he spoke. "If you can find them use the names Whiskey Echo, Yankee November, and India Tango."

"I know the Nimitz and her carrier task force is somewhere in the north Atlantic right now. The Navy stationed it there to prevent the Russian fleet from moving this way. The task force commander is a friend of mine

JOURNEY THROUGH A LONG WINTER'S NIGHT 265

and I know I can trust him. Why don't you get some rest while I'm checking on that? I'll wake you up in a couple of hours."

"You're right, I'm really tired, Admiral." Van Horne fell onto his cot several minutes later without removing his shirt or jeans. He didn't dream or have nightmares of the war as he thought he might while he slept. Instead, his mind found peace during an uneventful and quiet period of rest.

After what felt like only a minute, he was awakened by a hand on his arm and he looked up to see Spencer. "Its eleven thirty, Robert. Time to get ready."

Van Horne slowly lowered his head back onto the pillow. "I don't think I'm ready for this mentally, or physically, Admiral. I'm so worried right now I've got the shakes." He lay on the cot for several minutes before walking to the area where his men were sleeping to wake them.

Chapter Fourteen

At 12:15 A.M. Saturday morning, Van Horne and Spencer walked toward the fort's conference room together. They stopped in the fort's main entrance built with large gray stone blocks that formed an arched ceiling over their heads. They stood in the darkness and watched the heavy rain falling onto the large floodlights shining on the fort's exterior walls. The bright lights make the raindrops shimmer as if they were diamonds.

Van Horne stared at the steam rising off the floodlights when the rain evaporated, and it reminded him of mornings in Vietnam. Then he suddenly felt the same emotions he experienced before battles in Vietnam and Iraq as his adrenaline began flowing, and his excitement increased. "Here, this is for you," he told Spencer as he pulled an envelope from his jeans pocket and handed it to him.

"What's this?"

"My will, I wrote it a few minutes ago."

"You what?"

"I never took the time to a have a lawyer put one together for me. If anything happens to me I want you to have the tree farm, it's yours. Use the trees to generate some income and turn part of it into a camp for kids with emotional and physical problems. Maybe we can still make a difference in the world, Admiral."

Spencer stared at the rain falling in the floodlights for several seconds. Then he said, "When I flew to Virginia I only wanted you to come here as my advisor, Robert. I never intended for you to get this deeply involved." He paused and Van Horne seemed shocked by his next comment as he watched Spencer's silhouette in the darkness as the rain seemed to increase in intensity. "You know my wife could never have children. But if I had a son, and he turned out anything like you, Robert, or any of those other men you brought here, then I'd be very proud of him today."

Van Horne didn't know how to respond to Spencer's surprising comment. "Thanks, Admiral. We're

JOURNEY THROUGH A LONG WINTER'S NIGHT   267

doing what we think is right here, nothing more than that." Van Horne watched Goat Island as he thought about the impending battle, and he tried to push Spencer's words of praise from his mind. He knew he wasn't a hero, just an unlucky bystander caught up in the crisis.

"All right, Robert," sighed Spencer after he looked at his watch, "let's find your men." He knew that no matter what he said he couldn't get close to Van Horne as he mentally prepared for combat. Spencer remembered Van Horne always became cold, unemotional, and detached as his mind dealt with the possibility his men might be killed. They walked into the conference room and found the men waiting for them dressed in jeans and combat boots, and black knit shirts Spencer delivered to the fort with the other supplies. Every man was wearing a black nylon shoulder holster they found packed in the wooden boxes with the weapons.

Kevin Ryan motioned to Spencer and then led him to a quiet corner of the large conference room. As Ryan leaned against the stone wall with white paint peeling off; he clenched his hands together nervously. Ryan was stationed in Saigon as a Green Beret advisor during his second tour of Vietnam, and that was where Spencer first met him. Spencer remembered Ryan married and had three children after returning to the United States. "How are you this morning, Kevin?" asked Spencer.

"I'm OK," replied Ryan as he attempted to conceal his nervousness, but then he confessed, "Actually, I really have the jitters, Admiral. I'll get over them when things get hot on the island, and someone starts shooting at me. I know you're busy, Admiral, so I won't keep you here too long."

Spencer smiled at the comment as a father would after a similar statement from his son. "You're doing a big job here, Kevin, and you have every right to be nervous. Now, what can I do for you?"

"If anything happens to me while I'm on that island, you know what to do with this, Admiral," said Ryan after he reached under his shirt and pulled out a large white, sealed envelope stuffed with papers. Ryan stared

268 D'ONOFRIO

at the hand printed name on the envelope for several seconds then handed it to Spencer. "I hope this isn't asking too much of you this late into the operation."

"Nonsense, Kevin, I'll take care of it," said Spencer after he saw Ryan had printed his wife's name on the envelope. "You watch your head on that island. I'll give this back to you after the operation is over and we're sitting together having a drink."

"Thanks, Admiral, you don't know how much I appreciate this. I feel a lot better now." Ryan shook Spencer's hand and then managed a quick smile. Spencer felt deeply moved by several other similar requests and realized he held the men's last thoughts to their families and loved ones before they entered the inferno of combat.

"Have you all picked the men for the teams?" Van Horne asked Owen and five other team leaders after he walked to where they were standing beside the satellite image of the island.

"We've picked our men and the designators we'll use during the attack," replied Owen as he opened his notebook. "You'll be using Trojan Guide. We'll be using South Cycle, Jilted Hinge, Bravo Kilo, and Romeo Alpha. Here's a list of the men assigned to each team."

"These look good," commented Van Horne after he carefully read the names. "How's everyone holding up under the pressure? If anybody looks like they're too nervous or agitated to take with us we'll leave them behind with Admiral Spencer."

"We're all nervous, Major, but I think we're ready," commented Howard as he quickly looked around the room. "Everyone knows the risks, and what has to be done. No one is coming apart yet."

Marlowe and his men walked into the conference room and he made his way to where Van Horne was standing with his team leaders. "How's it look in the tunnels?" Van Horne asked as he handed him the sheet of paper with the team members printed on it.

"We'll have everything ready by the time your men are in the tunnels. My men are wrapping up some last minute details right now."

"Good, you're the key to getting us onto that island."

JOURNEY THROUGH A LONG WINTER'S NIGHT 269

"You'll be using the designator Midway Barber in the church steeple," Owen told Marlowe as he pointed at several lines on the piece of paper. "That's Midway Barber."

Van Horne looked around for Spencer and saw him standing off to the side, listening to the conversation. "Did Dupont find you a safe place so you can coordinate the attack?"

"There's an operational command center built two hundred feet under the Newport Naval Base. The Navy built it so they could maintain control of the Atlantic fleet during a nuclear war. Dupont and sixty of his men will be in that command center with me."

"That's a little close to Goat Island for me, Admiral. What're you going to do if they detonate the bomb? Why didn't Dupont find another site for you further from Newport?"

"We can't risk moving a large group of men and equipment anywhere right now, Robert, someone might get suspicious. The command center is nuclear explosion proof and they have enough food to wait it out in there for a few weeks. If the area is contaminated with radiation they have protective clothing we can use to get out of the command center. While your men are moving into position on the island, Dupont's men will update maps and diagrams as they monitor your progress. Stop worrying about me, Robert."

Van Horne raised his arm and bit the skin of his wrist, an old nervous reaction to stress, as he thought about the situation. "When you get to the command center I'd like you to contact your staff in Washington. Use a scrambled communications line and tell them to watch for anything unusual after the attack begins. If we're right, someone in that city may try to run. If we're wrong, there's going to be a lot of pissed off people in Washington gunning for you tomorrow."

"I was already planning to do that. When word gets back to Washington the island is under attack, somebody may panic and give themselves away. We'll know if anyone is involved in this if they try to run."

The group looked toward the stone doorway when

270 D'ONOFRIO

Holloway and his team walked into the conference room. "It raining like the dickens out there, Van Horne," shouted a concerned Holloway. "Do you still want to go ahead with the attack tonight, or postpone it until tomorrow night after the rain stops?"

Van Horne and his men were pleased with Holloway's reaction to the inclement weather and they immediately began laughing. "That rain may keep you alive tonight. We're going tonight, and its time to start handing out the weapons."

Taylor and Howard began handing each man a dark green backpack. Van Horne lifted a green combat harness that resembled suspenders and studied the wide green belt attached to it. Attached to each pistol belt were six green ammunition pouches designed to carry a total of twenty four extra ammunition magazines. The lightweight harnesses would also provide a place for the men to fasten their bayonets. It would also provide a place to attach the hand grenades the men planned to carry onto the island. Van Horne handed each man a nine millimeter handgun, and a silencer which was one inch in diameter and four inches long. The silencer attached to the end of the handgun's barrel and could suppress the weapon's noise to a whisper when fired. Five men stood and lifted shotguns from a long table along with a bandoleer of thirty shotgun shells.

Marlowe's men carried several wooden boxes of concussion grenades into the conference room and placed them on the stone floor. The grenades emitted a momentary flash of brilliant light that would temporarily blind enemy soldiers. A deafening explosion to further confuse the enemy soldiers would accompany the blinding light. The Seabees carried cases of white phosphorus grenades into the conference room next. These grenades hurled small pieces of burning metal chips into the air when they exploded. The burning metal caused excruciating pain when it struck human flesh, and was difficult to extinguish. The third type of grenades brought into the room were the regular explosive models with five second fuses.

Marlowe and his men opened the brown canvas bags

JOURNEY THROUGH A LONG WINTER'S NIGHT   271

they brought to the fort and began unpacking small blocks of gray C-4 plastic explosives, detonators, and electronic triggering devices. The soft plastic explosive could be molded like clay, and was impervious to both fire and gunfire. The men carefully packed the plastic explosives, detonators, and the triggering devices into their backpack.

Marlowe's men then carefully carried the wooden crates of full ammunition magazines into the conference room from the fort's hallway. Each man took additional ammunition magazines for their handguns and rifles and placed them into their extra ammunition pouches and backpacks.

Owen then began distributing the rocket propelled grenades for the forty millimeter launchers mounted under the barrels of some rifles. The men quickly inspected the grenades and then pushed them into another green nylon harness they placed around their necks.

Black plastic boxes containing radios no larger than a pack of cigarettes were then attached to each man's pistol belt. The radio headsets consisted of a narrow steel wire which held a small earphone, and a small adjustable boom microphone. A thin black wire connected the speaker and microphone to the radio. After the men adjusted the radio headsets they lowered them and allowed them to hang around their necks.

"This is a map of Goat Island that's similar to the satellite photograph we used during our planning meetings," explained Van Horne as he pulled a handful of small red cards from a cardboard box and displayed them to the group. "The Admiral assigned a reference number to every building and structure on the island. They're sealed in plastic so they can't get wet, and they may be helpful if we get into trouble."

"The AT-4s will be waiting at the escape tunnel for you two," Owen told Foran and Lee. Then he pushed a magazine of bullets into his handgun and slid the weapon into his shoulder holster. "After you knock out those trailers you've got to destroy the Stingers. We don't want to worry about someone shooting down the

272   D'ONOFRIO

Admiral's helicopters if we get lucky enough to find the President."

"Earlier tonight I asked Admiral Spencer to arrange for a few Navy jets to be in the area when we hit the island." Van Horne told his men as he pointed at an area of the large map fastened to the wall. "He's contacting the Nimitz and trying to get three F-14 Tomcats into the air if we need them. If you need a loud diversion contact the Admiral and see if the jets are available."

Van Horne was curious as he watched James Howard walk to the rear of the conference room to speak to Marlowe. The two men laughed together and then Howard lifted a fully loaded backpack. "What's in that backpack, Jim?" Van Horne shouted.

"Some extra supplies for the team hitting the garage, Major. I want some extra blocks of plastic explosives and Claymore mines."

"I want all the maps, pictures, and any notes we made about the attack burned before we leave here," Van Horne told the men as he checked his rifle. "It won't take long for someone to figure out what we're going to do if they get in here and see all of this."

"Its time for me to get back to the base, Robert," Spencer told Van Horne after he looked at the clock. "I'll take Marlowe's men with me and they can get to the church from there."

"Take care of yourself, Admiral. I'll be seeing you."

As Spencer shook Van Horne's hand he said, "Good luck, I'll see all of you after this is over. Don't get careless up there." As he walked out of the conference room he wondered if he would see any of the men again.

Spencer climbed into his limousine and listened to the torrential rain falling onto the black metal roof. He watched the streams of water running down the windows for several seconds, then looked at the fort's wet exterior walls lit by the floodlights. "How's everything going, Bill?" Spencer asked William Carson, the limousine driver charged with protecting Spencer for the night.

"Everything you asked for is ready, Admiral. Our men in Washington are already in position in the government office around the city."

JOURNEY THROUGH A LONG WINTER'S NIGHT 273

"What about Reynolds and the other officials still at the base. How are we going to handle them?"

"I'll deal with them myself after you're in the command center, Admiral. I've already talked to a few of our men and they're going to help me round them up. Hell, I've never kidnapped a government official before."

"They may give you a problem so be ready for anything," warned Spencer as he lifted the limousine's telephone and asked to be connected to the Flight Operations Center at the Quonset Point Naval Air Station. Several minutes later, a man answered the telephone, and Spencer immediately recognized his voice. "This is Admiral Spencer, I want to talk to Rolling Thunder."

"This is Rolling Thunder." The man was courteous, but very brief.

"We're moving Van Horne's men to the base in a few minutes. Are you ready?" Spencer asked as he turned on an overhead light and pulled a map out of his briefcase.

"We just finished checking our equipment. We're good to go on our end. You tell us when to move and we'll be ready to drop fire on those bastards wherever they are."

"I'll contact you when we're close to beginning the attack. Don't forget what I told you. If anyone shoots at you, you make sure they die!" Spencer replaced the telephone as he felt the rain water that soaked his hair running down his neck and into his shirt. "Lets get moving, Bill. I can contact the Nimitz and check on those fighters while you're driving."

Chapter Fifteen

"If everyone is ready we'll move out to the Admiral's trucks. I'll feel better after we're all in Luce Hall," Van Horne told the group, then he and Holloway led everyone into the fort's stone corridor. The heavy rain formed large deep puddles on the stone floor in the areas where the ceiling was collapsed. The group walked through them as they made their way through the winding hallway until they found five men waiting beside an open door at the rear of the fort. "I'm Van Horne, lets get these people out of here."

Van Horne's abruptness and the tone of his voice seemed to startle the men and none of them replied. Then one said, "Admiral Spencer told us to use the back roads through the city so we won't be seen from Goat Island. We've got six trucks parked outside so we can put some of your men into each one."

Van Horne carefully studied Spencer's men and wondered if he could trust any of them as he looked into their eyes. He thought about the risks then told his men, "Load your weapons. We could get ambushed anywhere between here and the base. If anyone hits us, kill them!" The group then climbed into the back of the large military trucks where they pulled down the canvas flaps to protect them from the torrential rain.

At 1:47 A.M. the trucks arrived at the Luce Hall parking lot, and Van Horne led the group through the rain and into the building. As he walked down the marble steps that led to the basement he remembered his feelings during the ambush. Those terrifying memories seemed to make him angrier and more anxious to attack the island. He knew he had a chance to avenge the deaths of Mahoney and the others by ambushing the enemy that attempted to kill him.

"All right, lets move into the tunnel," Van Horne told the group as they stood in the darkened basement beside the escape tunnel's stone doorway. "Switch to your radios when you're in the tunnel so we don't have to shout down there. Lets get moving." Van Horne

JOURNEY THROUGH A LONG WINTER'S NIGHT   275

touched the brown stones of the tunnel doorway as he walked through it and he momentarily thought about Sullivan. The image of the frail old man caused him to smile for a moment.

As Van Horne led the group into the tunnel, Marlowe and his men were moving their equipment into Saint John's Church steeple. Marlowe's body trembled from fear as he slowly led his men up a steep, narrow, and dimly lit circular wooden staircase built into the center of the towering church steeple. A gray and green mold covered the wooden stairs in some areas and produced a musty smell. Each cautious step Marlowe took on the old wooden stairs produced a loud creaking sound. Marlowe's handgun trembled as he slowly climbed the stairs ten feet ahead of his men, heeding Van Horne's warning of a possible ambush.

When he reached the top of the staircase Marlowe found the weathered oak door filled with knots the church's pastor described to him. He darkened the top of the staircase by reaching up and twisting the dim overhead light bulb. Then, as his hands trembled from both fear and anxiety, he slowly unlocked the door and pushed it open after he knelt on the wooden steps. He stared at a large wooden platform built in the center of the steeple dimly lit by the orange glow of the street lights below. As Marlowe stood he listened to the torrential rain falling onto the roof built over the platform to protect the original church bell from the inclement weather.

Marlowe cautiously walked to the edge of the wooden platform and stood in the rain and estimated he was two hundred feet above the ground. He motioned his men onto the platform and they stood silently beside him in the darkness. From this position they could see the buildings on Goat Island, which were three thousand feet away. The men did not speak for several minutes as they watched the well lit island and the buildings on it with their binoculars.

"Sheeet, it's a god darn long shot from here to that hotel," commented an apprehensive George Drake with his southern accent. "This dang wind could be a prob-

276 D'ONOFRIO

lem for us if it picks up. Right now it's nothing more than a dang nuisance." Drake's concerns also troubled the other men in the steeple and they wondered what would happen if the wind prevented them from hitting their targets on the island.

"We'll just have to compensate for the wind," said Marlowe as he lowered his binoculars and wiped the rain water off the lenses. "We told Van Horne we could handle this part of the attack, and I know we can pull this off. Schwartz, get that damn cannon of yours unpacked. I think we're going to need it."

Spencer sat back in his chair in front of an electronic console and watched the activity in the underground command center cluttered with various types of equipment. Eighty volunteers from Dupont's staff frantically finished preparations to plot the progress of Van Horne's men as they attacked the island. Some of the men and women stood around eight large individually mounted Lucite panels in the middle of the command center. Drawn onto two panels was an outline of Goat Island and the buildings located on it. Drawn on several other panels were the exterior of the hotel building, and the other prominent features such as the outdoor swimming pool area, the tennis courts, and the seawall behind the hotel. Other panels contained drawings of the hotel's convention center complex, indoor swimming pool, lobby, restaurants, and the layout of several other hotel floors.

Spencer turned when he heard a man shouting in the command center behind him. A frown formed on his face as he watched Carson and four of his men pushing Coleman, Jamison, and Reynolds against a wall. The officials appeared shocked and confused when they saw the men and equipment in the command center. When Spencer saw the handcuffs around each man's wrists he immediately stood as he thought, "My god, Carson, what have you done?"

"There's Spencer," Coleman told the others when he saw him walking across the command center. Coleman turned and looked toward the command center's entrance when the nuclear explosion proof door

JOURNEY THROUGH A LONG WINTER'S NIGHT 277

closed with a resounding thud and slowly locked in place.

"I want to know what the hell is going on in here, Spencer," shouted an angry Jamision. "Your men just pulled us out of bed at gun point. Then they handcuffed us and dragged us here with our staff. I don't even know where my people are right now."

"You could be in a lot of trouble here, Admiral," warned Reynolds as Carson pushed him back against a wall. "Why did you do this?"

"Why don't we just throw them in the supply room with their staff and keep them there until this is over, Admiral?" asked Carson as he kept his handgun pointed at Reynolds' chest.

"No, we need them, Bill. Get their handcuffs off so I can talk to them."

"What's going on down here, Spencer?" asked Coleman as he looked around at the men and women frantically working near him. "Have you lost your mind?"

"We're getting ready to attack Goat Island," replied Spencer without further explanation he thought was unnecessary.

"You're what? Why didn't anyone tell me we're using the military option. I thought that option was dead?"

"It was, until we discovered some disturbing new information yesterday. I don't have time to explain everything to you right now. I have a tape recorded message I want you to listen to. After you hear it you can decide what to do. If you don't want to get involved in this you can sit it out in a conference room in the back."

Reynolds stared at the white concrete floor after he listened to the intercepted conversation between Murtagh and Barnes. "I'm in, Admiral," he said after a long sigh. "What can I do?"

"If you want to help you can give Marlowe and his men a hand. But that means you'll be in the city during the entire attack. You could be killed if they detonate that bomb."

"I've had it up to here with everything that's happened on that island, Admiral. Show me where Marlowe is and I'll take my men and help him."

"What about you two?" Spencer asked Coleman and Jamison.

278 D'ONOFRIO

"Do you know how risky this is, Spencer?" asked Jamison as he quickly looked around the command center. "What if you're wrong? What if your involvement here makes the situation worse?"

"Then I guess Benson is going to fire me," said Spencer as he nervously looked at his watch. "I don't have time to stand here and discuss this with you. I know this is a tough decision, but you've got to make it now. You can either help us stop what's going to happen on that island, or you can sit back and watch. Whatever your decision, we're committed and we're going ahead with this attack."

"I'm with you, Admiral," replied Coleman. "You're so god damn convincing that I don't have a choice."

"Me too, Admiral," added Jamison reluctantly. "If you're wrong, we can all look for jobs together. Get our people out here and tell us what can we do to help you."

"Midway Barber, this is Trojan Guide," said Van Horne as he stopped and watched his men walking past him in the tunnel's dim yellow light. "What's the weather look like up there?"

"It's raining like hell," replied one of Marlowe's men as wind driven rain blew against his face. "You were right about the rain, we can't see any Russian soldiers on the island. They must all be inside the buildings."

Van Horne smiled to himself as he began walking beside Michael Kearns. "Now I'm convinced those soldiers on the island aren't really Russian paratroopers. You know as well as I do combat hardened Russian soldiers would be patrolling the island on a night like this. They'd know this is the perfect night for an ambush, it's Charlie's Weather, and they wouldn't be trying to stay dry in the hotel right now."

"You're right, Major," agreed Kearns as he adjusted his rifle on his shoulder. "We're not going to know who or what the heck we're really up against until we have a few bodies on the surface."

The group walked from the area lit by the clear light bulbs into the area where Spencer's men installed the red bulbs in the ceiling fixtures. The red light bulbs created an eerie sensation in the catacomb like tunnels as

JOURNEY THROUGH A LONG WINTER'S NIGHT   279

it cast bizarre shadows on the rock walls and metal racks. When the group was about one hundred feet from the first escape tunnel Van Horne held up his hand and everyone stopped. "I want the Bravo Kilo team up at the front with me now."

Marlowe walked into the tunnel and Van Horne almost laughed when he saw his clothes. They were saturated with rain, and the water dripping onto the floor formed a puddle under him. "Good thing we didn't have to do this in the middle of the winter. My balls would be frozen solid by now, Van Horne."

Van Horne briefly smiled as he watched Gene Depietro and the members of his Bravo Kilo team walk out of the group. "You're going to be alone at the other end of the island, so you'll have to take care of each other there. If you get into trouble I don't know how much help we'll be able to give you."

Depietro was almost as large and muscular as Van Horne and the two men shook hands. "Good luck, Major, I think we're all going to need it."

"Let me know when you're in position, Gene. We'll start cutting through the plate when you're ready."

Van Horne told his men to relax and then he and Marlowe walked to the first escape tunnel. Van Horne was surprised to see the three level camouflaged metal scaffolding the Seabees assembled in the vertical escape tunnel so they could work under the steel plate. They also attached additional red lights to the vertical shaft's stone walls so they could see in the tunnel. Van Horne watched two of Marlowe's men preparing their equipment on the tunnel floor. He looked up and saw another working on top of the ten foot wide work area at the top of the scaffolding.

"How does it look up there, Carlson?" Marlowe asked his man in charge of preparations in the tunnel.

"It's not as bad as I thought it would be up here." Carlson raised a flashlight and directed the bright beam onto the bottom of the metal plate. "I've drawn a chalk mark on the metal where we're going to cut through it with the acid. We should have a three by four foot hole for them to crawl through if the plate comes down like I think it will."

280 D'ONOFRIO

Van Horne suddenly heard his name in his radio headset. "Trojan Guide, this is Bravo Kilo. My team is in position. Over."

"Roger Bravo Kilo, you can relax for awhile. Midway Barber, this is Trojan Guide. How does it look on the island? Over."

Marlowe listened as his men in the steeple replied to Van Horne. "We just saw three sentries walking near the seawall behind the hotel. Another group is standing guard at the end of the destroyed access bridge. That's all we can see from up here, Trojan Guide. Over."

"Is that sentry still on the hotel roof, Midway Barber?"

"Roger that, he's still up there, but he's not walking around. He's trying to stay dry under the elevator shaft roof. Over."

"Damn it," Van Horne mumbled as he looked at Marlowe. "I was hoping that bastard would be gone by now. All right, it's time for you to get my men onto the island."

Marlowe climbed to the top of the scaffolding with Carlson. There he saw ten large blue plastic tubes of acid that measured two inches in diameter by six inches long. Printed on each tube in large red letters were the words "Danger-Acid." Marlowe quickly pulled on rubber gloves and carefully removed the cap from one tube as he precariously balanced himself at the edge of the scaffolding. Working in the glow of the red lights the two men touched the tip of the tubes to the chalk line on the metal plate and squeezed the soft plastic containers. An almost translucent acid mixture one half inch in diameter flowed from the nozzle and immediately stuck to the bottom of the metal plate. After the acid was applied to the steel it immediately began bubbling. Seconds later liquefied metal began falling onto the top of the scaffolding.

"This acid is eating through the steel faster than we thought it would," Marlowe whispered into his microphone as he looked down at Van Horne. "You better move your men up here and get them ready."

Van Horne spoke into his microphone as he motioned the group forward in the tunnel's red light. "Tac

JOURNEY THROUGH A LONG WINTER'S NIGHT 281

Com, this is Trojan Guide. We're almost through the plate. It's time to get our diversions into the air. Over."

"Roger, Trojan Guide. I'll take care of it. Tac Com, out. Get me the commander of the Nimitz on the line," Spencer immediately told a man seated in front of the communications console beside him.

"I've got the Nimitz, Admiral. I've piped it into your headset."

"This is Tac Com. Things are moving faster than we anticipated here. I think you should push up your timetable and get your aircraft into the air. Over."

"Roger, Tac Com, I understand," replied Captain Athena as he stood on the aircraft carrier's bridge and watched the torrential rain beating against the windows. The Nimitz's bridge was filled with the ship's navigational controls and more than sixty men. "I'll have my task force fully airborne in twenty minutes. Good luck, Admiral, out." Athena walked to the front of the ship's bridge and looked at the carrier's long flight deck now lit by red floodlights mounted overhead. "What's our current status?"

"The flight bridge reports we're ready to launch, Captain," Athena's executive officer replied with a concerned tone in his voice. "I wish you'd reconsider what you're about to do here, Skipper. You don't have any idea what's really happening in Newport, and you're putting yourself in a dangerous position." The officer paused for several seconds and studied several instruments on the navigational console. Then he added, "but I would be doing just what you're doing right now Skipper. I just wanted you to know we're all behind you on this."

Athena bit the skin on the inside his jaw as he watched the flight deck for several seconds. "Thanks, Phil. Let's get the E2C airborne and see if there's any other ships out there. If it's clear we'll get the tanker and the Tomcats airborne."

Athena watched the carrier's flight deck as the crews began working in the heavy rain. Steam lit by the overhead red floodlights rose eerily in the rain from the ship's catapult as the flight crews prepared a gray and white E2C Hawkeye for launching. The radar plane was eas-

282   D'ONOFRIO

ily recognized by the gray rotating radar dish mounted on top of the airframe. The pilot would use the designation Rusted Anvil for all the communications during the attack. After they completed the aircraft's final equipment checks the flight crew ran from under it and knelt on the deck. As the pilot increased the aircraft's engines to full power the noise on the flight deck became deafening. Seconds later, the steam catapult threw the aircraft off the carrier's deck.

Several minutes later, a telephone rang on the Nimitz's bridge. After a short conversation one of the officers told Athena, "CIC reports the surface is clear around us for four hundred nautical miles Skipper."

Athena was relieved the ship's Combat Information Center, which controlled the ship's defenses, and the missions of its aircraft, reported their were no other ships nearby. "Lets get the KA6 and the fighters off the deck before the weather gets any worse," replied Athena as he turned several switches on a panel and listened to the conversation between the carrier's Flight Control Bridge and the pilots in their aircraft.

"Roger, Eagle Sidewinder, after you're off the deck assume a primary heading of one eight four. Good luck, Eagle Sidewinder." Athena watched through the window as the steam catapult propelled the KA6 refueling tanker off the carrier's deck. A strong gust of wind buffeted the tanker and Athena held his breath as he watched the aircraft suddenly tip to the left. The pilot quickly regained control of the aircraft and moments later it disappeared into the darkness and clouds.

The first of three F-14 Tomcats was quickly moved into position on the flight deck. When its engines were screaming at full power the catapult propelled it off the carrier's deck. The aircraft contained the mission commander who was using the designator Whiskey Echo. Moments later, the Nimitz was a speck of fading light in the rain and darkness as Whiskey Echo flew into the clouds. Yankee November was the designator of the second F14, and thirty seconds later, the jet was following Whiskey Echo into the clouds. Athena watched the flight crews preparing the third F-14 know as India Tango.

JOURNEY THROUGH A LONG WINTER'S NIGHT 283

He watched the catapult propel the aircraft off the deck, and he stared at it as it disappeared into the darkness. Athena smiled as he watched his flight crews huddle together in the middle of the flight deck and cheered loudly.

Athena watched the torrential rain falling against the bridge windows and wondered what history would record about the events of the night. It would either brand him as a fifty-three year old traitor, or it would list him as a reluctant hero who helped save his nation.

Chapter Sixteen

Six men stood apprehensively around a military radio laying on the cement floor of a dimly lit aircraft hanger on the grounds of the Quonset Point Naval Air Station. None of them spoke as they listened to the conversation between Van Horne and Spencer. As heavy rain fell onto the building's metal roof it created a loud and constant background noise, a contrast to the near silence inside. The men's excitement and anticipation seemed increased as they listened to the descriptions of the activities occurring around, and under Goat Island. The man known as Rolling Thunder slowly pulled a crumpled pack of cigarettes from his flight jacket as he visualized what was happening under Goat island. Then he struck a wooden match against the side of a small box and quickly moved the flame to his cigarette. The yellow flame displayed his hardened face and black eyes, but offered no insight into the man's thoughts. He immediately looked at the other men when they suddenly heard an excited Marlowe say, "The plate is coming down Trojan Guide! It's on its way down now!"

Van Horne motioned his men forward and they moved around the base of the scaffolding in the glow of the red light bulbs. He suddenly became very excited when he saw water seeping through two of the acid cut lines in the steel. Van Horne quickly motioned to four of his men and said, "Watch the top of the tunnel after they pull down the plate. If anyone looks into the hole, shoot them." The men immediately attached the silencers to their handguns and pointed them at the top of the tunnel.

As the acid quickly cut through the metal, Marlowe and Carlson each lifted a two inch thick metal bar wrapped with black electrical tape. The bars were eighteen inches long and had a large black suction cup attached to each end. The two men positioned the suction cups against the bottom of the plate and pushed up on the bars, attaching the devices to the steel. Van Horne remembered Marlowe explained the suction cup bars

JOURNEY THROUGH A LONG WINTER'S NIGHT   285

would provide the Seabees with a way to hold the smooth metal plate and lower it onto the scaffolding.

Van Horne watched nervously as Marlowe and Carlson pulled down on the metal bars, but the plate did not appear to move. After they pulled down on the bars a second time, more rain water began seeping into the tunnel through the acid cut lines, and the plate seemed to shift position. Marlowe nodded at Carlson, then he violently pulled down on the bar with all his strength and body weight. Marlowe rested the one inch thick plate on his shoulder after one end unexpectedly dropped into the tunnel. During the previous hours, the heavy rains created large puddles of standing water on the grass above the escape tunnel. When Marlowe pulled down the plate, the water began flowing into the tunnel covering him and Carlson, and splashing onto the men standing around the scaffolding.

The sound of a frantic man's voice in everyone's radio headset suddenly broke the silence in the tunnel. "Trojan Guide, this is Midway Barber! Stop whatever you're doing and don't move! Don't say a word! I say again, stop whatever you're doing and don't move. Two Russian sentries just walked in the parking lot near you."

"Fuck me," thought Van Horne as he watched Marlowe and Carlson struggling to hold up the metal plate. "First I want the god damn plate out of the way,and now they've got to hold it up so the Russians don't find us. We get this far and then get fucked by two wandering sentries who don't know enough to get out of the rain."

As the acid completely cut through the metal Marlowe and Carlson struggled to balance the heavy plate on their shoulders. The loosened dirt around the plate mixed with the rain water flooding into the tunnel covered the two men with a brown mixture as they struggled to hold the thick piece of metal. The muddy water fell onto the top of the scaffolding and the brown mixture showered Van Horne's men below, spattering their faces and arms.

"I don't know if I can take this pain for too much longer." Marlowe thought as his arm and leg muscles began to burn and cramp under the plate's weight. "I

286   D'ONOFRIO

will not give in to the pain. If this plate falls onto the scaffolding, or onto the tunnel floor the Russians will hear it and we're all dead."

Van Horne's heart pounded in his chest as he waited for another report from the men in the steeple. Twenty seconds later, he looked at the tunnel ceiling when he heard the message, "Trojan Guide, this is Midway Barber. The Russian sentries have moved out of the parking lot. You can keep working. Midway Barber, out."

Marlowe and Carlson immediately lowered the plate and placed it onto the top of the scaffolding. As they were removing the suction cup devises from the plate they looked up after the dirt over the escape tunnel collapsed onto them. As the two men prepared more equipment Van Horne climbed the metal escape ladder attached to the rock wall and unscrewed the red light bulbs.

After he darkened the vertical escape tunnel, Van Horne was shocked by what he saw above him. The lights on the buildings and city street in Newport were creating an orange glow over the island as they reflected off the falling rain and low clouds. It was an eerie scene at the top of the darkened tunnel, and Van Horne thought it resembled the doorway to another world as heavy rain fell into the hole. He watched Marlowe and Carlson silhouetted in the darkness with the orange clouds behind them as they assembled a metal ladder on top of the scaffolding. "Tac Com, this is Trojan Guide. We've opened the escape tunnel. Trojan Guide, out."

Van Horne pulled his rifle over his shoulder and quickly climbed to the top of the metal scaffolding. Then he slowly climbed the ladder the Seabees assembled as streams of ground water flowed into the tunnel and saturated his clothes. He crouched down at the top of the ladder when his head was just below the surface of the ground. Then he slowly raised his head until his eyes were above the surface and checked the surrounding area for Russian sentries. *Nothing, no patrols, no god damn sentries. I'm not surprised, I knew they wouldn't be here,"* he thought.

Van Horne was pleased the escape tunnel was only twenty feet from the hotel parking lot in the center of

JOURNEY THROUGH A LONG WINTER'S NIGHT 287

the island. The grassy area was not brightly lit by the orange street lights. Directly ahead Van Horne saw the darkened buildings and shops in the center of Newport, across the harbor water where the raindrops were creating millions of tiny circles. Van Horne looked to his right and saw the well lit marina and condominium buildings. He smiled with a sense of accomplishment when he looked to his left and saw the lit hotel complex.

Van Horne grasped the cut edge of the steel plate and carefully pulled himself through the opening. He fell onto the wet grass five feet from the hole and watched for enemy soldiers in the torrential rain as the members of his first team climbed out of the tunnel. After Willey crawled out of the tunnel he reached back into the opening and lifted out a bundle of six AT-4 rocket launchers Carlson handed him. Van Horne motioned to the men and they quickly moved between the cars in the well lit parking lot.

"Trojan Guide, this is Midway Barber. I can see you in my starlight scope," said a spotter in Saint John's Church steeple as he watched the shadowy figures moving in the heavy rain. "There's no one around you."

Van Horne and the others watched the surrounding area as the second team quickly crawled out of the tunnel. He motioned them toward the well lit parking lot as he lay in a deep puddle beside the hole waiting for the next team. His body stiffened and he suddenly became terrified when he heard the message, "Trojan Guide, this is Midway Barber. Stop moving. There's three Russian soldiers walking near the seawall behind you. Don't move or they're going to see you. They may have already." The sound of the heavy rain prevented Van Horne from hearing the approaching sentries. His entire body trembled with fear as he lay on his stomach while watching a tall church steeple lit with blue floodlights in the center of Newport.

Moments later, after what seemed to be an hour of anguished waiting, a voice broke the silence. "Trojan Guide, this is Midway Barber. The sentries just walked into one of the condominium buildings. Out."

Van Horne crawled to the hole and frantically pulled

288 D'ONOFRIO

Holloway out of the tunnel, then he motioned him down on the wet grass. Van Horne helped the other members of Holloway's group out of the hole and they fell onto the ground beside their leader. None of Holloway's staff had ever trained under such severe conditions and it took several minutes for them to become acclimated to the darkness and torrential rain. At times the heavy rain fell in wind driven sheets and made the situation even more intimidating as it covered their faces, temporarily blinding them and making breathing difficult. The vivid lightening streaks crossing the dark night sky and reverberant thunder from a nearby storm added to their anxiety and uneasiness.

Van Horne led Holloway's team to the parking lot and looked at his watch after he knelt beside Foran and Lee. Both men were accustomed to working under such severe conditions and preferred this type of weather for an ambush. "I've got to start moving the others toward the hotel or we'll bunch up in this damn parking lot. Can you two help the others out of the tunnel?"

"No problem, Major," whispered Foran who was now confident he and his partner could handle any task after getting onto the island without being detected by the Russians. "We'll take care of them, count on it."

"If any of the Russians bastards find the tunnel get rid of them," said Van Horne. Foran unexpectedly grabbed his arm and startled Van Horne when he displayed a closed fist. Van Horne looked at him and made a fist which the two touched together, and then briefly smiled.

Van Horne quickly led the three teams between the cars and vans in the well lit parking lot as he ran crouched over at the waist. The group stopped every fifteen feet and checked for Russian soldiers until they were one hundred feet from Barnes' three supply trailers. Van Horne slowly raised his head above the hood of a red sports car and looked into the three trailers through their open doors. He saw men sitting and laying down inside the trailers while others were smoking outside in the parking lot. Then he motioned everyone lower and the groups continued moving toward the hotel.

Foran and Lee helped the other men out of the tun-

JOURNEY THROUGH A LONG WINTER'S NIGHT   289

nel, and then Lee reached in and took another bundle of AT-4 rockets from Carlson. He and Foran carried them to the parking lot and placed them beside the bundle Willey already pulled from the tunnel. The two men sat on the wet asphalt as torrential rain fell onto them and they quietly prepared the rocket launchers.

Van Horne led the teams to the end of the parking lot where everyone crouched down between the cars in the heavy rain. The only obstacle separating them from the convention center was the two lane access road used by the trucks making deliveries to the hotel's rear loading docks. Large bright floodlights mounted on the hotel roof lit the road with an orange tinted light. The light made the heavy rain glisten and sparkle as it fell and splashed on the road.

Van Horne turned to the men kneeling behind him as he wiped the rain water from his hair, slicking it down to his head. "You wait here until I check behind the building. I'll signal you when it's safe." After quickly looking around for sentries Van Horne quickly ran across the lit road and jumped behind the large evergreens planted beside the building. His heart raced wildly with excitement as he waited for nearby Russian sentries to shout a warning after seeing him running in the bright light. As the seconds passed, he realized no one had seen him. There were no sentries, and no warnings were sounded.

Van Horne quickly crawled toward the rear of the convention center through the deep puddles and mud, in rain so heavy it made hearing difficult. When he reached the rear corner of the building he suddenly stopped breathing when he thought he heard voices. The sound of the heavy rain falling onto the access road made him unsure of what he really heard. Van Horne grasped the oozing mud with his fingers and pulled himself forward slowly until he could look around the building's corner. He was surprised to see two sentries standing together in a dimly lit area under a canvas canopy no more than fifteen feet from him.

These bastards should probably be patrolling behind the hotel. They just don't want to walk in the rain. I don't

290   D'ONOFRIO

have a choice damn it, he told himself. As he slowly stood mud fell off his shirt and pants, then he quickly stepped around the corner with his handgun drawn. Van Horne startled the two soldiers when they saw someone suddenly step from the shadows behind the building. Van Horne quickly fired two bullets that ripped through one sentry's chest and killed him before he could scream.

After the bullets knocked his companion's body backward, the second Cuban fumbled for his machine gun. Van Horne frantically aimed his handgun, but fear and excitement caused his hands to shake, and the single bullet he fired tore through the flesh of the sentry's throat. Van Horne fired a second bullet after the wounded man cried out loudly and reached for his throat. The bullet struck the sentry's head and it seemed to explode as the brass projectile ripped away most of the skull after tearing through the brain.

Van Horne was shaking almost uncontrollably as he knelt and checked the two bodies while he thought, *I've got to settle down. My fear affected my aim. Letting this one live an extra second was a fucking stupid mistake that might have been fatal for everyone. It won't happen again*, he thought as he ran back to the building's corner and signaled his men to move across the access road. After the first team was behind the building Howard's men escorted Holloway's frightened team across the road.

Decker hid in the shadows behind the convention center and was terrified as her heart pounded so hard she thought it would explode. Bright lightening streaked over the island, and the resonant thunder frightened her, adding to her growing apprehension. She was more afraid than she had ever been at any other time in her life. She gasped for air as her breathing became erratic and her chest tightened. She looked at Holloway kneeling beside her and wanted to tell him she was too afraid to continue. *I'm going to die on this island*, she told herself. The rain water ran down her face and into her shirt, between her breasts, and then into her green pants as she knelt on the wet asphalt. *Why did I ever come here? I want to go home. I can't do this. I can't do it.*

JOURNEY THROUGH A LONG WINTER'S NIGHT   291

A vivid bright streak of lightening accompanied by a tremendous clap of thunder, momentarily lit the bodies of the dead sentries laying nearby. Decker covered her mouth with her hands after she saw the faceless corpse laying on its back as rain fell into the shattered skull. Holloway saw Decker's horrified reaction and he grasped her wrist tightly and pulled her hands away from her face. "Come on, Maggie, get control of yourself," he whispered as another loud crack of thunder startled everyone. "You can do this. You're not going to die here, I won't let you."

Van Horne motioned a thumbs up signal to Howard and pointed toward the far end of the hotel building. Then he led his team to where the convention center's rear guest rooms were located. "You've got to be shitting me," he mumbled when he saw the balconies he and his men had to climb to reach the building's roof. Moments later, Van Horne climbed up the first balcony wall and threw a leg over the railing as the torrential rain made the climb treacherous.

Fifteen minutes later, Van Horne cautiously climbed onto the highest of the building's balconies and stood on the narrow painted metal railing. He reached up and grasped the edge of the building's roof with both hands. When he tried to pull himself onto the roof the torrential rain caused him to his grip and he suddenly slipped off the wet railing. Van Horne suddenly dangled helplessly from the roof by one hand sixty feet above the ground. The heavy rain that fell into his face added to his momentary fear and caused him to panic. As he pulled his arm back his body twisted and he saw a lighthouse in the distance, and the well-lit Newport Bridge only two miles away.

"Shit," was Van Horne's only thought as he quickly turned his body and grasped the building's roof with his other hand. His arm muscles burned while he dangled with the additional weight of the weapons and ammunition on his back. Then his hands began to cramp as he struggled to pull himself onto the roof. As bright streaks of lightening lit the sky over the island Van Horne's anger flared and he raised his leg and threw his foot onto the roof. Then he

292   D'ONOFRIO

painfully pulled himself onto the roof. He lay in a deep puddle on the roof for several seconds, then knelt and began pulling his men onto the roof. "That was too damn close," he whispered to the others as they crouched down and began walking across the convention center roof.

Howard nervously watched Van Horne dangle from the roof, and then climb onto it: "Lets find our staging area. I don't like standing around here in the open. Long, Mahoney, watch yourselves when you hit the garage. You don't know how well they've got it guarded."

Edward Long and Robert Mahoney suddenly felt isolated and vulnerable as they watched their team disappear into the heavy rain and shadows behind the hotel. They both volunteered for the risky assignment of attacking the garage's front entrance, hoping to distract the enemy soldiers inside it. They crouched behind a trash dumpster in the shadows and several minutes later, Mahoney tapped Long on the shoulder after Nielson's team ran behind the convention center.

"Did you have any problems back here?" asked Nielson as he knelt beside Mahoney while wiping the rain off the face of his watch.

"No problems except for those two," Mahoney replied as he pointed at the two bodies. "Everything is going good. How's your team doing?"

"We're here for the party. Where's Howard and Holloway's group?"

"They're already moving toward the back of the hotel garage." Mahoney listened to the heavy rain falling on the dumpster's metal lid, then he confessed. "I really hate being wet. I hated it all the time I was in Vietnam, and I still hate it today." "Yeah, but this rain might keep us alive tonight shit head," replied Nielson, then he stood. Nielson led the team known as Jilted Hinge, and he began moving his men toward the end of the island where the hotel's outdoor swimming pool was located. The team cautiously moved past the convention center's cement loading docks as they remained in the building's shadows. They immediately stopped moving each time a bright flash of lightening lit the island, then they continued forward.

JOURNEY THROUGH A LONG WINTER'S NIGHT   293

James Howard carefully led his men, and Holloway's group, toward the garage's rear entrances. He motioned the group behind some large evergreens in the building's shadows and crawled to the edge of the team's first obstacle. Located directly ahead was a wide grassy area and the convention center's rear access doors. Three large floodlights mounted on the building's roof brightly lit both the grass and the doors. Howard knew his team had to move across the well lit area to get to the garage's rear entrances as he stared into the darkness beyond the lit area.

Howard's men immediately raised their rifles after he suddenly crawled backward and hid behind a large evergreen bush. As heavy rain struck the evergreen's needles and splashed into his face, Howard slowly pulled the branches apart so he could see the building's access doors. He held his breath when he saw two heavily armed soldiers walk into the doorway. One of the soldiers pulled a pack of cigarettes from his pocket and offered them to the other. Howard frowned when he heard them speaking Spanish and thought, *Russian soldiers speaking Spanish. What the hell?*

Howard turned toward his men and raised two fingers, then he pointed at Bruce James and Bob Jarvis.

James slowly pulled out his bayonet as Jarvis crawled beside him. Howard reached into his pocket and slowly pulled out a piece of steel wire two feet long with a small wooden block attached to each end. Howard grasped the blocks as James and Jarvis waited beside him. Holloway's team members hid behind the bushes and tried to determine if they were going to be discovered.

Two minutes later, the Cubans finished their cigarettes and walked into the torrential rain with their machine guns pulled over their shoulders. James and Jarvis ran from behind the bushes first. Jarvis grasped one startled sentry from behind, gripping the man's chin with his large hand. Then he pulled the struggling man's head backward with all of his strength. James unmercifully plunged the full length of his bayonet into the soft flesh of the struggling Cuban's throat. As warm red blood covered his hands, James violently pulled the

294 D'ONOFRIO

bayonet forward and severed the man's jugular vein. Streams of red blood suddenly sprayed onto James' chest as he pulled the bayonet from the man's throat and let the body fall onto the wet grass.

Heavy rain fell into Howard's face as stepped behind the second surprised sentry and wrapped the thin steel wire around his neck. Howard pulled on the blocks of wood with all his strength and tightened the thin silver colored wire until it was cutting the flesh of the man's throat. The sentry's weapon fell off his shoulder as he frantically reached for his throat. He frantically pulled at the constricting wire as warm blood began to flow from the cut flesh. The soldier struggled for several seconds but died when James suddenly stepped in front of him and drove the full length of his bayonet into the man's chest over his heart with a resounding thud. James and Howard then dragged the body into the shadows and left it beside his dead companion.

"Tac Com, this is South Cycle. Two sentries killed behind the hotel. South Cycle, out." Howard pointed at two of his men and they quickly ran across the lit area ahead of the group. They immediately hid in the shadows behind the bushes when they were in a darkened area again. When he was sure it was safe, Howard moved the remainder of his men and Holloway's team across the lit area. The group continued moving forward in the heavy rain until they reached the corner of the building. Howard cautiously looked around the corner and studied the large parking lot behind the hotel. The orange glow from six large floodlights mounted on the hotel's roof brightly lit the parking area filled with cars and vans.

Howard motioned to Bruce James, and he and four men cautiously crawled around the corner and under the large wooden deck near the garage's two rear entrances. The wet wood mulch under the deck smelled of pine when the men crawled through it. During the day, the hotel used the wooden deck as an outdoor restaurant. It stood five feet above the ground which sloped upward under the deck. Howard's men sat on the higher ground under the deck so they would not be seen by Russian soldiers who might be walking in the parking lot.

JOURNEY THROUGH A LONG WINTER'S NIGHT   295

Within minutes, Howard and Holloway's teams were sitting in the wet mulch under the deck. The smell of the wood mulch immediately reminded Howard of his days at work as a tree cutter. He thought about sunny and peaceful days when he cut towering trees in his native South Dakota. He was distracted by the heavy rain pounding down onto the wooden planks above, and the rain water running through the spaces between the planks which fell onto him and the others.

The garage's two rear doors were only thirty feet from the deck. When Howard heard men shouting to one another inside the garage he wondered how many enemy soldiers his small team would be attacking. The overhead fluorescent lights in the garage cast a bright white glow on the black asphalt driveway outside the two rear doors. This was a sharp contrast to the parking lot's orange floodlights.

Jarvis and James immediately began unloading the backpack filled with explosives the Seabees prepared for them. Jarvis cautiously stood beside the deck and positioned a Claymore mine so it was pointing at a wide glass access door that opened into the hotel. Then he quickly attached five more Claymore mines to the deck's railings as the torrential rain fell onto his face. As loud thunder made him shudder, Jarvis carefully activated the remote controlled detonators which he fitted into the back of each mine. At the same time, James carefully attached six large blocks of plastic explosives to the bottom of the deck with black electrical tape, then he pushed a remote detonator into each of them.

"Tac Com, this is South Cycle. My men and Holloway's team are in position and ready. Out." Howard watched the heavy rain falling onto the cars in the parking lot in the orange tinted light as he thought about the attack. He wondered which of his men, if any, would walk through the garage doors into the morning daylight. He quickly pushed the thought from his mind as he listened to the sounds of the soldiers talking and laughing inside the garage.

Chapter Seventeen

Nielson and his team ran forward in the shadows beside the hotel in the heavy rain. They quickly crawled beside the bushes planted near the building when they found the two sentries Howard's team killed. As his team watched for a roving enemy patrol, Nielson studied the grassy lit area ahead. "I knew these overhead lights were here, but I didn't know they would be so bright!" Nielson whispered to his men as they huddled behind him. "I don't have a good feeling about this!"

Gatting looked over Nielson's shoulder at the lit area. "They must have men in this area and they may see us in that light," he whispered as he motioned toward the two dead bodies.

"He's right, we've got to find another way," as he quickly looked at his watch and realized his team was late getting to their staging area. He looked to his left and saw the concrete sea wall one hundred feet from where he was kneeling. "Lets move back a little to where its darker. We'll move to that seawall and climb over it. Then we can crawl across the rocks on the other side and make it to the end of the island that way. It'll be slower, but I think it's a lot safer!"

The team cautiously moved back to a dimly lit area behind the hotel building. After checking for Russian sentries they quickly ran toward the seawall as lightening streaks accompanied by loud thunder lit the sky over the harbor. As they ran through the unlit area, a floodlight that lit the access road behind the building suddenly engulfed them in orange light. Moments later, Nielson jumped onto the seawall and crawled across the wet and rough concrete surface. Seconds later, he and his men jumped off the barrier and landed on the rocks on the other side.

"What the hell?" thought Nielson after he suddenly realized something was laying on the rocks beside him in the darkness. When his eyes became accustomed to the dim light he was horrified when he saw a young woman's severed head laying on the rocks. A large wave

JOURNEY THROUGH A LONG WINTER'S NIGHT   297

crashed into the rocks and washed the woman's long red hair as her eyes remained open in a glassy stare.

"Fuck me!" Nielson mumbled as he crawled backward against the seawall after recognizing the overpowering stench of decaying human flesh.

A vivid streak of lightening momentarily lit the rocky area and all the men seemed appalled when they saw dead hostages lying around them. Barnes and the Cubans used this area as their personal dumping ground and threw the bodies of the women and children they barbarically mutilated onto the rocks in this area so they could not be seen from the city. Nielson closed his eyes for a moment and let the rain fall onto his face when he realized decaying bodies covered the rocks as far as he could see. Although Nielson and his men saw dead bodies in Vietnam and Iraq, they were disgusted by the number of innocent people butchered by the enemy soldiers.

Nielson motioned to his men and they began crawling across the rocks as their shock quickly turned to rage. The torrential rain and ocean waves constantly wet the large rocks and made the footing slippery. This forced the men to pull their rifles over their shoulders so they could walk on their hands and knees to prevent from falling. Large waves crashed onto the rocks ten feet to their right and sometimes covered the men with salt water.

In one area the men carefully crawled between the bloated and intertwined severed limbs of decaying female corpses. Nielson noticed all of the dead women were naked, and he guessed they were raped before being murdered. Nielson suddenly stopped when he saw the body of a woman he guessed was in her early thirties. He stared at the woman's agonized face and held his breathe when he realized how much she resembled his wife. "If things were a little different, that could be Tracey laying here. How could anyone human do this to a helpless woman?" As he studied the body he saw someone used a bayonet to cut the woman's chest open before ripping out her heart. The woman's killer then pulled an almost full term baby out of

298   D'ONOFRIO

her body through her mutilated abdomen. The umbilical cord still connected the two bodies together and Nielson had to look away when he saw the face of the dead fetus laying on the rocks.

Fifteen minutes later, Nielson's team reached the end of the seawall and they quickly crawled onto the grass at the end of the island. This area was not lit and they could move easily in the darkness. As they looked ahead they saw the lit city streets and town dock in Newport across the water. Nielson used the lights in the city to search for enemy soldiers in the darkened area in front of the group as he watched for moving silhouettes.

Nielson shaded his eyes from the heavy rain with both hands when he thought he saw something in the shadows beside the hotel's tennis courts. He turned and displayed a clenched fist to his team and then pointed to the right. Moments later, everyone saw a small red light momentarily appear in the darkness between the outdoor tennis court and the side of the hotel building. They knew a sentry was standing in front of them smoking a cigarette as his hat sheltered the burning tip from the rain.

Nielson pointed at David White, and he crawled forward and disappeared in the darkness and torrential rain. White slowly crawled into a deep puddle beside the chain link fence that surrounded the tennis courts. When he saw the sentry standing beside the building, lit by the city street lights in the distance, White stopped moving. As loud thunder startled him, and heavy rain fell onto his body, White remembered the mutilated bodies he climbed over on the rocks. He carefully attached the silencer to his handgun, then carefully aimed the weapon and fired a bullet that struck the soldier's stomach. The Cuban soldier immediately grasped his stomach and fell back against the brick wall. Then White quickly fired three more bullets that ripped through the Cuban's abdomen and knocked him onto the wet grass. White stood and ran toward the Cuban as he fired four more bullets into the body.

White radioed Nielson while dragging the sentry's body behind the large bushes beside the building. He

JOURNEY THROUGH A LONG WINTER'S NIGHT 299

met the group as they ran past the tennis courts to the other side of the island. The floodlights shinning onto the hotel's exterior brick walls lit the grassy area between the building and the water ahead of the group. Two hundred feet ahead was the team's target, the hotel's Greenhouse Restaurant. Nielson pointed to the group's left when he saw five sentries standing on the remains of the destroyed access bridge and he and his men immediately fell onto the wet grass.

"I can't see any hostages inside the restaurant!" Nielson whispered to his men as he shaded his eyes from the rain and stared at the restaurant's exterior glass wall. "That damn glass must be tinted, and the rain is streaking it so much I can't see through the windows!"

"Maybe they've moved the people out of there," whispered Guay as he watched behind the group for enemy soldiers. "Maybe they know we're on the island."

"If they did, we'd be dead by now! Lets crawl behind the bushes next to the building and get a look through those windows. Keep an eye on those sentries on the bridge. We don't need any more surprises."

Jim Owen motioned to his team huddled between the cars in the hotel parking lot, then they all ran across the access road and knelt together in the shadows behind the convention center. George Neville and Kevin Ryan displayed a thumbs up signal to Owen and then crawled behind the trash dumpster with Long and Mahoney. They watched as Owen and the other members of their team disappeared into the shadows behind the hotel. Neville and Ryan were to create a diversion behind the convention center by destroying the building's loading dock doors when the attack began. Owen hoped the noise and confusion created by the explosion would distract the Russians guarding the hostages and allow his men to enter the building undetected.

Five minutes later, Owen's team was squatting behind the bushes beside the lit grassy area, and the building's open rear access doors. They instinctively raised their rifles when they suddenly heard a large group of men walk to the door and briefly discussed the rain in a foreign language. Then the men walked back into the

300 D'ONOFRIO

building. Owen heard more men's voices and laughter inside the building and he motioned his men around him. "It sounds like we're going to have a problem getting in through these doors. It might be safer if we move in through the front doors." The men all nodded their approval and the group quickly moved back to the end of the building where they hid behind the dumpster with Neville and Ryan.

As Van Horne and his men walked across the roof a vivid streak of bright lightening and loud thunder from a storm located almost directly over the island startled them. Five minutes later, they knelt at the bottom of an inclined roof pitched at a seventy degree angle which ended just below the balcony of the President's suite.

The men adjusted their equipment and then cautiously began climbing the inclined roof's wet and slippery shingles. As they climbed higher they found three balconies built into the roof line, and they rested on each for several minutes. As he held onto a balcony railing Van Horne saw the lit Newport Naval Base in the distance. When he looked to his left through the heavy rain he saw the unlit steeple of Saint John's Church where Marlowe's men were watching the island. Then he looked down at the edge of the island and watched the large ocean waves crashing onto the rocks, and for a moment he was at peace. Van Horne's anger flared after he watched several large waves wash two dead bodies off the rocks in another area of the island.

He motioned to his men, and ten minutes later they were kneeling at the top of the inclined roof below the President's balcony. Two of the men clasped their hands together and lifted Robert Preston over the balcony's white railing as the others watched the hotel windows warily. Preston pulled the handgun from his shoulder holster, and watched the roof and the penthouse suite's closed curtains for Russian soldiers from behind a large plastic chair. When he was sure none of the Russians saw him, Preston pulled the others onto the balcony. They crawled behind the various pieces of white furniture on the balcony in the torrential rain and unpacked the plastic explosive charges for shattering window glass.

JOURNEY THROUGH A LONG WINTER'S NIGHT   301

Schwartz carefully adjusted several knobs on his rifle in the dimly lit church steeple as four of Marlowe's other sniper's watched him. "Where the hell did you ever get a fifty caliber rifle?" asked one of the them as Schwartz attached a one foot long silencer to the end of the rifle's barrel, making the weapon almost six feet long.

"I made this while I was in Saudi Arabia during Desert Storm, before they assigned me to your group. I took this fifty off a Jeep that an officer totaled in Riadade. Don't forget, I'm an armorer and they trained me to repair weapons for our units building airfields in the booneys! I built this beauty for firing armor piercing rounds through the turrets of Iraqi tanks during the ground offensive," he added as he attached a two foot long telescopic night vision scope to the weapon. Schwartz lifted the rifle and carefully rested it on the steeple's wooden wall. As he supported the rifle with one hand Schwartz pulled a six inch long bullet from a canvas carrier and forced it into the weapon's breach.

"Did you every shoot anyone with this?" asked Leon Frey, Schwartz's spotter for the attack.

"No, not straight on. I made it for stopping the men inside tanks! After a bullet passes through a turret it just bounces around inside the tank until everyone is dead!"

"Did you every kill anyone, Schwartz?" a nervous Frey asked to Schwartz. "When you were in Iraq, did you ever kill anyone?"

The twenty-two year old Schwartz hesitated before he answered. "No, I knocked out some tanks, but I never saw the bodies inside. I never wanted to see what I did," Schwartz added as he moved his eye away from the telescopic sight and looked at Frey.

"Are you going to be able to kill the Russians?"

"I know what I have to do here, and I'll do it." Schwartz looked through his telescopic sight and aimed the weapon at the sentry sitting on the air conditioner duct on the hotel roof. Several minutes later he became alarmed when the sentry suddenly stood and began walking on the roof that was dimly lit by the glow of the lights on the island below. "Frey, get Van Horne on the

302 D'ONOFRIO

radio and tell him what's going on!"

"Trojan Guide, this is Midway Barber. The sentry on the roof is walking toward you!" When Van Horne's men heard the message they all aimed their handguns at the roof which was only fifteen feet above the balcony. "He's moving straight toward you, Trojan Guide! Above you and to your right!"

Van Horne quickly made a decision he hoped was correct. "Midway Barber, get rid of him from where you are! Do it now before he sees us on this balcony!"

The Cuban sentry walked to the edge of the roof and shaded his eyes from the heavy rain as he looked toward the center of the city. "What's he looking at?" Frey asked Schwartz as he watched him through his binoculars. "Our guys are ten feet below him and he doesn't see them down there!"

Schwartz moved the cross hairs of his night vision Starlight scope over the sentry's chest, then he slowly squeezed the rifle's trigger. The weapon's silencer muffled the gunshot, but did not slow the large bullet that struck the sentry's chest, and violently knocked him off his feet as it ripped though his body.

"Shit, shit, I've got something moving fifty feet to the right of that body!" Frey told Schwartz when he saw another man frantically run across the hotel roof.

When Schwartz pulled open the rifle's breach a smoking brass bullet casing flew into the air and fell onto the platform's wooden floor. Schwartz frantically forced another bullet into the weapon as a Cuban Army officer knelt beside his fallen sentry. The officer's mouth opened in horror when he saw the man's extensive wounds, and he reached for the portable radio hanging from his belt to warn Vazques.

Schwartz knew Van Horne's men on the island were now in jeopardy as the upset Cuban officer raised the radio to his mouth. Schwartz squeezed the weapon's trigger and fired a bullet that struck the man's right side and ripped through his abdomen. The bullet propelled the dying man's body across the roof after severing his spinal column.

Frey and Schwartz watched the hotel roof for more

JOURNEY THROUGH A LONG WINTER'S NIGHT   303

sentries but no one else ran from the shadows. "Trojan Guide, this is Midway Barber. We just got rid of two sentries on the roof. Midway Barber, out."

Van Horne and his men crawled across the balcony in the heavy rain and lay beside the brick columns that supported the penthouse's five foot wide plate glass windows. They carefully placed a four inch long, two inch wide plastic explosive charge onto the bricks at the base of every window.

"This is Trojan Guide. Are all teams in position?" Van Horne whispered into his radio microphone as he cupped it in his hand so he would not be heard by anyone inside the suite.

Gene Depietro was the first team leader to report. "This is Bravo Kilo. We're in position and ready to go in the tunnel under the marina. Out."

"Trojan Guide, this is South Cycle," reported James Howard. "We're in position and ready to hit the garage. Holloway's team is here with us. Out."

"This is Jilted Hinge. We're in position near the Greenhouse Restaurant. Out."

Jim Owen was the last of Van Horne's team leaders to report. "This is Romeo Alpha. We're in position behind the convention center. Romeo Alpha, out."

Van Horne was relieved to hear Marlowe's voice in his radio headset. "This is Midway Barber. We're ready in the steeple. Watch yourself up there Trojan Guide! Out."

"Trojan Guide, this is Tactical Commander. We're all set on our end. Tac Com, out," reported Spencer.

"This is Trojan Guide. Hold your positions. Out."

Spencer quickly depressed several buttons on the console in front of him. When he knew Van Horne could not hear him he contacted the team designated as Rolling Thunder. "Rolling Thunder, this is Tac Com. Van Horne and his men are ready to attack the island. Over."

"Roger, Tac Com. We're on the way. Rolling Thunder, out."

General Franklin Maxwell first used the designator Rolling Thunder while serving as a division commander in Vietnam with the First Air Cavalry. His innovative

304   D'ONOFRIO

ideas were crucial to the development of the principles for supporting ground combat troops with attack and supply helicopters. His innovative theories and philosophies were so widely accepted and extolled, the Army commanders promoted him to commander of the First Air Cavalry after the conflict in Vietnam ended disastrously. Maxwell spent years refining and reworking his air assault tactics for the new generation of sophisticated and more versatile attack helicopters. During the Iraqi war, he and his pilots received thirty commendations after his Air Cavalry helicopters easily destroyed enemy tanks while suffering few casualties.

Now the fifty-seven-year-old two star general was risking his life and career on Spencer's speculation and suppositions. After Spencer explained what he knew about the situation on Goat Island, Maxwell adamantly refused to help him. But, after he heard the tape recorded message Van Horne's men deciphered, Maxwell knew he had to provide air support during the attack to ensure its success. Spencer realized he was lucky Murtagh moved Maxwell and his unit to the Quonsett Point Naval Air Station with the Third Special Forces Group.

Although many people considered Maxwell's personality abrasive and abrupt, he had great compassion for the men and women in his command. He cared about each of them as a father would his sons and daughters, and took time to know each of them. During the previous day, he met with his most trusted pilots and their crew members. He explained everything he knew about the situation on Goat Island, and Spencer's plan to attack the island. He emphatically warned his staff their actions during the attack might be considered treason if Spencer's intelligence information was incorrect. Then Maxwell told them he would be flying one of the helicopters.

"It's time for us to drop fire on the bastards on that island," Maxwell shouted as the sound of a loud alarm suddenly filled the huge aircraft hanger. He turned and watched the hanger's two hundred foot long green steel door slowly slide open. "Light up the runway! It's time

JOURNEY THROUGH A LONG WINTER'S NIGHT   305

to stop this insanity and help those people!"

Large floodlights mounted on the hanger roof suddenly flickered to life and Maxwell saw fifteen helicopters sitting on the runway in the heavy rain. Then he turned and looked at the seventy five men and women standing behind him after the hanger's internal lights were turned on. Forty five of the men were volunteers Maxwell recruited from the Third Special Forces Group. The others were his helicopter crews and ground support teams. "Lets show the bastards on that island what the Iraqi Army all ready knows! You can't screw with us and expect to go home with your balls in one piece!"

Two pilots and two crew members ran to each of the Black Hawk helicopters in the heavy rain. The helicopter's armament included fixed machine guns mounted on either side of the airframe, door mounted machine guns, and wire and laser guided missiles. The Apache helicopters also carried a four man crew. Their armament consisted of fixed machine guns, cannons, and wire and laser guided anti-tank missiles. Infra-red systems allowed the pilots of both model of helicopters to see in the rain and darkness.

"This is Rolling Thunder. We'll take the eastern route out over the ocean. Then we'll hit the city from the north after Spencer's men destroy the Stingers. They won't hear us coming until it's too late to stop us! Good luck to everyone, and God be with all of you."

Maxwell watched the Apache gunships lift off the wet asphalt and hover in the rain to the right of the runway. He assigned the Apache's the designator Arc Light, Echo Romeo, Lexington, and Whiskey Papa. The Black Hawk gunships used the designators Rolling Thunder, Echo November, Charlie Hotel, India Lima, and Xray Foxtrot. After the Black Hawk helicopters were hovering above the runway the entire airborne attack force flew toward the ocean with Maxwell in the lead.

Van Horne and his men stepped beside the two foot wide brick columns that supported the suite's plate glass windows on the balcony. They hoped the narrow columns would provide protection from the flying glass when the explosives shattered the windows. "This is

306 D'ONOFRIO

Trojan Guide. Fifteen second warning," he whispered into his microphone.

When his men heard Van Horne say, "This is Trojan Guide, five seconds!" in their radio headsets they leaned forward and depressed the detonator buttons on the explosive charges. Then they stepped behind the brick columns and stood in the heavy rain with their hands covering their faces as they waited for the explosions.

Chapter Eighteen

Lee felt his heart pounding as he knelt behind a car in the hotel parking lot moments before Van Horne warned the attack was about to begin. As wind swept rain fell onto his face he suddenly looked to the right and saw the orange tinted clouds drifting over the buildings in the city. *"If I'm going to die, then tonight is the night it should happen,"* he thought. *"I've always found peace in the rain, and maybe it'll bring me the luck I need to survive the night."* Lee suddenly seemed to find tranquility in the scene. He leaned back against the car and looked at Foran who was kneeling beside three AT-4 rocket launchers, and signaled he was ready.

Lee's personality was opposite that of his partner. Foran immediately volunteered to destroy the trailers when he discovered the extreme risk factor associated with this crucial portion of the attack. While he was in the Army, Foran craved the exhilaration of high risk assignments in enemy held territory. Now the adrenaline was again flowing in his veins, providing him with the excitement and tension he enjoyed. *"I'm in the middle of an enemy occupied island and I can destroy anything with this,"* he thought as he wrapped his hand around a green rocket launcher that measured four inches in diameter. As a vivid streak of lightening crossed the sky overhead he stared at the three foot long rocket while rain ran down his face. Although he never understood why, Foran was both amazed and frightened by the sound and devastation he could create with explosives. *"I'm ready,"* he thought as he lifted the rocket and nodded to Lee.

Thirty seconds later, the explosive charges Van Horne's team attached to the hotel windows detonated, creating a resounding concussion at the top of the hotel. Van Horne pulled his hands away from his face after the shattered pieces of window glass flew across the balcony. The wind blown rain suddenly seemed to suffocate him as he shouted, "Go! Go! Go!" into his microphone. Moments later, all the teams began the simulta-

308 D'ONOFRIO

neous attack of Goat Island. Every man knew there was no way to stop the attack, and no way to get off the island. Every man knew his job, and for a brief moment the fears and concerns in the men's minds faded as they were relieved the attack was beginning.

"What the hell was that god damn noise?" Leland asked himself after he was awakened by the explosion several floors above. "It must be those Cuban shit heads firing their rifles again." He looked at his watch and realized Barnes was in charge, so he closed his eyes and went back to sleep.

As heavy rain fell onto him, Foran leaned over the hood of a car and aimed an AT-4 at the side of Barnes' communications trailer. The trailer's aluminum exterior appeared orange when it reflected the glow from the nearby parking lot lights. Ten surprised Cuban officers inside the trailer shouted at one another after they heard the explosions at the top of the hotel and a few ran to the trailer door. The others used the radios inside the trailer and attempted to contact Vazques and their men for more information.

Foran attempted to steady the black cross hairs of the rocket's sight on the side of the trailer as his excitement and erratic breathing interfered with his aim. He took a deep breath and then slowly squeezed the weapon's trigger. Flames suddenly shot thirty feet behind him and the rocket flew from the launcher with the sound of rushing air. A flaming red streak lit the cars in the parking lot as it flew over them. When the rocket struck the trailer a tremendous explosion ripped it into hundreds of pieces. A blinding flash of bright white light and a deafening concussion accompanied the explosion. Then a huge swirling cloud of billowing black smoke mixed with bright orange flames as it violently rose into the sky above the destroyed trailer. Burning fragments of the trailer began falling on the automobiles in the parking lot.

When the rocket struck the trailer the tremendous explosion propelled hundreds of pieces of burning aluminum outward and they struck the President's helicopter. The flaming debris easily pierced the aircraft's

JOURNEY THROUGH A LONG WINTER'S NIGHT 309

sheet metal body and Lee appeared shocked when the helicopter was suddenly engulfed in flames. The concussion of another tremendous explosion seconds later blew the helicopter apart after the tanks of aviation fuel ignited.

The sounds of the large explosions on the island startled Barnes and he immediately looked around. He quickly climbed off Sharon Lingard, the President's event secretary, whom he was raping as she screamed hysterically on his room's carpeted floor. He appeared startled again when Vechesloff suddenly burst through the room's door as he pulled on his pants.

"What was that explosion I just heard?" Vechesloff asked as he ran to the open balcony door. "It sounded like something exploded in this building, and at the other end of the island."

"How the fuck should I know what it was," replied an irritated Barnes as he looked through the room's windows that faced the city. "Get your gun and we'll find Trembulak and Vazques."

During the week, Vazques used one of Barnes' three trailers as a supply area and sleeping quarters for the soldiers guarding the area behind the hotel. The violent explosion which destroyed the communications trailer two hundred feet from them woke the fourteen men sleeping inside the trailer. The sleepy and confused soldiers cursed one another and pushed each other aside as they frantically rushed toward the trailer's door.

Lee rested his elbows on the hood of a car as the torrential rain bounced off the polished red metal surface and splashed into his face. He fired a rocket at the center of the trailer just as the Cubans rushed into the doorway. The rocket trailed flames over the cars and another powerful explosion rocked the island moments later. The explosion engulfed the trailer in flames and lifted it off the ground with the screaming men trapped inside. A brilliant orange fireball billowed above the parking lot after a second, and a seemingly more powerful explosion suddenly ripped the entire trailer apart. A deafening concussion accompanied the explosion which shattered many of the car windows in the parking lot.

310   D'ONOFRIO

Dismembered pieces of bodies began raining down onto the island along with the burning fragments of the trailer.

Five seconds later, another rocket trailing long red and orange flames flew across the parking lot and struck the side of the third trailer. The issuing explosion lifted the trailer off the asphalt and then the aluminum walls were suddenly blown outward by a tremendous flaming explosion accompanied by searing flames. The devastating effects of the explosion destroyed cars parked within a sixty foot radius. An enormous swirling cloud of black smoke and orange flames quickly rose into the sky over the island as flames engulfed many of the automobiles in the parking lot. The searing heat caused the paint to bubble from some automobile's exterior before they exploded violently.

Lee and Foran watched the raging flames consuming the remains of the trailers and cars scattered across the parking lot in the heavy rain. As a wave of spreading yellow flames quickly rolled across the parking lot the gas tanks of many more automobiles began violently exploding. The heavy rain falling onto the flames created clouds of steam that rose off the asphalt and was quickly dissipated by the winds.

Lee pointed to the right when he saw four Cubans run wildly across the parking lot with their clothing covered in flames. The fires in the parking lot were so bright Foran saw other Cubans numbed by the sudden and unexpected attack running toward the destroyed trailers to search for their comrades. Both men found their rifles and began shooting at the dazed Cubans. Lee killed three Cubans trying to help another severely injured soldier, as Foran shot at another group of startled soldiers.

"That's it for the this part of our job," shouted Lee as he pushed a full magazine of bullets into his rifle. He quickly looked over the hood of the automobile after more vehicles engulfed in flames violently exploded. "They sure as hell weren't expecting us. They didn't think anyone was stupid enough to get to this island."

"Come on, we've still got to get rid of those Stingers so we can bring in Spencer's helicopters," shouted Foran

JOURNEY THROUGH A LONG WINTER'S NIGHT   311

as he checked a magazine of ammunition, and then pushed it into his rifle while nervously looking around. Lee agreed and the two men pulled their rifles over their shoulders and lifted as many rockets launchers as they could carry.

Depietro and his men waited anxiously for the attack to begin in the five foot wide tunnel near the steel plate under the United States Yacht Club's marina. The red overhead light bulbs cast an eerie glow on the tunnel's rough walls and floor. Depietro thought about his wife, and the times they shared together before she died in an automobile accident. He touched the ridges in the rough rock wall and studied the shadows created by the red lights as he pictured her in his mind. Then he smiled when he visualized his daughter standing beside her mother at her college graduation a month earlier.

Gallo was sitting on the floor and watched Fuller pull a picture from his pocket. "That your family, Paul?"

"Yeah, I took it six months ago," replied Fuller with a deep sigh. "I started my own company so I could make some money to take care of them. Now I hope I get a chance to see them again."

"You will. This'll be over before we know it."

"If anything goes wrong and I get lit up, make sure you fry the bastard that does me."

"You're not going to get hit up there, Paul. None of us are. We're going in hard and fast, and then we're all going home."

Depietro raised his hand and turned to his men when he heard Van Horne warn the attack would begin in fifteen seconds. "This is it. Everyone down on the floor facing away from the end of the tunnel. Keep your heads down until after the explosion."

The Seabee assigned to help Depietro's team was already laying on the tunnel's hard rock floor. When he heard the explosions, and Van Horne's message to begin the attack, in his radio headset he pushed an electronic detonator's button. A deafening concussion suddenly filled the tunnel when all the explosives attached to the bottom of the steel plate detonated. The explo-

312 D'ONOFRIO

sion's concussion filled the narrow tunnel with a violent wind that blew over the men carrying dust and smoke as it shattered all the light bulbs above them.

The powerful explosion and concussion startled and dazed Depietro and his men, and they slowly stood after it. They ran fifty feet through the smoke and dust that now filled the darkened tunnel toward a column of dim light directly ahead. Light filtered into the dust filled tunnel through the hole above. When Depietro found the old steel escape ladder fastened to the rock wall he began climbing it.

At the top of the ladder he clumsily pulled himself through a seven foot wide hole and rolled onto a hardwood floor. Smoke and dust filled the large room and Depietro readied his rifle as his men climbed out of the tunnel behind him. The explosion killed ten Cubans in the building's dining room located directly above the metal plate. One Cuban died when the force of the explosion drove a three foot long piece of hardwood flooring through his chest. Depietro quickly looked around and saw the explosion destroyed all the room's elegant wooden tables and chairs, and some of the dark mahogany paneling lining the walls. The explosion also destroyed many of the room's ceiling lights. "There goes the first trailers." Depietro heard someone behind him comment after the sound and vibrations of a tremendous explosion shook the building.

Depietro's team was laying on the floor beside the dead bodies when a group of frantic Cubans ran into the dining room. Depietro fired his rifle first, filling the room with deafening gunfire and killing the two men leading the group. A startled Cuban fired his handgun at the attackers and then stepped behind a wall to reload the weapon. Fuller fired a full magazine of bullets at the wall and they shattered the plasterboard into several pieces and killed the soldier standing behind it.

Depietro and his men quickly stood and ran to both sides of the dining room's doorway that opened into the building's large lobby. Depietro pointed at Fuller and Gallo after he saw two enemy soldiers run through a door behind the lobby's front desk. "Those two are yours,

JOURNEY THROUGH A LONG WINTER'S NIGHT   313

get rid of them. We'll check the other rooms on this floor and then we'll clear the second floor."

Fuller and Gallo ran across the thirty foot wide lobby decorated with large models of sailboats and stood on both sides of an office door. "It's too risky to go in through here partner," shouted Gallo as the sounds of a large machine gun suddenly filled the building. The entire building suddenly seemed to shake when another powerful explosion destroyed a trailer.

After Fuller pulled the pin from a hand grenade Gallo kicked the thick wooden door open and quickly stepped aside. Bullets from a Cuban machine gun immediately ripped through the walls that surrounded the door frame. "Damn it," shouted Fuller after fragments of wood struck his face, then he reached forward and tossed the grenade through the open door. When the grenade exploded the concussion blew the door and large pieces of the wall into the lobby. Fuller and Gallo rushed into the destroyed office and immediately lowered their weapons. They saw two men laying on the floor in a large puddle of blood beside pieces of a shattered wooden desk and chairs.

As they stepped back into the lobby they heard the sounds of more automatic weapons in other areas of the building. "I just saw someone running across the parking lot," shouted Foran as he ran to the marina's front doors. "I'll take care of them and catch up to you." He kicked the marina's front doors open while pulling the pin from a grenade, then he threw on the driveway toward the running Cubans. When the grenade exploded the concussion knocked five soldiers onto the wet asphalt in the torrential rain. Shrapnel and the explosion immediately killed two Cubans, and the others died minutes later.

"Any problems taking care of those two we saw in the lobby?" Depietro asked Gallo when they met in a large first floor library.

"They're history. Fuller is taking care of a some loose ends in the parking lot."

"Good, we've already got this floor cleared. Let's clear the second floor and start moving toward the condos."

314   D'ONOFRIO

Depietro and Stephen Shepard cautiously walked up the wide wooden stairs that led to the conference rooms and offices on the building's second floor. Both were startled when a Cuban soldier unexpectedly ran to the top of the stairs and began shooting at them.

"My leg. My leg," screamed Shepard after five bullets ripped through his left thigh above the knee, and shattered the bones. "Help me," he screamed as he dropped his rifle and immediately grasped his leg with both hands while falling onto the stairs.

As bullets splinted the varnished wooden steps in front of him, and the white painted walls beside him, Depietro angrily pulled his rifle's trigger. He watched as bullets struck the Cuban's abdomen, then the soldier's back seemed to violently explode outward. Bright red streaks of blood and pieces of flesh soon covered the foyer wall behind where the dead Cuban lay on the floor.

"See if you can stop that bleeding," said an upset Depietro when he saw the large amount of blood flowing onto the stairs from Shepard's leg. Depietro and Shaw then pulled the pins from two hand grenades after they sat on the steps. Depietro threw his grenade to the rear of the large foyer at the tops of the stairs, and Shaw tossed his grenade into the center.

The explosions covered both men with broken pieces of hardwood flooring and drywall as they knelt on the steps with their hands over their heads. Shaw quickly loaded the grenade launcher under his rifle's barrel as he and Depietro cautiously crawled up the stairs covered with debris. "There's two dead over there," said Depietro when he saw bloody, dismembered bodies laying on the floor. Two wide corridors led from the foyer to the rooms on the second floor. The dark green painted walls and the few light bulbs not destroyed by the grenades created an immediate sense of foreboding.

"Get down," shouted Shaw as he suddenly pushed Depietro down on the stairs and fell beside him. Moments later deafening gunfire filled the building as hundreds of bullets shattered the white plaster ceiling and walls in the staircase above the men. "Are you all right?" Shaw asked after the shooting stopped.

JOURNEY THROUGH A LONG WINTER'S NIGHT   315

"Yeah, yeah, I'm all right. I didn't even see that machine gun," said a shocked Depietro as he brushed pieces of plaster off his head and neck.

"I saw the door open, but I didn't have time to warn you. They must have a god damn fifty in there. I hate machine guns."

"Can you get a clear shot at them with your grenade launcher? If you can't, we're going to have to rush the fucking door." Depietro suddenly ducked down when the machine gun fired again and bullets destroyed more of the walls above him.

Shaw raised his rifle over the top step with one arm and fired a forty millimeter grenade toward the room where the machine gun was located. The grenade's explosion destroyed the wall with a deafening concussion and filled the room behind it with shattered pieces of drywall, varnished wooden trim, and shrapnel. The explosion instantly killed three Cuban soldiers standing on the other side of the wall aiming their weapons at the door. The explosion also wounded eight other Cuban soldiers inside the room. Shaw reloaded and fired a grenade through the hole in the wall that exploded inside the large room. Depietro and the others covered their ears when the wall and door suddenly and violently exploded outward, scattering debris into the hallway and foyer, and onto the stairs.

An angry Cuban soldier in another room pulled open the wooden door and shouted at Depietro and Shaw, hoping to lure them into a trap. As the Cuban dove onto the floor and reached for his rifle Shaw fired another grenade. A deafening concussion filled the building as the explosion destroyed the entire wall and filled the room with debris. The explosion and debris killed six armed Cubans standing in the room waiting to ambush their American attackers. It also severely wounded several other Cuban soldiers laying on the floor.

As Depietro's men quickly checked the other rooms Gallo found a locked room door. He slowly backed away from the door with his rifle pointed at it and waited for the others to join him. Sharpe met Gallo in the dimly lit hallway after he finished wrapping bandages around

316   D'ONOFRIO

Shepard's leg wound. "This is the only locked door up here. I don't like the feeling I'm getting, and I don't want to kick it in."

"You know, if this operation is illegal I'm going to lose my damn license to practice law," said Sharpe as he quickly pulled a block of plastic explosive from Gallo's backpack. "I finally graduate from law school and then I come here with Van Horne, blow up half a goddamn island, and wipe out the Russian Army," he added as he split the explosive into two smaller pieces.

Sharpe cautiously pressed one piece of explosive around the door's brass knob and pushed a pencil shaped detonator into it as the group backed away. As the men looked away a loud explosion destroyed the room's thick door and a large section of the wall, filling the already darkened hallway with more dust and debris. Without looking into the room Depietro threw a grenade through the hole. The explosion killed three Cubans planning to ambush the group as they walked down the steps to the building's first floor.

"This building is clear. Let's find Fuller and hit the condos," Depietro told his men as they ran down the stairs. "Tac Com, this is Bravo Kilo. We've secured the marina. Shepard was wounded and we're leaving him here as a guard. Out." The group pushed open the marina's front doors and stood in the heavy rain as they looked around for Fuller.

As Fuller checked the Cubans he killed with the grenade in front of the marina, he saw more enemy soldiers run into a long, one story building located two hundred feet ahead. Fuller ran across the parking lot and hid in the shadows beside the front of the building. He cautiously stood outside a convenience store's large front window as a vivid streak of lightening, and loud thunder startled him. *If I go in through that front door I'll be dead in two seconds.* Fuller thought as he stood in deep mud and pulled the pin from a white phosphorus grenade. He raised his rifle and fired several bullets that shattered the store's large front window, then he jumped up and tossed the grenade through the opening. Immediately after it exploded Fuller heard men screaming as

JOURNEY THROUGH A LONG WINTER'S NIGHT 317

the hot metal chips burned into their skin.

Two screaming Cubans frantically pushed open the store's front door and ran toward the harbor water with their camouflaged clothing smoldering. As Fuller shot the men on the driveway an uninjured Cuban suddenly burst through the store's front door and ran out of the building carrying a large machine gun. Fuller knelt in the mud as he fired the remainder of the ammunition in his rifle at the Cuban. The soldier died after the bullets shattered the thick glass door into thousands of pieces before striking him.

"*Shit, these bastards are all over the place,*" thought Fuller when he heard more men shouting warnings to one another inside the convenience store. He immediately reached up and threw another grenade through the window and then quickly backed away from the opening. When the grenade exploded the concussion destroyed the front of the store and showered the driveway with shattered pieces of wood, glass, and aluminum siding.

Fuller watched billowing black smoke from several fires drifting through the front of the destroyed convenience store as he backed away from it. He looked into a marine parts store and a car rental agency office, but couldn't see enemy soldiers in either. When he reached the end of the building he looked around the corner and saw the condominium parking lot guard house thirty feet from him. As he watched the building he saw three frightened Cubans kneeling on the floor raise their heads and look through the large glass windows.

Fuller slowly pulled the pin from a grenade as he cautiously walked forward in the building's shadows. He tossed the grenade toward the guard house and then dove into a deep puddle as he covered his head with his hands. When the grenade exploded it shattered all the guard house's large windows and collapsed two of the building's white walls.

The powerful explosion killed one Cuban soldier, and the concussion violently threw another out of the guard house. The terrified man lay on the road screaming from the pain after the grenade's shrapnel shattered

318   D'ONOFRIO

his left leg. The third dazed Cuban lay on the guard house floor in pain after a large wooden ceiling beam fell onto his chest and shattered three ribs.

Fuller ran to the darkened remains of the guard house and saw the injured Cuban laying on the floor holding his chest. "No, no, stop," Fuller screamed as the injured man frantically reached for his machine gun. Fuller realized he would not surrender and he showered the Cuban with bullets, killing him instantly. Then Fuller saw the other wounded Cuban sitting against the guardhouse wall attempting to reload his machine gun. Fuller squeezed his rifle's trigger and fired all the bullets in his rifle through the building's flimsy wall. Seven bullets struck the Cuban and the impact knocked him into a puddle on the driveway where blood flowed from his mouth, nose, and back.

Fuller looked to his left when he suddenly heard something shatter a rear window of the car rental agency office. His eyes widened in panic when he saw an enemy soldier aiming a machine gun at him in the light of a nearby streetlight. Fuller didn't have time to reload his rifle and he began running for cover in the heavy rain. Before he ran six feet, nine bullets struck Fuller and opened large wounds in his back and chest as the impact knocked him down. As Fuller lay screaming face down on the wet grass in excruciating pain, the image of his wife and daughters slowly faded from his mind as he died in agony.

As they ran toward the building together in the heavy rain, Shaw and Depietro heard the sounds of an automatic weapon. Then they watched helplessly as Fuller's body was knocked to the ground. "Destroy the fucking building," said Depietro as he pushed a full magazine of ammunition into his rifle. "Take down the whole fucking thing."

Shaw fired a grenade that exploded when it struck the building's long roof. The large explosion ripped a thirty foot wide jagged hole in the middle of the shingles and plywood. A Cuban soldier hiding inside the marine parts store began screaming as a large section of the roof collapsed and killed him. Shaw fired another gre-

JOURNEY THROUGH A LONG WINTER'S NIGHT 319

nade that flew into the front of the convenience store. The explosion violently blew out the building's side wall and collapsed more of the roof. As several fires began burning inside the long building, Shaw fired a third grenade that struck the front of the car rental agency and exploded. The concussion destroyed all of the building's roof and sent shattered pieces of the structure flying high into the air. As the fires quickly spread through the structure the Cubans hiding inside the building began climbing over the wreckage to get out. Depietro and his men unemotionally began shooting them after they ran out of the burning building.

As the men watched the red and orange flames consuming the building rise higher into the night sky, they heard large explosions inside the marine parts store when cans of paint and varnish began exploding. As the flames engulfed the entire building Depietro led his men to Fuller's body. Gallo and Sharpe knelt beside Fuller and mourned the death of their friend. "Come on, we've got to get out of here," Depietro told them as the nearby orange flames brightly lit the group.

"You're right," replied Gallo with a sigh of desperation as he stood and shook his head. "We've still got a job to do."

"Those are the two condominium buildings we've got to secure," Depietro told his men as he pointed ahead. Suddenly several bullets struck the wet black asphalt driveway near the men and they immediately raised their rifles and looked around for the enemy soldiers shooting at them. More bullets suddenly struck the damaged walls of the destroyed condominium guard house but the group could not see any enemy soldiers on the island near them.

"Behind those cement barricades," Depietro shouted when he saw the gray cement blockades installed along the roadway to prevent cars from driving into the harbor water. Ten seconds, later the men were laying behind the cement barricades lit by the flames and the nearby street lights.

"Tac Com, this is Bravo Kilo. One of my men was just killed. We're pinned down by a sniper somewhere

320 D'ONOFRIO

on this fucking island. We can't find the bastard and we need some damn help right now. Over."

"Roger, Bravo Kilo. I'll get some help to you as soon as I can. Out."

"Everyone take an area and start looking for him," Depietro shouted to his men. As they lay on the street in the torrential rain they searched for the sniper in the buildings on Goat Island as the battle continued around them.

Chapter Nineteen

Lets get this damn thing going Van Horne! What the hell are you doing up there? thought Howard as he and his men sat uncomfortably in the darkness under the deck in rivers of rainwater. Adding to their discomfort were the swarms of mosquitos that annoyingly flew around them after they disturbed the wood mulch piled under the deck. As he listened to the sound of heavy rain falling onto the deck over him Howard thought, *I told myself I would never get into this situation again. Why the hell am I here risking my life again? After the war I swore I would never take another man's life, and now I'm back in the same situation! What the hell am I doing here?*

Howard checked the area around the deck lit by the large overhead orange tinted floodlights as he remembered the bodies of the hostages he saw laying on the rocks. *Who am I trying to kid? I couldn't have blown out of here and left the people to die after I found out what was going to happen! These men are all the best, and I know we can stop them!* he thought as he looked at his team crouched behind him and displayed a clenched fist.

When Howard's team heard Van Horne's explosives detonate in their radio headsets they immediately crawled to the edge of the shadows under the deck and waited. Several seconds later, the thunderous roar of an AT-4 destroying the first trailer rocked the island and echoed through the garage. Howard motioned to his men and led them into the bright overhead lights and rain, to the first of the garage's two rear entrances. His men nervously knelt against the building's exterior brick wall and watched the parking lot filled with cars for enemy soldiers. At the same time Howard leaned over the automobile blocking the garage entrance and saw thirty to forty soldiers standing inside staring at the front entrance. He estimated the garage was one hundred feet wide and two hundred feet long.

Howard nervously stepped back and leaned against the brick wall when the deafening sound of an explo-

322 D'ONOFRIO

sion destroying the second trailer echoed through the garage. Ten terrified Cubans immediately ran to the garage's front entrance and up the ramp that led to the hotel's front doors. The others nervously shouted questions to one another and waited for their companions to report what they saw.

I hope those explosions don't trigger the bomb's vibration sensors, thought Howard as he watched his men pull the pins from their grenades. James quickly reached around the corner and tossed a concussion grenade toward the garage's left corner, then threw the second grenade toward the right corner. Jarvis leaned into the doorway and rolled a grenade across the concrete floor behind a group of Cubans staring at the garage's front entrance. Howard rolled another concussion grenade across the floor toward the center of the garage.

Moments later, Howard was startled when the sound of an exploding concussion grenade in the concrete walled garage was louder than the sound that accompanied the destruction of the trailers. The shocked Cubans held their hands over their ears as the second concussion grenade exploded. The brilliant flash of light that accompanied the deafening noise temporarily blinded many of the men. The grenade Jarvis threw into the garage exploded several seconds later. Its concussion and shrapnel killed several nearby soldiers and shattered many of the long florescent ceiling lights, darkening a portion of the garage's interior.

Immediately after the explosions, Howard and his men stepped behind the automobile blocking the garage entrance and began firing their rifles at the dazed Cubans. The deafening sound of automatic weapons suddenly filled the garage and caused the Cubans to scatter frantically. Within seconds, Howard's men fired all the bullets in their rifles and wounded eleven Cubans as they ran for their weapons. Howard and his men then knelt behind the automobile blocking the garage doorway. They reloaded their rifles in the heavy rain and glow of the orange overhead floodlights as the Cubans scattered through the garage.

"If we don't get into that garage in the next few min-

JOURNEY THROUGH A LONG WINTER'S NIGHT 323

utes we're not going to have a chance to disarm the bomb!" Holloway told his team. "Murphy, Becker, March, we're going to give Howard some help! Miller, you stay here with Decker and the equipment." Howard was shocked to see Holloway and his men crawl behind him as he knelt on the wet asphalt to reload his rifle. He frowned when the four men stood and ran to the second garage door as more of the Cubans began shooting at their attackers.

Long and Mahoney were the two members of Howard's team assigned to attack the garage's front entrance. They stood beside the convention center's front corner in the darkness when the communications trailer suddenly exploded violently to their right. "Shit!" was the first word out of Long's mouth moments after the tremendous explosion startled him. He shielded his face with his arm when the President's helicopter unexpectedly exploded violently into a brilliant billowing fireball that rose three hundred feet into the sky. The explosion and fire were so intense both he and Mahoney felt the heat on their arms and faces as they watched the blazing inferno.

Long cautiously bent forward in the heavy rain and looked around the building's corner toward the hotel's front entrance. He was again startled when the second trailer violently exploded in a huge fireball behind him. Four hundred feet ahead he saw the garage's front entrance. Then he found the large decorative white planter located forty feet from the garage's entrance in the center of the hotel's wide driveway. "There's our planter straight ahead! I don't see anyone in the parking lot, but there's some Russians standing near the garage entrance."

"God damn it, we're a lot closer to those trailers than I thought we'd be!" commented a nervous Mahoney after a huge explosion destroyed the third trailer, and automobiles engulfed in raging flames began exploding. Both men turned quickly and raised their rifles after they heard gunshots behind them. They immediately lowered their weapons when they saw Owen's team moving toward them beside the convention center wall in the heavy rain.

324 D'ONOFRIO

"Time for us to go," Long told his partner after he heard the sounds of explosions and automatic weapons coming from the garage. As the two men ran across the parking lot toward the planter in the driveway Long saw something moving in the convention center's glass enclosed entrance. "Mahoney, trouble coming at us from the left!" he shouted as rain fell onto his face and made seeing difficult.

The convention center's entrance was a modern foyer thirty feet wide and twenty feet high with walls and doors constructed of thick plate glass panels. As two Cubans pushed open the outer foyer doors Long fired his rifle and watched the glass panels explode inward and shower the men with a cascade of needle like fragments. The bullets fatally wounded the two Cubans in the doorway and propelled their bodies backward and onto the foyer's tiled floor. The bullets also shattered one of the foyer's tall glass walls and created a sound that resembled rushing water when thousands of pieces of glass fell onto the two dead men.

"I've got them!" Mahoney shouted when he saw more Cubans run into the foyer as Long reloaded his rifle. As Mahoney fired his rifle a Cuban soldier was knocked backward after a bullet struck his shoulder. The man screamed in agony after he fell onto a two foot long piece of thick glass which sliced through his back and extended from his stomach. Bullets struck another Cuban's body and his neck was broken when the impact violently pushed him through a foyer wall as glass fell around him.

Mahoney and Long began running in the torrential rain again. When they reached the large planter they knelt back to back behind it and quickly checked the surrounding area for enemy soldiers. The octagon shaped planter built with cement blocks was four feet high, ten feet in diameter, and was filled with dirt. A variety of ornamental trees and flowering bushes were planted in it. As both men gasped for air after their long and frantic run across the parking lot they realized they were lucky to be alive. They also knew the most dangerous part of their assignment remained to be accomplished.

JOURNEY THROUGH A LONG WINTER'S NIGHT   325

Marlowe raised his binoculars as he knelt in the church steeple and scanned the large windows that surrounded the hotel's rooftop lounge. Suddenly everyone turned and aimed their weapons at the darkened doorway behind them after they heard the wooden steps in the steeple creaking. Marlowe's hands trembled as he slid down against the wooden wall and pointed his handgun at the doorway while the other men aimed their rifles at it. Moments later, Reynolds and four of his Secret Service agents stepped through the doorway with their handguns drawn. "Wait, don't shoot them! What the hell are you doing here, Reynolds?" Marlowe shouted.

"Spencer told me you and your men were up here. We're here to help you!"

"Stay where you are! If Spencer didn't send you, you're dead!" Marlowe was relieved to learn Spencer told Reynolds his team was in the church steeple.

Reynolds used a pair of binoculars Marlowe handed to him to watch the lit streets on the island. Then he quickly scanned the hotel windows. He suddenly stopped breathing and pointed with one hand when he saw three men standing together in a hotel window, watching the activity on the island below. "Up there on the top floor, I've got three men in a window. The one without the hat is the bastard killing the people on the island!"

Andres Vazques stood beside the large plate glass windows that enclosed the hotel's elegant night club at the top of the building. Two of his senior officers stood beside him dressed in their camouflaged uniforms and wearing hats. "What's going on down there?" Vazques screamed as he watched the island with his binoculars. "How did the Americans dogs get onto the island without our sentries seeing them? They must have disabled Barnes' mines and come ashore in rubber boats!"

"It sounds like American commandos are all over the island, Colonel!" shouted one of Vazques' frantic officers as he watched a howling fire storm destroying the long building near the marina. "I can't reach any of our men on the radio! None of them are responding! What should we do?"

"Keep trying to contact them!" Vazques shouted as

326   D'ONOFRIO

he watched a cloud of billowing flames rise into the sky beyond the convention center. "I must speak to my commanders so I can tell them how to defend the island against the Americans!"

"Neither of us can contact our men on the island, or those in the trailers, Colonel! We've got to get off this island or we'll all be killed by the Americans."

"You incompetent fools!" Vazques shouted at his men as he pulled the radio from one man's hands. Vazques didn't know Spencer's electronic jamming of all radio frequencies except the one Van Horne and his men were using, prevented him from contacting his men on the island.

As Reynolds watched Vazques in the window, Marlowe rested a rifle on the steeple wall and located the three men in the telescopic sight. "I can't get a clear shot at him because the others are standing in front of him!"

"Shoot any of the bastards! I don't give a shit which one you hit," said Reynolds as he looked up after the wind caused the nearby tree branches to bend back as the leaves rustled. "It's one less we have to worry about!"

Marlowe immediately moved the cross hairs of his rifle's telescopic sight over the head of the officer standing in front of Vazques. The large plate glass window beside the Cuban officer violently shattered inward, creating the sound of a loud explosion. Before the shattered glass fell onto the floor the bullet tore through the Cuban officer's throat and splattered Vazques' face and neck with blood. Vazques instinctively fell onto the carpeted floor as the other officer stared at the body of his dead companion in shock. The only sound in the lounge was the strong wind whistling through the shattered window. "What are you looking at? He's dead, get down." Vazques screamed at the standing Cuban officer who was shielding his face with his arm. Moments later, a third bullet struck the officer's chest and knocked him to the floor where he died several minutes later.

The Americans have the advantage for the moment! Vazques thought as the strong wind whistled through the shattered window. *When I find them I'll kill all of them! I've got to find my men and organize them so we*

JOURNEY THROUGH A LONG WINTER'S NIGHT 327

can counter attack and kill the Americans!

"Damn it, I couldn't get a clean shot at him," a frustrated Marlowe told Reynolds, then he angrily fired bullets through ten of the lounge's plate glass windows and shattered them. He didn't know the thick panels were shattering with sounds that resembled loud explosions. Or that thousand of pieces of shattered glass were falling onto Vazques as he frantically crawled toward the lounge door.

"I hope this rain keeps up so we have some cover," thought Nielson as his team lay on the wet grass three hundred feet from the Greenhouse Restaurant. In the moments before the attack began he looked to his left at the lit city streets across the harbor water. He quickly found the darkened steeple where Marlowe's team waited for the attack to begin. Then he briefly looked up when he heard the explosions on the balcony almost directly upward above him.

Nielson's group cautiously ran one hundred feet ahead and knelt in the mud and puddles behind several large bushes in the shadows beside the building's well lit exterior brick walls. Nielson studied the glass walled restaurant with his binoculars, but all he could see were baroque styled wooden tables and chairs inside the large enclosure. "I still can't see anyone inside that damn restaurant! The only way we're going to know if there's any hostages inside the other part of the restaurant is to blow out those windows and get in there."

Gatting tapped White on the shoulder when the sound and vibrations of a large explosion rolled across the island. Then the two began running beside the building toward the restaurant's glass enclosure. The other members of their team raised their rifles and watched for enemy soldiers when they heard a second thunderous explosion when the Presidents helicopter was destroyed.

When Gatting and White reached the black metal framework of the glass enclosure they fell onto the wet grass beside it. The restaurant's overhead tiffany lights and the decorative floodlights that washed the building's exterior helped to light the grass. When the two men raised their heads and looked through the win-

328 D'ONOFRIO

dows they saw soldiers standing over their hostages in a larger section of the restaurant inside the main hotel building.

"The gad darn Russians are inside the older section of the restaurant with the hostages," Gatting radioed Nielson with his Texan accent. "Stand by you boys, we're gonna blow these dang windows."

Gatting and White pressed several gray plastic explosive charges against the enclosure's black metal framework and then pushed an electronic detonator into each charge. Several streaks of vivid lightening crossed the sky, and when the accompanying thunder caused the enclosure's glass panels to vibrate it startled the two men. As Gatting and White crawled away from the enclosure in the bright lights and torrential rain a Cuban soldier saw them. He screamed a warning to the others and ran to the enclosure's glass wall where he aimed his machine gun at the two men. Then he shouted victoriously to his companions he was about to kill some of the American attackers.

Gatting pressed the detonator and a powerful explosion lifted he and White off the ground, and covered them with shattered pieces of glass. Gatting brushed broken glass off his hair and neck as he quickly rolled onto his back. As he shaded his eyes from the rain with his hands he saw the explosives completely destroyed the glass walls. The enclosure's entire metal frame was now a twisted mass of black metal bars resting on piles of shattered glass. The explosion destroyed all of the hanging tiffany lamps and the restaurant was now dark. Many of the exposed electrical wires used to power the overhead tiffany lamps created red and blue sparks in the rain for several seconds before they shorted out. Then Gatting saw the dead soldier's body under the twisted wreckage and he thanked his God for saving his life.

"Lets give them some help," shouted Nielson, then he and the others ran to the restaurant's destroyed enclosure. "Gatting, White, watch the doors that open into the other section of the restaurant while we move in!" shouted Nielson as he cautiously stepped over the

JOURNEY THROUGH A LONG WINTER'S NIGHT   329

twisted metal and shattered tables and chairs while walking on piles of shattered glass that cracked under his shoes.

As the sound of gunfire intensified in the garage on the other side of the planter they knelt behind, Long told Mahoney, "I can't see any Russians soldiers around here."

Mahoney crawled to the edge of the planter and looked at the garage's inclined front entrance when he heard automatic weapons and explosions. He quickly jumped back when he saw five Cubans laying on the driveway.

"Americans! Americans!" shouted one of the Cubans as he pointed wildly. Then another fired a machine gun whose bullets struck the front of the planter and shattered many of the white concrete blocks.

After the shooting stopped, Long looked over the planter and then quickly knelt beside his partner with a terrified look on his face. "They've got a rocket launcher!"

Moments later, two Cubans fired an anti-tank rocket and the sounds of a tremendous explosion rolled across the island when it struck the planter and exploded. The explosion propelled large pieces of the planter's shattered concrete walls through nearby hotel windows. The explosion's concussion also shattered many other hotel windows. Five of the planter's walls toppled onto the wet asphalt driveway and released the dirt and plants they held back. The section of the planter that Long and Mahoney hid behind remained intact and undamaged.

"Fuck me, that was too close!" said Mahoney after he painfully sat on the asphalt in the heavy rain and felt warm blood running from his left ear. "My body feels like it just got run over by a tank!"

"They probably think that explosion killed us! Look at this damn blood," said Long as he splashed water from a shallow puddle in his face to wash away the blood flowing from his nose. "Let's throw a couple of grenades over this planter and see if we can do some damage!"

Twenty seconds later, the Cubans soldiers laying on

330   D'ONOFRIO

the driveway saw two grenades fly over the planter in the overhead floodlights. The frightened soldiers immediately stood when the grenades landed twenty feet from the garage's inclined entrance and rolled toward them on the wet asphalt. The grenades exploded seconds later and covered the driveway and garage entrance with burning phosphorus chips. Some of the wounded soldiers ran into the garage screaming in agony with their skin and camouflaged clothing smoldering. This helped to distract the other Cubans defending the garage against Howard's men attacking through the rear doors.

"That did it!" shouted a relieved Long. Then he shot two screaming Cubans frantically rolling on the wet driveway as they attempted to smother the burning metal fragments embedded in their flesh. Mahoney shot another Cuban as he and Long ran to the top of the garage's inclined entrance and knelt behind the concrete wall that surrounded three sides.

"I never thought we'd get this far without getting killed!" Long suddenly confessed to Mahoney as he looked around in the bright overhead lights and reloaded his rifle.

"That's a fucking comforting thought. Why the hell didn't you tell me this before?"

"For what? You know, if they detonate that damn bomb we're standing on top of it! I always wanted to go out with a bang!" Mahoney smiled and shook his head after he heard his partner's gruesome comment.

Please, please dear God, don't let me get shot right now! thought Nielson when the broken glass he stepped on in the destroyed greenhouse enclosure made a loud cracking sound. Then he carefully climbed over the twisted and bent black metal supports that once held the Greenhouse Restaurant's windows, and the remains of destroyed tables and chairs. Nielson cautiously knelt in the rain beside a brick wall and a doorway that opened into the older section of the restaurant inside the main hotel building. "I can hear women and children crying in the next room," he whispered to his men as the heavy rain fell onto the group.

The Cuban soldiers standing in the inner section of

JOURNEY THROUGH A LONG WINTER'S NIGHT   331

the restaurant were nervous after their commander was killed in the explosion that destroyed the greenhouse enclosure. Now the sounds of gunfire and explosions from the front of the hotel and the garage made them more nervous and panicky.

The terrified hostages in the restaurant looked around frantically as the sounds of gunfire intensified around them. A young woman lay quietly in a corner with her face resting on a pair of children's red sneakers as she stared unemotionally at the restaurant wall's white patterned wallpaper. During the second day of their captivity she pleaded for more food for her five-year-old daughter. The Cubans taunted the woman and forced her to watch as they murdered her husband and then gang raped her daughter. The Cubans then murdered the child as a way to punish the woman for disturbing them.

"I've got to get a look inside," Nielson whispered to his men. He motioned them to remain where they were kneeling in the heavy rain, then he looked around the door frame. He quickly fell backward when a Cuban soldier immediately began shooting at the doorway after seeing him. The sounds of the automatic weapons and the bullets bouncing off the brick wall added to the hostage's hysteria. Many of them began screaming and shouting loudly, and that added to the Cuban's confusion.

Nieves and Guay ran past the doorway and knelt beside a second doorway that opened into the older section of the restaurant. "Shit mon, we're sitting here and they can hit us through either door!" Nieves whispered in a Jamaican accent to Guay as he slowly pulled the pin from a hand grenade. As streaks of rain water ran across his black skin, he placed it on the floor and held it between his knees.

"What the hell are you doing?" asked a shocked Guay.

"If I get killed, I know I'm going down onto the floor mon! If I go down this'm grenade 'll get released and explode! I'll get the bastards anyway, mon!"

"Don't forget that damn thing is there if we have to run!"

332 D'ONOFRIO

We can't risk rushing into the restaurant while the Russians are standing over the hostages, thought Nielson as he looked around for a solution to his problem. *The hostages we're here to rescue are only a few yards away, but there's nothing I can do to help them! I need a new plan, and I need it right now!*

Chapter Twenty

Where the hell are all these fucking Russians coming from? thought Howard as he knelt beside the car blocking the garage's rear entrance and reloaded his rifle. What he didn't know was that twenty Cubans in the hotel lobby heard the gunfire inside the garage. They immediately used the hotel elevators and traveled to the garage to help their comrades to defend the area. The wind suddenly forced the smell of burned gunpowder out of the garage and Howard momentarily remembered scenes from Vietnam as the torrential rain fell onto him.

"Grenade," shouted Jarvis when he saw a Cuban soldier dressed only in his white underwear step from behind a cement column. Jarvis firéd his rifle as the soldier pulled his arm back to throw the grenade, and several bullets struck the man's shoulder. As the soldier screamed in agony and reached for his wounds the grenade fell out of his hand. It landed on the garage floor near a group of Cubans firing their weapons at Howard. When the grenade exploded the concussion propelled the men's bodies across the garage and enraged the other Cubans who watched their friends die.

The closest Holloway and his team came to combat was during Desert Storm, and that was far from the actual fighting. They waited miles behind the advancing front lines to disarm any nuclear weapons the collation forces located. The loud noise of the automatic weapons and the sound of bullets bouncing off the garage's concrete walls and ceiling startled all the men. Hundreds of bullets ripped jagged holes in the sheet metal body of the car they knelt behind, creating a ringing noise. The bullets shattered many of the car windows and covered the men with glass.

Two screaming Cubans suddenly began running toward the automobile Holloway and his men knelt behind. Holloway's hands shook almost uncontrollably from both fear and apprehension as he aimed his handgun at one of them. *I've never killed a man!* he thought in the moments before a primitive survival instinct com-

334 D'ONOFRIO

pelled him to pull the trigger. He reluctantly fired two bullets into one Cuban soldier's chest when he was ten feet from the garage door. As the second Cuban fired his machine gun at him, Holloway fired three bullets at the soldier. The wounded soldier abruptly fell onto the concrete floor screaming after two bullets struck his right leg and tore through the flesh.

Murphy knelt beside Holloway and his body shuddered with fear as he frantically shot at the screaming Cuban rolling on the garage floor. Two bullets tore into the Cuban's back and he screamed loudly for several seconds and then died. Murphy saw the Cuban's machine gun laying on the garage and he quickly looked around, then he suddenly stood and ran into the garage. He grabbed the weapon and lifted it, but quickly discovered its strap was still wrapped around the dead Cuban's wrist. *Move, or you're going to die in here!* Murphy thought when bullets struck the floor near him. As he frantically dragged the dead man's body toward the garage door, a wide streak of red blood stained the concrete under it.

Murphy dragged the body around the automobile and knelt beside it in the heavy rain as he trembled uncontrollably and struggled to control his breathing. "I didn't think I was going to make it," he laughed almost hysterically while he and Becker quickly removed the machine gun and other weapons from the Cuban's body.

"Holloway," shouted Howard as he attempted to be heard over the sounds of the automatic weapons echoing inside the garage. "Throw those grenades into the garage when I tell you. Long, Mahoney, where the hell are you two freaking clowns? We're getting our asses pounded and you're out having coffee."

"We're stuck at the top of the inclined ramp!" Long screamed into his microphone, moments after bullets struck the cement wall he was kneeling beside. "We can't get into the garage from here! The bastards have a fifty caliber machine gun at the bottom of the ramp!" Pieces of concrete suddenly flew into the air as Long and Mahoney leaned against the outside wall and listened to the machine gun's distinctive noise.

JOURNEY THROUGH A LONG WINTER'S NIGHT   335

We're taking way too much time to get into this garage! thought Howard as he knelt beside the car and watched the rain water running down the sides of a grenade he held. "I can't worry about the sensors on the bomb detecting an explosion! I've got to take the risk or we're never going to get into this garage, and they'll detonate that bomb anyway!" Howard made his decision and pulled his microphone closer to his mouth. "Long, Mahoney, roll your grenades down that inclined ramp when you hear ours explode!"

"What the hell," shouted a startled Howard as he struggled to remain kneeling after a man's body suddenly fell onto him. Jarvis saw Bruce James' body fall to the side, and he grabbed his close friend's arm and slowly lowered him onto the driveway. "Shit, he's dead!" Howard shouted after he felt James's neck for a pulse. Then he made a fist and hit the side of the car when he remembered the deaths of many friends in Vietnam.

As Jarvis stared at the heavy rain falling onto his dead friend's face he quickly became enraged and immediately wanted revenge. A loud crack of thunder startled Jarvis as he suddenly placed his rifle on the wet asphalt driveway and pulled off his backpack so he could unload the extra ammunition magazines. "Becker, take my rifle! I'm not going to need it!" he shouted to Holloway's men.

Howard could see the combat hardened Jarvis appeared devastated by James' death and was planning to attack the enemy soldiers with only his handgun. Howard immediately began stacking his own ammunition magazines on the driveway beside Jarvis'. While Jarvis removed the weapons and ammunition from Bruce James' body, he stared at the tranquil expression on the dead man's face as the rain fell onto it. Howard grasped Jarvis' shoulder and looked into the desperate man's eyes. Jarvis seemed oblivious to the streams of rain water running down his face. "Take this, you're going to need it!" Howard shouted at Jarvis as he pushed James' handgun in his hand.

"I'm going to kill every one of those bastards myself! Let's get in there and kill all of those fucking bastards

336 D'ONOFRIO

before someone else gets lit up out here!" Howard had seen the same look on men in combat before, when their only concern was to avenge the deaths of their friends. He knew the need for revenge that filled Jarvis' mind was pushing him to attack the enemy soldiers, even if it meant losing his own to kill the enemy.

"We're going in there together, Jarvis, but you watch yourself! I didn't come to this hell hole to die, so you use your fucking head and keep both of us alive!" Then Howard turned and shouted, "Holloway, throw your grenades to the left and the right sides of the garage. Keep them away from that fucking bomb!"

Fifteen seconds later, one loud explosion followed another until seven grenades exploded inside the garage, silencing almost all of the Cuban's automatic weapons. Then Howard heard three more large explosions at the other end of the garage. "Those are Long and Mahoney's grenades. Let's move in!"

The explosions and shrapnel in the confined garage wounded most of the Cuban soldiers. Many of the injured men lay on the cement floor screaming in agony. A few others were only slightly wounded, while several other soldiers appeared only dazed by the explosions. A wounded Cuban stood holding his bleeding abdomen with one hand as he tried to raise his machine gun with the other. Jarvis pointed both handguns at the wounded man and fired the weapons several times. The bullets struck the man and ripped his chest apart as they knocked him backward and onto the floor.

At the same time Long and Mahoney ran down the garage's inclined front entrance. They shot four partially dressed and dazed Cubans they found laying beside the blue Cadillac blocking the doorway. Mahoney killed two wounded Cubans dressed only in their camouflaged pants he found laying on the cement floor. As he quickly looked around he saw an uninjured group of six enemy soldiers running toward the garage elevators as they shot at Howard's group. Mahoney lifted a large machine gun off its tripod base and fired it at the fleeing Cubans, but the bullets missed and struck a cement wall behind them.

JOURNEY THROUGH A LONG WINTER'S NIGHT   337

The Cubans huddled behind a wide concrete support column and began shooting at Mahoney. They forced him to leap onto the floor and frantically crawl over seven dead bodies as he dragged the machine gun with him. As he lay on the floor behind the cement column, he suddenly realized the warm red blood of the wounded and dead men covered his hands. He stood and wiped the red fluid coating his hands on his rain saturated jeans. *Where the hell are they going, the lobby?* he thought after he looked around the column and saw the Cubans running into an elevator.

"Get your hand grenades ready!" shouted a frantic Cuban as the others dropped their automatic weapons onto the elevator floor. "We'll use them to kill the Americans, then we'll find Colonel Vazques and find a way to get off this island!" After they pulled the pins from their grenades the terrified Cuban saw Mahoney running toward the elevator and one of them shouted, "Shut the door! Close it before he gets here!"

Shit, they're going to get away! thought Mahoney after the elevator doors closed tightly. In frustration, Mahoney suddenly fired the machine gun and watched the bullets create jagged holes in the elevator's polished outer metal doors. Many of the bullets struck the Cubans inside the rising elevator and knocked the grenades from several men's hands. The grenades exploded seconds later in the confined elevator and blew both metal doors into the garage with a loud concussion that startled everyone. Mahoney ran to the elevator and swallowed hard when he saw bloody and dismembered arms, legs, and hands spread across both the garage floor and the bottom of the elevator shaft. Vivid wet streaks of running blood and fragments of flesh covered the elevator car's bright white walls and ceiling.

As he turned away from the sickening sight Mahoney suddenly realized the shooting in the garage stopped. Some of the Cubans wounded during the attack lay on the floor moaning and screaming for help as their pain became unbearable. Mahoney lifted a rifle from the floor and looked down at a Cuban whose shirt was saturated with blood. He stared at the red blood pumping between

338 D'ONOFRIO

the man's fingers he pressed tightly against a bullet hole in his chest. The Cuban lifted a blood covered hand toward Mahoney as he pleaded for help in Spanish several seconds before he died.

"Thanks for your help out there," Howard told Holloway as the group began gathering the Cuban machine guns and handguns. Howard didn't want an enemy soldier fighting death to lift a weapon and kill one of his men, or Holloway's. "This was a lot tougher than I expected! I think it's safe for you to move the rest of your team and equipment in here now. These aren't the ideal working conditions, but at least you have light to work with near the bomb," Howard added after noticing how many of the overhead ceiling lights were destroyed by the bullets and grenades.

As Mahoney and Long pointed their rifles at the hotel's rear parking lot and watched for enemy soldiers, Holloway motioned Decker and Miller to join him. They quickly crawled through the wet mulch under the deck and ran into the garage with some of their backpacks in their hands. Then Miller quickly ran back to the deck with Mahoney. As Miller gathered the remaining backpacks, Mahoney lifted the remote detonators.

"Everyone take a door and set up your own defenses!" Howard told his men as he checked the three garage entrances and wondered if he had enough men to defend the area. "If they come back for this bomb we better be damn sure we can stop them!"

"I'll grab that heavy machine gun at the top of the driveway and put it on the hood of this car." Long told Mahoney as he leaned against the blue Cadillac blocking the garage's front inclined entrance. "We'll need it if they try driving a truck or car down this ramp." Mahoney agreed and they both ran to the top of the inclined entrance and carried the machine gun and antitank rocket launcher into the garage.

Long expected an enemy attack as he loaded the Cuban machine gun with ammunition. Mahoney knelt on the concrete floor and leaned against the Cadillac as he prepared the rocket launcher. "This is insane! I thought the world was finally moving toward peace, but nothing has changed! We haven't learned a damn thing!"

JOURNEY THROUGH A LONG WINTER'S NIGHT   339

Holloway's team quickly inspected the exterior of the bomb's gray metal case and were shocked by what they discovered. "Tac Com, this is Holloway. This bomb has yellow lettering and instructions written across the case in English! It even has a United States' serial and inventory control number stamped on it! No wonder the Russians didn't want us to get a good look at it when we were on the island! This is an American MARK-7 tactical plutonium bomb!"

"That doesn't surprise me. I would be more shocked if you told me it is a Russian bomb. Can it still be detonated with a remote transmitter?"

"Right now it can be triggered from up to twenty miles away! It uses an unjamable satellite signal to receive the remote detonation code. We've got to get inside this case!"

"I've got an idea, Holloway!" said Dupont as he lifted a microphone while looking at a map. "Can you move the bomb outside the garage so one of helicopters can pick it up and dump it into the ocean away from the city?"

"Negative! They rig these bombs with motion detectors to detonate if they sense someone is moving it. We've got to find a way inside so we can get at the detonator!"

"I don't even know where to start!" said a frantic Miller as he squeezed his shirt and allowed the water to fall onto the garage floor. The tension quickly increased when no one had any idea how to open the bomb's gray metal case. "Let's take a chance and remove a few of the access panels so we can get a look at what's behind them."

"Could be risky, Commander!" warned Becker almost immediately as he rubbed his finger over a five inch round access panel held against the bomb's gray case by five screws. "They could have micro-switches hidden behind any of these access panels!"

"You're right. Miller's idea is risky, but if we don't get into this bomb soon they'll detonate this thing before we can disarm it!"

Becker held his breath as he inserted a small screwdriver into an access panel's gray screw. Holloway startled him when he suddenly shouted, "Hold it! Hold it! I can see a small access panel under the bomb. It

340 D'ONOFRIO

shouldn't be where it is."

"How are you doing?" Howard asked Jarvis as they knelt beside the garage door watching the heavy rain falling into the hotel's rear parking lot. "We all feel invincible when the shooting starts and bullets are flying. I'm sure James' death must be a shock."

"I never expected him to get it. I thought I was the one who was going to die here, not him! I just didn't expect it, and I didn't take it too well! It was like being back in combat when my friends died in my arms, and I just couldn't handle it!"

"Things like James getting killed make you stop and think about everything we take for granted every day. Like what the hell are we doing on this island."

"I was just thinking the same damn thing. I left my safe office as vice-president of corporate planning to get shot at here. I'm the luckiest guy in the world with three daughters, and a terrific wife, and I'm risking all of it right now."

Howard suddenly reached out and grabbed Jarvis' black knit shirt, then he violently pulled the startled man forward and onto the garage floor. Bullets from several machine guns suddenly splintered the garage's wooden door frame and ricocheted off the outer concrete wall. "There's a group of Russians on the deck we used for a staging area!" said Howard as he stood and pulled Jarvis off the floor by his wrist. Howard stepped through the garage door and hastily fired his rifle at three Cubans standing in the orange glow of the overhead floodlights. The bullets flew past the Cubans and struck some ornamental Birch trees planted beside the deck, cutting them in half.

Three enraged Cubans wanted to kill the Americans who attacked their comrades in the garage. Several seconds later, nine more heavily armed soldiers burst through the deck's open glass door and joined the others shooting at the garage in the heavy rain. Then they all began shooting at the garage entrance with their automatic weapons.

"Now we've got a real problem!" said Howard after he looked around the corner, and then quickly stepped

JOURNEY THROUGH A LONG WINTER'S NIGHT   341

into the garage as more bullets struck the cement wall and door frame. "Some of them just jumped off the deck! They're going to rush us!"

"The ones on the ground are yours! I'll take care of ones on the deck," said Jarvis as he lifted a detonator off the floor.

Howard stood with his back against the door frame and checked his rifle, then he nodded at Jarvis. The deafening and distinctive sound of exploding Claymore mines suddenly echoed behind the hotel, and then across the harbor. The anti-personnel mines projected thousands of short steel rods outward with the force of bullets when they exploded. The rods killed the Cubans on the deck as they ripped through their faces, chests, arms, and legs. The explosion destroyed the wide sliding glass doors that opened into the hotel from the deck. The force of the exploding mines threw metal fragments and pieces of shattered glass and brick sixty feet into the hotel building injuring several other Cubans inside.

Immediately after the mines exploded, Howard stepped onto the driveway and into the heavy rain. He saw four panicking Cubans who fell onto the wet grass when the mines exploded slowly standing in the overhead floodlights as gray smoke engulfed the area. When the Cubans saw Howard they turned and began running for the seawall. Howard held his finger on his rifle's trigger, and seconds later all the men lay dead on the grass.

"That was too god damn close for me," Jarvis confessed to Howard as they knelt together inside the doorway and watched the parking lot. "I can hear automatic weapons all over this island. I wonder how our guys are doing out there?"

In the minutes before the attack began, Owen and his team waited in the shadows behind the convention center for Van Horne's signal. Immediately after he heard the explosives attached to the penthouse windows detonate in his radio headset, Owen pointed at Neville and Ryan. "You know what you have to do. Make it good."

"All right, lets move up to the front of the building," Owen then told the others, then he led the group forward

342   D'ONOFRIO

in the shadows beside the convention center building. The communications trailer suddenly exploded in a huge fire ball to the right and the blast startled the men. Immediately after a violent explosion suddenly destroyed the President's helicopter, Owen motioned his men down behind the bushes as a raging orange fireball billowed into the sky. As Owen knelt in the mud, he watched Long and Mahoney standing at the front of the building, checking the area toward the front of the hotel.

As Malin knelt in the mud behind an evergreen bush he shuddered when another powerful explosion destroyed the second trailer with the Cuban soldiers trapped inside. He squinted into the wind driven rain when six frantic Cubans suddenly ran from behind the convention center shouting at one another. The excited soldiers stopped on the access road and frantically pointed at the destroyed trailers as a rocket suddenly struck and destroyed the third trailer. The excited and confused Cubans didn't see Malin stand behind the bushes that were now brightly lit by the raging orange flames consuming the exploding cars in the parking lot. As rain fell onto his face Malin fired all the bullets in his rifle's ammunition magazine, and the dead Cuban's fell into the deep puddles beside the road.

The sounds and concussions of the three trailers being destroyed rolled across the island as Neville and Ryan attached plastic explosive charges to the two forty foot high steel doors on the convention center's loading docks. Neville surprisingly thought about the woman who had been his wife for five years and became angry when he remembered finding her with another man. "I can't think about her right now. I've got to stay alert or I'm going to get killed!"

Both men ran from the doors in the torrential rain and knelt behind a cement staircase thirty feet from the loading docks. Then they both pushed remote detonators almost at the same instant. Several huge explosions shook the entire convention center building and shattered all the windows facing the harbor. The explosions propelled pieces of the twisted gray metal doors beyond the seawall which was located sixty feet away.

JOURNEY THROUGH A LONG WINTER'S NIGHT   343

The explosion also ripped a large piece of one door from its frame and it flew across the loading dock. The twisted metal violently crashed through a block wall where it extended eight feet into the building's exhibition hall, killing thirty of the hostages. The upper section of the second metal door bounced loudly across the loading dock's cement floor and shattered a flimsy plywood office. The explosion projected other large fragments of the door outward and they ripped through several tractor trailers like grenade shrapnel.

"That should shake up the bastards," Owen whispered to his men after they heard the explosions while waiting at the building's front corner. They cautiously stepped around the corner and ran fifty feet to the well lit glass foyer that was the convention center's main entrance. They were all surprised to see the shattered glass and bleeding bodies of the Cubans Mahoney and Long killed as they ran across the driveway.

"Lets get inside before someone sees us out here!" Owen told his men, then they carefully stepped through the steel frames of the foyer's shattered windows. They walked into a large lobby with a long red cherry counter and elegant wooden chairs and couches. Owen suddenly made a tight fist and displayed it to the group as a signal of potential danger, then he pointed at a wooden door ahead. His team immediately stepped against the walls covered with a white and gold patterned wallpaper when they heard men shouting behind the closed mahogany door.

As Owen cautiously walked toward the door, a Cuban soldier suddenly ran from a narrow hallway that led to convention center's executive offices. The Cuban was angered by the American's unexpected attack, and the deaths of his fellow soldiers, and he aimed his machine gun at Owen as he screamed profanities in Spanish. Willet fired his rifle first and the bullets struck the Cuban's chest and head, and knocked the body onto the floor.

Owen looked at Willet and thanked him by nodding at him. Then Owen stepped beside the door that opened into the hallway where the entrances to the convention

344 D'ONOFRIO

center's three ballrooms were located. He held his breath as he looked through the door's small window and estimated the hallway to be seventy feet wide and four hundred feet long. Red carpeting, white wallpaper, and large mirrors gave the illusion the hallway was immense. Adding to the illusion were six large cut glass chandeliers hanging from the ceiling. Large glass windows along the right side of hallway formed the building's outer wall, and they faced the hotel's front entrance and the garage's inclined entrance.

Owen quickly stepped away from the door when the thunderous noise of an anti-tank rocket exploding in the front of the hotel shattered many windows of the hallway. "I count at least twenty in the hallway on the other side of this door. I don't know how many are in the ballrooms."

Neville and Ryan carefully walked up the cement stairs with their rifles pointed into the darkened loading dock area. They cautiously walked into an immense and brightly lit storage area filled with cardboard and wooden boxes. Ryan was surprised no one was guarding this area of the building and asked his partner, "Why don't they have any guards out here? Where the hell are all their guards?"

Neville shook his head as he opened one of eight wide white doors that opened into the convention center's enormous kitchen. He and Ryan knelt down and quickly crawled across the white tiled floor and hid behind a long stainless steel food preparation counter. They saw counters littered with decaying food, dirty pots and pans, and swarms of cockroaches and ants devouring piles of spoiled food. The Cubans used the kitchen to prepare food for themselves during the week, and fed the scraps they did not eat to the hostages.

"Those must be the doors that open into the ballrooms," whispered Ryan as he pointed at the sixteen wide white doors at the far end of the kitchen. The two men crawled across the filthy kitchen floor, and Ryan grabbed a mop as he knelt six feet to the right of one door. He pushed the mop handle forward and forced the serving door to swing open into a ballroom, then he

JOURNEY THROUGH A LONG WINTER'S NIGHT 345

fell onto the floor.

Hundreds of bullets fired from Cuban machine guns in a ballroom ripped apart the wooden door and nearby walls, and forced the men to cover their heads with their hands. Adding to the noise in the kitchen were the bullets striking the metal pots and pans hanging from hooks, and those on the counters. The pots flew across the room with a resounding racket, and many bounced off the walls and floors. The bullets also shattered both empty and full glass jars of food on metal storage shelves, spilling the contents and projecting jagged fragments of glass through the air. Several bullets punctured a large hot water pipe in the kitchen's rear wall, and scalding water and steam suddenly began spraying into the room.

A group of Cubans in a ballroom reloaded their machine guns as they screamed warnings and congratulation to one another. They were confident they killed the American attackers they believed were trying to ambush them from behind. One of the frantic Cubans suggested someone should check the kitchen, but none of the other soldiers wanted to walk into an area where a wounded American commando might still be alive.

"There's a lot of them in the damn ballroom!" whispered Neville as he raised his rifle and aimed at the remains of the shattered wooden door after the gunfire stopped. He suddenly looked at Ryan with a pulled expression on his face after he heard automatic weapons and hostages screaming in the ballroom.

"They're shooting the hostages!" said a shocked Ryan as he looked back at the shattered door with a terrified look on his face.

"Romeo Alpha, this is Neville. They're shooting the hostages in the ballrooms. We've got to get in there and stop them!"

"We're coming at you right now. Wait for my signal and then hit them from your side." As Owen watched his men attach plastic explosives to the wall around the wooden door that opened into the hallway he thought, *I wanted to have the people in those ballrooms freed by now! Now I'm listening to them dying.*

Owen motioned to his men and they crouched be-

346 D'ONOFRIO

hind the heavy furniture in the lobby. Manley pushed a detonator's button and the wooden door and a large section of the wall disappeared in a blinding flash of light accompanied by a tremendous explosion. The explosion was so powerful it blew large pieces of the wall and door into both the small lobby and the convention center hallway.

The powerful explosion and accompanying concussion jarred and bruised Owen and his men. They wearily stood in the lobby now filled with dust and smoke and cautiously made their way to the fifteen-foot-wide jagged hole in the wall. With his team standing behind him, Malin tossed two concussion grenades through the hole and into the hallway. The explosions filled the hallway with blinding flashes of light and deafening explosions.

Owen then stepped through the hole and saw four Cubans laying on the floor twenty feet from where he stood. The explosion killed one soldier and wounded the others. Owen shot at three confused men who were frantically crawling across the floor, and they began screaming after they were struck by bullets.

Chapter Twenty-One

As the smoke and dust cleared in the convention center's wide hallway, the frightened Cubans screamed warnings to one another. Manley shot at two terrified Cubans who dropped their weapons after hearing the explosion and frantically ran toward a ballroom's open doors. Bullets struck one soldier's body and propelled it backward and against a large mirror that was shattered by the impact. Several bullets struck the other soldier and severed his spine. He immediately fell onto the red carpeted floor and began screaming to the others for help. As he frantically crawled across the carpet, dragging his useless legs in agony, Manley fired three more bullets that killed the wounded soldier.

An angry Cuban kicked one of the ballroom's ornate double doors open and screamed at the Americans after he ran into the hallway and fired his machine gun at them. Willet fell to one knee and began shooting at the soldier and the bullets struck the Cuban's legs. The sudden and severe pain caused the soldier to fall backward onto the carpeted floor as he held his finger on his weapon's trigger. Bullets ripped large holes in the hallway's white suspended ceiling and struck a large glass chandelier that suddenly crashed onto the floor and shattered into thousands of pieces. Owen fired several bullets and they killed the soldier as he grasped the bleeding wounds in both legs.

A horrified group of Cuban soldiers standing at the far end of the long hallway watched helplessly as their comrades died. They immediately turned and ran through the glass doors that opened into the area of the convention center that housed the hotel's indoor swimming pool. As bullets fired by Owen's men shattered the thick glass doors behind them, the terrified Cubans fell onto the cement floor behind a large hot tub filled with water. They lay there and frantically looked around when they heard automatic weapons and explosions around them.

Owen's men quickly split into two groups and ran

348 D'ONOFRIO

to both sides of the wide hallway. Both teams cautiously walked toward the first ballroom's double doors with their rifles aimed at it. All of the men were outraged when they heard the sounds of automatic weapons and hostages screaming beyond the ballroom doors. "We've got to get in there and stop them," shouted Owen. "Malin, use your grenade launcher and take down the doors."

"Hit the deck." Willet suddenly screamed when three Cubans stepped into the convention center's hallway through the large hole in the wall created by the plastic explosives. "They're moving in behind us."

Fuck me, thought Malin as he turned and fired a grenade that struck the wall behind the Cubans. The explosion and deafening concussion shattered many of the hallway's windows and knocked the Cubans onto the floor. Pieces of shrapnel struck one soldier and the jagged hot metal cut through his camouflaged shirt. It ripped apart the flesh of his shoulder and arm, and released a flood of deep red blood. The explosion dazed the other soldiers, and they lifted their weapons as they stood while their wounded companion lay on the floor screaming beside them.

Malin fired another grenade at the Cubans and it exploded with a blinding flash of light six feet in front of them. The concussion lifted the men's bodies off the floor and propelled them against the wall with such force they shattered the thick wallboard. As the men's broken bodies fell onto the carpeted floor, large red blood stains covered the wall above them.

"Let's get into that ballroom," shouted Owen when he heard automatic weapons and people screaming again. "Neville, Ryan, keep your fucking heads down. We're coming at you two."

As the members of his team looked away, Malin fired his rifle's grenade launcher. The deafening explosion shattered the ballroom's thick mahogany double doors, and the surrounding walls, into large pieces. The explosion hurled pieces of the debris into the large ballroom, and shattered two large crystal chandeliers over the doorway. Shreds of shattered and broken glass rained down onto both the hostages and their frightened Cu-

JOURNEY THROUGH A LONG WINTER'S NIGHT 349

ban guards. A huge cloud of dust and smoke filled the passageway as many of the four hundred frightened hostages laying on the ballroom's red carpeting began screaming hysterically. Owen's team rushed through the haze and knelt on the carpet when they had an unobstructed view of the ballroom's interior.

The first Cuban soldier Owen's men saw was a young officer dressed in a camouflaged uniform standing over the bodies of thirty dead hostages he shot only moments before. The explosion distracted the officer, but he was determined to carry out Vazques' orders and began shooting the men, women, and children laying around him as they screamed in terror. Within seconds he killed twenty more of the hostages and then frantically began reloading his machine gun. The other Cubans in the ballroom also began shooting the hostages laying on the floor at their feet. This caused the ballroom to be filled with loud gunfire, and screams of terror, all of which added to the confusion.

Willet became incensed when he saw the blood spattered bodies laying on the ballroom's floor. The people lay on large stains of their own blood with their faces and clothing filled with holes. He immediately raised his rifle and fired a single bullet that ripped through the Cuban officer's left arm above his elbow. The wound immediately forced the soldier to drop his weapon, and as he reached for the wound he cried out in pain. Willet fired five more bullets that ripped through the Cuban's abdomen and knocked him to the floor on top of the dead hostages. "Fuck you too," Willet shouted at the officer as he lay on the floor screaming in agony.

Immediately after they heard the explosion destroy the ballroom doors, Neville and Ryan rushed through the kitchen serving doors and killed four Cubans. The Cubans were kneeling beside the wall, preparing to ambush Owen's men. Ryan painfully leaped onto the ballroom's wooden dance floor beside the hostages and killed two Cubans running for the kitchen doors. As he rolled onto his back on the hardwood and began reloading his rifle he saw something moving to his left.

"Behind you Neville!" he screamed when he saw

350   D'ONOFRIO

more enemy soldiers.

A female hostage's hysterical screams and gunfire in another part of the ballroom momentarily distracted Neville. He suddenly felt something hot strike the left side of his body, then he had the sensation someone hit him with a baseball bat. The unexpected impact forced all the air out of his lungs and he violently fell onto the carpeted floor on his stomach. He could see the hysterical people screaming as they frantically crawled away from him, but he couldn't move. Neville died several seconds after ten bullets from a Russian machine gun ripped into his back.

Ryan rolled onto his side on the floor and shot the Cuban who killed Neville. Several bullets passed through the man's chest and covered the wallpaper behind him with streaks of blood and torn flesh. Tears formed in Ryan's eyes after he quickly crawled to Neville's body and saw the bullet holes and blood covering his shirt. As tears filled his eyes, Ryan crawled to a woman who was naked to the waist, and cut the twine tied tightly around her wrists. When he heard someone screaming his name, Ryan immediately crouched forward to protect the terrified woman, then he heard three loud gunshots behind him. He quickly turned with his handgun drawn and was surprised to see Manley standing over the body of the same Cuban soldier he shot after he killed Neville. Although he was severely wounded, the Cuban wanted to kill Ryan before he died.

"This ass hole almost shot you in the back you dumb fuck!" Manley shouted as he extended his hand and pulled a dazed Ryan off the carpet. "Get your ass back in gear so you don't get your head shot off, or ours!"

"I want everyone to listen to me," Owen shouted to the frantic hostages in the ballroom as he quickly walked between them. "I want those of you who have been freed to free the others. See if you can help the wounded people until we can get some medical help for them. I don't want any of you to leave this ballroom. We've got to keep moving, but we'll be close by to keep you safe."

"We've got to get out of here," an anxious Owen told his men after he looked at his watch. "We've been in

JOURNEY THROUGH A LONG WINTER'S NIGHT 351

here fifteen minutes and we've only cleared this ballroom. We've still got two left." The men ran out of the ballroom and quickly moved to both sides of the second ballroom's doors. "Malin, Willet, toss in a concussion grenade after I kick the doors open," Owen told them. "We don't have surprise on our side this time."

Immediately after Owen kicked the mahogany doors open, Malin and Willet threw their grenades into the ballroom and they exploded with blinding flashes of bright light and two deafening explosions. Some of the twenty Cubans inside fell onto the light brown carpeting beside the three hundred fifty terrified hostages they were guarding. Moments later, Owen's team rushed into the ballroom and killed eight confused Cubans as the deafening sounds of their automatic weapons terrified the hostages.

"There's more on the floor between the hostages." Malin shouted as he shot at a Cuban soldier laying on the carpet bedside a group of screaming hostages. The bullet inadvertently struck and killed a male hostage laying on the floor beside his wife and five children. Malin fired again and a bullet struck the Cuban's chest. The impact propelled his near lifeless body onto a nearby woman, who screamed hysterically when she felt blood running onto her back.

Some of the other Cubans panicked and dropped their weapons before they ran toward the kitchen's white doors. As Owen's team shot at the fleeing soldiers; bullets shattered the walls behind the Cubans, and moments later the men's red blood splattered the white wallpaper. Owen and all his men seemed pleased that thirty seconds after entering the ballroom they were freeing the hostages. " Everyone stay in here until we come back for you. Don't move into the hallway." Owen shouted as he knelt beside an elderly man and carefully cut the twine around his wrist with his bayonet.

Owen's team ran to the third ballroom's wooden doors. The men looked at one another after they heard strange noises coming from the other side. Inside the ballroom four Cubans were left alone to guard two hundred hostages after their six companions ran to help de-

352   D'ONOFRIO

fend the garage. Bruce Powell, Donald Skinner, and Craig Glass realized they would soon be killed by their terrified captors. The three men watched their nervous guards shout to one another in Spanish from where they lay on the room's green carpeting. The three hostages quietly twisted the twine around their wrists as the Cubans nervously aimed their weapons at the ballroom doors.

Powell was a thirty-six-year-old weight lifter who worked in the hotel's security department. During the week several drunken Cubans severely beat the two hundred fifty pound, six foot tall man, to prove they were stronger than any of the hostages. Powell's left eye was now almost swollen shut and the skin around it seemed purple and full of blood. Dried blood still covered the left side of his face and stained his white shirt which was torn during a two hour beating. As Powell attempted to ignore the pain of three broken ribs sustained during a two hour beating, he rolled onto his stomach and placed his forehead on the carpet. Powell then pulled his hands apart with all of his strength until he broke the weakened twine.

Skinner was a twenty-six-year-old electrician who was much smaller than Powell, but as his anger and apprehension increased, so did his strength. Skinner painfully pulled his wrists apart and broke the twine, but not before it created deep and bloody gashes in his hands and wrists.

Glass was the oldest of the three men at fifty-one, but the Vietnam veteran was still in good physical shape. The gray haired man's anger increased as he thought about the abuse he endured during the week. He clenched his teeth in anger and tightened his fists as he pulled his wrists apart and broke the twine. Then he nodded to the other two men who knew they would probably be killed, but were determined they would not die without a fight.

Powell watched a shirtless Cuban soldier dressed in camouflaged pants backing toward him with his machine gun aimed at the ballroom's doors. When the frightened soldier was standing two feet from him, Powell rolled onto his back as the other startled hostages

JOURNEY THROUGH A LONG WINTER'S NIGHT 353

watched around him. Powell quickly pulled his knees over his chest and then kicked forward with all his strength. His feet struck the soldier's lower back and violently knocked the confused and disoriented man forward, and onto the carpet. As the confused Cuban lay on his stomach he reached out for the machine gun knocked from his hands. Powell quickly stood and jumped onto the Cuban's back, crushing the man's face into the carpet.

Skinner was terrified as he stood and crouched as low as he could while running across the twelve feet that separated him from another Cuban. Then both he and the soldier fell onto the ballroom's hardwood dance floor after he tackled the soldier around the waist. Another terrified Cuban ran across the wide ballroom to help his companions as he screamed warnings at the hostages in Spanish and fired his machine gun into the ceiling. Glass surprised the soldier when he suddenly jumped up and tackled the running man, forcing him down onto the carpeting.

As the remaining Cuban ran between the hostages to help his screaming companions, a female hostage suddenly pushed her left leg foreword and tripped him onto the floor. Several men, and a few partially clothed women laying around him, began kicking the Cuban as he struggled to stand. As blood ran down the man's face from a broken nose he screamed to his companions in the other ballrooms for help, unaware they were already dead.

Powell struggled to his knees after the Cuban soldier rocked him off his back. As the Cuban was kneeling beside him Powell savagely punched the man's face with his large fist and knocked him onto his back. The Cuban swore in Spanish as he reached to his boot pulled out a long knife, forcing Powell to leap forward and grasp the soldier's hand. As the two men struggled for control of the knife, Powell turned the long metal blade until the tip pointed at the struggling soldier's chest.

"Die you animal!" an almost deranged Powell shouted as he pushed down the man's hands with all his strength. The man screamed in pain as Powell drove

354   D'ONOFRIO

the entire length of the knife into his chest. Then Powell twisted the knife embedded in the soft flesh as blood quickly filled the screaming man's mouth. A great sense of satisfaction flooded over Powell as he momentarily looked at the dead soldier's face. Then he quickly pulled the knife from the man's chest and ran to where Skinner was fighting with the Cuban he tackled to the floor.

Powell raised the blood covered knife over his head, spattering himself and several hostages with the dead soldier's blood. He drove the knife downward and into the Cuban soldier's back as he stood over Skinner with a handgun pointed at him. The shocked Cuban's eyes suddenly opened wide when he felt the excruciating pain in his back. He dropped the handgun and frantically reached backward wildly with both hands, searching for the embedded knife as he turned toward Powell. Then the soldier fell forward onto the carpet. Powell pulled Skinner to his feet and ripped the knife from the dead soldier's back. Then the two men leaped onto the Cuban fighting with Glass.

Fifteen angry hostages viciously kicked at the fourth Cuban tripped onto the floor as the injured soldier frantically tried to push them away. A naked woman the soldier repeatedly raped during the week stood and barbarically kicked the man's face with her feet. Eight other hostages managed to stand with their hands still tied behind their backs. They all began kicking the dazed Cuban, then some began freeing each other. Two other women the Cuban raped during the week stood over the screaming man and began kicking his groin and legs with their bare feet.

As the Cuban tried to stand another woman used two hands to lift his machine gun off the floor by the barrel. She swung the weapon as though it was a baseball bat and struck the back of the soldier's head with it. The disoriented and now almost unconscious soldier fell forward onto the floor again. Then an aggravated male hostage took the weapon from the woman and began striking the Cuban's head with it. The other hostages laughed and cheered as the man repeatedly struck the man's head with the weapon's butt. The dead sol-

JOURNEY THROUGH A LONG WINTER'S NIGHT 355

dier's head quickly became an indiscernible mass of torn flesh, shattered bones, and gray brain matter, all of which was oozing blood. The elated hostages suddenly began kicking the dead man's body, showering one another with blood and fragments of the man's skull as they laughed and shouted hysterically.

Owen and his men heard the screaming in the ballroom and thought it was the Cubans celebrating after they killed all their hostages. Manley kicked the doors open and when the group rushed into the ballroom they were shocked to see the almost hysterical men and women with their faces, arms, and hands covered with wet red blood.

"Who, who're you?" Powell asked Owen ominously as he walked forward while blood dripped from the knife in his hand. A group of fifty enraged hostages wanted to kill more of their captors and they quickly gathered behind Powell as they studied Owen and his men.

"We're members of an American rescue team." Owen swallowed hard after watching a smiling naked woman smearing blood on her chest and long blonde hair while kneeling beside a Cuban's body. "What the hell happened in here? Where are the soldiers who were guarding you?"

"We killed all of those animals ourselves," replied Powell, then the crowd unexpectedly began cheering and shouting jubilantly behind him. "We couldn't take any more and we had to fight back before they killed us. They beat us and raped the women, so we had to kill them."

"There's four dead on the floor," Malin told Owen as he cautiously walked through the crowd of agitated hostages.

"Shit, they're a lot more than just dead," added Ryan as he shook his head while he cut the twine around several hostage's wrists.

"We have to get out of here so you're in charge while we're gone," Owen told Powell as he looked at the blood covered knife held firmly in the dazed man's hand. "Don't let anyone come in here unless they're Americans. We'll be back to help you as soon as we can."

As Owen and his men continued clearing the con-

356 D'ONOFRIO

vention center, Holloway, and Becker lay on the garage's concrete floor in their wet clothes. Holloway carefully twisted the second screw holding the three inch square access panel under the bomb, as Becker held his fingers on the plate so it would not move. After Holloway removed the screw Becker lowered the panel and both men were puzzled by what they saw.

"There's a small mirror attached to the panel," Holloway explained to the group. "I can see some small switches in the mirror."

Decker knelt on the floor and looked at the image of the switches reflected in the mirror. Then she opened a manual and quickly flipped through it until she located a specific section. She turned the book so Holloway could see the page as he lay on the floor. "That panel looks like the one in this picture. Those are the switches that activate the hydraulic pump to open the case. If we set the switches to the correct positions the cover should open. If they're not set correctly the bomb will detonate."

Holloway studied the picture, then the switches under the bomb. "The switches look exactly like the ones in that picture. Does the manual give the switch positions?"

"Someone may have altered those switches."

"We don't have any other choice. What do the rest of you think?" No one else spoke, but they all nodded their head and agreed with Holloway's risky method for getting into the bomb.

Decker became more nervous as she read each switch setting. "Now, there should be a small button on the left side of the panel. Push it and the cover should open."

Holloway pressed his trembling index finger against a small red button, and seconds later everyone heard sounds inside the gray metal case. Holloway quickly sat on the concrete floor beside the bomb and pressed his ear against the metal case. "Those sounds could be the bomb getting ready to detonate. There's no sense running. If we've made a mistake this'll all be over in a couple of seconds." The group watched the bomb's gray metal case with growing apprehension, and most of them were startled and jumped nervously after they heard a tre-

JOURNEY THROUGH A LONG WINTER'S NIGHT   357

mendous explosion nearby on the island. None of them heard Miller praying silently as he stared at the bomb.

A partial smile formed on Holloway's lips after the bomb's two inch thick cover slowly shifted, and a small crack began to form as the cover slowly rose into the air. The group immediately knelt beside the gray metal case and used their flashlights to study the bomb's internal components as the case continued rising. They saw hundreds of feet of multicolored colored wires snaking through the case. A ten inch round silver disk etched with black timing symbols slowly rotated, and several lights flashed inside the bomb, reminding everyone the device was deadly.

As the bomb's cover slowly opened, Murphy began reading disarming instructions to the others from a small manual. Holloway and his staff immediately began attaching long red, green, blue, and yellow wires that extended from their instruments to the printed circuit boards inside the case. As the others worked beside them, Decker and Miller carefully removed three access panels from small brass conduits inside the bomb's case and began studying the multicolored wiring they found inside.

"We've been working in here for sixteen minutes." Holloway told his group as he quickly looked down at his watch. "I don't understand why they haven't detonated this thing yet."

Sixteen minutes into the attack and we're still waiting here for help, thought Nielson as he stood in torrential rain in the Greenhouse Restaurant enclosure's twisted black metal remains. He motioned to Walsh and Gatting, and they stepped onto the grass and ran beside the building's brick exterior wall lit by bright floodlights.

"We're sure as hell not going to get into that restaurant from here." Nielson told them as he held up his plastic coated map and studied it. He occasionally rubbed away the raindrops on it that obscured his view of the diagram. "I need you two to move around the outside of the building and come in through the lobby. I know it's dangerous, but we've got to try hitting them from behind."

358   D'ONOFRIO

"That's a dang bull shit plan, Nielson," Gatting commented almost immediately. "You know they're going to be waiting for us in the dang lobby." Then Gatting paused and wiped the rain water off his red hair when he saw the hopelessness in Nielson's face. "You're right, there's no other way to get into that freaking restaurant. We don't have a gad dang choice."

"All right, get moving," said Nielson as he handed them his four grenades. "You might need these on the way. Let me know when you're in position."

Walsh and Gatting ran across the soggy grass and stopped beside the building's corner. Walsh cautiously leaned forward and checked for enemy soldiers in the heavy rain. "Come on, there's no one in the parking lot ahead." They quickly ran through the parking lot to the next corner of the building two hundred feet ahead. "Wait till you see this shit," Walsh said with a surprised tone in his voice after he looked around the corner. He was shocked to see the torrential rains washing the dirt across the black driveway from the shattered remains of the white concrete planter.

"It looks like they hit that thing with a rocket. That must have been the explosion we heard a few minutes ago." They didn't know they were looking at the planter Long and Mahoney hid behind before attacking the garage.

As the two men were about to run toward the hotel's front doors, Walsh grabbed Gatting's shoulder from behind after he heard a loud shrill noise behind the building. "Claymore mines. I'd know that sound anywhere."

The two men ran along the lit front of the building in the heavy rain and knelt beside the brick wall near the entrance to the hotel lobby. Then Walsh quickly looked around the corner and saw the hotel's eight lobby doors constructed with brass frames and thick glass. Another set of identical doors twelve feet beyond the outer doors formed a large foyer with a brown marble floor and walls.

"I've got some shit head with a machine gun standing between the doors," Walsh told Gatting as he raised

JOURNEY THROUGH A LONG WINTER'S NIGHT   359

his rifle and pulled out the ammunition magazine to check it. He pushed it back into the rifle and then stepped around the corner. The foyer's outer glass doors suddenly exploded inward after bullets shattered them with the sound of thunder. As the startled Cuban soldier ducked for cover six bullets struck his body. The impact violently propelled his body backward and through the foyer's inner glass door that shattered into hundreds of small pieces.

Gatting watched the lobby's elegant chairs, sofas, and other furniture directly ahead of the doors as he reloaded his rifle. He instinctively aimed his rifle at a young Cuban soldier who suddenly ran into the lobby from the hallway that led to the Greenhouse Restaurant. Gatting could see the young man appeared frightened by the expression on his face, and he couldn't shoot the soldier. The Cuban unexpectedly stopped running and suddenly began shooting at Gatting with his machine gun as he screamed at him. As bullets struck the wet sidewalk, Gatting leaped to the side and fell onto the concrete sidewalk, bruising his elbow.

"What the hell was that?" Walsh asked as he looked around.

"There was some kid in the hallway who looked so scared I couldn't shoot him. The bastard just tried to kill me."

"That wasn't too smart ass hole. Now he's probably waiting for us in there."

"That little shit probably is. Lets find the mother and kill him," replied an angry Gatting, then both men cautiously stepped through the foyer's door frame. As they knelt on the glass covered foyer floor, both men shot at the young Cuban after he went into the lobby again. The bullet's impact lifted the soldier's body off the floor and it shattered a large stained glass window behind him. After the soldier's body fell forward onto the floor, streaks of blood ran down the white wallpapered wall.

"He's out of the way," said Walsh moments before he heard footsteps and voices in a section of the lobby located fifty feet to the left of the hotel foyer's doors.

360   D'ONOFRIO

Walsh pulled the pin from a grenade and quickly tossed it around the corner without looking. The grenade's explosion destroyed elegant wooden chairs and all the windows of a small gift shop located in the lobby. Walsh quickly looked around the corner and saw the bodies of three soldiers laying beside the shattered remains of a large chandelier that crashed down onto the marble floor.

Another Cuban soldier suddenly ran from the hallway that led to the Greenhouse Restaurant to investigate the explosion, and Gatting was the first to see him. He immediately pushed Walsh onto the marble floor as he and the Cuban began shooting at one another.

Chapter Twenty-Two

Walsh immediately covered his head with his hands after one of the foyer's glass walls exploded into thousands of pieces which fell onto him after bullets struck it. Gatting suddenly felt an intense burning sensation after several of the Cuban's bullets tore through the flesh. Gatting clenched his teeth and his face contorted as his pain suddenly became so intense his eyes began tearing. A second later, five bullets struck the Cuban's stomach, knocking the dying soldier onto the floor. "I need some dang help!" Gatting shouted before he dropped his rifle and then fell beside the weapon as he grasped his bleeding leg.

"Damn it, I don't like the way this looks," said Walsh as he knelt beside Gatting and saw the red blood oozing between his fingers. "Lets get you to a chair and see if we can stop that bleeding." He helped Gatting off the floor and steadied him as he hopped to an ornate wooden chair in the foyer.

"The bullet went right through my gad dang leg!" moaned Gatting as his partner carefully cut the denim with a bayonet. Gatting momentarily looked away when Walsh pulled back the material and exposed the mutilated and blood covered flesh. "I don't think you're going to be able to stop that dang bleeding."

"I'm sure as hell not going to let you bleed to death, you jerk," Walsh replied as he began cutting strips from the long blue curtains in the foyer to make bandages. After he tied several long pieces of curtain tightly around Gatting's leg, they seemed to slow the bleeding.

Both men's heads quickly turned after they heard men's voices in an area of the lobby to the left. Without speaking, Walsh crawled beside the foyer' inner polished metal door frame and pulled the pins from two grenades. Then reached around the corner rolled them across the marble floor, toward the center of the lobby. Six surprised Cubans shouted warnings to one another when they saw the grenades, and they frantically climbed over the hotel's long wooden guest service counter. The grenades

362   D'ONOFRIO

were three feet from the counter when they exploded and the concussion blew out all the lobby windows and covered the hotel driveway with shattered glass. The explosions also shattered the long oak service counter and killed the Cuban soldiers laying behind it.

"Come on gad damn, we've got to hold this area. Help me to that dang chair in the lobby and I can watch your back while you try to get into the restaurant." Gatting painfully hopped across the foyer on his uninjured leg as he held his rifle in one hand. Walsh helped Gatting to a finely upholstered chair and eased him into a sitting position. "Now get going. Nielson is expecting us to be knocking on that restaurant's gad dang front door, and I don't want to listen to him bitch if he thinks we're late."

John Foran and Raymond Lee, the AT-4 team, ran into the unlit area near the hotel's outdoor tennis courts. As Foran watched for enemy soldiers, Lee opened the twelve protective metal cases that housed Stinger missiles. After the cases were open, Lee raised his rifle above his head and smashed each missile's sophisticated electronic components. Without the sophisticated tracking systems the missiles could not track and destroy airborne targets.

"That was the last of the missiles. I counted forty seven," Foran commented as the two men knelt in the shadows and he moved the radio microphone beside his mouth. "Tac Com, Tac Com, this is the AT-4 team. We've neutralized all of the Stingers on the island. We're going to move around the hotel and see if we can help our men. AT-4 team, out."

As the two men ran on the brightly lit access road behind the hotel in the heavy rain they heard sporadic automatic weapons fire. Then they heard several large explosions at the far end of the island. When the men were running beside the guest rooms at the rear of the convention center, they stopped and turned after they heard the sound of an automobile engine starting in the hotel's rear parking lot. Lee raised his arm and pointed when he saw a van speeding through the large parking lot behind the hotel. The driver turned on the head-

JOURNEY THROUGH A LONG WINTER'S NIGHT   363

lights as the van's wheels screeched onto the access road Foran and Lee stood on.

Foran shot at the approaching van with his rifle as it sped toward two men at over sixty miles an hour. The combination of van's bright headlights and the heavy rain blinded Foran, and he lowered his rifle and began reloading the weapon. "I can't see a fucking thing in those headlights. I don't think we're going to be able to stop him."

"This shit head isn't going to get past me," shouted Lee as he squinted into the headlights and glare off the surface of the wet access road, while he aimed an AT-4 at the van. Bullets suddenly struck the road after the Cubans leaned out the van and began shooting at the two men they saw standing in front of them. "This one is personally delivered ass hole," Lee shouted as he pulled the At-4's trigger and a rocket flew from the launcher and struck the front of the van below the windshield.

When the rocket exploded raging orange flames suddenly engulfed the van and trailed behind the speeding vehicle. Moments later, all the van's windows and doors exploded outward violently as raging orange flames burst through the openings. The van's driver door landed on the grassy area behind the hotel, while the passenger side and rear doors bounced off the cement seawall and slid across the road. As the flaming van sped toward them, Lee and Foran ran into the shadows beside the hotel building. They watched pieces of the bumper and fenders break away after the van careened into the cement seawall. Both men shaded their faces after the vehicle's gas tank unexpectedly exploded and created a fireball that billowed into the night sky. The fierce explosion toppled the van onto its side and it slid onto the grass behind the hotel. Burning gasoline now covered the vehicle, the access road, and a large area of wet grass.

"No one could have lived through that explosion," said Lee as he tossed the rocket launcher on the grass.

"No one did," replied Foran as he cringed when he saw a man's body lying on the grass covered in

364   D'ONOFRIO

flames. "Come on, let's find our guys and see if they need our help."

"Midway Barber, this is Bravo Kilo," a frustrated and angry Depietro shouted into his microphone as his team still lay behind the cement barricades to avoid the unseen sniper's bullets. "We're still pinned down here and we can't move. We've been here for ten fucking minutes, and we need some god damn help right now."

"I understand your problem, Bravo Kilo," replied Spencer as he wrote another note on his pad. "I'll get back to you after I find a team that can help you out."

Marlowe and Reynolds listened to the conversation between Spencer and the desperate Depietro, and they looked toward the area of the Goat Island where the team was pinned down. "Bravo Kilo, this is Midway Barber. Do you have any idea where your sniper might be located? Over."

"I don't fucking believe this. We're getting shot at and this beauty wants us to find the fucking sniper for him." Marlowe looked over at Reynolds and smiled when they heard Depietro's frustrated comments. Depietro quickly covered his head when a bullet suddenly struck the front of the cement barricade he was laying behind with a resounding sound. When he realized where the bullet hit the barricade Depietro's eyes widened in shock.

"Midway Barber, the sniper isn't on this island. I think the bastard is somewhere in the city." As the heavy rain fell onto his face, and bright overhead lightening and thunder momentarily startled him, Depietro cautiously crawled into a deep puddle so he could see beyond the cement barricade. Then he watched the buildings in the city for several minutes. "I think I just saw a muzzle flash in that tall steeple lit with the blue floodlights. That one that's in the center of the city."

Marlowe and Reynolds immediately found the towering steeple of Trinity Church in the city. Marlowe estimated the church was located less than half mile from Goat Island. One of Marlowe's spotter focused his powerful binoculars on the lit wooden shutters that enclosed the upper two thirds of the steeple. Several minutes later, the excited spotter said, "There he is. I can see a rifle

JOURNEY THROUGH A LONG WINTER'S NIGHT 365

barrel sticking out between the shutters."

"He must have been in there all the time," said a shocked Marlowe as he watched the sniper fire a single bullet and then pull the rifle back through the shutters.

"He must not know we're here, or he would have tried to stop us by now."

"Why don't we try taking him out from here, Commander?" asked Schwartz after he checked the distance to the steeple with a laser range finder. "He's within range."

"Tac Com, this is Midway Barber. We found Bravo Kilos's sniper in a church steeple in Newport. Are your helicopters in the area to give us some help? Over."

"Roger, Midway Barber, they're moving in from the ocean right now. Their commander is using the designator Rolling Thunder and he's on the line with us."

"Rolling Thunder, this is Midway Barber. We have a fire mission for you. Over."

"Roger, Midway Barber. I'll send the Lexington and Excalibur to help you. Give me the target coordinates. Over."

"We've got a target in the city to check out." James Tyler, the Excalibur's pilot, told his crew as the helicopter flew over a residential area ten miles north of Newport.

John Havaneck was the Lexington's pilot and he studied a map of the city in the glow of the cockpit's red overhead lights as his co-pilot flew the helicopter. Maxwell believed Havaneck was one of the few pilots capable of pushing an attack helicopter to its aerodynamic limits during combat operations. He once watched the skilled Havaneck weave an Apache helicopter through forty Iraqi tanks to destroy a crucial fuel supply prior to the Desert Storm ground offensive. As they flew toward the city, Havaneck stared at the lit and deserted city streets below as he thought about what his commander was asking of him. *I may have to destroy some of the historic buildings in this city. I don't know if I can do that. I'm not fighting in a war a million miles from home in the middle of a desert. I'm not ready for combat in a city like the one I grew up in.*

366   D'ONOFRIO

Havaneck thought about the plutonium bomb on Goat Island, and the men risking their lives to disarm it. *I can't be worried about those things right now. My only concerns should be helping our men on that island and keeping my crew safe. I've just got to do the job no matter what gets destroyed down there.*

Havaneck turned and watched the men preparing their weapons in the red glow of the red ceiling lights mounted in the rear of the helicopter. He watched his crew chief and door gunner leaning on their machine guns as the ten members of the Blue Light team checked their automatic weapons. Havaneck turned and took the helicopter's controls as he watched the city momentarily lit by vivid lightening through the heavy rain streaking the aircraft's windshield.

"We should try to knock out that sniper before the helicopters get to church," Marlowe told Schwartz and the other men. Schwartz and another men knelt on the platform in the heavy rain and stared through their telescopic sights until they saw the sniper's rifle extend through the shutters. Schwartz fired a fifty caliber bullet that struck the white shutters and created a hole one foot in diameter in the white wooden slats.

Marlowe watched the steeple through his binoculars as two other of his snipers began firing their rifles at the steeple with Schwartz. As he watched several white shutters shattered by the bullets fell away and into the cemetery beside the church. Marlowe ground his teeth together when he saw the sniper's rifle suddenly slide through the shutters and fall to the ground below. "Excalibur, this is Midway Barber. The steeple is yours. We got the sniper. Over."

Tyler depressed a radio transmission button on the helicopter's controls and spoke to Havaneck using his radio. "We're up, John. You take the lead and I'll back you up. Over."

"I've got the target in sight and I'm turning toward it." Radioed Havaneck as he slowed the helicopter's forward speed, and slowly guided it around the two hundred foot high white steeple bathed in blue light.

The door gunner studied the hole in the white shut-

JOURNEY THROUGH A LONG WINTER'S NIGHT   367

ters three hundred feet from the helicopter as he nervously aimed his machine gun at it. "I can't see anything moving in there skipper. It looks like everyone is dead."

As Havaneck flew beyond the church and over the city, Tyler slowly guided his helicopter around the steeple. When the helicopter was slowly flying past near the hole in the steeple, five of Barnes' men suddenly began firing a machine gun at it. As Barnes men shot at the helicopter they were unconcerned they were shooting at members of their own armed forces. Instead, they enjoyed the challenge of defeating the forces they considered inferior. Murtagh told his men everyone was to be considered the enemy in their quest to gain control of the nation, and anyone who resisted should be killed.

"Pull out! Pull out!" Tyler's crew chief screamed as bullets ripped large holes in the helicopter's sheet metal tail. The bullets then severed the hydraulic and oil lines in the engine compartment, covering the men in the rear of the helicopter with scalding fluid. Barnes' men aimed the machine gun into the rear of the helicopter and killed the crew chief and all the members of the Blue Light team. Tyler struggled with the helicopter's controls and as he flew away from the steeple while hundreds of machine guns bullets struck the engine.

"Jesus Christ, look at that," shouted Marlowe as he watched dense black smoke lit by the city lights trail behind Tyler's helicopter.

"Lexington, Lexington, we're hit," Tyler screamed into his microphone as he struggled to control the damaged helicopter. "They're still in that steeple. It was an ambush. We're going down heavy."

Havaneck quickly turned his helicopter and watched helplessly as the Excalibur suddenly exploded in a fireball over the hotel parking lot littered with the remains of the three destroyed trailers. Burning pieces of the aircraft and men's bodies flew from the huge fireball and fell onto the cars below with the torrential rain. When the fuel aboard the helicopter ignited, it formed a cloud of scalding flame that fell onto the automobiles parked below, causing many of them to burn and explode.

368   D'ONOFRIO

Havaneck and his crew were in shock as they stared at the helicopter's burning debris scattered across the island. The crew chief covered his mouth with his hand as he watched for movement on the ground, but he knew everyone on the helicopter were dead. Neither Havaneck, nor his crew were concerned the snipers were hiding inside a building considered a religious gathering place. Havaneck increased his helicopter's speed as he flew over the rooftops of the city's houses and stores. He then maneuvered the aircraft until he was hovering two hundred feet from the rear of the steeple. "Castile, blow the shit out of that fucking steeple."

Robert Castile was the helicopter's door gunner and he aimed his five barrel machine gun at the white shutters at the top of the steeple. Castile was a devout Roman Catholic, but he knew he had to destroy the church to prevent other men from dying. "Forgive me father, I don't have a choice."

Castile depressed the machine gun's trigger and hundreds of smoking ammunition shells began flying into the air. The machine gun's five barrels quickly rotated as hundreds of bullets struck the steeple's white shutters and the walls below it. Castile directed the machine gun across the rear of the steeple' wooden clapboards. Hundreds of bullets passed through the steeple and ripped the wooden shutters and clapboards from the other sides of the towering structure.

Havaneck slowly turned the helicopter until the aircraft's nose was pointing at the steeple, then he squeezed a trigger and two large machines guns mounted to the side of the aircraft began firing. Havaneck directed thousands of bullets into the steeple's wide wooden base. Then he slowly moved the path of the bullets upward, hoping to kill any snipers who might be fleeing down a staircase built into the center of the steeple. Large black holes appeared in the lit steeple as bullets ripped through the structure, and shattered wooden boards and shutters fell from all the sides.

When his co-pilot saw Havaneck turn a switch that illuminated a red targeting display attached to his helmet, he said, "We're going to burn for this one skipper."

JOURNEY THROUGH A LONG WINTER'S NIGHT 369

"That doesn't mean shit to me right now, Kowalski. I'm sending all those cock suckers to hell myself." Havaneck armed the missiles mounted to the side of the helicopter as he moved the black box superimposed on a red targeting display over the church steeple. As the helicopter hovered above the shops that lined the city's historic Thames Street, Havaneck's crew heard him say, "This one is for, Tyler, who'll never see his kids again."

Havaneck and his crew were shocked to see a man suddenly knock several white shutters from the top of the steeple, then he began shooting at Havaneck's helicopter. Havaneck pushed a button as he ground his teeth together in anger and a missile flew toward the steeple in the torrential rain.

"This ones for you, fuck head," shouted Havaneck moments before the missile struck the steeple. It exploded ten feet below the hole in the shutters where the man was still shooting at his helicopter. The violent explosion threw shattered pieces of the burning white clapboard walls hundreds of feet into the air. Moments later, the top section of the steeple above where the missile exploded toppled off the towering structure and crashed to the ground. Havaneck fired a second missile and the immense explosion destroyed the wide base of the steeple, and most of the church building, raining pieces of wood onto the city streets and nearby buildings. The shattered remains of the steeple suddenly toppled forward and crashed down onto the cemetery beside the church, shattering all of the headstones. Havaneck slowly circled the church as his crew looked at the burning debris spread across the ground and city streets below. "I see three, no four bodies on the ground skipper," the crew chief reported to Havaneck.

"Midway Barber, this is the Lexington. Your sniper is history. Let me know if you need any more help. Out."

Depietro and his men were speechless as they watched the helicopter completely destroy the church steeple. They could see a cloud of black smoke rising into the sky as the remains of the church building began burning. "Come on, lets get our asses out of here,"

370   D'ONOFRIO

Depietro shouted as he stood. As the men ran through the nearby condominium parking lot in the torrential rain, several Cubans suddenly began shooting at them. Depietro and his men dove onto the asphalt behind several parked cars as bullets struck nearby automobiles and caused one of them to explode.

"I've got them," shouted Shaw as he pointed to the left in the rain. "They're in that long row of town houses near the water. They're in the second story window."

Depietro studied the structure that contained twenty condominium town houses built together in a single row. He knew his team needed help again. "Tac Com, this is Bravo Kilo. We're pinned down by some Russians in the long row of town houses. We need those helicopters again. Over."

Roger, Bravo Kilo. Give me the coordinates and I'll get some help to you."

Chapter Twenty-Three

Maxwell relayed the target coordinates of the town houses to his pilots, and then added the personal comment. "Blow that building and everyone in it right off the fucking island."

"I've got it. I've got a target. I can see men standing in the windows," reported the Arc Light's co-pilot as he watched the long building's black and white heat image in his infra-red weapon's sight. While the Apache helicopter flew toward Goat Island the co-pilot fired a missile. He guided it toward the building with electronic signals sent through a small wire the missile pulled from the helicopter. A strong gust of wind unexpectedly caused the missile to veer off course and it crashed into a large group of cars in the parking lot. The cars exploded violently in orange flames one hundred feet from Depietro as he and his men frantically ducked for cover. The flames which engulfed the automobiles in the parking lot lit the long condominium building as thick black smoke billowed above the island. A series of loud, bright explosions, startled Depietro and his men as more automobiles exploded after burning gasoline traveled across the asphalt under the vehicles.

Eight Cuban soldiers and four American Army officers from Murtagh's staff ran to the town house's windows, and watched the fire and explosions quickly enveloping the cars below. "So, those fuck head helicopter jockeys want a fight," laughed a young American lieutenant before he threw a wooden chair through a second story window. He briefly looked down with a smile when another group of cars suddenly exploded and created a swirling fireball. "We'll give them a fucking fight like they'll never forget. Then we'll bury the bastards just like we did to those a'holes in Iraq."

The Arc Light pilot fired another missile that struck the condominium building. It exploded one hundred feet from where the Cubans and Americans were shooting at the helicopter. The explosion showered burning building materials and destroyed household furniture onto

372 D'ONOFRIO

Depietro's team as they knelt behind cars in the parking lot and shot at the enemy soldiers in the condominium building.

The Black Hawk helicopter Easy Seven flew toward the island as the Cubans and Americans shot at it with their automatic weapons. The helicopter's entire Plexiglas windshield suddenly exploded inward after being struck by bullets which killed the pilot and severely wounded the co-pilot. The damaged helicopter flew over Goat Island as it descended and it crashed into several large sailboats docked in the harbor. The helicopter exploded in a large fireball that lit the water, and could be heard for miles. Depietro and his men were angered as they watched helplessly while several members of the helicopter crew attempted to swim to safety. Depietro made a fist and grimaced when the men disappeared in the flames immediately after several nearby powerboats exploded.

The angered pilot of the Arc Light flew toward Goat Island while the heavy rain streaking the aircraft's windshield blurred his view. As he flew over the island, the helicopter passed through the thick clouds of dense black smoke rising from the burning remains of three trailers. Using his infra-red night vision equipment the co-pilot aimed four missiles at the town houses as the door gunners on both sides of the aircraft began shooting at the building with their machine guns. The noise of the machine guns was deafening and the helicopter shuddered when the co-pilot fired his missiles. The co-pilot clenched his left fist around the controls and used them to guide a laser's light onto an area of the building where he could see the men shooting at his helicopter. The missile's sensors detected the laser's invisible light reflecting off the building's aluminum siding and flew directly toward it.

Two missiles struck the front of the building and the others crashed through the roof moments later. Four simultaneous and powerful explosions created a deafening concussion that destroyed all of the long building's interior walls. As the concussion roared through the wooden structure the entire roof and all

JOURNEY THROUGH A LONG WINTER'S NIGHT   373

the walls shattered into millions of pieces of flaming debris. The explosion threw pieces of burning building materials, clothing, furniture, and personal items six hundred feet into the air. Depietro and his men covered their heads and ducked down beside the automobiles when the building seemed to disappear in a tremendous fireball, and burning debris began falling onto the island around them.

The Arc Light slowly circled the remains of the condominium building that was now encased in a raging inferno after the missiles ruptured the island's main gas supply line. "I didn't think the missiles would flatten the whole building," said the shocked co-pilot as the helicopter hovered directly above Depietro. "I hope there weren't any hostages in there."

"I'm going to make sure no one's going to crawl out of there," replied the enraged pilot. Moments later, hot brass bullet shells began showering down onto Depietro and his men when the pilot fired his machine guns into the burning building, ensuring everyone was dead.

"Lets make a run for those condominiums," shouted Depietro when the Arc Light flew away. The flames consuming the condominium building, the building where the stores were located near the marina, and the exploding cars in the parking lots, brightly lit the island around the group. When the team reached the first six story condominium building they separated into two groups. There they cautiously stood beside both sides of the metal and glass doors that opened into the building's brick lobby where silver mailboxes lined the walls.

"I'm surprised that no one is here to protect this area. This doesn't make any tactical sense leaving this area unguarded," said Depietro as he looked around and expected his team to be ambushed at any second. He would never know most of the Cubans panicked when the attack began and ran to the main hotel building where they thought they would be safe.

"Come on, come on, get us in there," Depietro told Shaw anxiously as he watched him pressing plastic explosives against the metal doors. Thirty seconds later, the explosives detonated, destroying the door's thick

374 D'ONOFRIO

glass panels, the metal frame, and several of the lobby's brick walls.

Depietro and his men quickly climbed over the twisted remains of the metal door frame. They stepped into the building's lobby now filled with dust and smoke, and littered with shattered silver mailboxes. Depietro frantically pointed at his team after they heard men shouting as they approached the lobby through one of four inner doors. When two frightened Cubans suddenly ran into the lobby all of Depietro's men began shooting at them. The sound of automatic weapons in the lobby was deafening and seconds later, both Cubans lay dead beside a brick wall spattered with their blood. Depietro's men immediately searched through the building for more enemy soldiers as they assured all the hostages they found they were now safe.

"We're getting close," Holloway shouted across the garage to Howard, who was watching the heavy rain falling in the hotel's rear parking lot. As his team fanatically worked inside the bomb's gray metal case Holloway added, "We should be able to pull out the detonator in a couple of minutes."

Six thin blue and orange wires extended into the bomb's case from a small electronic instrument enclosed in a black plastic case lying on the concrete floor beside Stephen Becker. As he adjusted several knobs on the device a smooth red line suddenly appeared on the instrument's small blue display screen. "I've got a signal from circuit board 1169A, panel number one hundred twelve." Becker knew the solid red line was an electronic image of the electrical supply the bomb's sophisticated internal computer required to monitor its anti-tamper devices, and to detonate the device. Although it was a small electric current, the signal indicated the team located the power supply and circuits inside the bomb's case.

"I'm going to disconnect the power to the computer by following diagram eight Charlie." Decker told the others after she and Miller studied a manual and then carefully examined a circuit board inside the case. "If we're wrong, or if someone rigged the computer to detect a

JOURNEY THROUGH A LONG WINTER'S NIGHT 375

power loss, its dying instruction could be to detonate." Decker's hands trembled with apprehension as she carefully placed the tip of a small screwdriver into a screw. She held her breath and her body trembled as the others worked around her, then she slowly turned the screw to the left.

"Wait a minute, wait a minute. I'm picking up something strange here. I'm getting an increase in the electrical supply," explained Miller after the red line displayed on the instrument's blue panel begin to waver.

"Reset the screw to its original position. Then turn it in the opposite direction."

"I can't do that. That'll increase the power and the computer will sense the change and trigger the bomb!"

"Do it Decker," said Holloway as he stared coldly at her. "Listen to Miller, he may be right. They may have the power reversed to force the bomb to detonate if anyone got this far into the case."

Panic seemed to grip Decker and she swallowed hard as she slowly reset the screw to its original position. Then she began turning the screw in the opposite direction, a movement she knew was incorrect.

"Hold it! Hold it!" Miller shouted as he watched the smooth red line displayed on the instrument suddenly became jagged and broke apart into smaller lines. "That's it. We've isolated the power supply."

Decker smiled as she placed her hands on the bomb's case and rested her forehead on them as she felt the perspiration running down her neck. Her body suddenly jerked violently with fear when she heard explosions and gunfire nearby on the island, but she felt relieved that bomb's computer was no longer functioning.

"We've still got a lot of work to do here," commented Marlowe as he continued working. "We've got to get the detonator out of this bomb so it can't be triggered manually."

"Where the hell are you, Van Horne?" Spencer shouted angrily as he suddenly turned and looked at Dupont. The unexpected outburst from the normally calm man startled the naval personnel seated near him after he unsuccessfully attempted to contact Van Horne's

376   D'ONOFRIO

team again. "I wonder if the President is already dead, Stephen? I don't even know if Van Horne is still alive. I wonder if all this was for nothing. I don't know if I should continue with the next phase of the attack until I know Van Horne is still alive." Spencer paused and pictured Van Horne standing in a large command tent in Vietnam in his mind, and remembered how he used his ingenuity and imagination to survive in combat. "Van Horne is a god damn bastard, and I know he's still alive. I can feel it."

Spencer suddenly reached forward and angrily turned a switch on the gray communications console in front of him. "Sierra Xray, this is Tac Com. What's your present location? Over."

"We're fifteen miles north of the city, Tac Com. We're moving toward our staging area. Over." Charles Rusk was the thirty-seven-year-old pilot of the Apache helicopter known as Sierra Xray. The veteran of Desert Storm commanded the airborne task force assigned to carry the President to safety if Van Horne found him in the hotel. Rusk's rescue team consisted of three large Sea Stallion helicopters using the operational names, India Echo, Juliet Hotel and Delta Tango. The two escort Apache gunships used the names, Foxtrot Delta and Kilo Victor. They escorted the other helicopters to provide fire support if enemy troops on the island began shooting at them.

Rusk immediately contacted his other pilots as they flew over the eastern end of Newport Harbor and saw a towering lit bridge directly ahead. "This is Sierra Xray. Lets move under the bridge and wait there until we hear from Trojan Guide. Foxtrot Delta and Kilo Victor, I want you to take out any resistance on the island when we move to the hotel. All right everyone, good luck. Sierra Xray, out."

The helicopters flew toward the Newport Bridge and hovered under the highest section of the arched roadbed three miles from Goat Island. "Look at all the fires burning on that damn island," one of the shocked pilots radioed the others as he watched the infernos. "It looks like the whole island is on fire."

JOURNEY THROUGH A LONG WINTER'S NIGHT   377

"Now stay off this damn leg," Walsh warned Gatting as he finished wrapping more bandages he made from curtains around his friend's wounded leg in the hotel lobby. "The Army trained me to use explosives, not god damn first aide. I'm working on an electrical engineering degree in college, I'm not trying to become a doctor." Walsh briefly looked at the hallway that led to the Greenhouse Restaurant whose walls were covered with a white and blue streaked wallpaper. After he studied the finely upholstered chairs and sofas, in the lobby he pushed a full magazine of bullets into his rifle as he stood. "How are you feeling? You're starting to look pale."

"I feel a little shaky, but I think I'll be all right. Grab my rifle and then you get going Gatting. I'll be fine."

"Call me if you think you're going to pass out. If you hold on for a few more minutes, I'll get some help for you." Walsh stood and was careful not to make any sounds as he walked across the brown marble floor with his rifle pointed at the hallway. He was soon leaning against the corner of the wall, around which was the hallway that led to the Greenhouse Restaurant's front entrance. He held his breath as he listened to screaming women and children, many of whom were pleading with their captors to be released. They were the same sounds Walsh heard when he was standing in the rain in the destroyed greenhouse enclosure.

I've got to know if the Russians are in the hallway around this corner, Walsh thought as he tightened his grip on his rifle then quickly bent forward and looked around the corner. His eyes widened with shock when he saw two armed soldiers standing in the restaurant's doorway watching for members of the attack force. *Shit*, was his only thought as he quickly stepped backward and fell onto the hard marble floor. Bullets from the Cuban's machine guns suddenly ripped through the wall above him. They ripped apart the wallboard and caused several large pictures to fall onto the floor beside him and shatter.

As the terrified Cubans reloaded their weapons, Walsh quickly crawled away from the corner. As he lay on the floor he brushed pieces of white plaster board

378 D'ONOFRIO

and other debris off his blonde hair and face. "Jilted Hinge, this is Walsh," he said as he sat on the marble floor and motioned a thumbs down signal to Gatting. "I'm thirty feet from the restaurant's front doors. They have it pretty well covered and I can't get in there. Over."

"Walsh, this is Jilted Hinge. We can't use grenades from this end with the hostages in there. I'll contact Tac Com and have him get those jets up here. Sit tight until you hear from me."

"Roger, Jilted Hinge. I can have them here in a couple of minutes," said Spencer, he sighed heavily and shook his head when he realized the men were in trouble. "Whiskey Echo, this is Tac Com. What's your present location? Over."

"We're three hundred nautical miles south east of Newport. We just finished taking on fuel from our tanker. Over."

"We need you to make that flyby over the island, Whiskey Echo. Our men are having problems and they need your help right now. Over."

"Roger, Tac Com. That's what we're here for. We're turning toward Newport and we'll be there in a couple of minutes. We're going to make it loud, so keep your heads down. Whiskey Echo, out." The three pilots increased their aircraft's speed as their navigators entered the coordinates of Newport into the onboard flight computers.

Owen and his men knelt on the carpet in the convention center's long hallway beside the doors that opened into the room where the hotel's indoor swimming pool was located. He stared at the thousands of pieces of shattered door glass laying on the floor as he listened to Jilted Hinge report his team could not get into the Greenhouse Restaurant. "We're looking good here. I think we better give Nielson's men some help getting into that restaurant. Ryan, you and Malin see what you can do."

The two men cautiously pushed open an exit door and saw the hotel's front entrance two hundred feet ahead, across the driveway. They nervously checked the surrounding area in the heavy rain, and then quickly

JOURNEY THROUGH A LONG WINTER'S NIGHT 379

ran across the driveway in the rain. They were surprised to see the hotel's destroyed front doors, and the dead Cuban soldier laying on the floor in a pool of blood.

"It's Gatting," said a shocked Malin as he immediately lowered his rifle when he recognized the man sitting on the chair ahead. Ryan quickly looked behind when he heard a loud explosion on the other side of the building.

Gatting, who now felt as though he didn't have the strength to continue sitting, slowly lowered his rifle and motioned the men into the lobby. "I'm glad you're here. I don't know how much longer I'm going to be around."

"Lets get him over to that couch so I can take a look at his leg," Malin told Ryan as he pulled his rifle over his shoulder. When the two men lifted Gatting he was pale and almost unconscious. Malin appeared extremely concerned by the amount of blood that saturated the hastily made bandages. "You team up with Walsh and give him a hand. I'll take care of this," Malin told Ryan as he pulled down a long pink curtain to make a tourniquet.

"I'm not going to make it, am I?" said Gatting as his eyes tightened when the pain became unbearable.

"You're going to make it. We came onto this fucking island together, and we're fucking leaving together. You're not going anywhere before we do."

Ryan knelt beside Walsh who was sitting against the wall six feet from the corner with his rifle aimed at the hallway. "The Greenhouse Restaurant's front entrance is around that corner," whispered Walsh as he pointed at the debris on the floor and the bullet holes in the wall.

"It looks like they've got the advantage."

"For now they do. Those jets better get here soon."

At the same time, Owen led Willet and Manley into the large three story building room that housed the hotel's indoor swimming pool and several guest rooms. "This is where we heard those voices when we were waiting behind the building for the attack to begin. Let's watch our step in here," Owen warned as he walked across the cement floor painted blue to match the inte-

380 D'ONOFRIO

rior of the pool. Heavy rain pounded down onto the clear Plexiglas roof over the pool and vivid streaks of lightening cast bizarre shadows on the blue floor and pool water. "They must have lived in the rooms in this area during the week," he added when he saw dirty camouflaged clothing scattered across the floor. He immediately became angry when he saw the nude and blood covered body of a dead woman laying in the corner of the room.

Owen walked to a brick wall that formed the exterior wall of several guest rooms, and blocked his view of the remainder of the large room. He cautiously looked around the corner then quickly stepped backward as he shouted, "Get back." A group of Cuban soldiers standing on a staircase twenty feet away immediately began shooting at the brick wall after seeing him. Another group of partially dressed Cuban soldiers joined their comrades and they too began shooting as they shouted to one another.

Bullets ricocheted off the blue concrete floor and brick wall, and shattered windows on the other side of the room. "There's no way we can get around that corner. Let me see if I can get a shot at them with this grenade launcher." shouted Malin as he quickly loaded the launcher under his rifle's barrel as the deafening sounds of automatic weapons made him wince. He stepped beside the corner and when the shooting subsided he pushed the rifle beyond the wall with one hand and fired a grenade that struck the base of the metal staircase below where the Cubans stood. The base of the staircase was secured to the blue cement floor and the powerful explosion easily twisted the metal and ripped it away from the mounting brackets. Moments later, the entire staircase collapsed onto the concrete floor with a loud noise as the Cubans screamed in terror. Three of the men died instantly, while the other twelve were injured by the concussion and fall.

Owen, Willet, and Manley stepped beyond the corner of the wall and began shooting at the injured Cubans laying on the floor. Some of them were screaming as they lay under twisted metal. Others were struck by

JOURNEY THROUGH A LONG WINTER'S NIGHT   381

bullets as they were reaching for their weapons.

"Check the bodies. Make sure none of them are going to come back and haunt us," Owen told Willet as he quickly reloaded his rifle and looked around the room for more enemy soldiers.

"Most of them are dead." reported Willet after he walked around the fallen metal staircase with this rifle pointed at the men. "The others won't be around too much longer."

"Get down," shouted Manley as he suddenly pushed Willet and Owen backward when bullets suddenly struck the cement floor near them. The men fell onto the blue cement floor under the room's second story walkway as more bullets struck the nearby brick walls.

"Shit, I don't even know where that came from." Owen confessed as he stood with a disgusted look on his face and wiped the blood off his hands that had already pooled under the walkway from the dead Cuban bodies. He quickly looked around the room but could not see the enemy soldiers who continued to shoot at the cement floor near the group.

"You bastards," he mumbled to himself after he quickly looked up at the clear Plexiglas roof the size of a football field over the swimming pool. Floodlights mounted on the hotel roof lit the plastic roof and the metal supports under it. "I've got three up on the Plexiglas roof over the pool. They've opened two of the louvers up there and they've got a good position. We can't leave them up there, but I'm not sure if we can get a clean shot at them from down here."

"I can use my grenade launcher again," said Manley as he lifted his rifle and quickly reloaded it as he stood.

"Don't get too far out in the open. I don't want you getting shot or get hit when pieces of the roof start falling."

Manley knew he couldn't get a clear shot at the roof from where he was standing under the walkway. He quickly stepped from under it and fired the weapon upward as the Cubans began shooting at him. All the Cubans shielded their faces when the grenade struck the thick Plexiglas forty feet from them and blew a large

382 D'ONOFRIO

section of shattered plastic into the air. As they searched for their American attacker below they suddenly felt the Plexiglas roof cracking and shattering under them. Suddenly the roof's fatigued metal supports began twisting and buckling with a loud screeching sound, and moments later the entire roof began toppling into the large room.

"The whole thing is coming down," shouted Manley so he could be heard over the screeching sounds of the buckling and twisting metal roof supports collapsing into the room. Two Cubans screamed in terror as they fell into the room with the shattered pieces of Plexiglas and the metal supports. They died when they landed on the blue concrete floor around the swimming pool.

The upper portion of the third soldier's body fell into the swimming pool's water, but his legs struck the side of the concrete pool. The terrified soldier screamed for help as he frantically struggled to remain above the water while the weight of his broken legs dragged him to the bottom of the pool. The hysterical Cuban frantically grabbed for the water as he tried to get to the surface where he could see the lights reflecting on the water. He opened his mouth to scream, but his lungs filled with water and he died as images of his wife and baby daughter in Havana filled his mind.

"Look at this god damn place," said a shocked Manley as he looked around at the debris and the heavy rain falling into the room. "I didn't think the grenade would bring down the whole roof, and the supports too." He walked to the swimming pool and stared down at the body under the water as the rain drops obscured his view. "Here's one that didn't make it."

"You couldn't have known this was going to happen," said Owen as he placed his hand onto Manley's shoulder. "Even if you did, what other choice did you have? Lets get out of here and find the lobby."

Chapter Twenty-Four

Owen pushed open a glass door and was surprised to see a large and ornate garden. The garden was built inside a wide and long brick hallway that connected the main hotel to the convention center. Three foot high walls built with decorative bricks lined both sides of a ten foot wide curving walkway. The walls held back a variety of fragrant yellow and white flowers planted in the dirt. Fifty feet ahead the winding walkway turned sharply to the right, toward the hotel lobby.

Manley quickly moved ahead of the others after they heard several loud explosions whose vibrations rocked the building. After he cautiously looked around the sharp turn in the walkway, he was relieved no enemy soldiers were laying behind the brick walls. As he was about to signal to Owen it was safe to continue, he suddenly heard men shouting at one another. Then he saw three Cuban soldiers running through the hallway that led to the lobby just as they began shooting at him. Manley dove onto the brown tiled floor as Owen and Willet fell behind the brick wall forty feet from him.

Dirt thrown into the air by the Cuban bullets destroying the flowers above him covered Manley. He quickly looked around when he heard something rolling toward him on the tiled floor and he panicked when he saw a hand grenade. The grenade was five feet from him when it exploded and the concussion violently propelled his body against the brick wall as pieces of shrapnel ripped into his back and neck. Manley was conscious, but didn't have the strength to shout for help as the spasms of pain became so severe his hands began to cramp as he clenched them tightly. He rolled onto his back and lay in the puddle of blood now forming under him from his own wounds.

As the dense dust that filled the hallway began to clear Owen saw Manley laying motionless on the floor. "We've got to get up there and see if he needs help," said Owen as he suddenly seemed to disregard his own safety.

Willet grasped Owen's arm as he was about to crawl

384 D'ONOFRIO

forward, after they both heard Spencer's voice in their headsets. "This is Tac Com. I've just called the jets from their staging area. Get ready, they'll be here in a few minutes. Tac Com, out."

Colonel Mark "Archer" Chamberlain was the thirty-six-year-old pilot of Whiskey Echo. He glanced at the small picture taped to the side of the cockpit in the glow of his instrument's red lights. He smiled briefly when he saw his wife and daughter. This attack was more dangerous than any mission he flew in Iraq, and he was relieved his wife believed he was safe on an aircraft carrier in the north Atlantic. Chamberlain thought about his dead father and spoke to him as he checked his instruments. *I'm going to need your help to make it through this one dad. This one is for you, because you always knew I could do it.*

Torrential rain streaked across the jet's canopy as Chamberlain descended into the clouds while he watched the numbers displayed on his aircraft's guidance computer. When the aircraft emerged below the clouds he and his navigator could see the orange glow of Newport's lights on the horizon. "That city looks mighty peaceful up ahead," Chamberlain told his navigator as strong winds jostled the aircraft. "If that bomb goes off we're going to be flying into the brightest fireworks display you've ever seen."

"And the last," added the navigator with a laugh.

Chamberlain watched the city and guided the jet toward the raging fires blazing out of control on the island. He pushed the aircraft's control stick forward until he was flying nine hundred feet above the ocean water, then leveled the aircraft as he flew directly toward the hotel. Five seconds later, the F-14 passed over the length of Goat Island with a thunderous and ear shattering shriek while flying at almost twice the speed of sound. Chamberlain banked the jet sharply to the left and climbed into the clouds so the noise of his engines would be directed down onto the island below. The sound was deafening and many of Van Horne's men covered their ears as the entire building seemed to vibrate while many windows shattered around them.

The Cubans at the end of the brick walkway ap-

JOURNEY THROUGH A LONG WINTER'S NIGHT   385

peared terrified when the jet flew over the island. One of them began screaming when he thought Vazques detonated the bomb. Another dropped his machine gun and placed his hands over his ears as he tried to lessen the terrifying sound of the jet's engines. Moments later, Owen and Willet began shooting at the Cubans as they ran forward side by side. Two of the screaming Cubans died instantly. Owen aimed his rifle at the third Cuban laying on the floor with his hands still covering his ears. A terrified expression appeared on the raggedly dressed soldier's face and he died as he frantically reached for his handgun.

Owen and Willet ran to where Manley's body lay in a large puddle of blood. Owen shook his head when he realized his comrade was already dead. "Come on, we'll come back for him later. We've still got to find the damn lobby."

Nielson and his men checked their weapons as they stood in the twisted black metal supports of the destroyed Greenhouse Restaurant enclosure. In the distance they heard the faint rumbling of the approaching jets, and Nielson motioned to his men. At the same time Walsh and Ryan stood around the corner from the restaurant's front entrance. Everyone crouched forward as the intimidating and deafening sound of Whiskey Echo's engines filled the hotel. As the sound subsided while the jet flew into the clouds, Walsh and Ryan stepped around the corner and into the long hallway. Walsh fired first and his bullets struck a startled Cuban looking at the ceiling as he searched for the source of the ear shattering sound noise. Red blood splattered across the wall moments before bullets knocked the man's body to the floor. Another Cuban turned and ran through the restaurant's ornate wooden doors just before Ryan began shooting at him. Bullets splintered and ripped apart the hand carved door and frame, and struck the Cuban in the back. The bullet's impact knocked his body forward and his terrified companions watched helplessly as he lay on the floor screaming in agony.

Ryan suddenly began a loud primal scream as he shot at a Cuban soldier who ran into the hallway from

386 D'ONOFRIO

inside the restaurant. The bullets struck the Cuban's abdomen and the wounded man fell onto the floor screaming as he held his blood covered hands on his stomach. Thirty seconds later, the severely wounded eighteen-year-old Cuban soldier died.

Nielson and the men beside him heard the automatic weapons at the restaurant's front entrance. An instant later the unexpected noise of the second jet flying over the hotel briefly distracted all of them as they stood in the rain. Nielson and his men quickly stepped through the two brick doorways and entered the inner area of the restaurant where nine confused Cuban soldiers were shouting at one another. As Nielson's men began shooting at the Cubans from two areas, their bullets destroyed the restaurant's crystal light fixtures, and wooden tables and chairs. The Cubans wanted to surrender to Nielson's men, but none of them could speak English, their commander died when the explosives destroyed the greenhouse enclosure. Within seconds the Cubans were dead and their bodies were laying on the floor beside the hysterical hostages they abused and terrorized during the week.

"You're safe now. You're all safe," shouted Nielson while reloading his rifle. "As soon as you're freed I want all of you to move to the back of the restaurant and lay on the floor back there. We're going to stay here and protect you so no one else can hurt you."

An attractive young woman dressed in dirty and blood stained green silk pajamas painfully limped to where Nielson was directing his team. "I've got to find my husband. They took him out of here, and then they raped me every night. I haven't seen him in three days. I've got to find him."

"He could be anywhere in this building right now. We've found hostages all over the island. After we have the island secured you can look for him."

"No, no, I've got to find him now. I've got to know if he's all right."

Another badly beaten young woman staggered to where the almost hysterical woman pleaded with Nielson for his help while beating on his chest with her fists.

JOURNEY THROUGH A LONG WINTER'S NIGHT 387

"Come with me and we'll sit together until its safe," said the woman as she placed her hands on the frantic woman's shoulders. "Then we'll look for your husband together. I'll help you find him." The two women walked to the rear of the restaurant and they lay on the floor holding hands as they waited for the crisis to end.

Owen and Willet cautiously walked into the lobby and looked at the hundreds of bullet holes in the fine white wallpapered walls. Willett tapped on Owen's arm and motioned toward the bodies laying under the remains of the wooden customer service counter destroyed by the grenades. They saw Malin lower his rifle and motion them forward quickly as he knelt beside an unconscious Gatting on the couch.

"How bad is he?" asked Owen after he walked to the couch and studied Gatting's waxen face.

"We're going to need a doctor in here soon or he's not going to make it, Jim. I can't stop the bleeding."

"We don't have any medical people on the damn island yet. Tac Com, this is Romeo Alpha. What're the chances of getting a medic into the hotel lobby right now? Over."

"I don't know if that's a wise move yet, Romeo Alpha. We still haven't secured the island, and Holloway's team is still disarming the bomb."

"Well, what the hell is taking him so long?"

"They're doing the best they can. Take it easy. I haven't heard from Van Horne or his men. Have you been in contact with them? Over."

"Negative, I tried contacting them, but I didn't get any response. We started this attack twenty five minutes ago and I still haven't heard from anybody on that team."

"What do you want to do next, Romeo Alpha?"

"We can use some help holding this damn island. A lot of our men are in bad shape and already out of the picture."

"I have Blue Light combat teams aboard the helicopters flying over the city right now. We can move them onto the island and they can help you hold what you've already secured."

"That sounds good. Do it," replied a disgusted Owen

388 D'ONOFRIO

as he looked around at the dead bodies on the floor. "Gatting is in bad shape and I need a medic in this fucking lobby to take care of him now." Owen heard a helicopter fly over the island and he looked through a shattered window but could not see it in the darkness. "Where the hell did those helicopters come from?"

Spencer smiled at the question. "I'll explain everything to you after this is over." Then he leaned back in his chair and closed his eyes for several seconds.

The sound of the first jet flying over the island and the deafening engine noise echoing through the garage momentarily distracted Holloway's team. They stopped working inside the bomb's case and covered their ears with their hands as the noise became painful. They began working again, cutting the multi-colored cables that powered the bomb's computer. At the same time Holloway began removing the thick circular metal cover plate that protected the bomb's detonator. Five minutes later, Holloway and March exposed the bomb's detonator. It was a circular device eight inches in diameter and twelve inches high, constructed with electronic components and high explosives.

March and Becker slowly removed the ten large screws that held the detonator firmly inside the protective cylinder, knowing any of them could be booby trapped. As perspiration ran down Holloway's forehead, and his hands trembled, he carefully lifted the detonator out of the bomb. As he held it above the bomb his entire body seemed to tremble while Miller and Murphy cut the long multi-colored wires that carried signals to it from the computer. Holloway smiled triumphantly as he displayed the fifteen pound detonator and the wires dangling from it to his team. "Tac Com, this is Holloway. We've removed the bomb's detonator. I say again, we've removed the detonator from the bomb. Over."

"Good work, Holloway." Spencer suddenly began clapping as he was caught up in the jubilation and relief when loud shouts, applause, and whistles, suddenly filled the command center. "Are you going to destroy the detonator so it can't be used if the garage is recaptured? Over."

JOURNEY THROUGH A LONG WINTER'S NIGHT 389

"That's next, Tac Com. I'll get back to you after it's done. Holloway, out."

"I'll take the detonator from you," Howard told Holloway as he unexpectedly stepped forward and took the device from his hand. Howard placed the detonator on the cement floor beside one of the garage's rear entrances and reached into his backpack. When his men saw him loading his rifle, they all ran across the garage and gathered around him. "Who's guarding the doors?" he asked them with a surprised look on his face.

"Let the nuclear team guard the doors," said Long angrily after he realized Howard was planning to destroy the detonator without their help. "Where are you going with that?"

"Look, I told Van Horne I would get rid of this detonator myself. I can't let Holloway do it, and I won't ask any of you to risk your necks to help me. I'll take care of this, but I want all of you to stay in here where its safe."

"Fuck me, you're not going out there alone," Mahoney adamantly told Howard as he looked at the other members of the group nodding at him. "We made it this far together, and we'll fucking stick together until this operation is over. Let Holloway's people guard the garage for a few minutes, so we can get this shit over with."

Howard could see the determination on the faces of his men, and he realized he could not persuade them to remain in the garage. "Here's what I want to do. We'll take the detonator to that grassy area at the end of the island near the lighthouse and the tennis courts. That should be far enough away from the hotel, so we can destroy it there with plastic. After everyone checked their weapons, Howard led them into the heavy rain as he clenched the detonator in one hand and his rifle in the other.

When the group was one hundred feet from the garage's rear doors, five Cubans ran onto the wooden deck and began shooting at them. The bullets shattered a nearby car which showered the surprised men with broken glass. Howard motioned to his men and they dove onto the wet asphalt between several automobiles in the parking lot as bullets struck nearby vehicles and

390 D'ONOFRIO

caused several to explode in flames.

"Hit that detonator before this whole place goes up around us," Howard shouted as Jarvis frantically pulled an electronic transmitter from inside his rain saturated shirt.

Jarvis watched the deck as he pushed the detonator while the Cubans continued shooting at the cars around the group. He covered his face when the deck and the men standing on it suddenly disappeared in a blinding explosion that shattered many of the hotel's rear windows. The plastic explosives destroyed the entire deck and its supports, and projected burning pieces of shattered wood two hundred feet into the air. They began raining down onto the island with dismembered pieces of the Cuban's bodies. The explosion also destroyed a large section of the building's exterior red brick wall. Where the sliding doors once opened onto the deck was now a gaping hole fifty feet wide filled with dense smoke.

"Come on, come on. Let's keep moving," shouted Howard as he looked around at the burning pieces of wood covering the entire parking lot, and the automobiles in it. The exhausted men began running again, but suddenly stopped when they heard someone behind them shooting at a low flying helicopter passing over the hotel.

"He's on the third floor balcony behind us," screamed Long as he pointed upward and squinted to see in the bright glow of the orange overhead lights. The Cuban looked down and began shooting at Howard's group in the parking lot covered with burning fragments of the deck. Bullets fired by Howard's men struck the brick wall behind the Cuban, and then struck the soldier's body. As he dropped his weapon and clenched his chest the man fell from the third floor balcony and his body shattered the windshield of a car parked below.

A minute later, the men were gasping for air after they ran into the darkness that surrounded the grassy area at the end of the island near the lighthouse. Howard knelt on the grass and pulled a block of plastic explosive from his pocket as vivid lightening and loud thunder star-

JOURNEY THROUGH A LONG WINTER'S NIGHT   391

tled the group. Then he pressed the explosive against the detonator and molded it around the circular device. He pulled a pencil shaped detonator from his pocket and carefully pushed it into the plastic explosives. "I'm ready, you get the hell out of here. Find a place to hide between the cars in the parking lot and keep your fucking heads down. This is going to be a big one."

Mahoney knelt beside Howard with his rifle raised and watched for enemy soldiers. They watched the others run between the parked cars as they were silhouetted against the burning and exploding cars in the background. "We're out of here," Howard told Mahoney as he pulled the pin from the detonator. The two men immediately ran as fast as they could in the rain. Seconds later, they joined the others laying between several large automobiles in the parking lot as more cars engulfed in flames exploded nearby.

As Howard waited for the explosives to detonate, he saw a man run from the hotel building toward the detonator. He held his breath as he watched one of Barnes' men lift the detonator and inspect it. When the soldier saw the plastic explosives he just stared at it in shock. Howard covered his face with his hands immediately after the explosives detonated and caused blinding white lights to appear in his eyes. The concussion was so powerful it lifted all the men's bodies off the driveway and shattered most of the windows behind the hotel. The deafening explosion projected fragments of the metal detonator outward with such force they were embedded in the hotel's exterior red brick wall. Howard quickly looked for remains of the soldier's body, but he knew the man was ripped apart by the explosion's force.

"Tac Com, this is South Cycle. I've, we've, destroyed the bomb's detonator. Out," said a relieved Howard as leaned back against a car letting the rain fall onto his face. "I couldn't have done this without all of you. If I'd been alone I'd be dead right now. Thanks."

"Let's get back to the garage and take care of Holloway's team," replied Mahoney who felt thanks were not necessary. "Howard is starting to get sentimental on us, and it's making me sick." The men ran around

392 D'ONOFRIO

the burning debris that covered the parking lot and past the cars engulfed in flames. When they reached the safety inside the garage they congratulated the members of Holloway's team as they guarded the entrances.

While Howard and his men were fighting their way to the end of the hotel parking lot, Maxwell radioed instruction to his pilots, and one by one helicopters began landing on Goat Island near the marina. The area was now well lit from the flames still destroying the long building that contained the three stores. As each helicopter briefly landed on the island the Blue Light team members jumped through the open doors. After the team aboard Xray Foxtrot was safely on the island, the pilot flew toward the harbor. As Marlowe stood in the steeple he saw bright red tracers fly into the sky when someone in the marina fired a machine gun at the helicopter.

Moments later, Reynolds lowered his head and strained to hear a faint noise in the distance over the sounds of the heavy rain. Then he heard the sounds of several large engines starting. "They're getting ready to pull out," he told the others as he watched men frantically running across the wooden walkways and docks in the marina through his binoculars. "Two of the yachts just pulled away from the docks."

A shocked Marlowe lowered his binoculars when the ocean water suddenly surged three hundred feet into air, obscuring his view of the marina. Seconds later, the entire church steeple vibrated as the sounds of a thunderous explosion rolled through the city. Marlowe didn't know one of Barnes' men on a yacht remotely detonated a group of mines in the water in front of the vessel and created the unexpected explosions. Moments later, another one hundred underwater mines detonated with such force they propelled ocean water three hundred feet into the air. The explosion created large waves that crashed against the concrete docks in Newport and washed over the small park beside the Mariott Hotel.

Twenty two frightened Cubans and three of Barnes men stood on the deck of the Second Wave and watched the fires raging on the island to their right. Fifteen Cubans aboard the yacht Pale Horse, fired their weapons

JOURNEY THROUGH A LONG WINTER'S NIGHT   393

at the helicopters they heard flying over the island as raging orange flames lit the aircraft. Two of Barnes' men carefully piloted each yacht between the wooden docks and piers. Both groups planned to sail the yachts into international waters and then back to safety of Havana.

"There's no way we can stop them from up here," Marlowe told his men, then he spoke into his microphone. "Tac Com, Tac Com, this is Midway Barber. We can see some boats leaving the marina. Have you got anyone in the area to stop them?"

"I've got a team on the line, Midway Barber. I'll explain the situation to him and maybe he can help."

As Spencer was explaining what Marlowe saw in the marina to the Blue Light Two Niner team, the Cubans on the yachts continued shooting at the helicopters. Bullets suddenly ripped the tail section off a helicopter and it began spinning out of control five hundred feet above the island. The helicopter veered to the left and crashed onto the island's main road with a tremendous explosion, and swirling fireball that killed the crew.

"Those fucking bastards," shouted Captain Robert McCurdy, a Blue Light team leader, as Sergeant Charles Cranford knelt beside him. "That was our ride that just went down."

"Do you know where they are?" Cranford asked as a low flying helicopter passed over the island with all of its machine guns firing.

"They must be on those boats in the marina. Let's move up and see if we can stop them."

"Fire whenever you're ready. Don't let them get away," McCurdy shouted to his and Cranford's men after they knelt on a wooden dock in the torrential rain and loaded their anti-tank rocket launchers. McCurdy fired his rifle at one yacht's white hull, now fifty yards away and well lit by the raging flames destroying the nearby condominium building.

When an anti-tank rocket struck the same yacht, a powerful explosion easily ripped a hole in the side of the sixty foot long Second Wave's fiberglass hull. A second blinding explosion, accompanied by a deafening con-

394   D'ONOFRIO

cussion, destroyed the hull and shattered building windows in Newport. The explosion created a rapidly growing fireball and thick black smoke that billowed into the sky and briefly lit the island. The yacht's debris and dead bodies floated in the raging flames that now quickly spread across the water in the marina.

The Cubans on the Pale Horse frantically pointed at the shattered hull of the Second Wave as it quickly sank below the flames one hundred feet ahead of them. Knowing their vessel would be destroyed next, some of them frantically dove off the deck and into the water. Moments later, another immense explosion destroyed the Pale Horse after a rocket struck it. The explosion spread burning waves of fuel over the frantic and screaming Cubans as they swam to a nearby boat.

The wooden docks in the marina on Goat Island were now brightly lit by the flames on the water under them, and they soon began burning. As flames spread across the water and engulfed several other yachts in the marina, they exploded in massive fireballs that ignited others boats docked nearby. As the spreading fires destroyed the docks, Cranford ran toward his men in the heavy rain to congratulate them. McCurdy covered his face with his hand when the sounds of nearby machine guns frightened him. When he looked up he saw Cranford's motionless body laying in the torrential rain.

"Get down on that fucking dock and stay there," McCurdy screamed at the anti-tank teams as the bullets from large Cuban machine guns shattered street lights near the frightened men. Raging flames and more explosions one hundred yards away brightly lit the docks as one team ignored McCurdy's warnings and ran toward him.

"Get down. Get Down," he screamed at the six men as they stood. Before they could react to the warning they all died after they were struck by bullets. The second team lay on the dock in the heavy rain and waited there in terror, knowing they could not move without being killed.

McCurdy raised a radio microphone to his mouth as hundreds of bullets ripped apart the corner of the

JOURNEY THROUGH A LONG WINTER'S NIGHT   395

building he knelt beside, and the wooden walkway near the trapped Blue Light team. He watched the lit city across the water as he shouted into his microphone, "Dragon Six, this is Two Niner. We're caught in a fucking ambush beside the marina. The situation's getting terminal, and we need some fucking help fast. Do you copy, Dragon Six?"

"God damn McCurdy, I knew that dirt ball would get himself into trouble," said Major Peter Caserta, the thirty-four-year-old commander of six camouflaged Army Hummers made famous during Operation Desert Storm. "Let's get in there and bail out his sorry ass," Caserta radioed his vehicles as they swerved across the city's main street and violently crashed through the protective wooden fence built around the small park beside the Mariott Hotel. The drivers stopped the vehicles beside the water and all the soldiers saw the raging red flames consuming the docks, and the clouds of dense black rising off the water.

"Keep your head down, Two Niner, it's gonna get fucking noisy," Caserta radioed McCurdy as fifty caliber machines guns on the vehicles began firing across the water at several yachts in the marina. Caserta ran behind the Hummer as bullets suddenly shattered the vehicle's windshield, and he lifted another radio microphone. "Shearer, where the fuck are you, and my fucking diversion? We're getting pounded out here."

The Cubans suddenly stopped firing their weapons at Caserta's vehicles when they heard the approaching sounds of loud air horns in the city. As they and Caserta watched the lit city streets they saw a long blue and white city bus turn onto the road that led to the destroyed access bridge. "I told Shearer to hot wire a car, not a fucking city bus."

The Cubans suddenly started shooting at the bus as it raced toward the destroyed bridge at sixty miles an hour. Shearer, a sergeant in Caserta's team, pulled on the bus's air horn rope one final time as bullets created holes in the windshield. He screamed loudly while he knelt beside the driver's seat and steered the bus straight ahead with one extended foot holding the gas peddle to

396 D'ONOFRIO

the floor. Then he leaped through the bus's open door and dove out onto the grass beside the road, breaking his arm and both legs. He shouted triumphantly when the bus sent wooden fragments flying into the air after it crashed through the police crowd control barricades while traveling at close to seventy miles an hour.

The Cubans on the yachts watched the bus drive off the end of the destroyed access bridge and crash into the harbor water seconds later. Immediately after the bus broke the surface of the water hundreds of the unexploded mines began detonating around the vehicle, adding to the Cuban's confusion. Caserta shook his head as he watched a wall of water quickly move through the marina and spread the flames as his men continued shooting at the yachts. Bullets punctured several vessel's wood and fiberglass hulls and they began burning. McCurdy and his men on the docks covered their heads after an antitank rocket fired from a Hummer crashed into a large yacht and exploded, showering the marina with flaming debris.

"Shift six yards to the left, Dragon Six," McCurdy shouted into his microphone as the Cubans began shooting across the water at the six Hummers. Moments later, three anti-tank launchers fired simultaneously. They created a blinding and deafening explosion that destroyed the yacht the remaining Cubans were shooting from, and a group of large boats tied to the nearby dock.

Orange and red flames quickly spread across the water in the marina. They began burning the marina building, almost all of the marina's wooden walkways, and other docked yachts and boats. McCurdy turned and raised his rifle when a member of another Blue Light team suddenly ran out of the burning building with a man over his shoulder. "Who the hell is that?" McCurdy shouted before he ducked down after another large yacht exploded in a brilliant ball of flames nearby.

"One of Van Horne's men," replied the soldier as he turned with Shepard on his shoulder. "He's wounded pretty bad, but we can take care of him. We'll meet you in the parking lot in front of this building."

McCurdy nodded and watched as the white hulls of

JOURNEY THROUGH A LONG WINTER'S NIGHT 397

several destroyed yachts slowly sank below the flame covered water. He suddenly felt a great sense of satisfaction when he saw bodies floating in the raging flames that covered the water. "Welcome to hell," he angrily shouted as he emptied his rifle's ammunition magazine onto the floating bodies of the dead men, then he checked on the condition of his own men.

Chapter Twenty-Five

Spencer stared at a blue military clock hanging from the command center's gray wall as he crushed his thumb nail between his teeth. As he did, he thought about the day he flew to Virginia and asked Van Horne to accompany him to Newport. Then he swore at himself. "Why the hell did I ever get Robert involved in this?" Spencer asked himself as he remembered the rows of small trees planted in the endless fields of dirt, and the peace he seemed to find there for a few hours. "If anything happens to him, I'm responsible for it. I should never have asked him to come here, never. I didn't know what else to do. I didn't know who else to go too. What am I going to do if he gets killed? How will I ever live with that?" Spencer leaned back in his chair and remembered Saigon's main street, and places like Mister Magoos and Lucys. The bars where he and Van Horne often sat and drank beer as they exchanged their views about the war, and the world.

In the background an excited man was shouting his name, but Spencer didn't hear it. He was picturing the lush green foliage and picturesque mountains of Vietnam as he flew over them in a Huey helicopter. It wasn't until Dupont roughly grabbed his shoulder and startled him did Spencer hear him shouting his name. "Admiral, I've got Trojan Guide on the line."

After a radioman turned several switches on his console everyone in the command center suddenly heard a man's voice. "Tac Com, this is Trojan Guide. What the hell are you doing, sitting on your hands? Over."

"This is Tac Com. Did you find the President, Trojan Guide? Is he all right? Over." A great sense of relief seemed to flood over Spencer and the other men after they heard Van Horne's frustrated and exhausted voice.

"I don't have time to explain what's going on up here, Tac Com." Van Horne quickly wiped the water off his watch as he stood in the torrential rain on a hotel balcony high above Goat Island. Then he looked at the lit buildings and streets in the city. "We're on the top

JOURNEY THROUGH A LONG WINTER'S NIGHT   399

floor of the hotel and I need your helicopters up here right now."

"They're on the way, Trojan Guide. Tac Com, out." Spencer could sense the urgency in Van Horne's voice and immediately contacted the helicopters hovering under the Newport Bridge. "I wonder if Van Horne found, the President?" Spencer asked Dupont as he leaned back in his chair and looked at the clock. "What the hell has he been doing up there all this time?"

During the following days, Van Horne and his men would repeatedly describe their attack of the hotel to the nation's military leaders, the intelligence organizations, and selected members of the government. Although Van Horne and his men explained the details of the attack many times, the events and actions of the men never changed. Neither did the descriptions of personal sacrifice and heroism that occurred during a costly battle, which Van Horne and his men would never forget.

When the explosive charges his team attached to the penthouse windows detonated the loud explosions and concussion startled Van Horne. The shattered window glass glistened in the dim light as the explosion's propelled the millions of fragments across the balcony and into the air beyond the white metal railing. The heavy white plastic chairs and tables were toppled by the force of the explosion and thrown against the metal railing by the concussion. The first word that came to his mind after the explosion was, "Shit!" After Van Horne shouted the words to begin the attack into his microphone, he and Preston climbed over the destroyed window frame. They pulled back the suite's floor length white curtains and stepped into the suite where they believed the enemy soldiers were holding the President.

Two Cuban soldiers were standing in the suite's large living room when the explosives destroyed the windows, and they immediately fell onto the dark red carpeting. "I've got two behind the sofa," Preston shouted as he began shooting at the Cubans now kneeling on the carpet with their weapons. The bullets easily ripped holes in the sofa's fabric and splintered the elegant wooden

400 D'ONOFRIO

frame. Several bullets fatally struck one Cuban's chest and knocked him violently onto the floor. His companion died after three bullets passed through his neck. The impact knocked the soldier backward as blood and flesh spattered the furniture behind him.

"You can move in," Van Horne shouted to his men waiting in the torrential rain on the balcony as he and Preston checked the suite's master bedroom. Kearns, Grogan, Taylor, and Willey stepped into the suite and searched the other two bedrooms, but they could not find the President, nor his family. "I was sure they'd be in here," a disappointed Van Horne told his men after they all displayed thumbs down signals. "Now we're going to have to look for them up here, and that's going to get tricky and dangerous."

The six men immediately looked at the suite's destroyed windows when they heard the sound of a tremendous explosion rumble across the island after the AT-4 team destroyed the communications trailer. They were surprised to see bright orange flames reflecting off the windows in the city after the explosion. Then they heard the loud explosion when the President's helicopter was destroyed by a violent explosion.

"Sounds like the damn island is coming apart under us," commented Taylor nervously as he flinched when another loud explosion rolled across the island. "I'll bet any money my ex-wife would be crazy if she knew I was here."

"Why?" Grogan asked. "Does she want to get back together?"

"Hell no. If I get killed her alimony ends."

"Fuck her too," was the only reply from the normally placid Kearns as he quickly looked around the suite. His comments were a severe deviation from the normally calm exterior he exhibited while reporting the news on television in Texas. His short, blunt response, made the others momentarily smile as it broke the tension.

Van Horne turned quickly when three Cuban soldiers shouting to one another unexpectedly ran into the suite's foyer. They were rushing to investigate the

JOURNEY THROUGH A LONG WINTER'S NIGHT   401

explosions and appeared startled when they saw six heavily armed Americans dressed in jeans and black shirts standing over the bodies of their dead comrades. Van Horne and Grogan were standing beside the suite's oak liquor bar, and they began shooting at the Cubans who were now twenty feet from them. One Cuban began firing his machine gun at Van Horne as he frantically leaped onto the floor. The Cuban's bullets shattered the liquor bottles and glasses on the bar before Grogan's bullets struck his shoulder and head. Within moments, the three Cubans lay dead on the floor beside one another.

"Lets cover that door before some of these other ass holes rush in here," said Van Horne as he stood and pulled the empty ammunition magazine from his rifle. He tossed it onto the carpet while gray smoke poured from the end of his rifle's barrel. As he was pushing a full magazine of bullets into the rifle, he saw Preston lean against the pale blue wallpaper. The blood on his hand smeared across the wallpaper as he suddenly fell forward onto the floor. As the others aimed their weapons at the suite's door, Van Horne ran across the room and knelt beside his friend's body. It took only a second for him to find the bullet holes in the front of Preston's black shirt. "He's dead, damn it," Van Horne angrily told the others as he ran his hand through his own hair in frustration. "Let's find the fucking President and get out of here."

Taylor appeared extremely upset by Preston's unexpected death, and as he stared nervously at his friend laying on the carpet, his fears seemed to paralyze him. Taylor was jittery and nervous before the attack began, but he didn't tell his companions because he feared they might ridicule him. As he stared at Preston's lifeless body he thought, "I could be laying there beside him in the next few minutes. My life could be over in a minute." The thought of dying terrified Taylor, and he suddenly and vividly remembered almost dying in Vietnam several times. His body trembled with fear and he suddenly wanted to hide until the attack ended.

As Taylor watched the other upset men reloading

402 D'ONOFRIO

their weapons he thought, *I volunteered for this part of the operation, and they're just as frightened as I am. They're depending on me to help them, and I've got to do it.* He took a deep breath and then stepped beside the others as his body seemed to tremble uncontrollably.

Moments later, the group heard an enormous explosion and the entire building seemed to vibrate when the explosives destroyed the convention center's loading dock doors. Van Horne cautiously walked toward the suite's door that opened into the hotel's central hallway, and led to the other elegant suites on the floor, and the elevators. He and Willey knelt on the plush carpeting inside the suite's door as Kearns, Grogan, and Taylor stood behind them with their rifles pointed into the hallway.

Van Horne quickly looked around the door's varnished wooden frame and frowned when he saw several soldiers frantically run from one suite to another. Two terrified and frantic Cubans were arguing about how to get out of the hotel when they ran out of another suite and turned toward Van Horne and his men. Their eyes widened in horror when they saw the five Americans huddled together in the doorway twenty feet ahead of them.

"Get rid of those two bastards," said an angry Van Horne as the startled Cubans fumbled for their machine guns. Taylor and Kearns immediately began shooting at the two soldiers. Willey raised his hand and shielded his neck as hot brass shells fell onto him from their rifles. The two Cubans lay dying on the floor before they ran six feet in the hallway.

"What the hell were those explosions I just heard?" Leland asked Barnes after the two men physically ran into each other as they rounded a hallway corner. "I was sleeping when an explosion on the floor above us woke me. Then I heard some more explosions that sounded like they came from down below. Do you know what's happening?"

Barnes frowned and his anger flared uncontrollably after he heard another tremendous explosion and felt the vibrations when explosives destroyed the load-

JOURNEY THROUGH A LONG WINTER'S NIGHT 403

ing dock doors. "I don't know what the fuck is going on. Those explosions could be the fucking Cubans screwing around before we head for home tomorrow night."

"I'm going down to the lobby to find out what's happening outside. You better check on the President. We don't want anything to happen to him until we have to kill him."

Barnes became enraged after he heard another huge explosion on the island. He ran into his room and then onto the balcony where the torrential rain immediately began saturating his hair and clothing. Barnes' room faced the city, preventing him from seeing the hotel parking lot littered with the burning remains of the three trailers and the President's helicopter. His mouth opened in shock when he saw bright yellow flames reflecting off the building windows in the city.

Barnes' suddenly stepped back from the balcony's railing and shielded his face when explosives destroyed the Greenhouse Restaurant's enclosure directly below him. His anger seemed to increase after he realized Vazques' men were not prepared for an attack. "Someone is going to die after I find out who's responsible for attacking this fucking island."

Barnes suddenly heard a man's voice behind him in the room, and when he turned he saw one of Vazques' confused officers. Barnes slowly lowered his handgun as the excited man began shouting questions at him in almost inaudible English. "Who, ah who attacking the island? Military, uh, military attacking?"

"How the hell should I know what's happening out there you fuck head?" shouted Barnes as he walked back into the suite and pushed the unshaven man dressed in camouflaged clothing aside. "Murtagh didn't warn me our military was going to attack the island. Why the fuck am I even explaining all this to you? Get your fucking ass out there and see if you can find your commander. Maybe he can tell us what the fuck is going on."

Barnes walked to an ornate cherry desk and lifted a military radio microphone. As he tried unsuccessfully to contact the communications trailer in the parking lot

404 D'ONOFRIO

his anger quickly increased. "Fuck me," he shouted angrily as he lifted the portable radio and threw it against a large gold framed decorative mirror attached to the wall. As shattered glass and pieces of the mirror's wooden frame fell onto the carpet Barnes ran to a closet and lifted a large silver metal case which he carried onto the balcony. He knelt in the heavy rain and opened the case, then he pulled out a twelve inch round camouflaged satellite communications antenna and pointed it toward the clouds. Then he attached an antenna cable to a battery powered radio inside the case that would allow him to contact Washington using an unjamable United States' military communications satellite.

"Black Specter, Black Specter, this is Inca Atlas, Inca Atlas, over." Barnes screamed into the microphone as his anxiety quickly increased after hearing automatic weapons on the island below, and nearby in the building. "Come on answer, answer you bastards," he shouted irately as he listened to static coming from the radio's speaker and watched the rain falling onto the tranquil city through the balcony's white metal railing supports.

Barnes looked at the suite's door after he heard a loud explosion in the hotel that shook the building. Then he heard, "Inca Atlas, this is Black Specter two seven, over," come from the radio's speaker.

"This is Atlas, where the fuck is Murtagh? Why isn't he on this radio?"

"Are you crazy using this open frequency," asked the confused radio man in Murtagh's office at the Pentagon. "Anyone can hear this conversation if they're monitoring military communications channels."

"I don't give a fuck about that now. Where's Murtagh? I've got to talk to him right now!"

"The General is asleep in his office. Why do you want him at this time of night?"

"Wake him up you fucking bastard. Get him up."

"He left orders he wasn't to be disturbed, and you couldn't pay me enough to wake him! The General had a long day and he's resting so he'll be able to direct the last phase of the operation tomorrow!"

"If you don't wake him up right now I'll fucking kill

JOURNEY THROUGH A LONG WINTER'S NIGHT   405

you when I get back to Washington, you fucking cock sucker," Barnes screamed into the microphone as he wiped the wind driven rain off his face. He moved closer to the balcony railing and watched as several of Vazques' men frantically ran across a road firing their weapons toward the marina. He became more distraught when he heard an explosion behind the hotel and then another one at the far end of the island near the marina.

Barnes suddenly heard Murtagh's sleepy voice and he bent forward and closer to the military radio so he could hear his commander as water dripped off his hair. "Barnes, what the hell is so important it couldn't wait until morning? And why the hell are you using an open communications channel that can be monitored?"

"Someone is attacking this fucking island, General! I don't know who or how, but someone just hit this fucking island big time, with everything they've got!"

Barnes' comments confused Murtagh and his staff officers standing beside him, and he motioned to one of them to get him his uniform. "That's impossible, you must be dreaming. You haven't been drinking tonight have you?" Murtagh's aides laughed as they sat in his large and lavishly decorated outer office and drank coffee.

Barnes heard another large explosion on the island and he leaned against the balcony railing. As he looked toward the far end of the island, he squinted into the rain when the roof of the long building near the marina disappeared in a blinding explosion that threw flaming debris hundreds of feet into the air. "Don't tell me I'm fucking dreaming. Did you hear that explosion? Someone just hit this fucking island and we're getting overrun. They're already inside the hotel. Vazques' men are going down hard all over the fucking place," he shouted as he watched flames quickly engulf the building whose roof was destroyed only moments before.

A concerned look immediately appeared on Murtagh's face and he turned to several of his staff officers. "Double time over to the strategy room and see if anything unusual is happening there. Then get right back to me."

Heavy rain continued to fall onto Barnes' face as he

406 D'ONOFRIO

looked through the railing's metal supports at the orange tinted clouds hanging over the city. He stared at the clouds with a shocked expression on his face when he heard the sound of approaching helicopters. "They even have helicopters in the city. They have a fucking air assault team in the city, General."

As the two men spoke, Murtagh's aides ran back into his office two minutes later and told their commander nothing unusual was happening in the strategy room. Murtagh knew if anyone was attacking the island the room would be filled with military officers relaying instructions and coordinating the military force. "There's nothing going on here, Barnes. I want you to find Vazques and Trembulak and figure out what's going on there yourself. Then report back to me after you know exactly what's happening. I'm going to the strategy room to take a look around myself."

Raging anger fueled by Murtagh's unconcerned comments consumed Barnes's logic as he ran into the hallway that led to the elevators. He was startled when he was knocked against the wall by four of Vazques' frightened men who were running toward an emergency exit door. "Where the hell are you flaming shit heads going? Get back to your posts," Barnes screamed as he raised his handgun and shot one of the frightened men in the back. The impact knocked the screaming soldier against the hallway's light pink wallpaper, and then he fell onto the carpeted floor. The gunshot and agonized screams of their dying companion made the other terrified men run faster, but Barnes shot all of them before they reached the emergency exit. "Useless fucking cowards," was his only comment as he shot each of the wounded men in the head before stepping onto the elevator.

Murtagh pulled on his uniform jacket as he walked into the Pentagon's bleak white corridor with four of his aides. Several minutes later, they stood in the Pentagon's huge strategy room. Only hours before the military commanders had completed the evacuation of Rhode Island and portions of the surrounding states. Murtagh shook his head and doubted Barnes' report when he saw seven military officers in the room direct-

JOURNEY THROUGH A LONG WINTER'S NIGHT 407

ing the troops patrolling the evacuated areas to prevent looting. He couldn't understand how a military force could be attacking Goat Island while the officers spoke infrequently on their radios. *Barnes must be crazy. There's nothing going on in here.* he thought.

"What's the latest report from our men in Newport, Major?" Murtagh asked the duty officer as he walked between the rows of computer terminals and quickly read the information displayed on a large color monitor.

"It's quiet in the city this morning, General. We've evacuated everyone from the area, and we're waiting for dawn. Admiral Adams scheduled the next status meeting for zero six hundred hours this morning."

Murtagh looked at a large computer generated monitor attached to the wall and checked the status of the military forces around the world. It showed all United States' forces were on alert, but none appeared engaged in combat operation. "Get someone at the Newport Naval Base on the telephone, Major. I want an up to the minute status report from someone up there."

"We've already evacuated almost everyone from the base, General. I don't know who we'll find up there at this time of night. I have a copy of a printed status report if you'd like to review it, General."

"Get someone on that damn phone, Major, or I'll find someone to replace you who can follow my orders without giving me his personal assessment of my requests." The embarrassed officer immediately contacted the Newport Naval Base and then reported to Murtagh he had Admiral Dupont on the telephone. Murtagh angrily pulled the telephone from the officer's hand, "Dupont, this is Murtagh. What the fuck is going on up there in Newport?"

Spencer's heart suddenly began racing and he immediately turned in his chair and looked at Dupont after he heard Murtagh's comments in his headset. Then he stood and pointed at Jamison and Coleman to ensure they were listening to the conversation.

"What are you talking about, General?" asked Dupont as he tried to sound confused by Murtagh's question. "I'm not really sure what you're asking. Eve-

408   D'ONOFRIO

rything is quiet up here. Why?"

"I just heard an attack force is moving against Goat Island at this very moment. Neither I, nor any other military commander in Washington has authorized a military strike of that island. Why wasn't I notified before we began attacking that island?"

Spencer motioned to Dupont and turned a switch so he could speak to Murtagh through his radio headset. "General Murtagh, this is Herbert Spencer. How did you hear about an attack of Goat Island back there in Washington already?"

Murtagh wasn't prepared to hear Spencer's voice, or the unexpected question, and he suddenly realized he had made a costly and possibly devastating mistake. If the military officers in the Pentagon's strategy room were not aware of an attack force operating in Newport, then he should not have known about it either. The confusion and panic created by Barnes' frantic radio message caused Murtagh to question the attack when he should not have known about it. He immediately tried to dismiss Spencer's question as irrelevant while trying to intimidate him. "I just heard a rumor as I was walking through the Pentagon hallway, that's all. Are we attacking that damn island or aren't we? Just answer my fucking question, Spencer." shouted Murtagh as he attempted to intimidate Spencer, then he motioned his aides closer.

Spencer stood and stared at the gray console in front of him as anger uncharacteristically overtook his normally calm and tranquil personality. "There's no way you could know Goat Island is under attack, General. No way, unless you have a direct communications link to the enemy force on that island. Maybe you'd like to explain how you're the only man in Washington right now who knows we just hit Goat Island?"

The military officers in the strategy room didn't understand why Murtagh slowly lowered the telephone as he stared blindly at the huge monitors on the walls. "Kill all of them. I don't want any witnesses," were his only comments as he walked toward the door. Murtagh's aides immediately pulled handguns equipped with si-

JOURNEY THROUGH A LONG WINTER'S NIGHT   409

lencers from their uniforms and began shooting the military officers in the room. A few of the terrified men ran into the Pentagon's wide hallway screaming for help. Murtagh's men murdered them and several other military officials they found walking in the hallway. As Murtagh and his aides calmly walked through the Pentagon's wide hallway they killed another eighteen military men and women they encountered.

When he walked into his office Murtagh had specific instructions for his men as he opened a large wooden cabinet and loaded a handgun. "Contact our men in Washington and tell them we're switching to Operational Plan Lazarus. If we follow that plan exactly I'm sure the government, and the country, will be ours by noon. Then get Barnes back on radio and tell him I want him to detonate the bomb on Goat Island immediately. We'll come back for all of you on our way to the Capital. I want you all standing beside me when I take control of this pitiful government."

Murtagh's staff officers looked at one another after hearing Murtagh's confusing and inconsistent orders.

"I don't understand, General," said one of the officers.

"Major Barnes is still on Goat Island with the rest of our men. They'll be killed by the explosion if you don't give them time to get off the island."

"Barnes is an excellent combat officer and he always follows orders. The situation has changed drastically and we can't wait for them to get off the island. Unfortunately, he and his men will be the first casualties as we rebuild our nation, but their names will be revered by our future generations."

Several minutes later, Murtagh and a large group of his staff drove behind the Pentagon building to four helicopters that were slowly descending toward a lit landing pad. They flew directly to Andrews Air Force Base and the helicopters landed beside an enormous hanger in a remote area of the sprawling military facility. Murtagh smiled to himself when he saw Air Force One, the jet reserved for the President of the United States, sitting at the far end of the complex lit by large flood-

410 D'ONOFRIO

lights. He imagined how he would look standing at the top of the jet's walkway while waving to appreciative people of the United States who were cheering for him. Then he quickly followed his men into a darkened airplane hanger.

Back on Goat Island Barnes ran into the heavy rain falling on his balcony and lifted the radio microphone. "Black Specter, this is Inca Atlas, over."

He was surprised when he did not hear Murtagh's voice, but that of another man. "Inca Atlas, this is Black Specter six one. The General has put Operational Plan Lazarus into effect. He has given orders you are to detonate the bomb immediately."

"What the fuck, is he crazy? Doesn't he know I can't get off this fucking island? What the fuck does he think I'm going to do, blow the bomb while I'm still on the fucking island?"

"That's the General's direct orders, Barnes. He left with the others to destroy the White House and the other government buildings in Washington according to his Plan Lazarus. He said he wants you to detonate that bomb right now, so do it."

"Hey, fuck you, you brainless cocksucker. Contact my backup teams and tell them I need a way off this fucking island. I'll kill the President myself and meet them in the marina after I get the bomb's detonator from that cocksucker Trembulak. I'll set the bomb off after we're a few miles out at sea."

As Barnes spoke on the radio, Van Horne was contemplating what he and his team should do one floor above. His instincts, the ones he learned to listen to when he was in Vietnam, were warning him of danger. "I'm getting a bad feeling here. They're probably waiting in those suites down the hall to ambush us from both sides."

"Kearns, toss a concussion grenade to the right after I do. We'll move out after they explode." Ten seconds later, flashes of bright light and the sounds of two deafening explosions filled the hallway and suites. The grenade's distracting effects and the gray smoke that filled the hallway allowed Van Horne's group to move forward safely.

JOURNEY THROUGH A LONG WINTER'S NIGHT 411

Van Horne ran ahead of the group and knelt beside a set of double wooden doors, as the recessed lights in the ceiling above pierced through the drifting gray smoke like daggers. He quickly visualized the hotel floor plan in his mind and remembered the doors opened into another penthouse suite where he now hoped to find the President and his family.

Taylor and Willey rushed into a suite and found a stunned Cuban laying on the green carpeted floor near a large wooden coffee table. As the Cuban reached for his hand gun, Taylor pulled his rifle's trigger, showering the man with bullets and shattering a nearby wooden coffee table.

Kearns rushed into another large suite where the Cubans destroyed most of the wooden furniture and windows during the week. He quickly searched through the empty bedrooms, and as he rushed into the living room he was startled when a large, dirty, and raggedly dressed Cuban soldier knocked him to the floor. Kearns didn't have time to consider his imminent death when he looked up and saw the Cuban smiling as he pointed a handgun at his American attacker's chest.

Without thinking, and reacting only from instinct, Kearns raised his left leg and kicked the Cuban in the groin as hard as he could. The sudden and severe stabbing pain caused the soldier to reach downward with both hands, and as he did, Kearns savagely kicked the man's face and shattered his nose. The Cuban fell back against the wall with blood streaming over his mouth and chin from his nose. Kearns stood and pushed the soldier toward the balcony where he threw the large man through the thick glass panel door. Kearns was surprised to see the dazed soldier slowly stand up in the heavy rain as he pulled a long bayonet from its holder.

Kearns ran across the balcony and leaped into the air with his legs extended in front of him, knocking the Cuban violently backward and against the metal railing. Then he attempted to wrestle the bayonet from the Cuban's hand in the heavy rain. His enemy was much stronger and pushed the knife closer to Kearns' chest after he pinned him painfully against the railing. Kearns

412   D'ONOFRIO

knew he was going to die when the bayonet's point was one inch from his chest and could smell the Cuban's breathe as he crushed him against the railing.

Kearns suddenly pulled out his own bayonet with his right hand as numbing fear tried to override his logic. Moments later, he drove the steel shaft into the Cuban's right thigh until it struck a bone. The Cuban cried out and released his grip on his bayonet as soon as he felt the excruciating and stabbing pain. The Cuban continued screaming in terror when Kearns unexpectedly lifted his struggling body and pushed him over the railing. The man screamed as he fell toward the ground and then there was silence after his body crashed on the wet grass. Kearns wiped the blood flowing from a deep gash in his forehead with his wet shirt sleeve. Then he sat on the balcony's wet concrete surface and leaned back against the railing as he tried to calm himself. After his breathing slowed down, Kearns walked back into the suite and found his rifle as blood continued to flow from the wound.

After the group finished searching through the suites, they ran into the hallway and knelt behind Van Horne who was standing with his ear pressed against the wooden doors. "This is tough shit Major. What'd you want to do next?" Willey whispered to Van Horne as he watched the smoke filtering through the white wallpapered hallway.

Van Horne took the shotgun Kearns had pulled over his shoulder and motioned to him to break a block of plastic explosive into four pieces. The group watched the hallway as Kearns carefully pressed the gray plastic explosive charges against the doors, and pushed a green pencil shaped detonator into each putty like mass. "Grogan and Willey, you're out here in the hallway to watch our backs. Taylor and Kearns are with me." Van Horne told everyone as he looked at the ceiling's recessed lighting, and wondered how dark it would be in the hallway if the explosion destroyed them.

The group moved thirty feet away from the door and covered their faces with their hands as Kearns readied a remote detonator. Five seconds later, the explosives

JOURNEY THROUGH A LONG WINTER'S NIGHT   413

detonated and destroyed the two wooden doors and the surrounding walls. The concussion filled the hallway and suite with debris and dense smoke, and created a floor to ceiling hole twelve feet wide in the wall. The gray smoke and dust swirling through the hallway made seeing anything ahead almost impossible. As Van Horne slowly stood, a river of water flowing from destroyed hot and cold water supply pipes in the wall began flooding the hallway.

Van Horne covered his face later when bullets fired from machine guns fired through the hole, struck the wall on the other side of the hallway. As the shooting continued, Van Horne crouched down and ran forward as he squinted into the smoke and dust. When he was kneeling beside the jagged hole he pulled the pin from a concussion grenade and threw it into the suite. The shooting continued, but stopped immediately after the grenade exploded. Van Horne stepped through the hole and fired the shotgun at a stunned Cuban standing in the suite's destroyed foyer. The impact of the shotgun's pellets striking the soldier's chest knocked him backward and onto the floor. As the wounded man screamed from the pain, Van Horne fired the shotgun into his chest and killed him. Taylor immediately stepped into the suite behind Van Horne and killed another Cuban dazed by the grenade.

Van Horne tossed the shotgun onto the floor disgustedly and reached for his rifle as he stared at another doorway directly ahead. He motioned to his men and the group rushed through it and fell onto the floor of the suite's elegant living room that was littered with shattered mirrors and pieces of the large screen television. Van Horne and his men immediately crawled forward and knelt beside the two frightened hostages they found sitting on a sofa.

The Petersons still wore the clothing they were wearing the morning the Cubans attacked the island. They were both obviously relieved to see that it was not the Cubans returning for them. The Cubans used stiff metal wire to tie their hands together behind their back, and tape covered their mouths to prevent them from talk-

414   D'ONOFRIO

ing. Van Horne carefully pulled the tape from Ervin Peterson's mouth as Taylor carefully removed the gag from his wife's mouth. "Are both of you all right?" asked Van Horne who was angry they he had not found the President. Then he carefully cut the wire around the man's wrists with his bayonet.

"Yes, yes, we're OK. I don't know who you are, but you've got to stay here and take care of us," pleaded a confused and terrified Peterson. He turned and looked at a shattered window when he heard a loud explosion on the island below. "You've got to stay here and make sure they don't come back for us. Please, I'll give you all the money I have if you help us."

"We thought the President and his family were in here. Not finding this guy is really starting to piss me off. Do you know where they are?"

Peterson raised a trembling hand and pointed toward the suite's outer doorway as he stared at Van Horne almost in shock. "They took Joe and his family and moved them to the suite at the end of the hallway about ten minutes ago. Go back into the hallway and turn right, it's the suite next to this one. They know you're here, and they'll be waiting for you."

"Fuck'em," was Van Horne's only reply as he stood and lifted his rifle. His frustration, anger, and determination intensified as he thought about missing the President by only several minutes. "Grogan, Kearns, you stay here and take care of these two. I'll take Taylor and Willey with me to find the President."

Grogan and Kearns studied the wide hole in the suite's wall as two five inch round columns of water rose three feet above the broken pipes in the wall. "We'll never be able to hold this area if they rush us through this hole," said Grogan as he looked around the room at the furniture. "I had this same problem when a car crashed through the front of a building I was working in as a security guard one night. We can't make it this easy for them." Kearns knew what his partner was thinking and they quickly moved a long brown sofa, several upholstered chairs, and three large wooden tables across the opening. The furniture would prevent the enemy

JOURNEY THROUGH A LONG WINTER'S NIGHT   415

soldiers from easily rushing into the suite, giving the two men time to stop them.

Van Horne stood beside the last set of double wooden doors in the hallway and slowly twisted the doorknobs. His anger and frustration flared again after discovering they were locked. "We're not going to screw around with these bastards anymore. If they've got the President in here, they've got to know we're up here, and they're waiting for us. We may be able to distract them if we knock down these doors and the wall." He pulled a block of plastic explosive from Willey's backpack, then pressed the gray mass against the wall beside the door frame, and pushed a pencil shaped detonator into it.

Van Horne quickly moved twenty feet from the doors where he knelt on the floor with his men in the water running from the shattered pipes. He shielded his face with one hand as he pressed an electronic detonator's button. The violent explosion filled the long hallway with a fast moving cloud of dense dust and smoke after it shattered both wooden doors and destroyed a long section of the hallway wall. The explosion threw pieces of the doors, pieces of its metal frame, and shattered pieces of the walls into both the hallway and suite.

As a dense dust and smoke cloud swirled around him, Van Horne squinted as he stepped into the suite with Taylor and Willey following closely behind him. The three men stopped in the foyer and Van Horne looked through the doorway ahead of them, but they could not see anyone in a room with light beige walls. Van Horne ran to the doorway and dove through it, landing on the floor of the suite's large living room. What he saw forty feet ahead shocked Van Horne and caused him to instinctively raise his rifle as he knelt on the floor.

"Don't come any closer, or we'll kill these people," a man holding a handgun nervously shouted at Van Horne's group. "Put down your weapons and stay where you are or I'll kill these people."

"Taylor, Willey, pick a target and stay on it," Van Horne shouted to his men. They immediately raised their rifles and aimed them at the people in the room.

Van Horne quickly looked around and saw a nearly

416 D'ONOFRIO

unconscious President Rockwell slumped on a long red sofa in front of the sliding door that opened onto the suite's balcony. Severe bruises and blood covered Rockwell's face and the side of his neck. His left eye was swollen closed and blood covered his lips where they were crushed against his teeth during a savage beating. Blood stains also covered his torn shirt from the severe beating Vazques and his soldiers inflicted on the helpless man during the previous day while they raped his wife and daughter.

The President's naked wife lay unconscious on the long couch beside her husband with a blanket covering her body. Purple and red bruises covered her face, shoulders, arms, and legs. After Vazques men raped the women, the soldiers savagely beat them with long chains they found in the hotel maintenance office.

The President's daughter was laying on the floor with her hands covering her face as she wept hysterically. She was naked and the bruises created while the Cubans beat her with chains covered her body and face. She clenched a blanket tightly with two fists and tried to protect herself from further violators. After Barnes finished raping the young woman, thirty of Vazques' men took turns raping and sodomizing her on the grass beside her screaming mother.

Van Horne looked at Trembulak and Fasha Partyski who were standing beside one another behind the long couch, using the President's body as a shield. Trembulak quickly pulled on his pants after the first explosions awakened him. He now wore the Russian general's shirt, but looked ridiculous because he did not have time to button it or comb his hair. Trembulak was never in a situation where he was being pursued by an adversary. Normally it was his men who were murdering unsuspecting people with car bombs, or killing them in airports with automatic weapons, while he watched from a safe distance. Now his men were under attack and he didn't have any idea how to deal with the situation, or how to avoid capture. Although Trembulak didn't realize it, this was the same horrible sensation the innocent people his men attacked experienced before they died. The situation terri-

JOURNEY THROUGH A LONG WINTER'S NIGHT   417

fied him and he nervously looked around after hearing several loud and massive explosions, and automatic weapons, through the open balcony door.

Partyski stood barefoot in a short black skirt and a white blouse she hastily pulled on after Trembulak woke her. She was terrified by explosions she heard outside the building, and the sounds of men screaming on the island. Thoughts of being captured and put on trial in the United States for her role in the attack caused her body to tremble almost uncontrollably. She briefly thought about being sentenced to death for accompanying Trembulak to the island and she was panicked by the idea. As her body trembled she nervously looked at Trembulak hoping he would have a way off the island after she heard more loud explosions.

Van Horne kept his rifle pointed at Trembulak but knew he could not shoot at him, or Partyski, without risking the lives of the President and his family. Both Trembulak and Partyski pointed their handguns at the President's head and his wife's body, and Van Horne realized it was a standoff. Neither group could start shooting without jeopardizing their own lives. Van Horne saw a small black box with several flashing lights and an extended silver antenna that Trembulak held in his left hand. He immediately assumed it was the electronic transmitter needed to detonate the bomb.

"They're all over the island. The Americans are all over our island," screamed a frantic man as he backed into the suite through the open balcony door and stood behind the couch. Vazques knew the agonized screams he heard outside the hotel came from his men, and the thought they were dying incensed him. As another huge explosion rocked the building, Vazques turned and was stunned to see the three men within the suite with their rifles pointed at him. He panicked and raised his handgun as he was both surprised and confused by the clothing the men wore.

As Van Horne slowly stood with his rifle aimed at him, Vazques suddenly recognized him. His confusion and surprise was immediately apparent as his face contorted with anger. "How can you still be alive? Barnes

418 D'ONOFRIO

sent our best men to kill you after you came to this island."

"Barnes?" Van Horne thought when he heard the name. "That doesn't sound like a god damn Russian name. What the hell is this ass hole talking about." The entire building suddenly seemed to shake as the sound of another large explosion rolled across Goat Island, and Van Horne could see it terrified Trembulak and Partyski.

"Why don't we put down our weapons and talk about how we can end this stand off without anyone else getting hurt," suggested Van Horne as he lowered his rifle, but kept his finger on the trigger.

Vazques appeared confused by the statement as he stared at Van Horne, then he raised his handgun and pointed it at the large man's chest. He carefully studied the man's face to ensure he was the same one who toured the island several days earlier, and the one he sent his men to kill. "Barnes and Leland sent our best men to kill you in the building on your naval base. We knew you were in there planning how to attack this island. We knew you had to be killed after you saw the gas mask my man was carrying."

"Those men did get into the building," shouted an angry Van Horne as his chest tightened when he remembered the helpless sensation he experienced during the ambush. Then he became angry when he remembered Mahoney laying on the floor. "The bastards killed some people who were no threat to you. If you wanted me dead that much you should've sent those ass holes after me when I was alone, so no one would have gotten hurt."

"I don't care how many of the American pigs my men killed," Vazques screamed angrily as he spit saliva while rain water dripped onto the floor from his camouflaged uniform. "Why didn't they kill you in that building? I thought your military police captured them after they killed you. Barnes told me he was going to demand your government release my men tomorrow morning, or more hostages would be killed."

"The men you sent to the base and the ones you sent to the fort are dead. Right now I hope those bas-

JOURNEY THROUGH A LONG WINTER'S NIGHT 419

tards are burning in hell, and I'm sorry you're not there with them too."

"You killed all of my men?" Vazques screamed as a numbing sensation seemed to flood over his entire body. He slowly lowered his handgun and reached for the back of the couch to steady himself as his body began to tremble. "One of the men I sent to kill you at the naval base was my son. You killed my son, my only son." Vazques stared into Van Horne's uncaring eyes as the realization he would never see his son again seemed to paralyze him both mentally and physically. Images of his wife and his son when he was a young boy began flashing through Vazques' mind as he held onto the couch and stared at it in shock.

"How were you able to get onto this island?" Trembulak suddenly shouted after he heard helicopters flying over the city in the darkness, and several more loud explosions. Trembulak momentarily seemed to stutter with fear, then he began another sentence again as he tried to calm himself. "Barnes told us the plan for defending this island against your military forces was flawless. He assured us everything was considered and planned for."

"He obviously underestimated us, and so did you."

"He and Leland assured us none of Vazques' men would be harmed, and that they'd be home in a week. It was supposed to be so easy, and none of us would get hurt."

"It looks like someone has been using everyone on this island. You, and the hostages," said Van Horne with a disgusted tone in his voice. He was angry he was forced to listen to the man he came to the island to kill as he waited for an opportunity to attack. "Now you've got to decide what's going to happen next. You can either surrender your men, or we can take them off this island in body bags."

"Surrender to an inferior force of Americans? If you value your President's life you'll tell us how you got on this island, or you can watch him die as you stand there."

"I'll tell you what you want to know," said Van Horne, who was angered Trembulak was still bargaining with

420 D'ONOFRIO

human lives. Van Horne immediately raised his rifle and aimed it directly at Trembulak's head. "But, if you shoot any of those people, you'll be on your way to hell two seconds after you pull the trigger."

Van Horne momentarily thought about Holloway and his team, and wanted to give them more time to disarm the bomb as he spoke to Trembulak. "Whoever put together the plan to attack this island were amateurs, and did a shitty job. If they'd done more research they'd have learned this island is sitting on top of a tunnel system built by our nation during the Second World War. We opened the tunnels and moved onto the island, then we started killing your men."

"Where is this tunnel entrance located?" Trembulak screamed as he suddenly pointed his handgun at Van Horne's chest. "Tell me where it is, or I'll kill you, and then your President."

"And then what the fuck are you going to do? Walk through that tunnel and find a taxi at the other end, ass hole? There's armed men all over the island and at the Newport Naval Base. There's no place for you to run. You have two choices, either surrender here, or die here."

"You stupid American fools. You've watched too many of your John Wayne movies, and now you're trying to be the hero. Your President will come with me. He'll remain my hostage until we are safely out of this country and in another part of the world."

"He's not going anywhere, and neither are you ass holes. I came here for the President and his family, and I'll kill them before I let you take them with you."

"You'd kill the man you came to rescue? You're bluffing with your John Wayne rhetoric."

Frustration, exhaustion, anger, and the thought of Preston dying while he watched all contributed to Van Horne's reply. "Listen to me you fucking ass hole. If I can't free them, then I'll kill them myself to make sure this ends here and now."

Trembulak held up the detonator so Van Horne could see it. "You're bluffing. I can destroy your nation with one push of this button. I'm the one who will decide what will happen here, and you'll follow my instruc-

JOURNEY THROUGH A LONG WINTER'S NIGHT   421

tions or die. You will take us to that tunnel and lead us safely off the island, or I'll detonate the bomb."

"You came to this island to hurt and kill as many people as you could, not to kill yourself. Now you're standing here with the same sickening feeling I've felt a thousand times before. It's the feeling you get just before the enemy is about to run over you, and you know you're going to die. If you're ready to die then push that button, asshole. But I can guarantee you'll never hear the explosion. I'll spread pieces of your fucking head across that wall behind you with this rifle long before that bomb detonates. Then you'll really know what it feels like to die."

As Grogan and Kearns guarded the Petersons they stood at opposite ends of the gaping hole in the suite's wall as five inches of water covered their boots. After they turned off all the lights, the interior of the suite was now dimly lit by a few undamaged recessed ceiling lights in the hallway. The sound of water flowing from the broken pipes made it impossible for them to hear anything in the hallway. When Kearns saw a man's shadow moving toward him on the hallway wall, he quickly stepped backward and motioned to Grogan someone was approaching. Both men's hearts raced as they stood with their backs pressed against the wall and waited as resounding thunder seemed to shake the building.

Moments later, they saw the dim gray shadow of a man on the furniture that blocked the gaping hole. The man stepped over the debris in the dimly lit hallway and stopped to study the damage he saw inside the suite. Kearns and Grogan's eyes widened with fear when the man extended his arm into the room as he leaned against the couch. They both saw the large handgun he held firmly. As he trembled with fear, Grogan shifted his gaze and looked at Kearns when they both heard the shocked man angrily remark, "What is this? What the hell happened in here?" after he saw the Cuban's bodies laying on the floor in the water.

Grogan stood in the shadows against the wall three feet from the man, and struggled to control his breath

422 D'ONOFRIO

ing so he would not be discovered. When the man suddenly pointed the handgun toward where Kearns was standing, Grogan knew he couldn't allow his friend to be shot without doing something to prevent it. Grogan suddenly threw his rifle across the darkened suite and the sound startled the man when it struck a wall. As Grogan stepped from the shadows he made a tight fist and punched the man's wrist as hard as he could, effortlessly knocking the weapon from his hand. Then he grasped the shocked man's wrist with both hands and pulled him over the couch where he fell onto the floor in the dim light.

Leland painfully stood and immediately assumed a karate stance as water dripped from his saturated uniform. He defiantly stared at the two men silhouetted by the dim hallway lights while he shook off the pain from falling on his shoulder. Kearns and Grogan appeared surprised to see the man was wearing an American Army uniform. Neither wanted to mistakenly attack a member of a military rescue team that might have moved on the island after the attack began. "Who the hell are you?" a shocked Kearns asked the man who wore the bars of a military officer on his uniform.

"The one who's going to kill both of you bastards with my bare hands."

Kearns couldn't understand why an American solider was inside the hotel, and the man's threat seemed to enrage him. He quickly stepped forward and momentarily distracted Leland, allowing Grogan to unexpectedly strike Leland's face with his fist. The violent blow dazed Leland, and as he staggered backward and tried to maintain his karate stance Kearns savagely punched him in the face. While Leland staggered backward, Kearns kicked his chest and he fell onto a decorative wooden cabinet, which shattered and collapsed around him.

Grogan and Kearns lifted the dazed Leland and pushed him back against the wall. "I love it when shit heads like you threaten me, you son of a bitch." Kearns screamed with his face an inch from Leland's. Then Kearns pulled out his bayonet and placed the blade against Leland's jugular vein. "I don't really give a fuck

JOURNEY THROUGH A LONG WINTER'S NIGHT 423

who you are! I should cut your fucking throat and watch you bleed to death!"

"This piece of shit isn't worth it, Kearns," warned Grogan as he held Leland's shirt and nervously watched his partner, unsure of what he would do next. "Lets not kill him, lets break up this bastard a little and see what he knows."

"Go fuck yourself! I'm not telling you anything! You can both go to hell!"

"We know we've already got adjoining rooms shit head, so what we do here makes no fucking difference," screamed Kearns before he pulled back his hand and punched Leland's face. Several minutes later, Leland unconscious body fell onto the floor with his face and body severely bruised.

"I don't know who the hell this guy is, but I'm sure he isn't part of our military," Grogan told Kearns as he cut a piece of drapery cord and tied Leland's hands behind his back. "He probably thought our military forces were attacking the island, so he wore this uniform hoping he wouldn't be noticed."

"I owe you one for saving my ass back there," Kearns told Grogan as he knelt on the floor. "I thought I was dead." Grogan didn't answer as he lifted his rifle, but Kearns next comment brought a smile of satisfaction to his face. "I feel a lot better now that we beat the shit out of this guy."

As Trembulak was about to threaten Van Horne with the remote detonator again, he suddenly stopped shouting and a shocked expression quickly spread over his face. Reading the expression on Trembulak's face, and watching where he was staring, Van Horne suddenly turned expecting trouble. He frowned when an American Army officer dressed in a camouflaged uniform rushed through the hole in the suite's wall with a handgun clenched in his hand. Trembulak and Vazques recognized the man immediately, but Van Horne and his men were shocked to see the soldier and they immediately aimed their rifles at him.

"Whoa, whoa, take it easy. Take it easy," said the American Army officer who appeared surprised to see

424 D'ONOFRIO

the rifles pointed at him. He slowly raised his hands over his head as he briefly looked at Vazques and Trembulak with a puzzled expression on his face.

"Who the fuck are you?" a surprised Van Horne asked angrily as he stepped forward and pulled the handgun from Barnes' hand.

"Chill out. Chill out. I'm Major Shackleford, United States Army. I'm the one that should be asking you the questions right now sport." Lying had become a way of life for Barnes, and he was able to do it without feeling self conscious or guilty.

"Yeah, and I'm the one holding the rifle pointed at your fucking head, asshole. Let me tell you something, I hate it when people tell me to chill out! If you say it again I'll tear off your balls and stuff them up your fucking ass. Got it?"

Without turning away from the man he could somehow sense was his enemy Van Horne said, "Taylor, use your radio and find out what's happening."

"You're wasting a lot of my precious time up here trying to be a hero sport. I came here to rescue the President and you're stopping me from doing my job. What the hell are civilians doing inside this hotel with weapons while the United States' military is trying to free the President. Where the hell did you three come from? Were you hostages on this island who managed to get free?" Barnes remained calm as he spoke to Van Horne. He cautiously evaluated the situation and tried to determine how he could kill the three men and take the remote detonator from Trembulak.

"What unit are you with?" Van Horne asked Barnes as he studied the man's hardened face. The solider suddenly appeared so convincing and sincere that Van Horne momentarily thought he could trust him.

"I'm with the Fourth Special Forces Group! Those are my men chewing up the island while we're standing around here like dumb shits, jerking each other off while we're talking," replied Barnes as he extended his hand and reached for the handgun Van Horne was holding. "Come up, lets cut the shit and get the President out of here before someone comes in and wastes all of us."

JOURNEY THROUGH A LONG WINTER'S NIGHT   425

"Something is really flaky here, Major," Taylor suddenly warned Van Horne as he lowered his radio headset around his neck. "I've been listening to Tac Com and there's no military units operating on the island with us yet," Everyone suddenly looked toward the balcony door when they heard the unmistakable sound of a helicopter flying past the building with its machine guns firing.

Van Horne looked back at Barnes, and as his anger flared he momentarily lost control of the rage contained inside himself. For an instant the raging monster he struggled to control every day of his life suddenly surfaced. Van Horne quickly stepped forward and raised his arm, striking Barnes' face as hard as he could with the handgun he held. Barnes immediately fell against the suite's wooden liquor bar, knocking many of the empty bottles onto the carpeting as blood began flowing from his nose and mouth.

As Trembulak and Vazques watched helplessly, Van Horne struck Barnes' face with the handgun again and opened another deep cut in his cheek. All of the rage and anger Van Horne repressed during the week after seeing the dead hostages laying on the rocks suddenly shattered his normally reserved exterior. "Why don't you tell me who you are again," Van Horne shouted at Barnes as he savagely pushed Barnes' face down onto the top of the bar. Then he lifted the injured man by his uniform, turned him around, and pushed him back against the bar.

Van Horne savagely struck Barnes' chest with the handgun several times, and one of the more powerful blows broke one of his ribs. Blood continued to flow down the right side of Barnes' face and neck from his battered face as he fell onto the carpet. Van Horne threw his rifle onto the bar and suddenly pressed his handgun against Barnes' head. Then he reached into Barnes' pocket and pulled out a leather wallet.

Van Horne quickly fumbled through the papers until he found a military identification card, then his anger suddenly flared out of control. "So you're fucking Barnes. The brave fucking ass hole who tried to have me killed." Van Horne grabbed the injured Barnes' shirt and

426   D'ONOFRIO

dragged him to the center of the large room as loud thunder shook the building. Without concern for his injuries, Van Horne threw him onto the carpeted floor and kicked him in the chest as everyone heard another huge explosion on the island.

As Van Horne retrieved his rifle from the bar the President's daughter looked at the injured man laying beside her. She began crying hysterically as she pointed at Barnes' bruised and bleeding face. "That, that's the one who raped me first. He raped me before the others," Barnes slowly and painfully curled himself into a ball and held his chest, then he looked up at Trembulak and Vazques for help.

As everyone heard automatic weapons through the balcony's open door, Grogan added to the confusion in the suite when he pushed Leland in the suite. Leland's face and arms covered with blood, and when Grogan pushed him against the wall, red streaks smeared across the decorative white wallpaper. "We found this piece of shit out in the hallway, Major. He's dressed like an American soldier, but the bastard tried to kill us." Grogan suddenly pushed Leland forward and the injured man fell onto the floor beside the wall with his hands still tied behind his back.

Vazques showed little concern for Barnes or Leland as he stared at Van Horne and his men. As he thought about his son dying at the Naval Base a fanatical need for revenge seemed to fill his mind. "You've all killed my son! Barnes killed him with his lies, and you killed him in that building with your weapons. You're all responsible for his death! Now I'm going to kill as many Americans as I can to avenge him."

"Are you fucking crazy, Vazques?" Barnes painfully shouted at Vazques as he grabbed a nearby chair. Using it, he painfully and slowly stood as a helicopter flew past the balcony with a noise that distracted everyone.

"We'll all die here if you start shooting at them! Use your fucking head. I don't want you or that fucking camel jockey to do anything until I tell you to."

Barnes painfully turned toward Van Horne as he attempted to wipe away some of the blood running down

JOURNEY THROUGH A LONG WINTER'S NIGHT 427

his face, but only managed to smear it across the skin. "Do you have any idea what you fucking heroes have done here? Do you know what your being on this island has jeopardized?"

"I know that nothing on this island is what it appears to be. The only thing I'm sure about is that you've hurt a lot of innocent people," said Van Horne as his jaw tightened with rage. "After I find out who Black Specter is, I'm going to find the fucking bastard and kill him myself."

Barnes frowned when he realized someone had listened to his conversation with Murtagh. "You won't find out anything about Black Specter. It won't matter even if you do find out who he is. By this time tomorrow I'll be walking in the sunlight as a hero, and you'll either be in jail or dead." Even in defeat Barnes believed Murtagh's alternate attack plan would still give him control of the nation.

"You're gonna tell me who he is, or I'm going to cut your fucking throat."

"It's over, Barnes. Let it go," Leland suddenly shouted with an anguished and defeated tone in his voice while he knelt beside the wall streaked with his own blood. Everyone suddenly heard another loud explosion on the island, then they heard the sounds of men screaming in agony. "Listen to what's going on out there. We tried our best but it's not going to work. It's over for now, but we'll be back."

The radar operators aboard E2C Hawkeye flying south of Newport suddenly saw two mysterious aircraft flying toward the city on their screens. One of them immediately notified Whiskey Echo and reported contact with targets designated as Alpha and Bravo. Whiskey Echo then contacted Spencer and discussed the situation. "Negative, none of our aircraft are in the area," Spencer told Chamberlain. "Anything you find out there should be considered hostile."

"Roger, Tac Com. India Tango, check out those two targets. Find out what they are and then splash them."

India Tango slowly pulled away from the KA-6 refueling tanker and turned to the south. Although it

428 D'ONOFRIO

was dark and heavy rain created thick streaks of water on the jet's canopy, the aircraft's navigator was able to locate and identify the targets using his radar and infra-red imaging systems. "I've got two inbound birds flying toward the free fire zone around Newport. They look like they're Apache helicopters. What the heck are they doing out here?"

"Beats me, but we're not going to screw around with them!" replied the pilot as he flew five miles above the helicopters and briefly saw the fires raging on Goat Island ahead. "Arm your Sparrows and lets get rid of them." Neither the pilot nor his navigator knew American combat soldiers who served under Barnes at the Pentagon were piloting the helicopters. The helicopters were one of two emergency escape plans for getting off the island that Barnes developed for himself before the attack.

The jet's navigator fired a missile, and as it trailed flames in the darkness he watched an infra-red image transmitted by a camera in its nose. The navigator guided the missile toward the target with a control panel as it flew toward a helicopter from behind. "Perfect," said the navigator, then he held his breath as it closed the final one hundred feet and struck the helicopter's engine. He and the pilot immediately looked down through their jet's canopy and saw a large fireball plummeting toward the ocean below. The navigator launched another missile and it struck the second helicopter as the terrified pilots were trying to flee the area, abandoning Barnes on the island.

Chapter Twenty-Six

A series of horrifying images of his son dying in agony after Van Horne's men shot him filled Vazques' mind. As shock turned to realization, a burst of brilliant white light seemed to blind his mind's eye as he felt an over-powering and almost fanatical need for revenge. Suddenly he was no longer concerned about his men dying on the island below. He realized the only way to avenge his son's death was to destroy the men who murdered him, and exterminate as many Americans as possible. He was determined to destroy them even if it meant sacrificing his own life to destroy them.

"You shut your mouth you lying bastard, or I'll kill you before the rest of these American dogs," Vazques suddenly screamed at Barnes as he aimed his handgun at him. Then he raised his handgun and aimed it Barnes' chest. "It's because of you, you and you're lies, that my son is dead. You and all these other Americans are responsible for his death. You wanted to kill all the people on this island Barnes. You said you wanted to destroy your nation with the bomb. Now you'll have your wish, and I'll have revenge for my son's death."

Vazques' face was pale and drawn and his brown eyes were wide with anger and contempt as he unexpectedly stepped toward Trembulak. He pushed the startled terrorist against the sofa and frantically began grabbing for the plutonium bomb's remote detonator. "Give me that detonator so I can destroy the people who killed my son," he screamed as he began struggling with Trembulak in front of the balcony's open door. Vivid lightening suddenly streaked above the city, and loud thunder startled the others in the suite as they watched the confusing scene.

As Vazques frantically grabbed for the detonator, Trembulak continued to fight him off. Trembulak tried to keep his back to the raving Cuban military officer, forcing him to reach around his body for the detonator. Vazques suddenly grabbed Trembulak's wrist with his right hand and reached for the detonator with the other.

430 D'ONOFRIO

Trembulak dropped his handgun as he frantically tried to pull Vazques' hand away.

Vazques quickly became enraged when he could not reach the detonator, and suddenly wrapped his arm around Trembulak's neck as he stood behind him. Then he pulled back his arm with his other hand as he attempted to break Trembulak's neck. Trembulak's face suddenly turned a brilliant shade of red, and the muscles in his neck and face tightened as Vazques increased the pressure. "Help me, Barnes," he muttered as he began suffocating while he held the detonator out in front of him. "Stop him before he kills me." In the confusion, Partyski didn't know whether to shoot Vazques or keep her handgun aimed at Van Horne and his men.

"Are you fucking crazy, Vazques?" Barnes screamed as he watched the men struggling on the other side of the long sofa. "What're you trying to do, get us all killed?"

Trembulak's face quickly turned a deep shade of purple and his body began to slump forward in Vazques' arms. Vazques suddenly pushed the almost unconscious man against the sofa's high upholstered back. As Trembulak gasped painfully for air he suddenly lost his balance and fell to his right, violently knocking Partyski onto the floor.

Van Horne and his men watched the confusion quickly developing in front of them. They all knew they would never have a more opportune time to attack. Partyski looked up at the Americans immediately after she fell onto the floor. When she saw them raise their rifles she began screaming, "They're going to shoot us. They're going to shoot us!"

Partyski saw the handgun she dropped after Trembulak knocked her onto the floor. She lifted it and hastily aimed it at Van Horne as she sat sprawling on the floor, supporting her body with one hand. Moments later, everyone in the room appeared startled when she fired a single bullet that missed Van Horne and created a hole in the ceiling above him. The handgun's loud noise startled the petite woman and the recoil almost ripped the weapon from her hand. Although she always traveled with Trembulak, she never participated in any

JOURNEY THROUGH A LONG WINTER'S NIGHT   431

of his organization's killings. Now trembling with fear as she held the handgun with both hands she tried to aim it at Van Horne's chest.

Taylor aimed his rifle at the woman sitting on the floor ten feet from him as he shouted, "Don't do it." When Partyski looked at Taylor and saw his rifle pointed at her, she panicked and pointed her handgun at him. Taylor had never been in a situation where he killed a woman at close range, and for a brief instant he was indecisive about what to do next. He thought that he might be able to reason with the woman, but when she unexpectedly swore at him, Taylor knew she was determined to kill him.

Another single loud gunshot filled the suite when Taylor fired a bullet that struck Partyski's face to the right of her nose. A moment later, the bullet tore through the rear of her skull and knocked the woman's body violently backward as it did. Bone fragments, long streaks of red blood, and pieces of Partyski's brain, skull, and hair, spattered Vazques and Trembulak's face, arms, and clothing. Barnes wiped a large wet gray mass from his face and disgustedly threw it onto the floor after he saw it was a piece of the woman's brain. Gray brain matter, patches of long brown hair, and red blood streaked and spattered the white wallpaper behind the woman's body. The President's daughter began screaming hysterically after she saw the bullet destroyed most of the woman's skull. The now conscious President Rockwell immediately fell onto the floor beside his screaming daughter and wrapped his arms around her.

As the shocked Barnes, Vazques, and Trembulak stared at the woman's body, the sudden and deafening sounds of a low flying jet's engines startled them again. They immediately looked toward the balcony door as the ear shattering sound of the aircraft filled the suite. Twenty seconds later, the deafening sounds of another jet flying over the island added to the confusion and anguish in the suite.

Trembulak seemed to be in shock as he stared down silently at Partyski's lifeless body sprawled across the carpet. The woman he made love to only hours

432   D'ONOFRIO

before was now laying at his feet dead in a puddle of her own blood. The single bullet ripped away half of her head from the top of her skull to her chin. The one intact eye still in Partyski's face remained open as red blood poured from her shattered skull and stained the carpet under it.

Vazques showed no remorse that the woman he habitually refered to as a bitch and a whore was dead. He suddenly lunged forward and pulled the detonator from a dazed Trembulak's hand before pushing him backward against the blood covered wall. Vazques tossed his handgun onto the floor and then triumphantly held the detonator over his head with both hands. He slowly backed toward the balcony door with an almost comical smile on his face as lightening streaked the darkened sky behind him. "Now you're all going to die for what you did to my son. You and millions of other people in your country are going to die because of you."

"For Christ sake don't do it, Vazques," Barnes screamed as he painfully stepped forward and reached for the detonator.

A moment later, Vazques pushed the detonator's button and several red lights mounted on the black box immediately began to flash. As he jubilantly threw the detonator onto the floor he began screaming at the shocked men standing in front of him. "I hope the bomb kills millions of your people, especially their children, and destroys your mighty nation."

Van Horne knew he was going to die and his anger suddenly flared out of control until the rage trapped inside him became uncontrollable. He surprised everyone when he suddenly took two steps toward Vazques who was still screaming at him. He couldn't hear what Vazques was shouting at him as he thought, *If I'm going to die, then I'll at least have the satisfaction of killing the asshole that condemned me to death.*

Vazques stopped shouting and his eyes widened with shock after Van Horne raised his rifle and aimed it at him. "Fuck you too," said Van Horne moments before he fired three bullets into the Cuban's chest. The bullet's impact violently propelled Vazques' body backward

JOURNEY THROUGH A LONG WINTER'S NIGHT   433

and it shattered one of the floor to ceiling windows that opened onto the balcony. "I hope you rot in hell you mother fucker," Van Horne uncharacteristically shouted at Vazques as he stepped forward and fired ten more bullets into the body as it lay face up in the torrential rain. For a brief moment, Van Horne was angered the worst he could do to Vazques was kill him. He angrily pulled the empty ammunition magazine from his rifle and threw it onto the carpet as he stared at the body. Then he looked at Barnes and Leland who were watching him, as they tried to determine what the man who appeared to be insane would do next.

Van Horne's savage killing of Vazques, and his brutal shouts of retribution, terrified Trembulak. He immediately raised his hands above his head in terror and backed away when Van Horne suddenly looked at him. "You can't hurt me, I'm surrendering to you. I am a freedom fighter, and now I'm surrendering myself to you as a political prisoner of war. I'm protected by the laws of your own country."

"Shut up, you fucking bastard. I don't want to hear another thing out of you. " Van Horne looked at his watch and then his men who still had their rifles pointed at the group. He frowned after fifteen seconds passed and the bomb had not yet detonated. As he stared at the watch's second hand Van Horne thought, *I wonder what its going to feel like when that bomb explodes? I'm here in this room right now, and in another instant, in the time it takes to blink my eyes, I'm going to be dead.* Grogan startled everyone in the room when he suddenly and exuberantly shouted, "All right, god damn it. Holloway's group just disarmed the bomb. They must have finished just before that bastard pushed the button. We're home free, Major."

Van Horne showed no emotion after the announcement. Instead, he kicked Partyski's handgun out of his way and stepped over her still bleeding body as he walked toward Barnes who was leaning against the sofa. At the same time Grogan and Willey began helping the President and his daughter off the floor. Taylor quickly pushed Leland and Trembulak to a corner of the large room

434 D'ONOFRIO

and forced them lay face down on the floor.

Van Horne's body trembled with both rage and anger as he stared at Barnes. He knew he still had the problem of getting the President safely off the island. But, he wanted to deal with the man he felt was responsible for the killings on the island before he did anything else.

"Whatever you hoped to accomplish on this island has failed. Now I want to know what's really going on here, and who's behind all this."

"You can go fuck yourself if you think I'm going to tell you anything," Barnes angrily shouted as he painfully stood erect.

"You're part in this attack is over, so you may as well tell me what you hoped to accomplish by hurting and killing all these people." Before Barnes could react Van Horne savagely raised his rifle and struck the man's already abused face with the butt. The blow was so powerful it knocked Barnes backward and he fell over a wooden coffee table and onto the floor. Blood flowed onto his hands as he held his broken nose and several deep cuts in his face while he lay on the floor in pain.

Chamberlain and his F-14 pilots were cruising ten miles south of Newport Harbor when they heard another report from a radarman aboard the E2C aircraft. "This is Rusted Anvil. We have target Charlie moving north from the ocean at coordinates 118-Sierra-3. It looks like a surface craft moving toward Newport."

"Ah, Roger, Rusted Anvil, we see the target on our radar screens too. We'll check it out." Chamberlain contacted Yankee November and the pilot immediately turned toward the unidentified target with instructions to destroy it.

Several miles below a sleek speedboat with two powerful engines easily cut through the large and choppy ocean waves. It cruised into Newport Harbor and sailed toward Goat Island in the darkness and heavy rain. After the missiles destroyed the two helicopters flying to the island to rescue Barnes, another group of his men were now attempting to rescue him in the speedboat. Eight men stood on the deck and held onto the hand-

JOURNEY THROUGH A LONG WINTER'S NIGHT   435

rails as the speedboat crashed through several large waves that washed over the deck. As they squinted into the torrential rain falling into their faces they saw the large fires raging across Goat Island. When they were two miles from the city all of the men suddenly looked upward into the darkness and rain when Yankee November's engines screamed overhead at a low altitude.

As the fighter banked to the left and flew over the city, the jet's frantic navigator told his pilot, "They've fired a missile and its got a radar lock on us." The pilot immediately pulled back on his controls and the jet began a steep ascent into the clouds as it turned away from the city. The navigator activated the aircraft's electronic equipment designed to confuse the missile's radar system that was guiding it to the jet. Fifteen tense seconds later, as the pilot frantically flew an evasive pattern above the clouds, a green light appeared on the navigator's console which signified the missile's radar was no longer tracking the aircraft. The missile plummeted toward the earth and crashed into a sprawling shopping mall in the nearby town of Middletown. The huge explosion destroyed most of the building and immediately igniting many large fires.

The men on the speedboat frantically began working in the heavy rain preparing another Stinger Missile. When Yankee November was seven miles from the speedboat the navigator fired a Harpoon Missile.

"Any second," the navigator told the pilot. Moments later, they saw a large bright explosion below when the missile struck the speedboat and destroyed it in a huge fireball. Yankee November flew over the ocean water now covered with burning fuel, but neither the pilot nor his navigator could see the dead men's bodies floating in the flames.

Willey looked toward the open balcony door when he heard an explosion in the distance roll across the harbor. He lifted his radio headset and listened to Yankee November reporting to Whiskey Echo. "That last explosion we heard was a missile hitting a boat in the harbor. Our jets just destroyed it."

"That was your ride out of here, wasn't it?" Van

436 D'ONOFRIO

Horne asked Barnes as he watched the blood running onto the injured man's face. "You still don't think this is over, do you? You're so fucked up, you still think you're going to get out of this."

Everyone watched Barnes slowly pull himself to a kneeling position on the floor as he tasted the salty blood flowing into his mouth. Then he wiped his face and smeared the blood across his skin and the back of his hand. "You fucking bastards have jeopardized a plan to help this nation become the greatest power in the world. You're all fucking shit heads who have no idea how this country should be run. You're content to sit back and do nothing while spineless bastards like this fuck Rockwell leads this nation into ruin. We should be ruling the world, not struggling to feed our people."

"I'll never understand where people like you come up with these ideas. You're a fool, a god damn dangerous fool."

"Don't criticize me you fucking bastard. Don't think you've stopped us by what you've done here. Do you really think we're going to give the fucking politicians another chance to destroy this country? By this time tomorrow we'll all be heroes, and a new and powerful government will be leading this nation to greatness. Only Murtagh has the ideas and the plans that can make this nation great again."

"Murtagh is behind all this?" asked a surprised Van Horne immediately after he heard the General's name. Then Van Horne remembered Spencer's concerns that a high ranking member of the military or the government might be involved in the attack.

"Don't think that what you've done here is going to disgrace the only man who has the guts to save this nation. While you're here fucking around, he's already taking control of the government to help the people."

Anger seemed to flood over Van Horne after hearing Barnes' pathetic comments. "Murtagh doesn't give a shit about the people, you stupid bastard. If he did, he wouldn't have killed all the people on this island, and planned to destroy the nation he wants to lead to your so called greatness with a nuclear bomb."

JOURNEY THROUGH A LONG WINTER'S NIGHT 437

"The people we killed meant nothing to us. They were sheep, we sacrificed them to prove this nation needs a stronger government, a military government. I would have killed all of them if I thought their deaths would have helped us force the politicians out of office faster. If our nation doesn't find the greatness the General has planned for it, it's all your fucking fault."

"You're a stupid bastard if you believe any of that shit you just told me," Van Horne replied as he kicked Partyski's handgun onto the carpeting in front of Barnes. "This fiasco is over, and you and I both know what your options are right now, you fucking bastard. It's either that gun, or I'm going to drag your sorry ass downstairs and give you to the government you're trying to overthrow. Do you know what they're going to do to you for killing all of the hostages on this island?"

"The government? That useless bunch of lying fucks," Barnes laughed. "When Murtagh takes over the country today I'll be a hero."

Van Horne suddenly remembered how other criminals who were obviously guilty of inhumane crimes often avoided prosecution. As he stared at Barnes he thought, *There's always a chance some slick lawyer is going to claim this guy is insane. They can say only an insane man would kill the people on this island like he did to help his country. Or they might convince a jury Murtagh misled Barnes and he didn't realize the others were going to kill the hostages on the island. If that happens he'll never stand trial for killing the hostages, or betraying his country.* Van Horne's rage flared out of control, and he was determined that was not going to happen as he tightened his grip on the rifle.

Barnes slowly lifted the handgun with a blood covered hand as he tried to calculate how much time Murtagh needed to complete Project Lazarus. *I've got to get rid of this fucking bastard and the men with him,* he angrily thought as he stared at the handgun. *I can still kill Rockwell and his family, and get off the island. Before I leave, I'm going to cut that fucking Trembulak's throat for not helping me, that fucking, useless bastard.* Barnes slowly pressed the end of the handgun's barrel against

438 D'ONOFRIO

his head as he appeared to be starring down at the floor. In actuality he was studying where Van Horne's men were standing as he looked out the corner of his eyes. *My first shot has to kill their fucking leader, then I'll kill the others while the bastards are in shock.* Barnes suddenly pulled the handgun away from his head and aimed it at the men as he angrily screamed, "Fuck all of you."

Van Horne stood with his rifle cradled in his arms as he anticipated Barnes would not commit suicide, an event he was actually hoping would happen. Without moving he fired a single bullet that tore through Barnes' throat and ripped away the flesh to his shoulder. The bullet's impact knocked him to the floor and Barnes immediately grasped his mutilated throat with both hands. Spasms of agonizing pain racked his body and caused his legs to kick wildly and uncontrollably on the carpeted floor. He felt his own warm blood flowing onto his hands, then he saw the red fluid covering his arms as he attempted to stop the bleeding. Tears streamed from his eyes as the agonizing pain seemed to increase each second.

The bullet destroyed Barnes' vocal cords and the only sound that came from his throat was a watery gurgling as he rolled on the floor in agony. Leland looked away from the gruesome sight moments before he vomited onto the carpet after Barnes raised a blood covered hand to him while pleading for his help. Barnes' body began to convulse uncontrollably with painful spasms and he heard himself sucking air and blood into his lungs through the wound in his throat. He realized he was dying and he opened his mouth futilely to swear at Van Horne in defiance. His body shuddered violently as spasms of intense pain racked it, then Barnes' body suddenly stopped moving and his chest collapsed when he died.

"You're crazy, you're crazy," a wide eyed and frantic Trembulak screamed at Van Horne as he stared at Partyski and Barnes' bodies in terror. "Stay away from me. I'll tell you everything. I'm not a Russian soldier. My name is Casimir Trembulak, and I demand to be treated like the prisoner of war that I am."

JOURNEY THROUGH A LONG WINTER'S NIGHT   439

Van Horne suddenly pointed his rifle at the terrified Trembulak, and he frowned as he stared at the screaming man. He wanted to kill Trembulak, but he was already beginning to control his rage. He knew the man's death would serve no other purpose than to satisfy his own need for revenge and justice. "Shut your fucking mouth, or I'm going to blow your head off."

Van Horne looked at his watch then quickly pulled his rifle over his shoulder as he stepped beside Rockwell who was slowly standing beside his daughter. "How are you doing?" he asked as he helped Rockwell's crying daughter to a chair so the President could help his wife.

"I'll be all right. I don't understand how Murtagh can be responsible for all this. I don't understand it, and I'm not ready to believe it."

"I think you better start believing it, Mister President. It looks like Murtagh and the others like him think you're doing a shitty job running this country. We'll get some fucking answers from those other two after you and your family are off the island. Then I'll deal with Murtagh myself."

Van Horne realized how vulnerable the group was to attack and he immediately told his men to move the Petersons into the suite. He walked onto the balcony in the heavy rain and watched the lit city streets beside the water as he contacted Spencer. A great sense of satisfaction seemed to fill his mind and he made a fist and squeezed it, exhilarated with the realization his men infiltrated an island thought to be impenetrable. He sighed deeply and closed his eyes as he attempted to relax for several seconds while feeling the sheets of wind driven rain crash against his face. Then he opened his eyes and studied the hotel building's dimly lit exterior red brick wall and the roof twelve feet above the balcony. In the distance he heard the helicopters approaching in the darkness.

Van Horne turned and watched Sierra Xray circle the top of the hotel several times and then hover three hundred feet from the building, and sixty feet above it. After Rusk turned on the helicopter's exterior flood lights, they brightly lit the balcony, the roof, and the falling

440 D'ONOFRIO

rain. "Trojan Guide, this is Sierra Xray. How are you holding up?"

"I'm a lot better now that you're here. How the hell can we get the President and his family up to you?"

Rusk studied the building and discussed the situation with the pilots of the Sea Stallions now hovering around the top of the hotel. "It looks like we're going to need a sling and a basket. There's no other way to do it. We can hover over the balcony and lower a line down to you. It should only take a few seconds to get them into the helicopters, but watch out for the rotor down draft."

"Ok, we're going to need a basket to get the President's wife and daughter up to the helicopter. I'll be right back with them."

"There's a helicopter moving into position over the balcony to take you out of here, Mister President. We're going to use a sling to get you into it. Then we'll get your wife and daughter up there with you."

"No, my wife and daughter go first. Then you can take me."

"I heard him, Trojan Guide," said Rusk after hearing the comment in his headset. "The helicopter is thirty feet above the balcony and the basket is on its way down to you." The building seemed to vibrate as a large helicopter slowly moved into position over the balcony.

"All right, you're calling the shots. Lets get your family out of here." Van Horne carefully lifted the President's unconscious wife with the blanket wrapped around her body and gently carried her onto the balcony. The President shaded his eyes in the rotor down draft and oppressive noise, and led his daughter slowly onto the balcony with the blanket pulled tightly around her body. Rockwell looked up at a large helicopter hovering above the hotel. When he looked to his right a Cobra gun ship flew past the building.

Van Horne had trouble walking in the down draft created by the helicopter's rotors. He tightened his grip on the President' wife as some of the plastic furniture blew across the balcony. The noise of the overhead helicopter was deafening. When he looked up the force of the rotors made the raindrops feel like needles when

JOURNEY THROUGH A LONG WINTER'S NIGHT 441

they struck his skin. He carefully knelt on the concrete balcony and placed the President's wife into the metal rescue basket dangling from the bottom of the helicopter by a thick steel cable. Then he frantically motioned the President's daughter forward.

"You lay beside your mother and we'll get you up to the helicopter together," he shouted trying to be heard over the helicopter's noise. Mary Rockwell tried to look up at the huge black helicopter floating forbiddingly above, but the rain blinded her as it saturated her blanket. As Van Horne helped her she lay in the basket and held her mother, then he fastened several safety straps over both of them. "Take them up, they're yours." he radioed the helicopter's crew chief as he stepped back.

One long and tension filled minute later, the helicopter lowered a sling onto the balcony. "All right, it's your turn," Van Horne shouted to Rockwell as he grabbed the leather harness attached to a thick steel cable.

As he struggled to hover his small helicopter in the strong rain and wind Rusk thought he saw a piece of paper blowing across the brightly lit hotel roof. His heartbeat suddenly increased and Rusk pushed a button that activated the loudspeaker mounted beneath his helicopter as the co-pilot frantically pointed ahead. Several seconds later, he screamed, "Hit the deck, Trojan Guide. Hit the deck," Rusk shouted as he watched a man fumbling with a machine gun quickly run across the lit roof.

Van Horne was surprised by Rusk's voice bellowing from the loud speaker, and the unexpected warning of danger. He frantically looked around, but could not see an imminent threat approaching. He knew he could not defend both himself and the President, so instead of reaching for his rifle Van Horne wrapped his arms around Rockwell and tried to shield him from whatever was about to happen. Grogan heard the warning inside the suite and rushed onto the balcony with his rifle raised.

As streaks of lightening crossed the sky and loud thunder shook the hotel, Raw pictured his family in his mind while running across the well lit roof. *I know they'll understand I helped to attack the United States after their*

442 D'ONOFRIO

new government is formed. I know my actions here will bring honor and dignity to my family. If I can kill the American President it'll still give Murtagh a chance to gain control of the United States' government, and allow the attack to continue in Moscow. I can still save my country and people.

Raw ran to the edge of the roof and fired his machine gun into the tail section of the helicopter hovering over the balcony. The pilot immediately banked the helicopter away from the building, and as it plummeted toward the island below, the pilot and co-pilot wondered if they were going to die. The pilot pulled back on his controls and the helicopter suddenly leveled off ten feet above the ocean water. The pilot momentarily glanced back at the hotel's roof as he flew toward the naval base with the President's wife and terrified daughter aboard.

When he heard the gunshots Van Horne looked up and saw the armed man wearing a Russian military uniform at the edge of the roof in the heavy rain. He knew he couldn't do anything to prevent the Russian soldier from killing him and Rockwell, and he thought, *This is it.*

Fuck me, this wasn't suppose to happen, thought Rush as he instinctively squeezed a button on his aircraft's controls. Two machine guns mounted on the side of his helicopter began firing bullets under a Sea Stallion hovering near the balcony. Within seconds, hundreds of bullets cut a large hole through the building's roof and shattered many of the bricks above the balcony. Both Van Horne and Rockwell shaded their eyes from pieces of the flying bricks and then fell onto the balcony together. As they did, they heard an agonized scream from above as bullets ripped the large Russian soldier's body. Moments later, a large section of the roof collapsed into the hotel. It covered the furniture and carpeting with shattered building materials, along with blood covered broken bones and exposed internal organs from Raw's body.

"That was too fucking close," Van Horne shouted to Rockwell with a curious half smile the President didn't understand. Another helicopter slowly moved into posi-

JOURNEY THROUGH A LONG WINTER'S NIGHT   443

tion over the balcony, and Van Horne helped Rockwell place a sling under his arms which the helicopter lowered. A minute later, the President was safely aboard the helicopter, and it banked sharply to the left and flew away from the hotel in the darkness. Another large helicopter moved over the balcony and Van Horne helped the Peterson's climb into a metal stretcher. Then he watched as it lifted them to safety in the rain as vivid lightening streaked across the dark sky above.

"Drag those two pieces of shit out here," said Van Horne as he shielded his face from the wind while another helicopter moved into position. As he turned away from the rotor's powerful down draft, he watched as the men pushed Trembulak and Leland onto the balcony. Van Horne studied Leland's bruised face for several seconds as the rain water ran down the skin. Then he turned him around and tightened the cord around his wrists until it cut into the flesh and blood was washed from the wounds by the rain. Van Horne's anger flared, and he suddenly grabbed Leland's shirt and belt and pushed him violently against the balcony railing. "See those bodies down there laying on the fucking rocks. I should throw you off this fucking balcony for killing those people, but I need you to give me some answers." Then he strapped a sling around Leland's body and motioned upward with his hand.

Van Horne grasped Trembulak's shirt with one hand and dragged him to the center of the balcony while Leland was being lifted into the helicopter. He radioed the helicopter crew the warning, "Watch these last two. The one coming up to you right now looks like an American soldier, but he's a fucking traitor. I don't know who the hell this ass hole is. They're both part of the group that took over this island and killed the people. Don't believe a fucking thing they tell you." The six members of the Blue Light team forced Leland onto the helicopter's floor as he tried to explain he was an American Army officer sent to the island to rescue the President. Then they pushed Trembulak down beside him as the helicopter flew toward the Naval Base.

Van Horne stood on the balcony with his men and

444   D'ONOFRIO

watched as Sierra Xray and three other helicopters hovered seventy feet from the building. "Thanks for all your help, and for saving my ass up here," Van Horne radioed Rush as he shuddered when he pictured Raw standing on the roof with the machine gun pointed at him.

"You and your men did all the work, Trojan Guide. You saved the President, his family, and stopped them from using that bomb. We just came along for the ride, and the laughs. Can we give you a lift back to the base?"

"No thanks, we've got to check on our men down below." Rusk turned off the exterior floodlights and the helicopters flew toward the Newport Naval Base with the gun ships trailing behind him.

Van Horne turned and looked at Kearns, Grogan, Taylor, and Willy standing beside him as he listened to the relentless ocean waves crashing on the rocks around the island. "If only Preston had made it. I'd feel a lot better about what we just did here if he was with us."

"He knows what we just did, Major," Grogan suddenly told Van Horne as he smiled. "You know how he was. He always wanted to be in the middle of the action. He's probably sitting back right now with a beer in his hand telling us how sloppy we were when we hit this place and found the President. If he'd been with us you know he would've run into this suite with his god damn guns blazing, the little clown."

Van Horne and the others smiled at Grogan's comments, then they solemnly thought about their dead friend. "Lets find out what's happening on this piece of rock, then we'll head down to the lobby. Tac Com, Tac Com, this is Trojan Guide. The President and his family are headed your way. How are the rest of our teams doing? Over."

Spencer was elated Van Horne was not injured during the attack and he smiled to himself as he reviewed his notes. "Your men have secured most of the island, Robert. We're already moving Blue Light teams onto the island to help them."

"I think I know who's behind all this, Admiral."

"So do we, Robert. We intercepted a radio conversation between someone on Goat Island and the Pentagon. General Murtagh and his men have something to

JOURNEY THROUGH A LONG WINTER'S NIGHT   445

do with all this."

"You're right, Murtagh is responsible for everything that happened here. We grabbed one of his men and that Russian General, or whoever the hell he is. They're on a helicopter heading your way too. I'd like to find that fucking Murtagh and kill the fucking bastard with my bare hands." Van Horne's anger increased as he looked down at the edge of island and saw the bodies laying on the rocks beside the water in the rain. "That bastard deserves to die."

"Don't worry about him right now, Robert. I've got my men and everyone else in Washington looking for him and his staff. I've already contacted the Vice-President and told him about the attack, and what we've learned about the situation. This hostage crisis is a lot bigger than we ever imagined."

"Now we know why we couldn't figure our what was going on. By the way, Admiral, where the hell did all those helicopters come from?" asked Van Horne as he watched an Apache helicopter land in front of the hotel for several seconds while a Blue Light team jumped from it.

"I'll explain everything to you later, Robert. We still have some problems we've got to deal with."

Van Horne was becoming more excited about the success of the attack, and he became upset with himself after momentarily ignoring the remaining problems. "You're right, Tac Com. What's next on our list? Over."

"I've got some medical personnel ready to move into the hotel to help your men and the hostages. I'll fly over with them and meet you on the island. I'll open a communications channel so you can talk to your men. This is Tac Com, out."

"This is, Trojan Guide to all the teams. The President and his family are safe, and on their way to the Newport Naval Base. Lets all meet in the hotel lobby."

Ten minutes later, Van Horne and his men walked into the dimly lit hotel lobby where many of the recessed lights were destroyed by hand grenades. Van Horne carefully studied the destruction in the lobby. He shook his head when he saw the dead men laying in a large pool of blood under the shattered remains of the wooden counter.

446   D'ONOFRIO

"Christ, I'm glad to see all of you," said an ecstatic Van Horne as tears seemed to momentarily fill his eyes when he saw some of his men standing together talking. His joy quickly turned to concern when he saw one of the men quietly sitting beside the hotel's destroyed front doors. Many men had their rifles cradled across their laps and their faces buried in their hands. Others were sitting on the carpeted floor with their heads on their knees, while others were laying flat on their backs on the carpet beside the bodies of the dead Cuban soldiers. Each was now dealing with what he did on the island in his own personal way.

As more of his men walked into the lobby, they began congratulating one another. They watched the Blue Light teams guiding groups of uninjured hostages to the helicopters that would carry them to the Newport Naval Base. A woman dressed in a dirty and blood stained green nightshirt held her young son in her arms as she ran to where Van Horne and his men were standing. She began crying as she said, "I want to thank all of you for helping us. I thought we were going to die in this God forsaken place. Thank you for giving my son a chance to live." Van Horne and his men appeared deeply moved by the emotional woman's sincere words of thanks. For them, that was sufficient recognition for risking their lives during the attack.

Van Horne was watching another group of severely beaten hostages walking from the Greenhouse Restaurant when Spencer rushed into the lobby with two of his men. "How are you feeling. Robert?" Spencer asked as he helped several of the men pull off their weapons.

"I'm starting to get pissed off. What the hell did Murtagh think he was going to accomplish by hurting all these people? The part that really pisses me off is that we put him into a position of power where he could try to pull this off. Murtagh, he's just a fucking opportunist who hoped to get something for himself. We're the stupid ones that let him do this."

Spencer didn't have a reply for Van Horne's angry comments. He knew he could never justify or understand Murtagh's actions or the situation, so instead of

JOURNEY THROUGH A LONG WINTER'S NIGHT 447

replying he began helping the other man. Words of congratulations suddenly filled the lobby when Howard and his men, along with Holloway's team, walked out of the garage together. Van Horne watched the doorway Decker walked in with the group, and when she saw him she rushed between the men and hugged him tightly. He was relieved she was safe and he wrapped his arms around her body. Then he pulled her tightly to his chest while burying his face in her long wet hair.

Holloway made his way through the men until he was standing beside Van Horne, and Decker quickly stepped aside so the two men could talk. "Nice job in that garage, Holloway," said Van Horne as the two men shook hands. "They hit the detonator in the penthouse and I thought it was all over."

"We couldn't have done it without your men to take care of us. They did a great job saving these people. Every one of them would be dead if it wasn't for you."

"We're not taking all the credit. Every one pulled together and worked as a team, and it payed off. If it wasn't for your people we'd all be dead right now."

After the group talked for several minutes, Spencer raised his arm and displayed the face of his watch to Van Horne. "We should start moving your men off the island while its still dark, Robert. This place will be crawling with news helicopters and network reporters in a little while."

"Lets get Holloway's team off the island first, Admiral. Then we'll get our men out of here."

Spencer spoke to a military officer in the lobby and he immediately led Holloway's team to an evacuation helicopter. Then Van Horne found Owen standing in the group. "Do you have a status yet?"

"I'm not sure my list is complete, Major, but I think it's close." Owen sighed as he stared into Van Horne's eyes and saw they were glassy from exhaustion, the battle, and concern for his friends. He was reluctant to tell Van Horne what he wanted to know, but knew there was no way to avoid it. "The dead are Preston, Fuller, James, Manley, and Neville. That's five dead that we know of right now. The wounded are Shepard, Long,

448   D'ONOFRIO

and Gatting."

"That's a lot for such a small group. Those numbers are a lot higher than I expected them to be. I never should have gotten them involved in this fucking mess," he confessed as his eyes suddenly began to fill with tears.

Spencer heard Van Horne's angry comments and was soon standing beside him with his hand on his shoulder. "You knew this might happen, Robert. They all knew what might happen and they still chose to stay."

"We knew it might happen to any one of us, Admiral. That doesn't make it any easier for me to accept their deaths. I hoped none of them would get hurt, and instead they got killed."

"They did a dirty job with very little help, and without knowing who they could trust, Robert. They pulled off this attack on their own with almost no help from anyone else. They saved the President, the hostages, and a large area of our nation from destruction. I'd say they did one hell of a job here, and everyone should be very proud of what they accomplished."

"Nothing is worth having your friends get killed for, Admiral," Van Horne added as he wiped away the tears running down his cheek. "They were good men who deserved better than to die on this piece of rock because some asshole wants to rule the world."

"Come on, Robert, let's find a helicopter and get your men off this island. I'll take care of the ones who didn't make it." Van Horne began helping his men off the floor as he thought about his friends killed during the attack, and their families.

As Spencer led the men out of the lobby and into the torrential rain, they began talking and pointing when they saw the remains of the flower planter hit by the rocket. Then they saw the bodies of the Cuban's laying inside the garage's inclined entrance. They were even more shocked when they saw the boats, docks, marina, the three stores, and the row of townhouses totally engulfed in flames. They watched the orange flames and billowing smoke clouds turbulently rising above the island. Many of them pointed at the cars and vans still engulfed in flames, and those still exploding in several

JOURNEY THROUGH A LONG WINTER'S NIGHT 449

parking lots.

Everyone immediately looked up when a small helicopter flew over the hotel and a man seated in the rear of it pointed toward the group. After the helicopter landed on a road, Marlowe and Reynolds jumped out it. They ran toward the group with the orange and red fires scattered across the island raging behind them.

"Great job on this island, Van Horne," said Marlowe as he extended his hand to him.

"Your men did an outstanding job in that church steeple."

"We weren't alone up there. Reynolds and his men did a lot of the work."

"Thanks Reynolds, I'm not sure how you got dragged into helping us, but we all appreciate what you did up there. It was a hell of a risk sitting in that steeple, and we all appreciate what you did for us."

"Did you get rid of that piece of shit?" asked Reynolds, and Van Horne knew he was talking about Vazques.

"Personally," was Van Horne's only comment was he pictured Vazques' body shattering the door glass.

As the group impatiently waited for an evacuation helicopter to land, Van Horne looked over the seawall behind the hotel. He briefly smiled when he saw the lit stone walls of Fort Adams shrouded in the mist and rain. Then he looked at the lit buildings in the city and saw flames rising from the remains of the destroyed church. He was distracted when he heard the sounds of two large helicopters slowly landing on the island in front of the group. As he watched his men wearily climb into the helicopters he turned and looked at the hotel one final time as rain fell onto his face. Then he raised his hand and the crew chief pulled him into the helicopter.

Reynolds, Spencer, and Marlowe watched as both helicopters slowly lifted off the island and flew over the hotel toward the Newport Naval Base.

Chapter Twenty-Seven

Although the plan Murtagh considered flawless was now in jeopardy, he was confident his alternate attack plan would assure him military control of the United State's government. As Van Horne's men gathered in the hotel lobby on Goat Island, Murtagh's men worked in the brightly lit aircraft hanger and carefully inspected the equipment they would use for Project Lazarus. The name was an acronym Murtagh used when he described the rise of the new United States' military government after the death of the democratic government.

"Even if I radio our men in Maryland right now, they'll never have enough time to fire that missile at the White House. I'm sure Barnes has already detonated the bomb, and by now Newport is nothing more than a cloud of radioactive dust. Actually, I couldn't have planned this any better. That bomb will destroy all the evidence linking us to what happened on that island."

Murtagh thought about the situation and became elated when realizing the advantages of destroying the island ahead of schedule. "That bastard Spencer is dead too. Now I can deny I talked to him if anyone accuses me of contacting Newport."

"What about the men we burned in the Pentagon on the way out, General?"

"We'll say some fanatic officer cracked under the pressure of the crisis and killed his co-workers, and then himself, in the Pentagon. How can they prove anything different? That explosion is going to create so much confusion across this nation that we should be able to take control of our government by noon today."

As Murtagh and his men began pulling dark green aviation flight suits over their uniforms, he offered his philosophical views of the situation. "None of you should consider this minor setback a defeat gentlemen. When events seem to be going against us we should gain strength from them and look beyond today. Lets not forget our struggle here will benefit all the people of this glorious nation. Unfortunately, like the true soldiers we

JOURNEY THROUGH A LONG WINTER'S NIGHT   451

are, we must now take matters into our own hands and secure the objective. Now, lets help our nation rise out of the ashes we now find it in, and nurture it to a powerful force that can rule the world." Murtagh's men saluted their commander and ran to different areas of the large hanger as the building's huge steel door began sliding open slowly.

Murtagh's Project Lazarus called for the destruction of the most prominent government and historic buildings in Washington. His psychological warfare experts convinced him the destruction of the most well known buildings would symbolize the destruction of elected government. Murtagh was confident the symbolism and confusion immediately after the attack would allow him to seize control of the government. A large airborne attack force Murtagh's command staff secretly assembled at Andrews Air Force Base during the previous six months would be used to attack the city.

As Murtagh walked toward a huge transport airplane parked in the hanger, he smiled triumphantly as his men moved twenty heavily armed Apache helicopters onto the runway. During the previous month, Murtagh's men removed all of the official markings and United States' insignias from their exterior. The white painted image of a skull sitting atop two crossed swords now replaced the American flag on all the helicopters.

"Those helicopters aren't going to have any problem destroying the buildings my psychological people selected as targets. I'll have to remind the pilots to knock out any police or fire units they find on the city streets. After the people see the police are out of the way that may foster mass rioting and looting in the city. We can use the panic and fear to our advantage to keep the police busy. We've got enough ammunition and fuel stockpiled in here to continue the attack all morning if that's what it takes to destroy the city. Then we'll move in and eliminate the political tyrants destroying our nation." Murtagh smiled as he pictured a raging fire storm destroying all the buildings in Washington.

A pilot called to Murtagh as he opened a circular metal access door under the large green and brown

452 D'ONOFRIO

camouflaged transport airplane. After Murtagh climbed up a ladder and into the aircraft, twenty military officers joined him inside. The aircraft was a C-130H Specter Gunship, an airborne weapons platform that originally carried six large machine guns and a single one hundred five millimeter recoilless cannon. The aircraft was equipped with infrared and night vision systems that allowed the crew to locate and destroy enemy targets at night. Murtagh's combat engineers modified the aircraft and now seven additional rapid firing fifty caliber machine guns protruded from each side of the aircraft. They also fitted a second recoilless cannon into the aircraft's cramped tail section. Several remotely controlled machine guns and grenade launchers protruded from the aircraft's underbelly, while others hung from the wide wings.

Two pilots and an engineer climbed onto the aircraft's flight deck and began their pre-flight check list. Murtagh sat in the observer's seat directly behind the men and pulled the straps over his shoulders. "I'll bet Spencer's heroic task force in Newport was surprised as hell when Barnes exploded that bomb in their faces. I can just see that glowing mushroom cloud billowing over the harbor and city in the darkness. They all deserve to die for trying to prove they were more adept than us, those fools. Now we're going to wipe Washington off the map and set up a military government the way it should have been after the revolution. We'll rebuild this city after we're in control, and we'll build it the way I want it to look after I'm governing this great nation."

"We can begin the attack anytime you're ready, General," the pilot told Murtagh as the aircraft's four large propeller engines roared to life.

"Lets get this attack force off the ground. The people out there are waiting for us to save them from the politicians. The faster we get the job done, the more grateful the people will be after they're free of the tyrants trying to ruin their lives."

An Apache helicopter hovered above the runway with its exterior lights extinguished and flew toward the air-

JOURNEY THROUGH A LONG WINTER'S NIGHT   453

port's two hundred foot high control tower. The tower resembled a suspended ball of light two miles ahead in the darkness. The five air traffic controllers in the tower gathered around an electronic monitor when a fast moving aircraft suddenly appeared on their radar screens. As they stood at the windows attempting to locate the mysterious aircraft in the darkness, a missile trailing red flames struck the control tower and exploded in a huge fireball. Shattered and burning pieces of the building and bloody pieces of bodies began raining down onto the runway as flames consumed the top third of the control tower. Murtagh's assault force could now fly from the base without concern someone might warn the officials in Washington of their presence.

The other helicopters flew across the sprawling Air Force complex toward the sleek jet interceptors parked beside the long concrete runway. The Air Force stationed the interceptors and their refueling tankers outside Washington to protect the city and coast from approaching enemy fighters and bombers. Murtagh needed the jets destroyed so they would not interfere with his aerial attack of the city. Two of the helicopters fired their laser guided missiles and sixteen sleek F-15 fighters suddenly burst into flames ahead. The billowing red fireballs quickly rose into the sky and consumed five nearby aircraft. Within minutes, the helicopters destroyed all of the jet fighters, and clouds of flames billowed into the night sky as the aviation fuel burned on the runway. Using more of their missiles, the helicopter pilots then killed the interceptor's pilots and ground crews as they ran out of a building.

To ensure his pilots would help him destroy the buildings in Washington, Murtagh promised all of them high ranking positions in the military after he expanded its presence around the world. The combat pilots were intrigued by the idea they would be promoted to colonels immediately after the attack. All of them were eager to help Murtagh in his quest to assume control of the government so they could personally benefit from it.

Murtagh smiled confidently as he studied the hundreds of red lit switches, gauges, and display screens

454 D'ONOFRIO

that surrounded the pilots on the Specter's flight deck. His excitement increased when the aircraft began rolling out of the lit hanger and into the darkness. "With any luck I'll be the new leader of this suffering nation before noon." Several minutes later, the Specter was speeding down the runway with its four large propeller engines screaming. The aircraft flew into the darkened sky and turned toward Washington as the Apache helicopters flew over the treetops toward their target.

Murtagh contacted his helicopter pilots after the Specter pilot told him they were five miles from the city. "I want you to level the White House and kill everyone in it. I want Benson and all of his staff out of the way. After you're done there I want you to refuel and rearm, then target the Pentagon and destroy as much of that building as you can with your missiles. The more people you kill in there, the less resistance we'll have when I take over the government. Do the job and I'll reward all of you after this is over."

Murtagh became angry after a helicopter pilot radioed him. "Our men are still in your office, General. You told them to stay there until we went back for them."

"It's inevitable that loyal soldiers always die in combat," replied Murtagh who was not unconcerned the men who risked their lives and careers to help him would be killed during the attack. "I'm sure they're all willing to sacrifice their lives for our cause and the well being of our nation. I know those men will understand why they must die. Don't be surprised if you see them standing at the windows saluting you as you destroy the building with your missiles. After you've destroyed the White House, I'll use the satellite communications link aboard this aircraft to contact Chchenkoff. I'll personally tell him to begin the next phase of the attack in Moscow."

Murtagh smiled when he saw the towering and well lit stone obelisk of the Washington Monument on the horizon silhouetted against the early morning light in the east. He knew his conquest of the nation was only a few minutes away, and he suddenly felt indestructible and victorious as his fists tightened with enthusiasm. He squeezed the aircraft's intercom button and

JOURNEY THROUGH A LONG WINTER'S NIGHT 455

spoke to his men manning the machine guns and cannons on both sides of the aircraft. "As soon was we're past the Washington monument I want you to start destroying all the buildings on both sides of the Mall. We'll take out the Capital Building from up here with our own weapons. They won't know who the hell we are, and we'll tell everyone a Russian task force got in here and did all the damage."

The pilot banked the Specter sharply to the right and flew past the Washington Monument. Directly ahead Murtagh saw the long and wide grassy area commonly referred to as the Mall. The grassy area was six city blocks wide and extended from the Lincoln Monument to the steps of the United States' Capitol. Government and historic museum buildings that were a lasting tribute to the nation's independence and ingenuity lined both sides of The Mall. The Washington Monument, Smithsonian Institute, National Achives, and Senate offices were among the buildings Murtagh could see through the aircraft's windshield.

The pilot pushed forward on his controls until the darkened Specter Gunship was one hundred feet above the ground. The machine gunners on both sides of the aircraft began firing at the buildings after they heard the co-pilot say, "Select your own targets and begin the attack." Machine gun bullets struck the front of the Smithsonian Castle, the oldest of the historic museum's buildings. The bullets destroyed the fine stone exterior and shattered many of the priceless stained glass windows.

As thousands of smoking brass bullet casings dropped from the sides of the Specter, the men manning the two recoilless cannons in the aircraft's tail began firing at the buildings. "I always hated fucking history when I was in school," laughed an Army sergeant aiming a recoilless cannon. Then he fired at the National Achieves building, the most important of the buildings Murtagh wanted destroyed. Carefully preserved and protected inside the building were the nation's Declaration of Independence and the Bill of Rights, both of which Murtagh wanted destroyed. Murtagh considered the

456   D'ONOFRIO

documents obsolete because there would no longer be elections. He planned to personally select and appoint all government leaders after removing the politicians across the country from office. Those who opposed Murtagh's new government would be executed, he wouldn't have time for their interference as he implemented his plan to rebuild the nation. Murtagh's hands clenched tightly in satisfaction as he watched the well lit front of the Archives Building crash inward after the recoilless cannon's shell struck the large stone pillars and exploded.

Twenty seconds later, the Specter's pilot pulled back on his controls and the lethal aircraft screamed fifty feet above the well lit United States' Capital dome. The machine guns and grenade launchers mounted beneath the aircraft suddenly began firing downward and thousands of bullets shattered the building's large marble blocks. Ornate windows and thick wooden doors were violently blown inward by the bullets and exploding grenades. The explosions killed four guards as they ran through a corridor to their security office. Another twenty grenades suddenly struck the building's huge and well lit rotunda, toppling the tall statue positioned on top of the dome. It shattered into hundreds of pieces and slid down the side of the damaged rotunda. Other parts of the stone rotunda suddenly broke away and crashed into the building, destroying the sculptured stone walls and antiques below with a deafening noise.

As the Specter flew into the night sky another large section of the rotunda suddenly broke loose and fell into the building. It crashed down onto the ornate floor inside the Capital Building and killed six startled and confused guards inspecting the damage. The building that symbolized the nation's government since it was built more two hundred years ago was slowly being destroyed by the men who wanted to end democracy.

As The Specter pilot began a large circle to put him over the Capital Building again, Murtagh saw a large four engine passenger plane descending toward Washington National Airport. "Shoot down that damn jet. We can use the explosion and fires to help destroy the city."

JOURNEY THROUGH A LONG WINTER'S NIGHT   457

When the Specter was one mile from the passenger jet, the machine gunners used the intercom system to joke with one another about how many people they were going to kill. Their bullets easily ripped through the aircraft's thin sheet metal fuselage, severely wounding the pilots and flight engineer, and some of the three hundred passengers on the aircraft. Murtagh's eyes widened with delight when the jet's large left wing burst into flames. The wing suddenly ripped away from the aircraft's fuselage after hundreds of bullets passed through it. Some of the terrified and screaming passengers still strapped into their seats fell into the darkness through holes suddenly opened in the fuselage as the burning aircraft plummeted from the sky end over end. The flaming aircraft and burning wing crashed into a residential section of the city and both exploded in huge, billowing fireballs. The tremendous explosion and burning aviation fuel that covered many buildings momentarily lit the night sky with an orange glow. The explosions and fires killed thousands of innocent people who were asleep in the densely populated Georgetown section of the city.

Bullets and grenades from the Specter sent another large section of the Capital's stone rotunda, and a long section of roof, crashing into the building. Moments later, flashes of light appeared from both sides of the aircraft as thousands of machine gun bullets stuck the buildings lining the Mall. The bullets chipped and shattered the stones of the Washington Monument as a recoilless cannon shell slammed into the front of the Lincoln Monument and exploded. The explosion destroyed many of the tall stone columns and threw shattered fragments one hundred yards from the structure. The recoilless cannon fired again and destroyed a large section of the granite steps that led up to the monument. The explosion killed four guards who ran onto the steps as they tried to determine what was happening in the city.

"I wonder if the Apaches have finished destroying the White House yet?" Murtagh asked his pilots as he looked through the aircraft's side window.

The helicopter pilots planned to destroy the White

458 D'ONOFRIO

House with the same type of laser guided anti-tank missiles they used to destroy tanks in Iraq. Two pilots agreed to circle the nearby parking lots and kill anyone who managed to flee from the White House while the other pilots attacked the building. As the pilots flew over the treetops in the darkness they watched the buildings and lit streets under them. They joked about killing everyone inside the White House and reducing the historic stone structure to rubble.

Then they saw their brightly lit target in the distance. The well lit two story white stone building surrounded by a large lawn and sprawling gardens. Two helicopters flew over the tree tops toward the White House as the others hovered over several government buildings. One of the pilots studied a schematic drawing of the White House. Then, using his night vision equipment, he quickly located the two areas of the building's roof where Secret Service agents watched the surrounding area for potential problems. The pilot fired two missiles and watched as they flew toward the building's roof, homing in on a laser's reflected light. He smiled when a blinding flash of light signaled the missiles destroyed the glass enclosed area that housed four Secret Service agents. As flames and smoke rose above the White House, the pilot fired another missile that instantly killed five startled agents on another part of the building roof.

Another pilot veered his helicopter to the left and destroyed the entire roof of a nearby federal building with four missiles. He killed seven Secret Service agents who were preparing to fire a missile at the helicopter attacking the White House. The pilot then radioed the others and the helicopters began flying toward their target. Moments later, missiles crashed through the windows and roof of the White House's Executive Wing and exploded. Building materials and destroyed furniture were thrown seventy feet into the air as more missiles destroyed the Oval Office, and six offices adjacent to it. Two laser guided missiles exploded when they struck the lit granite blocks that formed the exterior walls and portico of the White House. They created a gaping two

JOURNEY THROUGH A LONG WINTER'S NIGHT   459

story hole in the building and destroyed many of the historic antiques housed inside.

As the joking pilots took turns firing missiles at the White House, the other helicopters circled above the nearby city streets and watched for approaching trouble. They could see Murtagh's Specter gunship flying above the city in the distance with their night vision equipment. They also saw the clouds of smoke rising above the burning buildings lit by both the street lights and early morning light. Four missiles suddenly struck the White House's second floor exterior wall. The explosions completely blew off the building's roof and threw debris two hundred feet into the air with a blinding flash. Three helicopters hovered around the White House as the pilots fired more laser guided missiles at the building. They created gaping holes when the explosions destroyed the windows and stone walls, and the building's interior walls and furniture. The White House's second floor was now completely destroyed and raging flames quickly engulfed the destroyed furniture and other historic objects.

"Lets make sure that flake Benson and everyone else with him are dead," laughed a pilot moments before he fired four more missiles at the building's first floor exterior wall. The explosions destroyed the walls and crashed into the building, destroying a formal reception area, the kitchen facilities, and a diplomatic dining area. As the building's first floor walls collapsed, much of the second story stone facade ripped away and crashed onto the lit lawn in front of the building.

The pilots circled the burning ruins of the White House and were confident Benson and everyone else in the building were dead. "Murtagh should be happy," one pilot radioed the others as he watched the flames quickly spreading through the shattered remains of the building. "I didn't know getting promoted in this man's Army could be so easy. I'll contact the General and tell him we're done here."

All of the pilots suddenly saw an orange streak fly into the sky from the trees located across the street from the White House. One pilot's mouth opened in horror

460 D'ONOFRIO

moments later when the orange streak struck the bottom of an Apache helicopter and an explosion destroyed the aircraft in a tremendous fireball.

"What the hell was that?" a confused pilot radioed the others as he watched the helicopter's shattered and burning remains fall onto the tall steel fence that surrounded the White House lawn. Moments later, the debris exploded again in another fireball that covered the grass and city streets with burning aviation fuel.

"That was Woble that just went down," one pilot radioed the others. "What happened to him? What knocked him down?"

"Here comes another one," screamed a pilot when he saw a second orange streak quickly rising into the darkness from between two buildings. It struck the bottom of another helicopter that was hovering over a street near the White House. An explosion ripped through the bottom of the helicopter and engulfed the startled crew in flames moments before another explosion destroyed the aircraft. The burning remains tumbled through the air and exploded again after crashing down onto the street, covering nearby cars with burning fuel.

"It's a fucking ambush," a frantic pilot radioed to the others after he determined the orange streaks were missiles. "We flew into a fucking ambush." The other pilots agreed, and two of them began firing their machine guns and cannons into the city park across from the White House. Trees, wooden park benches, and children's swings were the only things destroyed by the frantic pilots as explosions ripped apart the area.

The helicopter pilots were unaware that Spencer's National Security Agency, and the Central Intelligence Agency, had intercepted the radio conversation between Barnes in Newport and Murtagh in the Pentagon. Spencer's staff immediately contacted the Secret Service and told them Vice-President Benson and everyone else inside the White House was in imminent danger and should be evacuated. Benson and his advisors were now in the nearby nuclear explosion proof facility known as Weather Mountain, and were watching the helicopters attack the White House on closed circuit television.

JOURNEY THROUGH A LONG WINTER'S NIGHT   461

"Black Specter, this is Raven Three," a helicopter pilot shouted into his microphone. "We've flown into an ambush at the White House. They've destroyed two of our aircraft with missiles. We're breaking off the attack and heading back to base."

"No, no, keep attacking the White House until you kill everyone inside that building," Murtagh screamed into his microphone, angered by the pilot's concern for his own safety. "What are you, cowards? Keep attacking the building until they shoot all of you down, that's an order." The extreme stress and sudden realization his plans to gain control of the nation were collapsing around him confused Murtagh. He couldn't understand his pilot's concern about being shot at by an enemy he never expected to be in the city. He couldn't understand why his pilots weren't willing to sacrifice their lives to help him become the nation's greatest leader.

One helicopter pilot saw four men run out of a building and kneel together in the middle of a well lit city street. The co-pilot was watching the men through a side window when the pilot suddenly flew away from the White House. "They fired a missile," screamed the frantic co-pilot when he saw the orange flames rising into the sky toward them. "No, no," he screamed as he shielded his face with his hands moments before the missile struck the side of the helicopter and exploded.

The remaining pilots were shocked to hear a radio message broadcast to all of them. "This is the Secret Service. Land your helicopters on the streets around the White House immediately. This is the only warning you will be given. Land now, or you will be shot out of the sky."

"We can beat this," laughed one pilot as he suddenly flew between two tall buildings, and then began flying away from the White House as he skimmed the lit eight lane wide city street. "I got out of tighter situations than this in Iraq."

Directly ahead, six speeding police cars suddenly blocked the street and the pilot laughed as he fired his machine guns. Thousands of bullets killed eighteen police officers, and all the cars suddenly exploded in

462   D'ONOFRIO

flames seconds later. After the pilot flew through the smoke, he and his crew momentarily felt an unusual sensation as though something pushed the aircraft forward from behind. Moments later, an explosion blew their bodies through the helicopter's front windshield with a cloud of flames after a Stinger missile struck the aircraft's tail. Burning debris and twisted metal crashed down onto the city street and slide across the asphalt. Some of the burning debris crashed into parked automobiles and they immediately began burning and exploding.

The other pilots stared at the burning remains spread across the city street and immediately realized they could not escape. They began landing around the destroyed and burning White House, and the Secret Service and Washington police began arresting the men as they climbed out of their aircraft. In the distance they heard sirens as fire trucks raced to save the White House that was now completely engulfed in flames.

"Why the hell can't I get my helicopter pilots on the radio?" Murtagh shouted as he became angry when he couldn't contact them. "Those bastards must have turned coward and headed back to Andrews. God damn every one of them. Everyone I counted on has let me down except all of you and Barnes. Now we'll have to continue the attack ourselves."

The pilot banked the Specter in a sharp turn, and when the aircraft was one hundred feet above the Mall, the men manning the weapons began firing again. Murtagh leaned forward and stared through the aircraft's front windshield when he saw something moving on the brightly lit Capital's steps directly ahead. "Who the hell is that on the Capital steps? They're probably park police who think they're going to stop us with their handguns. Kill the useless bastards."

"I can't tell who they are, General," replied the Specter's co-pilot. "We'll use the machine guns under the aircraft to get rid of them."

"Kill all of them," replied Murtagh without regard as he smiled when he saw burning buildings to the left and right.

JOURNEY THROUGH A LONG WINTER'S NIGHT   463

The Specter pilot slowly pulled back on his controls so the aircraft would fly directly over the Capital. He and his copilot were shocked when they suddenly saw the orange flames trailing from a missile as it flew from the Capital steps. "They've fired a missile at us," the pilot screamed as he banked the transport plane sharply to the left, hoping to avoid it.

Murtagh's mind couldn't comprehend the startling news a missile was flying toward the aircraft. He was jostled in his seat when the Specter suddenly banked sharply again as the pilot attempted to avoid the missile. Only hours before Murtagh was on the verge of taking control of the United States' government, and now he was close to death. "What do those fools think they're doing to me?" Murtagh screamed as he unbuckled his seat belt and stood on the flight deck where he grasped a hand rail. "They're testing me! Testing me to see if I can lead this nation to greatness! They don't know who I am, or that I'm the only one who can save this nation! Nothing is going to stop us. Nothing!"

The last thing the pilots and flight engineer saw as they instinctively covered their faces with their hands was the bright flash of light when the missile struck the aircraft's nose and exploded. Then they all screamed in agony for a few brief seconds after the windshield shattered inward and pierced their flesh. The men experienced excruciating pain as flames instantly enveloped their bodies. The pain was so intense the men screamed loudly as the flames burned the flesh from their bones, causing their minds to almost explode from the agony. As fast as it began the pain subsided and then there was nothing, no pain, no sensations, then no life.

The flames completely engulfed Murtagh's body as he looked away from the explosion. His mind couldn't comprehend what he saw when the flames instantly and completely seared the flesh from his hands, exposing the skeleton. He suddenly began screaming in agony as the instruments around him exploded from the searing heat and flames that burned the hair off his head and caused his flesh to bubble and melt off his face.

The men manning the aircraft's weapons felt a

464 D'ONOFRIO

strange vibration when the missile struck the front of the Specter. Moments later, a cloud of scalding flame raced through the interior of the darkened aircraft. The men began screaming as boiling clouds of flames suddenly shot out of all the openings where the machine guns and cannons were located. Several seconds later, a tremendous explosion ripped the aircraft into several large pieces. Fragments of the fast moving aircraft and burning aviation fuel rained down onto the Mall and city streets in front of the Capital Building.

The Capital Building was where Murtagh planned to announce he was declaring martial law, and his plans to create a new government. Instead of walking up the Capital's stone steps triumphantly with large crowds of enthusiastic people cheering wildly, Murtagh's shattered and burned body lay smoldering on the grass surrounded by both the Specter's wreckage and the bodies of the men fanatically loyal to him. The brilliant military leader's dreams of conquest and power brought death and destruction to the nation, and ultimately himself.

Chapter Twenty-Eight

Immediately after the two helicopters landed beside the large hospital at the Newport Naval Base, five of Spencer's staff escorted Van Horne and his men into the facility. They were met by a group of thirty Navy doctors and nurses from the hospital who volunteered to remain in the underground command center with Spencer and Dupont during the attack. If Van Horne's men were successful and freed the President and the other hostages, the medical staff wanted to be nearby so they could provide immediate assistance if needed. Dupont arranged for the other doctors and nurses evacuated from the hospital to be waiting in transport planes filled with medical supplies at the Groton Submarine Base in Connecticut. Immediately after Holloway's team disarmed the plutonium bomb, Dupont contacted the pilots and told them to return to Newport. Thirty minutes after Van Horne's helicopter landed at the naval base, the doctors and nurses rushed back into the hospital and began caring for the hostages being evacuated from the island.

"Lets get rid of those weapons before we go any further gentlemen. We don't want any accidents in here," the hospital's senior doctor told Van Horne's men after he led them into a large storage room filled with wooden boxes. After they discarded their weapons the doctors gave each man a quick examination.

After their examinations the men changed into dry clothing they placed into canvas bags prior to the attack. All of them became upset when they saw the unopened bags which belonged to the men wounded and killed during the attack. The staff offered the men their congratulations as they passed out coffee and juices brought from the hospital's cafeteria. The exhausted men then sat on chairs and the floor in silence as they thought about what they did on the island. Some of them were elated, while others were extremely upset with the destruction they caused. When the hostages began arriving at the hospital the exhausted men unexpectedly

466 D'ONOFRIO

began helping them into the emergency rooms and admitting areas.

Van Horne helped several men suffering from broken arms and legs, and others whose faces were blackened with bruises received during the week. The Cubans beat the men unmercifully to frighten the other hostages into submission, and to injure the larger male hostages they considered a threat. All of the hostages were suffering from dangerous levels of dehydration after the Cubans refused to give them water during their captivity. The majority were severely and dangerously undernourished.

I can't remember how many hours its been since I had some sleep, Van Horne told himself as he lifted an elderly woman out of an ambulance and carefully placed her gently onto a stretcher. Then he stood and felt the light rain drops falling on his face from the gray clouds above. *I know I'm exhausted, I can feel it in my body, but I just can't settle down. Maybe it's seeing all of these suffering people. Maybe it's my mind trying to justify the men I killed on that damn island.* Van Horne's mind replayed vivid images of him killing Vazques and Barnes again and again, until he forced himself to concentrate on helping the injured hostages. He wondered if he would ever be able to forget what he had done on the island.

At eleven o'clock that morning, Spencer and Dupont arrived at the hospital. Dupont had already changed into a dress military uniform and Spencer was wearing a blue suit. This was in preparation for meeting the government and military officials they expected to be arriving in Newport within the hour. As they walked through the hospital, they found Van Horne and Owen carrying an injured woman laying on a stretcher into the emergency room.

"Everything seems to be under control in here," said Dupont as he watched the nurses and doctors attending to patients in the cubicles and on the hospital floor. "The Newport Hospital reopened and they're already helping to treat some of the people we're moving off the island. The Providence Hospital should be reopening soon, and we should be able to have everyone off that

JOURNEY THROUGH A LONG WINTER'S NIGHT   467

island by three o'clock this afternoon!"

"How's the President doing?" Van Horne asked both men as he placed a blanket over the women. "He didn't look too good when we found him in the hotel."

"He's going to be fine, Robert," replied a gravely serious Spencer. Then he added with a brief smile, "thanks to you and your men, and a lot of luck!"

"Blind luck, Admiral, she doesn't have favorites. Were your men able to find Murtagh in the Pentagon? I hope that bastard didn't have a way out of the country after he found out about the attack."

"We found him in Washington, Robert! Unfortunately, he and his men were able to destroy the White House before we could stop them."

"I'm sorry your men found him before I did, Admiral! I wanted to kill that fucking bastard myself before anyone else got to him. Now he'll claim insanity and start planning his next fucking operation in prison, if he even goes to jail."

Spencer smiled when several hostages laying on stretchers on the hotel's white tiled floor looked at one another after hearing Van Horne's comments. "I'm glad to say that's not going to happen, Robert. He and a group of his men were killed when one of my teams shot down a Specter gun ship they were using to destroy the buildings in Washington. We've already made a positive identification of his body. This mess is finally over!"

"Is it, Admiral? What about all the lives that have been destroyed here? What about these people who survived the attack? They'll never be the same mentally again."

"We got Murtagh, Robert. That's all we could do, and now he's dead."

"I thought I would be happy when I found out he either killed himself, or was killed by your men! Now I'm not really happy or overjoyed about it! It's a hard feeling to explain, Admiral. I guess I'm relieved he's dead because I know he's responsible for the suffering and deaths on that island!"

Spencer then had some sobering news for Van Horne, news that forced him to remember who was re-

468 D'ONOFRIO

sponsible for failure of Murtagh's plan. "I found the bodies of your men killed during the attack, Robert. I'm having them moved to the morgue here in the hospital. I knew all of them so I was able to give their names to the coroner."

"I don't think I can handle seeing them right now, Admiral. I'm not ready to deal with their deaths yet. Thanks for taking care of them."

"It wasn't a problem, Robert. I'll arrange for notifying their families and getting their bodies shipped home. I'll take care of everything."

"No, I asked them here, and I should be the one to call their families. It's the least I can do for them, and they'd expect it of me."

"We're going to have a news conference in two hours at the Mariott Hotel," Dupont then told Van Horne as he stepped aside when several nurses pushed a stretcher through the corridor with a young girl laying on it. "We have to tell the press something about the attack that freed the President and the hostages. I've already spoken to Admiral Adams so Marlowe, Holloway, and I, are off the hook. Do you want us to release your name and those of your men to the reporters during the news conference?"

"We joked about this before the attack, Admiral, when we were wondering if any of us would survive. We agreed we don't want our names released to anyone. We don't want to be connected to this attack in any way if we can avoid it. We just want to get back to our own lives! You'll have to come up with your own story about what happened here."

Spencer watched several of Van Horne's men carry a woman laying on a stretcher into the emergency room from an ambulance. "How are your men holding up, Robert? I haven't seen one of them speak since I've been here."

"I've noticed a few of them seem to be having problems dealing with what they did. I think they're going to need some help."

"Well, we'll get them all counseling if they need it, Robert. I'll find the money in my budget to provide it to those men. That's the least of our worries right now."

JOURNEY THROUGH A LONG WINTER'S NIGHT 469

"Thanks, Admiral, it'll really be appreciated."

"The Mariott Hotel just reopened so they can handle some of the crowds they're expecting in the city tonight. I've reserved a floor of rooms for you and your men, Robert. I'd like to get you over there so you can all get some rest!"

Van Horne watched some of his men leaning against a white nurses station in the hallway and he saw everyone was exhausted. "You're right, Admiral. We've helped out all we can in here. Now it's time we take care of our own people. I've got some calls to make myself this afternoon."

Van Horne walked through the emergency room and the patient admitting areas and gathered his men. He accidentally walked into a large white room where long white sheets covered the bodies on the tiled floor, stretchers, and silver metal tables. He shook his head as he slowly backed out of the room when he realized each covered the body of a hostage who died after arriving at the hospital. After Van Horne gathered all his men together, Spencer directed them to a civilian bus one of his men was driving. Then the driver took them to the hotel.

When the men walked into their rooms most of them took hot showers and then either collapsed on their beds or called their families. Some walked outside the hotel and sat in the sunlight that was beginning to stream through the breaks in the lighter white clouds overhead. Some sat beside the ocean waves crashing onto the mainland and watched the seagulls floating in the breeze as they searched for food. As the men watched the white foamy waves they experienced a strange sense of satisfaction. They were pleased they saved the hostages, and were thankful they were not injured or killed during the attack.

All of the men were amazed when they saw the burned out and charred buildings on the island and the remains of the destroyed boats and wooden docks floating on the blue ocean water. They looked overhead and watched the green military helicopters landing on the island to carry hostages to the hospitals. For many of the men their involvement in the attack now seemed

470   D'ONOFRIO

as though it was a dream, for some it was a long and vivid nightmare.

Van Horne awoke from a deep sleep at eleven o'clock the following morning after sleeping almost eighteen hours. He pulled back the curtains covering his balcony door and smiled when he saw the deep blue sky dotted with white puffy clouds. He walked onto the balcony in a strong, warm and humid breeze. From there he watched a large group of Marine engineers completing the construction of a floating bridge from the city docks in Newport to the shore of Goat Island. The bridge would temporarily replace the destroyed access bridge that connected the island to the city.

When he looked down at the city streets, and the small park beside the water, he smiled when he saw crowds of tourists that were already in the city. He sat on the balcony for thirty minutes enjoying the sensation of the warm sun on his face. Then he quickly walked back into the suite when he heard the telephone ringing.

"How are you feeling this morning, Robert?" asked a relieved sounding Spencer. He was unsure and concerned about Van Horne's mental condition after he had time to think about the destruction he caused on the island, and the death of his friends.

"I've felt a lot better than I do right now," Van Horne joked with Spencer, and both men immediately knew his mental condition was already improving. "I feel like I just woke up and this whole thing has been a nightmare. When I was laying in bed this morning, I wasn't sure if I'd really been on that island until I just saw the buildings we destroyed. It's a strange feeling, Admiral!"

"I can't even imagine what it's like, Robert."

"How are you doing this morning, Admiral?"

"I managed to get some sleep last night, but when I woke up this morning I still felt exhausted!"

"You've been through a lot with us during the past few days, Admiral! Not knowing who we were really fighting added to the tension. Speaking of that, were you able to get anything from those two we took out of the President's suite?"

"They've both been very cooperative! One of them is

JOURNEY THROUGH A LONG WINTER'S NIGHT   471

a member of Murtagh's personal staff at the Pentagon! His name is Leland. He's providing us with a lot of information about how they planned their attack, and what they hoped to accomplish. The other is some terrorist who's wanted by countries around the world! They told us those soldiers we thought were Russian, were really Cubans. They were helping Murtagh in exchange for financial aide for their country. It seems that Murtagh planned to appoint a military government and was going to make himself the leader of the nation for life!"

"Are you shitting me? That's why he killed all those people! So he could become the dictator of this country?"

"Not only that, Robert, some military men, and former leaders of the intelligence organizations in Moscow were planning to do the same thing there! They've already been picked up by the Russian officials."

"I'm sorry to say they almost pulled it off, Admiral."

"Murtagh's staff officers went through months of investigation and research preparing for the attack. They just didn't expect that a bastard like you would be coming after them! That was their only god damn mistake, Robert! If it wasn't for you, Murtagh and his men would be sitting in the White House this morning!"

"I can tell you're feeling better now that the pressure is off?" laughed Van Horne as he flipped through the room service menu and searched for something for breakfast.

"You're right, Robert, its over and I've learned this nation isn't prepared to deal with terrorist attacks. That's what I consider this entire incident, a terrorist attack. We've got to start working on a plan next week! A plan to defend ourselves against bastards like Murtagh, from within and outside our country!" Spencer pictured the rows of body bags he saw along the shores of Goat Island in the rain the previous day and promised himself it would never happen again. "Have you had breakfast yet?"

"No, I just got up. I was watching them working on the island when you called."

"Good, get dressed and I'll be there in half an hour to pick you up. We can have breakfast, or lunch, and

472   D'ONOFRIO

then I have some people who want to talk to you."

Van Horne took a shower and enjoyed the sensation of the hot water running down his skin. Then he shaved and dressed. For the first time since he arrived in Newport he decided not to carry a handgun inside the red shorts he pulled on, and that seemed to help him mentally. He still felt exhausted as he moved around, but he knew he couldn't sleep any longer.

When he heard a knock on the suite's door he was relieved to see it was Spencer, and not a reporter who discovered his involvement in the attack. "I'm arranging a dinner tomorrow night for your men, Marlowe's Seabees, and the members of Holloway's team. Just a little get together before everyone heads for home," explained Spencer as they walked toward an elevator.

"That sounds good. I'm sure everyone will enjoy getting together."

"You know, you and your men are going to have to stay here for a few more days to sit through some military debriefings, Robert. We want to document everything your men did on that island. I was able to postpone the first debriefing session until tomorrow morning so your men can get some rest today."

After Spencer and Van Horne finished eating in a crowded hotel restaurant they walked outside and stood in the bright sunlight watching the activity on Goat Island. "Do you know how many hostages they killed before we hit the island, Admiral?"

"Without a firm count my guess would be four to five hundred. We don't have a final count because we're still finding bodies inside the closets and rooms in the buildings on the island. The bastards didn't care who they killed! We found men, women, children, and even a few babies. A few of the doctors I spoke to at the hospital said the bastards raped more than a third of the women at least once during the week. A lot of them were raped more than once. That four to five hundred number doesn't include the thousands of people killed in Washington when Murtagh tried to destroy the city."

"We should have hit that damn island sooner," was Van Horne's only angry comment as they climbed into

JOURNEY THROUGH A LONG WINTER'S NIGHT 473

Spencer's limousine. The driver slowly weaved through the city streets already filling with spectators, and took the men to the Newport Naval Base Hospital. Two of the ten Secret Service agents at the hospital's main entrance checked Spencer's identification card and then allowed both men into the building.

"Why did we come back here?" Van Horne asked Spencer as he followed him into and elevator.

"The President wants to see to you this morning, Robert. He told me he wants to meet the man who saved his life, but never told him who he was," Spencer replied with a laugh. When the elevator reached the hospital's top floor, eight Secret Service agents in the hallway quickly stepped aside after they recognized Spencer. Spencer opened a door and led Van Horne into a large conference room with sanitary white walls filled with a long wooden table, comfortable chairs, several long sofas.

Neither man spoke as Van Horne leaned back against the table and Spencer sat on a chair. Several minutes later, a door opened and both men stood as President Rockwell walked into the room dressed in blue pajamas and a white robe. Large white bandages covered many of the bruises on his face and neck, and a large white patch covered the eye damaged during a beating. The President's wife and daughter wore long pajamas and red robes, and they slowly walked into the room behind him as they held hands and still appeared to be in shock. They smiled at Van Horne and Spencer and carefully, almost painfully, sat on a long sofa as the President slowly sat on a chair.

"Please, have a seat gentlemen. I'm sure you're just as exhausted as we are after the activities of the past few days. It's good to see you again, Admiral Spencer."

"How are you feeling this morning, Mister President?"

"Better, much better," he laughed as he took his wife's hand and held it. "We're all feeling a lot better today."

"Mister President, I'd like to introduce you to Major Robert Van Horne."

Van Horne immediately stepped forward after the

474 D'ONOFRIO

President extended his hand to him with a smile. "I think I've met the Major before. I'd like you to meet my wife Melanie and my daughter Mary. Please, sit beside them. We're very grateful to you and your men for saving not only our lives, but those of the other hostages. This nation will never forget what your men did on that island. Admiral Spencer has informed me of your request that no news releases be issued about you or your men. I'll honor that request, although I feel your men do deserve some type of recognition."

"That's really not necessary, Mister President! We knew what we had to do here, and we couldn't walk away from it."

"The Admiral told me you'd probably say something to that effect, Major. I've only had a few hours to think this over, but I'm going to instruct Admiral Spencer to write individual checks for each of the men who accompanied you onto that island, and the members of our military forces who actively supported your men during the attack. I realize that money can never repay those men for their bravery or sacrifice. But, I hope that one hundred and fifty thousand dollars for each man and woman will show how much we appreciate their efforts and sacrifice. I'll arrange for the money to be given directly to the families of those men killed during the attack."

The President's statement shocked Van Horne. "Thank you, Mister President. Money isn't necessary, but I know everyone will appreciate it. It was a tough operation and we agreed to do it without knowing how many laws we'd be breaking, or if we'd be considered criminals after it was over."

"Well, as far as we're concerned we don't even know who you are, Major, and in light of that, I don't know how you could have broken any laws! When we're feeling better, my wife and I will invite each of your men and their families to the White House for dinner. There won't be any reporters around so they won't have to worry about anyone discovering their involvement in this attack. My family and I want to personally thank each of you for helping us, and we'll be seeing you soon too, Major."

JOURNEY THROUGH A LONG WINTER'S NIGHT   475

The President looked at his wife and daughter and realized how fortunate he was to still be alive. "I just want to say thank you again, Major. We're still very tired, and I'm sorry, but I think we need some more rest right now. It's been a pleasure meeting you, Major," said the President as his family stood beside him. "Thank you again for your efforts, and please give my thanks to your men when you see them."

The President's wife reached forward and suddenly grasped Van Horne's hand with both of her hands. "Thank you very much for helping us! Please thank your friends and tell them we'll be praying for all of them. God bless all of you!"

Van Horne looked at the floor and smiled to himself as he and Spencer walked toward the elevator. "What's on your mind, Robert?"

"I feel a lot better after seeing the President. He's already looking a lot better then when I found him." The images of him killing Barnes and Vazques suddenly slipped from Van Horne's mind after he realized the President and his family were safe.

"You're starting to look exhausted again, Robert," Spencer told Van Horne after they climbed into the limousine. "How about if I take you back to the hotel so you can get some sleep?"

"This is a beautiful day, Admiral, I'm lucky to be alive. Besides, it's too nice a day to stay inside. I feel really good right now, and I don't think I want to spend the day in bed. I think I'll stop by the hotel bar and have a double scotch, then I'm going to take a long walk through the city and think about things. One thing is for sure, Admiral, it feels damn good to be alive."

When the limousine stopped in front of the hotel Van Horne stepped out and turned to Spencer. "That was one hell of an operation you pulled off on that island, Robert! You and your men should really be proud of what you did out there!"

Van Horne turned and shaded his eyes with his hands as he studied the charred and burned out buildings on the island. "Maybe this'll send a message to our elected politicians! Maybe they'll realize that it's not

476 D'ONOFRIO

politics like usual anymore! Maybe it's time for them to get off their asses, put their differences aside, and do something for the people!" He sighed and then turned and shook Spencer's hand as he said with a smile, "The next time something like this happens, and your ass is in a bind Admiral, don't even think about calling me!"

"I'll pick you up about seven for dinner, Robert. We'll find a nice quiet restaurant here in town and talk over things." After Van Horne watched the limousine drive out of the parking lot he made his way through the crowds of tourists and walked into the hotel's huge atrium restaurant which was now filled with people eating lunch. As he was looking for a free table he saw a familiar person dressed in a short denim skirt and a bright red blouse, reading a Cosmopolitan magazine as she sat at a table and sipped coffee. When Van Horne sat at the table a surprised Maggie Decker smiled as soon as their eyes met.

"I tried to call your room, but they said you already went out."

"What are you doing here? I mean, why aren't you at the base?" Van Horne asked as he took her hand.

"Holloway gave us the day off so we could all settle down. I thought I'd just relax with a coffee and catch up on some reading while I waited for you to get back. I thought you might have left already, and that I'd never see you again."

"I told you I'd find you after everything calmed down. I'm not leaving right now, not after everything we've been through together."

"How are you feeling this morning?" Decker asked as she leaned forward and kissed him.

"After surviving something like we just did on that island, your whole thinking changes, and the little things you took for granted every day suddenly become important to you. I know this sounds crazy but I'd love a scotch right now! Can I get you a drink?"

"No, it's too early for me," she laughed as she sat back and brushed her long hair to the side. "You have whatever you'd like and I'll have another coffee." Van Horne found a waitress and ordered, and as she walked

JOURNEY THROUGH A LONG WINTER'S NIGHT   477

away from the table, Van Horne looked into Decker's eyes.

"Spencer and I met with the President a little while ago."

"You did, you lucky bum!" replied Decker, a response that made him realize her mind was coping with what she saw and did on the island during the attack. "I'd give anything to meet him. How's he doing?"

"He's already looking better. He's making arrangements to pay each member of the rescue team one hundred fifty thousand dollars for saving the hostages."

Decker was stunned by the news, and she didn't speak for several moments. "I put in for my leave today, and it should come through sometime next week after the briefings are over. I'd like to see your tree farm, if that still sounds good to you."

Van Horne looked into Decker's warm eyes and rubbed the smooth skin of her hand with his fingers. "I'd like that very much. I'd like some time away with you, away from everything we've already been through." After the waitress placed the glass of scotch and the cup of coffee on the table, Van Horne slowly drank the liquor and savored the flavor as it burned his throat. After Decker finished her coffee, Van Horne took her hand as he stood. "Come on, let's get out of here."

Van Horne and Decker walked out of the lounge and into the lobby crowded with tourists. When nearby elevator doors opened and several people walked into the lobby, Van Horne pulled Decker into it with him. She quickly pulled her hand from his and she stepped out of the elevator. "Wait for me, I've got some clothes in the car!"

Van Horne smiled as he reached out and pulled Decker back beside him. Then he wrapped his arms around her and kissed her passionately. "And I told Spencer I didn't want to spend the day in bed!" he whispered into her ear as the elevator doors slowly closed.

About The Author

Richard D'Onofrio is a native of Connecticut, where he lives with his wife Nancy and their son Stephen. He is a veteran of the United States Army.

He attended Connecticut's Manchester Technical Community College where he received an Associates degree in Data Processing. He then attended Central Connecticut State University and received a Bachelor of Science degree in the field of Business Administration.

He was a Hospice volunteer in the community for several years, and later was a volunteer for the American Cancer Society.

The President of the United States is taken hostage in Rhode Island by Russian soldiers; only the first step in a sophisticated plan set in motion by top ranking military officials in both countries. As the governments of both nations collapse and the militaries prepare to seize control, the world races toward nuclear Armageddon.

Journey Through A Long Winter's Night

by
Richard D'Onofrio

Available at your local bookstore or use this page to order.

❑ 1-896329-19-5 – JOURNEY THROUGH A LONG WINTER'S NIGHT –
   $6.99 U.S./$8.99 in Canada

Send to: COMMONWEALTH PUBLICATIONS INC.
             9764 - 45th Avenue
             Edmonton, Alberta, CANADA T6E 5C5

Please send me the items I have checked above. I am enclosing $_____ (please add $2.50 per book to cover postage and handling). Send check or money order, no cash or C.O.D.'s, please.

Mr./Mrs./Ms._____

Address_____

City/State_____ Zip_____

Please allow four to six weeks for delivery.
Prices and availability subject to change without notice.